Clobbered by Camembert

AVERY AAMES

BERKLEY PRIME CRIME, NEW YORK

THE BERKLEY PUBLISHING GROUP
Published by the Penguin Group
Penguin Group (USA) Inc.
375 Hudson Street, New York, New York 10014, USA

Penguin Group (Canada), 90 Eglinton Avenue East, Suite 700, Toronto, Ontario M4P 2Y3, Canada (a division of Pearson Penguin Canada Inc.) • Penguin Books Ltd., 80 Strand, London WC2R 0RL, England • Penguin Group Ireland, 25 St. Stephen's Green, Dublin 2, Ireland (a division of Penguin Books Ltd.) • Penguin Group (Australia), 250 Camberwell Road, Camberwell, Victoria 3124, Australia (a division of Pearson Australia Group Pty. Ltd.) • Penguin Books India Pvt. Ltd., 11 Community Centre, Panchsheel Park, New Delhi—110 017, India • Penguin Group (NZ), 67 Apollo Drive, Rosedale, Auckland 0632, New Zealand (a division of Pearson New Zealand Ltd.) • Penguin Books (South Africa) (Pty.) Ltd., 24 Sturdee Avenue, Rosebank, Johannesburg 2196, South Africa

Penguin Books Ltd., Registered Offices: 80 Strand, London WC2R 0RL, England

CLOBBERED BY CAMEMBERT

A Berkley Prime Crime Book / published by arrangement with the author

PUBLISHING HISTORY
Berkley Prime Crime mass-market edition / February 2012

Copyright © 2012 by Penguin Group (USA) Inc.
Excerpt from *To Brie or Not to Brie* by Avery Aames copyright © 2012 by Penguin Group (USA) Inc.
Cover illustration by Teresa Fasolino.
Cover design by Annette Fiore Defex.
Interior text design by Laura K. Corless.

ISBN: 978-0-425-24587-3

BERKLEY® PRIME CRIME
Berkley Prime Crime Books are published by The Berkley Publishing Group,
a division of Penguin Group (USA) Inc.,
375 Hudson Street, New York, New York 10014.
BERKLEY® PRIME CRIME and the PRIME CRIME logo are trademarks of
Penguin Group (USA) Inc.

PRINTED IN THE UNITED STATES OF AMERICA

10   9   8   7   6   5   4   3   2   1

To my husband, Chuck.
You are the love of my life.
Thank you for your endless support
and your sense of humor.
And most of all, thank you for
encouraging me to believe in my dreams.

ACKNOWLEDGMENTS

Thank you to my husband for love and encouragement, and to the rest of my family for the same. I am so very, very blessed.

Thank you to the wonderful world of authors, both mystery and otherwise, who have offered their support, their opinions, and their wisdom. Thank you to my fabulous critique partners Krista Davis and Janet Bolin, both talented and successful writers in their own right. I don't know what I would do without you. Thank you to my culinary mystery blog mates at Mystery Lovers Kitchen for all the delicious recipes and foodie brilliance. Thanks to my blog mates at Killer Characters and to my pals at Cozy Promo, Plot Hatchers, and to all the Sisters in Crime guppies. Without you, I would have given up long ago.

Thank you to my publisher, Berkley Prime Crime, for wanting books about a cheese shop and for granting me the opportunity. Thank you to Kate Seaver, you are a dream editor. I am so lucky. And thanks to the rest of the Berkley team: Katherine Pelz, Kaitlyn Kennedy, Teresa Fasolino, Annette Fiore Defex, and Laura K. Corless. What a beautiful product you have turned out. {Beautiful in my eyes, certainly.}

Thank you to the support team of my sister, Kimberley, as well as Dana Kaye and Lindsey LeBret. Wow, is all I can say. Thank you to my agents, Bookends, specifically Kim Lionetti, for your enthusiasm. Thank you to the newest member of my "team," Marcella Wright, who is living her dream job with Murray's Cheese Shop, and to Marcella's fabulous Spaulding Gray (a feline "foodie"). Both have helped me with invaluable research.

Thank you to my sweet pets who are all watching over me from heaven.

And last but not least, thank you to all of you who are readers and fans. Thank you for wanting to read about Charlotte and her family and friends and the fictional world of Providence, Ohio.

Say cheese!

**Please visit me at my website, www.AveryAames.com,
or on my blogs at www.mysteryloverskitchen.com
and killercharacters.com.
I'm on Facebook, Twitter, and Goodreads as well.**

LIST OF CHARACTERS

Main characters

Charlotte Bessette—cheese shop owner, thirties, single

Amy, Claire—twin nieces (really first cousins once removed) of Charlotte, daughters of Matthew

Bozz Bozzuto—teenaged assistant and Internet guru in cheese shop

Delilah—owner of Country Kitchen, Charlotte's good friend

Freckles—owner of Sew Inspired and friend to Charlotte

Grandmère—Charlotte's grandmother, mayor of town, manager of theater aka Bernadette

Jordan Pace—cheese farmer

Lois Smith—owns Lavender and Lace B&B

Matthew Bessette—owner/sommelier, father of twins, cousin of Charlotte

Meredith Vance—teacher, best friend to Charlotte, engaged to Matthew

Pépère—Charlotte's grandfather aka Etienne Bessette

Prudence Hart—dress shop owner and local diva

Rebecca Zook—assistant in cheese shop

Sylvie Bessette—Matthew's British ex-wife

Umberto Urso—chief of police

Additional cast

Ainsley Smith the "Cube"—husband to Lois who owns Lavender and Lace B&B

Arlo MacMillan—local curmudgeon, owns chicken farm

Barton & Emma Burrell—cattle farmers

Chippendale Cooper—Ex-fiancé of Charlotte

Deputy Rodham—assistant to Chief Urso

Georgia Plachette—CFO of Clydesdale Enterprises

Ipo Ho—honeybee farmer

Jacky Peterson—sister to Jordan Pace

Kaitlyn Clydesdale—former resident, entrepreneur and Do-Gooder

Luigi Bozzuto—restaurant owner, Bozz's uncle

Octavia Tibble—librarian and Realtor, friend to Charlotte

Oscar Carson—workman at Ipo Ho's Quail Ridge Honeybee Farm

Quigley—reporter

Tallulah Barker—local animal rescuer

Tyanne Thompson—Hurricane Katrina survivor and friend to Charlotte

Violet—owner of Violet's Victoriana Inn

Animals

Rags—Charlotte's Ragdoll rescue cat

Rocket—Briard rescue, given to Amy and Clair by their mother

CHAPTER

"I thought I'd seen a ghost, Charlotte," Matthew said.

"It wasn't Chip." I popped off the lid of another Tupperware box of decorations we'd lugged from The Cheese Shop. "Chip lives in France, not Providence."

"He was blond, broad-shouldered, and fast."

"So are you."

"I'm telling you, the guy could run. What if it was him?"

I blew a stray hair off my face. "My ex-fiancé is not loping through the Winter Wonderland faire in the middle of February. Last I heard, he hated winter." And hated me, but that was water over the falls.

"I worry that he'll hurt—"

"It wasn't him. We have tourists. Lots and lots of tourists. One looked like him, that's all." A fog of breath wisped out of my mouth. I buttoned my pearl-colored sweater and tightened the gold filigree scarf around my neck to ward off the morning chill. Wearing corduroys, a turtleneck, and extra socks beneath my boots wasn't doing the trick.

Every year, in celebration of Providence's Founder's

Day, the Village Green transformed itself into a Winter
Wonderland faire. Farmers, vintners, and crafters from all
over Holmes County and beyond joined in the weekend fun
that would officially start on Friday evening. It was a tourist draw in a season when tourists should have been scarce.
Overnight, small white tents with picture windows, peaked
roofs, swinging doors, and fake green grass floors appeared.
Twinkling white lights outlined each tent.

I stood in the middle of ours and removed glittery
wedge-shaped ornaments from the decoration box. "Let's
change the subject."

"Okay, Miss Touchy." A grin inched up the right side of
my cousin's handsome face. He could be such a joker. He
plucked another taste of what I called ambrosia—he'd already eaten three—from a small platter of cheeses that I'd
brought to sample while we worked. "Hungry?" He waved
it under my nose. "Mm-mmm. This is a delicious cheese.
What is it?"

"Zamorano. A sheep's cheese from Zamora, Spain. Sort
of like Manchego. The milk comes from Churra sheep." I'd
eaten my fair share as an early morning snack.

"It's nutty and sort of buttery."

"Your new favorite," I teased.

"How'd you guess?" He slipped the cheese into his
mouth and hummed his appreciation.

While I decorated the tent with gold and burgundy ribbon looped through crystal wedge-shaped cheese ornaments, Matthew hoisted a box of wineglasses onto the
antique buffet that I'd brought in to serve as our cheese
counter and started to unpack them. We were setting up
Fromagerie Bessette, or Le Petit Fromagerie as we were
calling our little enterprise, primarily as a cheese- and wine-
tasting venue. For the first day we would offer Vacherin
Fribourg, a yummy cheese that's perfect for fondue, Haloumi
from Greece, which sort of tastes like a Mozzarella, and
the Zamorano. Our wines would include a creamy Mount
Eden chardonnay from Santa Cruz, a peppery Bordeaux,
and the boisterous but not over-the-top Sin Zin zinfandel.

Each customer would receive a burgundy souvenir plate embossed in gold with the words: *Say cheese*. For larger cheese purchases, we would direct eager customers back to Fromagerie Bessette. Gift items, crackers, and jams were available.

In between unpacking boxes, Matthew filched another sliver of cheese. "The Zamorano would pair well with the zinfandel, don't you think?"

I laughed. "It's good with all reds and even sherry."

"Hmph. Showing off?"

"You bet."

Matthew, a former sommelier and now my business partner, was doing his best to learn about cheese. In exchange, he instructed me about the complexities of wine. Our arrangement was what you would call a delicious swap.

"Well, it's killer," he said. "Truly killer."

A chill shimmied through the tent. I twisted the knob on the standing heater beneath the buffet table and cozied up to it. Once we opened the tent to customers, we'd have the heater on all the time.

The front door flew open and a dash of yesterday's featherlight snow fluttered inside.

Then Sylvie, Matthew's buxom ex-wife, entered. "Hello, love!" She bolted toward us, waving a handful of glossy flyers. A cool breeze swirled through the tent until the door swung shut.

"Speaking of exes," I said dryly as I felt my eyebrows rise.

"What are you . . . ?" Matthew sputtered. "Why . . . ?" He gaped at Sylvie with outright shock.

I didn't do much better. The lacy purple teddy Sylvie wore barely covered her ample chest and her you-know-what. I couldn't imagine that the purple muffler and ankle-high Uggs she was wearing provided enough warmth to bear the nip in the air. Her shoulders were dimpled with goose bumps.

"Did you forget to put on clothes?" Matthew managed to blurt out.

"I'm advertising, love," Sylvie announced in her clipped British accent as she waved the flyers.

Advertising what? I pressed my lips together to keep the snarky comment from escaping. Good business required tact, even with ex-in-laws.

Sylvie owned a women's boutique called Under Wraps. Many of the items in the store's window would make the sultriest vixen blush. A few years back, Sylvie abandoned Matthew and their girls to live with Mumsie and Dad in merry old England. A couple of months ago, she returned to Providence. Much to Matthew's vexation, she had wheedled her way back into their nine-soon-to-be-ten-year-old twins' lives.

"I've rented the tent next to yours." Sylvie fluffed her acid-white hair. Static electricity in the air made it stick straight up on top, but I didn't tell her, my silence giving me a wicked pleasure. "What better lure than the aromas of cinnamon and hot spun sugar from the neighboring tents, right, love?"

To increase business during winter months, the Igloo Ice Cream Parlor made all sorts of delectable treats. The Igloo had rented a tent near ours, and though the faire wasn't officially open, the shop was already selling its spicy winter version of cotton candy. Other scents like pine trees, cocoa, and brandy-laced crepes filled the air as well.

"C'mon, Mattie-Matt, sales are down," Sylvie said. "I've got to do something to make customers flock to my tent."

"Aren't you jumping the gun?" Matthew said.

"I like to be prepared." She sidled up to Matthew and ran a chocolate-colored fingernail down his sleeve. "Admit it. You always liked how I could coax a cow to croon."

Matthew's eyes turned as dark as lava. "Stop it." He nudged her away.

Coming to his rescue, I gripped Sylvie by the elbow and steered her toward the exit. "Sylvie, give me some of those flyers. I'll be glad to post these."

Some place. Maybe in Timbuktu.

"Thanks, Charlotte. Oh, did you hear—?"

"No time to gossip." I prodded her forward. "We're busy-busy."

Sylvie frowned. She prided herself on being Providence's gossipmonger extraordinaire. Gossip, according to her, flew rampant around a women's boutique. "But—"

"We've got to get back to decorating. Bye-bye!"

Before she could protest, I propelled her into the cold, not thinking twice about how she would keep warm. She was an adult—or at least she liked to think so.

The door lingered before closing, and I caught the strains of Kenny G's melodic saxophone playing a jazzy rendition of "My Funny Valentine." Our mayor—my darling, eclectic grandmother—insisted that easy listening music play non-stop during the Winter Wonderland celebration. Speakers had been set up at the corner of every aisle.

Matthew returned to the task of unpacking glasses and muttered, "Can you believe it? Sylvie rented the tent next to ours." On a normal day, my cousin was the most laid-back, generous man on the planet. But when it came to Sylvie, he turned sour. "Next to ours!" he repeated.

"Intimate, but not horrible."

"She's nuts. Certifiable. It's supposed to snow again."

"Not heavily." Another gentle storm was due tomorrow, the kind that would entice children to walk around with chins upturned, mouths open, and would make our white tents glisten with frost.

Matthew mumbled, "Looney Tunes," and I couldn't disagree. When Sylvie ran out on Matthew, he and the twins moved in to my Victorian home with me. Matthew and I had spent many nights discussing the repercussions of Sylvie's return. He worried that his children, by association, would start acting as crazy as she did. I assured them they wouldn't.

"C'mon, cuz." I nudged him on the shoulder. "No negativity, remember?"

"Yeah, yeah." Matthew brushed a thatch of tawny hair

off his forehead and grumbled his dismay. Our new Briard pup—a surprise gift to the twins from their capricious mother—couldn't have looked more chastised. "Found anybody to hire at The Cheese Shop?" Matthew asked as he inspected stemware for smudges.

"Not yet."

Business at Fromagerie Bessette—or The Cheese Shop, as the locals call it—was increasing at a steady clip, thanks to our burgeoning Internet business, multiple orders for gift baskets, and thriving wine sales. Taking off days to run Le Petit Fromagerie at the faire was making it nearly impossible for us to swing vacation time, even with the temporary help of my industrious grandfather. A few people had applied for the sales job, but none seemed like a good fit. I don't consider myself particular, but I do want whoever works for me to feel like family. Call me crazy.

"Say, did you see that ice sculpture shaped like a hound's tooth?" Matthew asked.

To lure more tourists to town, my grandmother had cooked up an ice-sculpting contest. Ten artists had signed up for the event. Two days ago, a truck delivered huge blocks of ice, and the artists set to work. The weather, as crisp as always in February, was cooperating and keeping the ice from melting.

"It's whimsical," he added.

"That's an understatement." The tooth sculpture was ten feet tall. I had a sneaking suspicion that the bubbly hygienist, a vocal advocate for flossing, was the artist. "Did you see the knight on horseback sculpture?"

"My personal favorite is the Great Dane cuddling a litter of kittens."

"It definitely wins the 'aw' factor."

The sculpture entries didn't have to be completed until Sunday, when the winner of the contest would be announced. I looked forward to seeing the other designs.

"Shoot." Matthew swatted the counter. "I left the wine openers in my car. I'll be right back."

As he exited through the tent door, Rebecca, my coltish young assistant, hustled in. Her long ponytail flew behind her like a jet stream. "Alert! Alert!" Her pretty face was flushed the color of Edam wax, her sweet forehead crimped with worry. She skidded to a stop on the fake grass.

"What's wrong?" I braced her slim shoulder.

"She's . . . she's . . ." Rebecca swallowed hard and caught her breath. "A woman bought the property next to Quail Ridge Honeybee Farm, and she's . . . she's—" Rebecca hiccupped.

I cuffed her on the back. "Calm down."

"She's starting a honeybee farm, too."

I understood her concern. Rebecca had a crush on our local beekeeper. To hear her talk, Ipo Ho had created the moon and the stars.

"She's going to ruin him."

"Relax. There's enough room in Providence for two honeybee farms. Ipo's honeybees dine on clover. Maybe the new owner will feed her bees wildflowers." Honey, with all its healing properties, had turned into a big business. Jars of Quail Ridge honey flew off The Cheese Shop's shelves.

"She's trouble, you watch."

Two years ago, Rebecca left her Amish community and moved to Providence with a rosy picture of what the "real world" would be. After a steady dose of Internet news and TV murder mysteries, she admitted that living in the modern world could be a challenge. But she wasn't leaving. Not any time soon. Because of Ipo Ho.

"Howdy-doo." A handsome and very tall woman in her fifties, wearing a jeans outfit and turquoise-studded cowboy hat and boots, ducked beneath the scalloped doorframe. Where was her horse? I mused. "Nice place," the woman said with a drawl as she dusted lacy snow that had fallen from the door's edge off her shoulders. "I'm Kaitlyn Clydesdale."

Aha! I stifled a giggle. She *was* the horse, complete with a cascading mane of straw blonde hair and a square jaw.

Rebecca gasped. "That's . . . that's her." She slunk back a few paces, as if standing near to the woman would mark her as a traitor.

"You're Charlotte, aren't you?" Kaitlyn jutted out a tanned hand.

Instinctively, I shook with her. Strong grip, perceptive eyes. I liked her. At least I thought I did. She radiated energy and enthusiasm.

Kaitlyn Clydesdale released my hand and roamed the tent, fingering the cheese ornaments and wine bottle labels. "Ah, the aromas. Love 'em. Exactly like I remember as a girl."

"Are you from around here?" I asked. I couldn't recall having seen her before, and she would be hard to forget.

"Lived here years ago. Moved to Texas in my twenties when I got married."

She wasn't wearing a wedding ring now.

Kaitlyn plucked a cheese card from a wheel of Vacherin Fribourg and read: "*Nutty. Melts great for soups, raclettes, and gratins.* Sounds fab." Over her shoulder, she said, "Maybe I could entice you to put together a cheese tasting party for my crew when we pass through town in a few months."

"Your crew?"

"The Do-Gooders."

I'd heard about the Do-Gooders, a volunteer organization that restored historic buildings in the Midwest. All the women wore turquoise-studded hats and turquoise-studded clothing. Their show of unity reminded me of the fabulous Red Hat Society ladies.

Rebecca whispered, "She's lying."

"Shhh."

Undaunted, she pinched my arm. "Ask her what's she doing buying the farm next to Ipo's."

I shot Rebecca a look. It wasn't like her to detest someone so out of hand, and truthfully I wasn't picking up any bad vibes from our visitor.

"Charlotte." Kaitlyn swiveled and met my gaze. "I knew your—"

"Achoo!" A fine-boned young woman with matted black curls scuttled into the tent. Her classic black wool coat swallowed her up; her five-inch platform-heel boots looked as clumsy as army boots.

"Bless you," I said.

"Sorry." Seeming as miserable as a wet poodle, the young woman dabbed her chapped nose with a wadded-up tissue and gripped her coat at her throat.

"I told you not to come inside, Georgia," Kaitlyn said. "Go back to the car."

The young woman flinched at the imperious tone but obediently shuffled out. How she balanced on those heels was beyond me.

"Forgive me," Kaitlyn said. "That was my CFO. She's under the weather. No need to be spreading germs."

"You hired a CFO for the Do-Gooders?" I said. Having one sounded pretty formal for a regional organization.

"Oh, no. She works for Clydesdale Enterprises." Kaitlyn replaced the Vacherin Fribourg cheese information card. "That's my main business."

Rebecca elbowed me. "Told you so."

Kaitlyn eyed Rebecca. "Am I missing something? Why are you upset with me? Who are you?"

"Rebecca Zook." Rebecca threw back her shoulders with youthful exuberance. "And you—"

I rested my hand on her forearm. "My assistant believes you've purchased the cattle farm next to the Quail Ridge Honeybee Farm."

Kaitlyn smiled shrewdly. "We're in negotiations."

Her revelation surprised me. Information about a place for sale should have surfaced in The Cheese Shop, if not from Sylvie, then from any of the dozen other people who liked to congregate at the shop to swap stories.

"'We'?" I said. "There's more than one of you at Clydesdale Enterprises?"

"My business partner and I. The seller is rather eager to close, so it should be final soon."

"You can't," Rebecca blurted.

"Young lady, I can do as I please."

Kaitlyn looked down her nose at Rebecca with a maliciousness that bordered on evil, and in a snap, my opinion of her changed. How rude. Nobody talked to my young friend that way. I got a weird feeling in the pit of my stomach. Maybe Rebecca's concerns were well founded. Maybe Kaitlyn intended to bury Quail Ridge Honeybee Farm. But why, for heaven's sake?

"Now, where was I?" Kaitlyn shook her head like a horse disgruntled with its rider and drew in a deep breath. "Oh, yes. Charlotte, as I was saying before, when we were interrupted." She glowered at Rebecca as though she were a gnat. "I knew your parents."

I fell back a step, shocked. Was that why she had come into our tent? Not to set up a cheese tasting for her crew but to talk about my folks? Most of what I remembered about them, I had learned from my grandparents. I was three when they died. I kept a hope chest filled with memories— my mother's linens, a copy of *Wuthering Heights*, my father's box of fishing lures, LPs of the Beatles, the Rolling Stones, and Elvis. A therapist had told me that with time the loss would soften, but I could feel my eyes welling with moisture.

"Such a tragedy." Kaitlyn strolled to me and patted my upper arm. "That darned cat."

I stiffened. "What are you talking about?"

Kaitlyn placed her hand on her chest; her mouth drew into a thin line. "Didn't you know?"

"Know what?"

"People, including your grandmother, said your cat was roaming around the car and distracted your father."

My stomach clenched as a streak of orange and white zipped across my mind. *Sherbet*. My cat. We'd owned a cat. Until now, I'd blocked the memory from my mind. Images flickered before my eyes. I was sitting in the backseat of our

Chevrolet. Sherbet was nestled in my lap. My father was driving fast and laughing. My mother laughed, too. Wind blasted through the car. We took one of the hills like a roller coaster, and my mother said, "Whee!" I whispered to Sherbet not to be scared. My father looked over the seat and winked at me. His face was full of lightness and joy. When he turned back to face the road, there was a blur. "Horses," my mother screamed. My father swerved.

I glowered at Kaitlyn Clydesdale. "No, that's not what happened. Sherbet was in the car, yes, but she was clutched in my arms."

"Are you sure?"

I willed away tears threatening to fall. Could I be sure? Had I forged my own memory? Had I blanked out the possibility that Sherbet had bolted from my arms and made my father swerve? Any reminder of Sherbet had been removed from my grandparents' photograph albums. Had my grandmother believed Sherbet was to blame? It was my fault that we'd had a cat at all. For months, I'd begged for a kitty. I'd whined until my parents had caved. *Oh, Sherbet. What happened to you?*

"Your mother was a darling friend," Kaitlyn went on glibly, as if she hadn't thrown an emotional boomerang into my life, and once again I grew uneasy. Who was she, anyway? Was Rebecca right to mistrust her? "We had such romps, she and I. She was a gifted singer, did you know? She would have been very proud of you and your accomplishments. Fromagerie Bessette is renowned." An alarm sounded from inside Kaitlyn's purse. She pulled out her cell phone. "Sorry, I must go. I have an appointment."

"Wait," I called, eager—even if I was put off by the woman—to know more about my mother, but Kaitlyn strode through the tent door without a look back.

No sooner had the door clicked shut than it reopened, and Sylvie sashayed in. At least this time she had the sense to wear a robe.

"I know something you don't know," Sylvie sang.

Refusing to rise to the bait and eager not to dwell on the

event that led to my parents' deaths until I could talk to my
grandmother and glean the truth, I said, "Rebecca, go back
to the shop and get those platters I need for the photography
shoot. We'll figure out what's up with Kaitlyn Clydesdale's
plans later."

"You bet you will," Sylvie said, triumph in her tone.

At times I wished I could pull out her wispy hair, strand
by strand.

"You're not going to like who her business partner is,"
she went on.

I strode to the buffet table cheese counter, removed everything from it, and polished it to a gleam.

Sylvie trailed me like a hard-to-lose shadow. "I heard
they want to take over Providence."

" 'They' who?" Rebecca said.

Sylvie kept mute. Obviously she wanted me to be the
one to beg for the answer. Well, she could choke on her
gossip, for all I cared. She didn't give a whit about Providence. Her main thrill in life was to upset Matthew and her
twins' lives. Selfish, that's what she was. Maybe *she* was
the partner. I could see her begging her doting mother and
father for cash to buy the property so she could make a
name for herself in a town that had snubbed her. Except,
thanks to reckless business judgment, her parents were
broke. La-di-dah.

"Who?" Rebecca demanded. "Tell us who."

Sylvie, the witch, didn't blab. Before scurrying out of the tent, she smiled a wicked grin and cackled. Give her a broom and she could celebrate Halloween three hundred and sixty-five days a year.

"Good riddance," I muttered. What I wouldn't do for a bucket of water.

For the next hour, I remained at Le Petit Fromagerie and photographed a variety of cheese platters—a square slate one, a raw-edged granite one, and a round teak one—each laid out with a different selection of cheeses. While I worked, I started to make a list of possible business partners for Kaitlyn Clydesdale. According to Sylvie, I wasn't going to like whoever it was. Prudence Hart, the town's self-righteous, style-challenged society goddess came to mind. She would do anything to make waves. I wouldn't put it past her to want to own a number of competitive businesses. She'd threatened to open her own cheese shop, except she wasn't fond of cheese. Arlo MacMillan, a curmudgeon of the highest degree, dreamed of expanding his

chicken farm, which lay to the west of Quail Ridge Honey-bee Farm.

"Move the wedge of Triple Crème Brie to the left, Meredith." I steadied my camera while Meredith, my best friend and schoolteacher extraordinaire, fiddled with the slate platter of cheeses.

With mid-morning light filtering through the tent's windows, I focused on the center of the platter, which I'd adorned with goat, sheep, and cow's milk cheeses, as well as crackers and a mound of luscious dates.

"How's that?" Meredith asked.

"A bit more to the left."

"You're as much of a sneak as you were in grammar school." Meredith whisked her shoulder-length hair off her freckled face. "How dare you wrangle me into a job with the promise of tasty tidbits and then renege. And I'm not talking about gossip. I was expecting f-o-o-d."

I chuckled. "Don't worry. You'll get some cheese. But I need to takes these photos in just the right light. Updated photographs on a website draw customers. And Rebecca is more than occupied on her break."

I glanced at Rebecca, who was supposed to be arranging jars of honey on the pair of baker's racks that we'd brought to the tent, but she was flirting with Ipo. She twirled a lock of hair around a finger and twisted the toe of her right ballerina slipper in the fake green grass. I couldn't fault her. The honeybee farmer, a transplanted Hawaiian and a former fire dancer at luaus, was not only handsome but a sweetheart. I gazed at my own heartthrob, Jordan, a local cheese farmer who had offered to help Matthew lug in boxes of wine. Muscles rippled beneath his work shirt. Per-spiration beaded on his chiseled face. He must have felt me looking, because he turned his head and gazed at me with such passion that heat swizzled to my toes. Over the past few months, we'd spent a lot more time together. And not only on dates. Fromagerie Bessette was in the process of adding a cheese and wine cellar beneath the shop—we wanted to offer the freshest cheese selections around as

well as preserve all our shipments of wine—and Jordan was helping us design it. As the owner of the building, he had even offered to foot half of the expense. He called it an investment.

"Yoo-hoo, where'd you go?" Meredith said. "As if I didn't know."

I yanked myself back to the photo shoot and clicked off a few more pictures using a wide-angle lens. "So, have you set a wedding date?"

Meredith and my cousin Matthew were engaged.

She said, "We're thinking that autumn would be—"

"Charlotte," Rebecca called. "What's that cheese you said Ipo would like?"

"That little round of Emerald Isles goat cheese. You know the one, from Emerald Pastures Farm." A charming artisanal cheese maker north of town owned Emerald Pastures Farm. She put her heart into her work. "It's got a luscious mushroom flavor. Very earthy. I've stored some in the refrigerator." In addition to the wine and cheese tastings we were offering in the tent, we planned to sell a modest selection of other cheeses and wines. I'd had a glass-fronted refrigerator delivered for the occasion. It stood between the baker's racks.

Rebecca pulled a hatbox-style cheese container from the refrigerator and plopped it into one of our pretty gold gift bags. "And what about the Brie?"

"I'd suggest using the same one I'm photographing. Rouge et Noir Triple Crème." It was a fabulously creamy Brie made by the Marin French Company, the oldest cheese manufacturer in the US. "And don't forget the Chevrot I told you about. It's young, so it's sweet."

"Like you," I heard Rebecca say to Ipo.

Warm breath caressed my neck. Jordan brushed my back with his fingertips, then kissed my cheek. "Ah, true love."

Desire crackled through me.

"I've got to return to the farm," he whispered. "Catch you later." He disappeared out the rear door.

Matthew followed him, saying he had business calls to make back at the shop.

"Earth to Charlotte." Meredith waved a hand in front of my eyes. "Are you ever going to tell me about your trip with Jordan? You've been pretty mum since you got home."

"It was wonderful, exotic, enticing." Jordan and I had spent a week in Switzerland, tasting cheese, sipping wine, and chatting. Well, doing more than chatting. Seven glorious days, six romantic nights. "I showed you pictures."

"Yes, you told me you listened to Alphorns and rode the funicular to Plan-Francey, and you toured the village of Gruyères and Chateau de Gruyères. But who is Jordan? Really?"

Jordan had lived in Providence for five-plus years, yet he had a mysterious past that I hadn't tapped. On our trip when I asked how he had learned to make cheese and, more particularly, how he had learned the art of affinage—the craft of aging cheeses, which he did in his huge caves for many of the smaller farms in the area—he told me a British cheese maker named Jeremy Montgomery had tutored him.

I related the story to Meredith.

"But Jordan isn't British," Meredith said.

"His parents were working in the American embassy in London."

"Aha, now we're getting somewhere. Doing what?"

"Not sure."

Meredith put a hand on her hip. "Where did he go to college?"

I took three pictures in a row. "Why are you grilling me?"

"Because he has a secret past."

"He likes the movie *The Godfather*. Matthew told me that any man who likes *The Godfather* is good by him."

Meredith offered her best schoolteacher-who-doesn't-believe-the-dog-ate-your-homework look. "Do you believe this story about the cheese maker?" She snickered. "What a silly question. Of course you do. You love him. Jordan could have told you he was formerly an Antarctic explorer, and you'd have believed him."

"And I'd have been captivated." I winked at her.

She grinned. "Okay, next round of questions. Who is this Kaitlyn Clydesdale that Rebecca was telling me about, and who is her mysterious partner?"

"Moi," a man said.

A shock wave of anxiety shot through me at the sound of the man's voice. I spun to face him as he entered the tent, and my heart skipped a beat. Actually it started to hammer my rib cage.

Chippendale Cooper, aka Chip Cooper, aka Creep Chef, let the door of the tent swing shut. He finger-combed his honey-colored hair and struck his typical jock pose. *"Bon soir,* Charlotte. I'm back from France." His sea green eyes sparkled with mischief. With as much humility as he could muster—which wasn't much—he added, "Long time, no spy."

Meredith clutched my hand in a death grip. "What's he doing here?"

I shook her off as deep-rooted anger surfaced. My hands balled into fists. Chip gazed at me warily and lowered his chin. Did he think I'd whack it? I couldn't top the damage that all the hockey sticks had done to it during high school. Not that I didn't want to try.

In response to my seething silence, he offered a devil-may-care grin. "Love your hair, babe. It's longer. The color suits you."

I self-consciously toyed with strands at the nape of my neck. I had grown my hair to chin length and had added gold highlights in the winter. It was flirtier; Jordan liked it.

Chip held up his iPhone. "Smile for the camera." He snapped a picture. "Beautiful."

Only Chip and Indiana Jones could have scars that turned into charming dimples. Jordan had a scar down the side of his neck—an ugly, jagged scar, usually hidden by the collar of his work shirt. I had discovered it one night during our trip to Europe—one intimate, lovely night. When I'd asked about it, he wouldn't tell me about the event that had led to it. I had attempted a guess or two, of course: a hard life on the street; a drunken brawl; an attack by an

angry ex-girlfriend? Jordan had cracked a smile at the latter but had offered no answers. Maybe a wayward penguin had attacked him on one of his Antarctica explorations, I mused.

Rebecca raced to my side. "What's going on? Who's the hunk?"

"Chippendale Cooper," Meredith said, as if that explained it all.

Rebecca gasped. "Creep Ch—"

"Chip," I said. "Call him Chip."

"Of all the gall." Rebecca flung her ponytail over her shoulder and glowered at *the hunk* as if she was the one he had maligned.

Chip took a quick picture of Rebecca, then hitched his head. "Can we talk outside, babe?"

"We have nothing to talk about." The level of bitterness that crawled into my throat surprised me. If I wasn't careful, tears would surface. No way was I going to let that happen. Chip could make all the snipes he cared to; I'd remain stoic. "Rebecca, I'm going back to Fromagerie Bessette. You close up the tent. Meredith, would you give her a hand?"

I strode toward the exit. Chip raced ahead of me and held back the tent door. While tightening my neck scarf, I sidled out, doing my best not to breathe or touch him as I passed. I didn't want to remember his musky scent. I didn't want to remember his fingers stroking my neck, my cheek.

Cool air blasted my face as I headed south through the Village Green.

Chip hustled behind me, stating the whys and wherefores of his decision, on one fateful winter's night years ago, to flee to France. He begged me to forgive him. "I was young."

"You were thirty."

Dodging hordes of folding tables and chairs, boxes of crafts, and clothing racks, I snaked through the white tents. I sped past a security guard for the Winter Wonderland faire, who tapped the brim of his hat with a fingertip in

greeting. Too angry with Chip, I failed to respond to the guard. I would have to apologize another day.

"Thirty is a formative time in a man's life," Chip said, keeping pace.

"In a woman's, too," I hissed.

"Tick-tock, yes, I get that."

"Not tick-tock. Not that at all."

"Don't you want children?"

I blasted past the ice sculpture of the Great Dane and kittens. Sure, I wanted kids. Yes, I was nearing my mid-thirties, and yes, every dratted magazine on every dratted magazine stand displayed some kind of article about the risk of having children over the age of thirty-five, but I ignored the articles. I did. I had eons of time. I was healthy, vibrant. I exited the Village Green and skirted around a man offering authentic Amish horse and buggy rides to tourists. Chip followed and gingerly scruffed the horse's nose as he passed.

"Then what is it, Charlotte?" Chip pressed. "Why are you so mad at me?"

I stopped on the sidewalk near the Country Kitchen diner. Every red booth inside the diner was filled with patrons. All seemed to be staring at us. I said, "You've got to be kidding."

"What?" Chip threw open his hands like a petitioner waiting for me, the judge, to deem him innocent.

I waggled a finger. "We are not having this conversation."

"I've come home to tell you I love you."

"Home? This is not your home. You abandoned the town. Your folks have moved away. You have no heritage here. Go back to France."

He shrugged. "There's nothing for me in France."

"There's nothing for you here, either." I folded my arms across my chest. Defensive, sure, but I needed armor, which seemed to be sorely missing. Maybe I had left it at the dry cleaners.

Chip jutted his hip like a cocky teenager, but he didn't fool me. I had shocked him with my tirade. His eyes

shuttered rapidly like a camera lens on the blink. "Don't you want to hear my plan? Why I became Kaitlyn Clydesdale's partner?"

"Not really."

"She ran into me at Le Creperie on Avenue Italie in Paris. She said I made the best crepes she'd ever tasted."

He did make good crepes, as light as clouds. I would never forget the time, right after college, when he had brought me crepes in bed, on a tray decorated with a rose in a vase. But that was beside the point. He had walked out on me. In the middle of the night. A man doesn't do that and return expecting instant forgiveness. Or any forgiveness, for that matter.

I squelched my emotions, found my spunk—sans the armor—and started across the street. Chip grabbed my arm. I wrenched free and glowered at him.

He threw his arms wide. "Hear me out, please."

He gazed at me with imploring eyes, and something stirred. Mind you, I didn't exactly melt, but I was curious. I said, "Thirty seconds."

Townspeople scuttled by on either side of us. The gentleman who owned the Igloo Ice Cream Parlor gave me a guarded look, as if to ask if I was all right. I offered a reassuring nod. He moved on.

"Kaitlyn said she had a hometown business she wanted to start." Chip laced his fingers behind his neck.

Was he flexing his muscles to impress me? Oh, please.

My right foot started to tap, and I smiled to myself. My grandmother did the same thing when listening to a fish story. *Liars never prosper,* she said.

"After a year running her business," Chip continued, "Kaitlyn will back me so I can open my own restaurant."

"Your own restaurant?"

"Yeah, you know, the one I've always dreamed of starting. Chip's Creperie." He swiped his hand in front of him as if painting the sky with neon. "Doesn't it sound swell?"

Swellheaded, more likely. "Aren't there enough creperies in France?"

"Here. She'll back me here. In Providence. I'm moving home. For good. The restaurant won't be on the main square, of course. Retail space is at a premium. But I'll find a location on the north side. Someplace with lots of foot traffic."

I stiffened. No, no, no. I needed a clean break. I needed to move forward with my life. I did not want my ex-fiancé hovering over my shoulder and judging my relationship with Jordan. My head started to throb. What horrible thing had I done to deserve such a lot in life?

"What the heck do you know about bees?" I demanded, sounding shrewish, but I couldn't help myself. If the rumor was accurate and Kaitlyn Clydesdale intended to turn the cattle farm into a honeybee farm, then according to Chip, she expected him to run it. But that wasn't possible. "You hate the sight of spiders and ants and all sorts of tiny creatures. How in the heck will you suit up in a beekeeper's uniform and cultivate the buzzing horde?"

"I've been studying up on bees. They're docile."

"Are you kidding me?" My voice grew louder. "They're not docile. What if you get stung?"

"I'm not allergic."

"You're impossible."

"But adorable." He traced a finger down my sleeve.

I recoiled. "Goodbye, Chip. Good luck." With my insides quivering in confusion, I strode across the street. When I entered The Cheese Shop, I could feel him gazing at me, but I didn't look over my shoulder. I gave myself a mental pat on the back for my keen resolve.

* * *

"*Chérie.*" My adorable grandfather, Pépère, stood behind the cheese counter, fiddling with the buttons of his navy blue jacket that appeared close to bursting. After a second, he gave up and ruffled his feathery white hair. "Bah. It is not cold enough to bother. Come here while there are no customers." He beckoned me to the kitchen at the rear of the shop. "It is nearly three o'clock. Load me up."

"Just a sec." On my way through the store, I tweaked the displays. I turned out the labels of the jars of jams and the many gourmet vinegars on the shelves, and reassembled hatbox-style containers and waxed rounds of cheeses on the five weathered barrels that graced the floor. I nudged in the ladder-back chairs by the marble tasting counter and, using the elbow of my sweater, polished a smudge from the glass front of the cheese counter. I would never forget my grandfather telling me, when I had started working at Fromagerie Bessette, that everything in the shop should appear as appealing as a piece of art.

Before entering the kitchen, I took one last glance around, admiring how well the Tuscany gold walls went with the hardwood floors and how inviting the archway leading to the wine annex looked. Matthew and I had made a smart decision to redecorate. The only thing that was uninviting was the curtain of heavy plastic that covered the door to the basement, but it was a necessary evil. If someone accidentally left the basement door ajar while we were revamping the cellar, the plastic would prevent dust from seeping into the shop. Thankfully the dust was almost nonexistent since we had completed the framing and were waiting for workers to begin the next phase.

"Load me up." Pépère removed the lid of a two-gallon cooler that sat on the floor. "What else do you want me to take? I don't want to be late to Le Petit Fromagerie. You'll give me what for."

I tweaked his elbow. "Oh, yeah, like that has ever happened."

His eyes crinkled with delight. "I have more of the Emerald Isles goat cheese, Zamorano, and Rouge et Noir."

"Perfect."

"Oh, and as you suggested, I set out a platter with the Two Plug Nickels' cream cheese on the tasting counter." Two Plug Nickels, another artisanal farm north of town, made the most fabulous lavender goat cheese and now a cream cheese that was silky smooth. "I put a bottle of the hot pepper pickle sauce beside it. The two are so tasty together, *non*?"

"Absolument." At Fromagerie Bessette, we offered samples at the tasting counter daily. Because I was focused on educating our customers about cheese platters, I had decided the cream cheese–hot pepper creation was a study in simplicity. The cheese, smooshed on a cracker and drizzled with sauce, was melt-in-your-mouth scrumptious.

"Take along these knives to the tent, as well." I handed him a few boxes of silver, braid-handled spreaders. They were a popular item to purchase. "While you're there, will you make sure I have enough serrated knives?"

"Mais oui."

Not wanting to haul a ton of cutting implements to the tent at the last minute, I had taken many over in batches.

I smoothed my grandfather's collar and kissed him on both cheeks.

As he exited, Rebecca scuttled in. So did a handful of customers. While we served them, Rebecca plied me with questions about Chip—why he was in town and whether I still had feelings for him—until I grew so weary that I snapped at her to mind her own business.

A half hour later, as the shop emptied of customers, Rebecca joined me at the prep counter against the wall by the kitchen. She cleared her throat. I ignored her and continued dicing Liederkranz into half-inch cubes. It was a pungent cheese that had all but disappeared from the array of cheeses until its rebirth in Wisconsin. Same recipe, new cultures. I had devoted the month of February to creating exotic cheese trays for my customers. To start this particular display, I had adorned a broad blue-banded porcelain plate with a mound of rice noodles. Around the noodles I had scattered clusters of cashews.

"Charlotte," Rebecca began.

"No," I said instinctively and plopped a handful of dried apricots on top of the lacy mound.

"I'm not going to ask you about Chip." She jutted a bony hip. "I got the hint when you snarled at me."

"What, then?"

She started to giggle. The nervous laughter increased.

She tapped her fingertips on her lips in an effort to stop from tittering, but the sound burbled out of her.

"Spill," I ordered, "or you'll burst."

"Ipo is coming over tonight." She danced a jig. The hem of her peasant blouse fluted around her hips. Her winter skirt swished side to side. "And we're going to do it."

I gulped.

"Not *it*, it," she blurted. "We're going to kiss." Her fingers skirted to her neck, then her chest. A red flush decorated her pale skin. After a moment, a sob caught in her throat and she grabbed my wrist. "Charlotte, what if I don't like it?"

She had never kissed a boy. Ever. Her Amish upbringing had kept her at arm's length from all men. She had admitted to liking a lanky boy when she was thirteen, but the farthest they had ever gone in their relationship was holding hands—forbidden before marriage in some sects.

I squeezed her shoulder. "You will like it. Promise."

"I hoped you'd say that." She eyed the platter I was putting together. "That's pretty. What cheeses are you adding to the Liederkranz?"

A few months ago, I had attended a cheese conference and had taken seminars to enhance my understanding of the art of plating. Cheese can be so varied in taste and texture, but many are pale. Adding fruits, nuts, olives, pickles, and meats, in a variety of colors, will brighten a tray and enhance the tasting experience.

"Yarg Cornish Cheese and Roaring Forties Blue," I said.

"I love Yarg," she gushed. "Did you know that Yarg is Gray spelled backward because Gray is the name of the couple who came up with the recipe for the cheese? Wait, of course, you did. You told me. The flavor of nettles is so unique," she went on. "And I adore the Roaring Forties Blue. The nutty finish is divine."

The front door chimes jangled, and Arlo MacMillan skulked in, all one-hundred-and-forty pasty pounds of him. His overcoat looked two sizes too big.

"Morning, Arlo," I called.

He gazed at Rebecca and me from beneath his hooded eyelids and gave a hint of a nod. Then he shuffled toward the barrel that was stacked with jars of homemade raspberry jam. Every week Arlo graced the shop with his gloomy presence, but in all the years I had known him, I couldn't remember him purchasing cheese more than three times—and then it was only Provolone cheese. I had tried to talk him into other selections, but he wouldn't budge.

Two tourists and a bevy of children, each dressed in a heavy winter coat, trooped in behind Arlo, all chattering at once. They bustled toward the counter, and the man who I assumed was the father scanned the chalkboard menu behind me. At the insistence of a few tour guides, we had added a limited array of pre-made sandwiches to the other foods that we offered. When we sold out, we sold out.

"That Collier's Welsh Cheddar, turkey, and cranberry croissant looks good to me," the woman said to the man. "American cheese and salami on wheat for the kids, and include a wedge of that blue cheese." She pointed at the Roaring Forties Blue. "We'll add it to tonight's salad."

As I was wrapping their purchase in our special cheese paper—waxy on the outside, plastic on the inside—the front door flew open.

"Charlotte!" Tyanne Taylor swept inside. She stamped her tennis shoes on the carpet to clear them of debris, darted around the family, and scooted behind the counter. Runny black mascara streaked her pretty cheeks. Smidgens of it had dripped onto her snug cinnamon-colored jogging suit. Tyanne had worked hard to get rid of unwanted weight, and now she had what health magazines would call a supertoned body. "Sugar, he's leaving me," she drawled. "My Theo is leaving me and the children."

"Why?" I asked in a gentle voice, hoping she would follow my lead. I didn't want to scare off customers with talk of divorce, but I also wouldn't turn away a friend in need. I finished off all the sandwich packages with our gold seals,

slipped the sandwiches and the wedge of Roaring Forties Blue cheese into a handled bag, and gave the bag to
Rebecca. "Ring them up, thanks."

"Can't yet. I think the dad has hit it off with Arlo."
Rebecca hooked a thumb.

Indeed, the father had joined Arlo by the barrel that held
a display of rounds of Camembert, assorted goat cheeses,
sourdough crackers, and jars of pesto, and they were chatting like old friends, which blew me away. Arlo didn't like
anyone. At least I hadn't thought he did.

"I'll pay," the woman said.

I steered Tyanne toward the coat rack at the rear of the
store.

When we were out of earshot, Tyanne said, "It's . . .
another woman." She rolled her shoulders back. Her jaw
drew taut. "But I won't let him get the better of me. I won't.
I don't need him. *We* don't need him. I saw you were hiring." She paused, her bravado weakening, and tucked her
lower lip under her teeth. "I thought I'd better come and
ask. Can I . . . Will you? I did all the marketing and computer output for the fresh market grocery down in New Orleans before . . . before . . ." She started to shake, unable to
finish her sentence. Before Hurricane Katrina had turned
her life topsy-turvy. After trying to make a go of it in rav-
aged New Orleans, her husband gave up and purchased his
uncle's insurance business in Providence and had moved
the family lock, stock, and barrel. No debate.

I gave her a hug. "You're hired." I couldn't think of anyone I would like more to work in the shop. She was a survivor. Salt of the earth.

"Oh, sugar, that's such a blessing. Thank you." She
sighed. "I feel like such a cliché. He's leaving me for his
assistant, for heaven's sake." She blew a strand of hair off
her face. "What did I do wrong? I lost weight. I streaked my
hair like he wanted." She shook her glossy layered locks.
"Did I let my mind go flabby or something?"

I squeezed her elbow. "It's not you. Sometimes we can't
fix things."

Exactly when had I started to believe that? After Chip ran out, I guessed. I had poured my all into our relationship. A therapist told me the breakup wasn't my fault. Prior to Chip, I had thought I could fix anything.

"When do I start?" Tyanne asked.

"Now. Bozz is tied up with senioritis at school."

"It's only February."

"All the seniors check out mentally once they've heard from the colleges of their choice." At first, I'd only hired my teenage guru, Bozz, to help with Fromagerie Bessette's website design, but over the course of the past two years, he had grown into an invaluable employee, knowledgeable about cheese, marketing, and so much more.

"Where has Bozz been accepted?"

"To Providence Liberal Arts College."

PLAC was the first college ever in Providence, and its debut freshman class would start in the fall. My pal Meredith was bubbling with excitement about the prospect. Her efforts to convert the old Ziegler Winery into a liberal arts college were coming to fruition. Bozz intended to work through college, but he had asked if he could cut his hours from sixteen to eight. I would miss seeing him as often.

I turned to Rebecca. "Would you bring Tyanne up to speed at the cheese counter and in the kitchen? A while later, Tyanne, I'll walk you through the website, the newsletter, et cetera. Around here, we all pitch in with everything."

"Might I freshen up, sugar?"

"Of course. You know the way."

She headed toward the back of the shop.

As she disappeared, Prudence Hart marched in, her dark mood matching her charcoal coat, her prunish face twisted into a knot as always. "This Founder's Day celebration, or Winter Wonderland faire, or whatever we're calling it this year, has got to stop." At times, she reminded me of the Wicked Witch of the East. She shook her fist overhead as if blaming the gods.

"The festival hasn't started," I reminded her.

"It makes a mess. Trash flying everywhere. And the

riffraff." Riffraff was one of Prudence's favorite words. Everyone not of her social status was riffraff. She stomped to Arlo, who was once again standing alone, and nudged him with her bony elbow. "Don't you agree?"

Like Prudence, Arlo's ancestors were some of the first settlers in Providence, but that didn't mean he had to be friends with Prudence. He muttered something, pulled his overcoat tight, and scuttled away from her. Prudence harrumphed. "And have you seen that woman prancing around in the cowboy hat, bragging that she's going to change things around here? Who does she think she is?"

I said, "Don't you recognize her?"

"No, why should I?"

As if summoned by Prudence's negative spirit, Kaitlyn Clydesdale swept into the store. "Why, Prudence, are you telling me you don't remember me?" She smiled broadly. "It's me, Kaitlyn. Katie C."

"No!" Prudence said, taking in Kaitlyn with narrowed, disbelieving eyes. "Can't be."

"It is." Kaitlyn ran a finger across the brim of her hat. "A few pounds thinner and wrinkles older. You dated my little brother, Kent."

Prudence's face grew reflective. She wasn't married and was known as a penny-pincher who would never share her wealth with a man. Did she actually have a soft spot for someone on this planet? This Kent guy? Prudence hurried to Kaitlyn and gripped her by both arms. "How is he?"

"Married, four kids, living in California. He told me to look you up. I heard you're in charge of the Providence Historical Museum."

"I am."

"I'm in charge of an organization that helps renovate such institutions."

Prudence's eyes brightened, and if I hadn't seen Kaitlyn Clydesdale in action earlier, snubbing Rebecca and practically taunting me with the memory of my parents' deaths, I would have sworn she was a nice woman. But I knew differently. She dropped bombs with ease, like the Red Baron.

"We'll talk, Pru." Kaitlyn broke free of Prudence and strode toward the counter.

As she did, Arlo shuttled toward the exit. He bumped into Kaitlyn as he passed and grimaced as though the contact stung.

Before the door closed behind him, my lively grandmother breezed inside, her purple crocheted poncho billowing up with vigor. She flipped off the hood of her homemade patchwork coat and plucked at her short hair. "Kaitlyn, there you are. I—" When Grandmère spotted me, she skidded to a stop, and a flush of embarrassment colored her aging crepe-paper-wrinkled skin. In my gaze, she must have detected that Kaitlyn had dropped the bombshell about my parents' deaths. She held up a finger to me as if to say we'd talk later, and I blew her a kiss, letting her know that I wasn't mad about the story. She knew best what I could handle at the time. I didn't believe that, at the age of three, I would have devoured myself with guilt, but perhaps I would have, and that guilt could have altered my life's journey.

With a sigh of relief, Grandmère skated toward Kaitlyn and slipped her fingers around Kaitlyn's elbow. "Charlotte, I see you've met my dear, dear friend Kaitlyn."

Dear, dear, I thought. Since when?

"We have known each other for years," Grandmère went on. "She was one of your mother's first friends. What was it you both loved to do?"

Kaitlyn said, "Climb trees."

"Oui." Grandmère petted Kaitlyn's arm. "And scrape your knees."

"Pfft," Prudence sputtered and glowered at Grandmère. Was she jealous that Grandmère and Kaitlyn were best buds? Was Grandmère purposely fawning over Kaitlyn to irk Prudence?

"By the way, Charlotte, did Kaitlyn tell you?" Grandmère said. "The Do-Gooders are going to invest in the Providence Playhouse."

"No!" Prudence gasped.

Grandmère stood as tall as her five feet two inches could make her. "It is a historical building worth saving, Prudence Hart, no matter what you may think." In addition to being the mayor of our fair city, my grandmother also ran the theater. Five years ago, she'd campaigned for a new set of loge chairs and had succeeded at raising the funds, but the structure was old beyond old. The walls had cracks. The bases of the walls were weathered. The wiring was faulty. "It is going to get a makeover," she crowed. "We have found our saint."

"Angel," I corrected her.

"Whatever. Are we not lucky? Our first production in the newly refurbished building will be . . . Wait for it." She held her finger up. "The musical, *Chicago*."

"But that's so mainstream," I said. My grandmother was known to do plays or musicals with a twist.

"Nothing like shaking things up by keeping them normal." Grandmère winked.

Prudence sputtered. "But Kaitlyn just promised to help renovate the Providence Historical Museum."

"Don't worry, ladies. I'll be doing both." Kaitlyn offered her megawatt smile. "I have every intention—" Her cell phone rang. "Excuse me." She fished the phone from her purse and answered. As she listened, her smile turned taut and her gaze steely. Though she cupped her hand around her mouth and the phone's mouthpiece, she could still be heard. "You listen to me. You'll do nothing of the kind! Do you hear me? I'll ruin you." She flicked the cell phone shut and flung it into her bag. As fast as her smile had vanished, it returned. "Now, where were we? Do-Gooders to the rescue."

CHAPTER

3

"Aunt Charlotte, I'm ready!" Amy hurtled down the stairs of my two-story Victorian, her eyes frisky with excitement.

She and her sister, Clair, weren't actually my nieces. Their father was my cousin, so the girls were first cousins once removed, but I could never bring myself to call them that. Matthew and I settled on using the terms *niece* and *aunt* the day the twins were born.

"Oops." Amy nearly missed the last step. She hit the floor and skated on one foot toward me, while I was struggling to put a leash on Rocket, the Briard pup that the twins' mother, Sylvie, had so sweetly dumped on my doorstep . . . and on me. Looping the choke chain over the dog's overly active head was always a challenge. The dog barked as a warning.

"Sorry," Amy said.

"Keep your head steady, pup," I added.

Rags, my Ragdoll cat, scooted into the foyer, batting an empty box of Camembert like a hockey puck. He sailed it into the dog. Rocket leapt backward and barked again. Rags

hissed. Rocket hunkered down and growled. I grinned. I had a house full of kids and none but the cat were mine.

"Sit, Rocket!" I ordered, though I had to admit I didn't sound very tough. Rocket didn't mind me. I said, "Sit!" more sternly. Rags, the rascal, did a victory cha-cha then scooted away. "C'mon, Rocket. Sit or you don't get your evening walk." Begrudgingly he obeyed. I slipped on the leash.

"How do I look?" Amy tugged the hem of her blue and yellow polka-dot sweater over the hips of her Capri pants then fluffed her blunt brown hair.

"Cute." I zipped up my parka and snugged my gold filigree scarf around my neck. "But why the fuss? It's just rehearsal."

The twins and ten other girls their age had been selected to sing in this year's Winter Wonderland chorale. A recital "hall" tent stood in the middle of the Village Green, near the town's wishing well and clock tower. The songfest would be the highlight of Saturday evening's festivities.

Amy's mouth quirked to a smile. "Because."

"She likes a boy," Clair said from the landing. "He's going to be at the Winter Wonderland faire." She tucked a book under her arm and took the stairs cautiously as she always did, but once she hit the hardwood floor in the foyer, she became as animated as her sister. She poofed her bangs and plucked lint off her floral sweater.

"Who is the boy?" I tilted my head.

"Thomas Taylor," Clair blurted.

Amy thwacked her. "I told you not to tell."

"You said don't tell Dad," Clair said with pixielike glee then adjusted her mini ponytail. "You didn't say I couldn't tell Aunt Charlotte."

"Does Thomas know?" I asked, surprised that Amy was the one who liked him. He was a shy boy and seemed better suited to Clair.

Amy shook her head. "Boys are dense."

"Why will he be at the faire?" I asked. "It's not officially open yet."

"His father is carving one of the ice sculptures. It's the one of a horse with a knight on it."

The sculpture I had admired, which shocked me. I didn't think that Tyanne's soon-to-be ex-husband had an ounce of creativity in his bones. "Well, you look very nice, and Thomas would be a dolt not to flirt with you."

"She calls him Tommy," Clair taunted.

Amy blushed. "C'mon, Clair. Daddy's waiting in the car." She yanked her sister by the elbow.

"Hold it. Don't forget your jackets and your dinners." I retrieved two brown paper sacks from the bench by the front door, each bag marked with a name.

"Grilled cheese like you promised?" Amy grabbed a blue jacket off the coat rack.

I nodded. "Yours has sliced cornichon pickles, Swiss, and prosciutto." I focused on Clair, who was shrugging into her aqua green jacket. "And yours is made with salami, Redwood Hill goat cheese, and homemade gluten-free bread." I had landed on a great gluten-free bread recipe that, once baked and sliced, lasted in the freezer. "I've wrapped them in foil so they should stay warm," I added, though I didn't think it would really matter. The girls liked cold pizza.

The pair whistled their thanks and whizzed out the door. Amy yelled, "Bye. Have fun at yoga class after your walk!"

"Let's go, boy." I picked up Rocket's leash and gave a gentle yank.

Rags zipped into the foyer at a clip and yowled like an alley cat: *Take me, me, me.* Up until a few months ago, he had been an indoor cat because of an attack when he was younger, but his agoraphobia disappeared whenever he walked alongside Rocket. However misguided, I think he believed the dog would defend him against another assault.

"You don't deserve a walk," I teased, "but all right." I slipped a jewel-studded leash around his furry neck, stroked his mismatched ears, and the three of us headed into the cold, moonless night.

Yesterday's snow was now nothing more than a mixture

of glistening ice and slush, highlighted by the glow of streetlamps. As we drew near to Lois's Lavender and Lace, the bed-and-breakfast next to my house, I was surprised to see Barton Burrell, a local cattle farmer, on a ladder. Not only was the hour well beyond dusk, but Lois's husband, whom I had dubbed The Cube due to his square shape, usually did the chores around the inn. Barton hammered nails into a wobbly flat of white lattice that abutted the wall. Sweat dripped off his oversized nose. I called out a hello, but he didn't respond.

The screen door of the bed-and-breakfast squeaked open, and Lois, looking so frail that the wind might blow her over, shuffled out to the porch carrying a tray. Her fluff-ball of a Shih Tzu, Agatha, traipsed beside her and gave a yelp. Lois spotted me. "Hello, Charlotte. Have time for a cup of tea?" She set the tray on a wicker table.

"I don't want to intrude," I said. Most nights, Lois and her husband drank tea outside and watched passersby. Weather never thwarted the ritual.

"You're not intruding, dear." Lois beckoned me with spindly fingers. "Ainsley is at a hockey game, don't you know. Got him the tickets myself."

I headed up the path with my four-legged buddies, who were content to go wherever I did. As I neared, I smelled the lovely aroma of nutmeg-laced scones, and my mouth started to water. "Yum," I said.

Lois beamed. She made heavenly scones in assorted flavors. She bent to greet my pals. "Hello, sweet things. I have home-baked treats for you, too." She hustled inside and returned with a large bone-shaped dog biscuit and a handful of bite-sized tuna morsels. Rags and Rocket set to work.

"Mr. Burrell," Lois called. "Time for a break, young man."

Barton descended the ladder and tramped up the steps to the porch. He looked leaner and shaggier than when I'd seen him last, and he had grown a mustache, but he also appeared less sure of himself, as if something was bothering him. A pang of concern shot through me because Barton, who moonlighted as one of Providence's local the-

ater stars, was usually a ham and full of bravado. He had been known to stand on a street corner and spout poetry or lines from Shakespeare's plays. Was he suffering a financial crisis? Was that why he was working for Lois? Perhaps Kaitlyn Clydesdale was in negotiations to buy his property. His cattle farm abutted Quail Ridge Honeybee Farm.

Lois poured Barton a cup of tea from a Haviland moss rose china teapot. She added a lump of sugar and offered it to him.

Barton blew on the tea, then drank two sips and whispered, "Thanks."

"Aren't you going to say hello to Charlotte?" Lois said.

"Nice to see you," he muttered. Air no longer hissed through the gap in his front teeth; he'd had the gap fixed last year. But that wasn't what disconcerted me. Something in his gaze made me think he was upset with me.

As he retreated to the ladder, I wondered if he was embarrassed to be seen taking on extra work.

Lois said, "Let's go inside. It's brisk. Do you think the puppy and cat can stay out here with Agatha?" She shuffled ahead of me and held the door open with her leg.

"It would be better if they could nestle in the foyer, just inside the doorway. Rocket is so young, he might bolt otherwise."

"Sure, sure."

I led Rocket and Rags into the entry and commanded them to sit. They did. Agatha marched in front of them like a sentry, daring them to make a move, which probably had something to do with their near-perfect behavior.

A warm wave of heat swirled around me as I followed Lois into the great room. The temperature was too hot for my taste, but the bed-and-breakfast was successful, so Lois probably knew what her guests enjoyed. The room reminded me of a hunting lodge, its walls packed with sports memorabilia as well as winter sports equipment. In the spring, the snowshoes, skis, hockey sticks, commemorative pucks, and slalom flags would come down and be replaced with garlands of flowers and glorious pictures of

Holmes County. Lois prided herself on decorating according to the season. She said it made her guests' stay that
much more unique.

A fire crackled in the stone hearth. I settled in one of the
many wingbacked chairs in the cozy room and inhaled
deeply. Lois must have laced the wood with sticks of cinnamon, which burned like incense and imbued the room
with a spicy scent.

Lois adjusted the eye patch over her weak eye—she
had recently decided that handmade decorative patches
were the *rage*—then she nestled into the chair opposite me
and placed a lavender crocheted throw that matched her
lavender warm-up suit over her knees. "Ainsley," she said,
referring to her husband as if we hadn't had a break in conversation. "He adores his hockey, don't you know. He was
a player, back when. An ace shot. I'm thinking of having
his game stick bronzed for his next birthday, but, hush,
don't tell him." She pointed to a hockey stick with three red
stripes on the handle that was hanging on the wall. "I love
surprises."

"So do I," a man said from the hallway.

Not her husband. Chip.

He emerged in the archway, and I groaned. How did I
not sense he was staying right next door to me? He swaggered into the room, his randy gaze drinking me in.

Why did it take all my mettle to look away? Dang.

"Ahhh," he said, eyeing the display on the wall. "Remember the first hockey game you ever attended, Charlotte?
Slap shot!" He mimed a powerful shot, raising his arms behind him and following through with flair.

How could I forget? The team had won because Chip
had made three goals—a hat trick. The high school crowd
went wild. Girls had thrown themselves at him, but he had
sneaked off with me—his science lab partner—in his Mus-
tang. Talk about chemistry! The next day we went for a
hayride, with church bells clanging in the background. He
said there was nothing more fun in life, and at the time, he
had been right.

"Remember?" he repeated.

Oh, yeah, I remembered. He was my first kiss. We had necked for two hours. I wondered if Rebecca was enjoying her first kiss right about now.

"Time flies, doesn't it?" Chip glanced at his watch. "Speaking of time, I'm off to the Village Green to watch the ice sculpting. Want to join me?"

"I'll pass."

"You don't know what you're missing."

But I do. I did. I had. I wouldn't make the same mistake twice.

He strutted out the front door and stopped in the foyer to give my pets a good nuzzle—the traitors yipped and purred their delight—then Chip exited and jogged down the steps laughing.

As his laughter faded, Lois said, "Have you heard about Kaitlyn Clydesdale's plans to start a new honeybee farm?"

Was that why she'd asked me in for tea? To ply me for gossip? I said, "Only rumors."

"Well, it's a shame, you ask me. That sweet Ipo Ho and his Quail Ridge Honeybee Farm won't be able to compete."

"Why not?"

"First off, Kaitlyn will update everything. Then she'll produce twice as much honey at half the price. I've heard that's what she does."

Not following, I said, "She owns other honeybee farms?"

"And cattle farms, goat farms, wineries, and more." Lois bobbed her head in rhythm. "I overheard her talking when she was staying here. She loves to update everything. She hates to let things remain behind the times."

"Kaitlyn was a guest here?"

"For one night. She moved to Violet's across town. Good riddance." Lois swatted the air.

Violet's Victoriana Inn was Lois's competition, and Lois was quite vocal about not liking Violet's sense of style. The inn was less homey than Lavender and Lace and a heap more expensive, although it did have a number of perks. Violet had hired a full-time masseuse and hairdresser.

From what I could tell, Violet's place was more Kaitlyn Clydesdale's style—brash and aloof.

Lois clucked her tongue. "She's not to be trusted."

"Violet?"

"Kaitlyn Clydesdale. Mark my words. I knew her years ago. She'll eat up this town." Lois looked at least five years older than Kaitlyn. Had their age difference colored her view? "She was a terror as a girl. Willful."

I knew a lot of willful people, but that didn't make any of them a terror.

"Willful," Lois repeated, and left it at that.

* * *

The sugary aroma of freshly made toffee in the Igloo Ice Cream Parlor snaked its way up the stairways, beneath the doors, and into the brightly lit yoga studio where my girlfriends and I were attending class. My stomach grumbled like a volcano. Sitting in the butterfly pose invariably made me hungry—don't ask me why. My pal Freckles, a button of a woman dressed in neon orange workout clothes, giggled at the noise. Meredith, Delilah, and Jacky joined in. I hushed them all with a glare. Freckles stuck out her tongue.

"Real mature," I whispered.

"Lie flat on your mats," the stick-thin yoga instructor said.

All of us un-pretzled our bodies and obeyed.

"Hands beneath your buttocks and lift your right leg. Inhale up, exhale down. Now, the left leg. Inhale up . . ."

I breathed out my earlier frustration with Chip, and focused on Jordan's winning smile and gentle hands and delicious kisses. I wondered if he would be free later. Would it be too brazen if I called?

"Plow pose. Raise your hips over your head. Touch your toes to the ground."

Jacky, Jordan's darkly elegant sister who glowed with new mommy joy even though, for the first time in her life,

she was battling tummy bulge, only made it halfway in the plow pose. She moaned with frustration and tried harder. Freckles, who had recently given birth to a second daughter, moaned as well.

"Psst." Despite the odd position, Meredith turned her head sideways. Her flexibility had something to do with regular exercise, I was pretty sure—something I needed to do more of. "Ipo will have to work things out for himself regarding the new competition with Clydesdale Enterprises, I'm afraid."

"She's right," Freckles chimed in.

Before entering the classroom, I had told my friends about my chat with Lois.

"Does Ipo have any recourse?" Jacky asked.

"There's nothing in the town's bylaws that states someone can't have a competing business," Delilah said. She would know. A number of competitors had tried to lure customers away from the Country Kitchen.

"Ladies, quiet," the yoga instructor said. "Silence is good for the soul."

"But silence won't solve the world's problems," I whispered.

Freckles tittered. "You're bad."

Delilah laughed, too. So did Meredith. The instructor gave us the evil eye.

While still attempting to achieve the perfect plow pose, Jacky said, "Meredith, when's the wedding?"

"We're thinking autumn. The college will be up and running by then." Meredith's enthusiasm was contagious.

"I love fall weddings," Freckles gushed.

Meredith had hired Freckles and her staff at Sew Inspired Quilt Shoppe to sew all the dresses for the wedding, mine included. But when was the wedding going to be? Autumn was such a nebulous time frame. Did Meredith mean September, October, or November? A girl needed to plan ahead. I didn't want to lose five pounds in August for nothing.

"Delilah, how are things going with Luigi?" Meredith

asked, switching subjects deftly. Luigi Bozzuto was the owner of Providence's only four-star restaurant, La Bella Ristorante.

"Great. He's helping me divine some new grilled cheese sandwich recipes." She made a humming sound as she often did when talking about food. "How does Vella Dry Jack, bacon, red onions, and syrup sound?"

"Decadent," Meredith said.

"Utterly." Delilah grinned. "Luigi said I should call it the *Godfather*, after . . . Charlotte, you tell them."

I said, "Ig Vella was considered the godfather of American artisan cheese—a term he hated, by the way. His father founded Rogue Creamery with the help of J. L. Kraft."

"Wow," Meredith said.

"Luigi is such a card." Delilah laughed. She hoped to host a grilled cheese contest in Providence someday. In an effort to create the most unique sandwiches imaginable, Delilah had sought Luigi's advice. Within a week, Luigi and she had started dating. Though Luigi was at least twenty years older than Delilah, he could keep up with her intense pace and he loved to dance. The level of dance ability didn't matter to Delilah. Good, bad, or indifferent at the skill, a man's job was to get her out on the dance floor.

"How are things with Urso?" Delilah asked Jacky, who had achieved the plow pose—just barely.

"Unfurl, ladies, and roll onto your stomachs," the instructor advised. "Arch your back in the cobra pose."

As we all obeyed the command, Delilah said, "Yoo-hoo, Jacky . . . Umberto Urso . . . hello. I asked you a question."

Jacky drew in a deep breath but kept mute. The day after she found out she was pregnant by insemination, she started dating Providence's chief of police, who was one of my best friends. Had they broken up? I couldn't remember having seen them strolling together or holding hands in quite a while. I would hate it if they split up. Urso had seemed so happy. Jacky, too.

"Cat-cow," the instructor said.

We all drew to our knees, inhaled, and rolled our backs toward the ceiling.

"Fine, don't talk about Urso," Delilah said. "Charlotte, where's Rebecca? Why hasn't she joined us in this no-talking zone?"

"She's consoling Ipo," I answered.

"That's not what I hear," Freckles said. "I hear they're going to do it."

"Wahoo." Delilah whistled under her breath.

I groaned. How many people had Rebecca confided in? "Not *it*, it," I said. "They're going to *kiss*."

That earned laughter and a round of "Uh-huh, right," from Meredith, Delilah, and Jacky.

"Ladies, please, no talking, or I'll have to ask you to leave," the instructor said. "This is a relaxing environment."

"I'm not talking," Freckles said. "I'm laughing."

"No laughing, as well."

Delilah flat-out guffawed. I couldn't hold in my chuckles any longer, either.

The five of us scrambled to our feet, gathered our things from the rear of the room, and hustled into the foyer of the yoga studio. Our laughter chorused above the burbling water fountain. Lyrical music, designed to make those who entered the hallowed studio calm, filtered through speakers, but we simply couldn't be serene.

"I'm so sorry," Freckles said, still chuckling.

"I'm not." Meredith patted Freckles on the back. "None of us were reaping the benefit of the class for some reason."

"My twelve-year-old told me there's hyper-electricity in the air. Winter brings it on." Freckles was always packed with trivial information. She and her husband homeschooled their daughter. "Frenchie and hubby are doing a physics experiment on the topic this very minute with our other munchkin watching from the stroller."

"I wasn't talking about physics," Delilah said. "I was talking about chemistry." She turned to Jacky. "C'mon, give. What's up with you and Urso?"

At least they had backed off discussing Rebecca and Ipo's situation.

"Nothing." Jacky tucked her yoga mat under her arm. "I mean, things are fine. Everything's fine."

As Delilah pleaded for more, Meredith tweaked my elbow and whispered, "By the way, I Googled the guy that Jordan said taught him to make cheese—Jeremy Montgomery."

Her presumption that I would want to know made me prickly—was I that easy to read? I glanced at Jacky to see if she was listening in. She wasn't. She seemed intent on stalling Delilah's interrogation. I said, "Go on."

"I'm worried," Meredith said.

"Why?"

Meredith chewed on her lower lip then proceeded. "He died before Jordan was born."

My insides percolated with apprehension. Why would Jordan lie to me? "Are you sure?"

Before she could respond, the front door of the yoga studio burst open.

Bozz, my teenaged Internet guru, hurtled inside. Chest heaving for breath, he brushed longish bangs off his forehead and gasped. "Miss B! I just got a text."

Big deal. I would bet he received nearly two hundred texts a day.

"It's from Chief Urso!"

My heart snagged in my chest. "What did it say?"

"He . . . He"—Bozz bent over and sucked in air—"he couldn't reach you." He stabbed a finger in the direction of my purse. We were required to turn off all cell phones for the yoga class.

"It's about Rebecca." Bozz offered me his phone.

I snatched the phone from his palm, and as I read, my knees went weak.

Kaitlyn Clydesdale was lying dead in Rebecca's cottage.

CHAPTER

While I hotfooted it to Rebecca's, my boots spanking the wet pavement, selfish thoughts zipped through my mind. Whether I had liked Kaitlyn Clydesdale or not, I had been hoping to ply her for more information about my mother. I knew so little. My mother's parents had died of natural causes soon after the crash. My mother had no sisters or brothers. The few friends she'd made had married and moved away. Kaitlyn claimed to have been one of those friends. I was hoping that, during the time she was in town, she would tell me more about my mother—her secrets, her passions, what had made her tick. During my childhood years, Grandmère had done her best to fill in the blanks, but a friend who had known my mother for years would have been so much better. With the link gone, I felt a loss deep in my soul.

By the time I reached Rebecca's red-shingled cottage, a crowd had gathered. Many were popping up and down, trying to see over the heads of someone in front. Rebecca rented her darling abode from my Realtor friend, Octavia

Tibble, who owned a half dozen such cottages around town and rented them only to single women who Octavia decided had promise. I looked for her among the crowd but didn't spot her. She adored Rebecca. Maybe she was already inside demanding Rebecca's rights.

Heart pounding, I veered toward the white fence that was cluttered with barren rose vines. I slipped through a break in the fence and stole to the front porch.

The top half of the Dutch door hung open. I would lay odds that our illustrious chief of police was already inside. He hated a stifling hot room. Everyone else within the cottage had to be freezing.

As I drew near, Grandmère sidled to my side. "Oh, *chérie*." Tears streaked her cheeks. She pulled the ends of her knit burgundy scarf to tighten it. "I am so glad you are here. It is a shame, *non*?"

"Yes. Tell me what happened."

"Chief Urso believes our sweet honeybee farmer killed Kaitlyn Clydesdale."

"Killed? This is a murder scene?"

Neither Urso nor his deputy had hung the yellow *Police Line—Do Not Cross* tape yet. At any moment, they might order the crowd to retreat. Before that time, I needed to learn all I could.

"The jury is out," Grandmère said. When my grandparents moved from war-torn France, they had adapted quickly to the American way of life. Grandmère loved to use Americanisms. "*Regarde.*" She pointed at the living room, visible from our spot near the Dutch door.

Kaitlyn, wearing the same getup she had worn in The Cheese Shop, lay on her back on a red braided rug. Her body was wedged between an Amish rocking chair and a ladder-back chair; her head was close to the leg of the coffee table. Rebecca's furnishings were sparse. She and I had gone garage sale hunting one day and had picked up most of the items. She had saved an entire month's earnings to buy the ruby red love seat upon which Ipo and she were sitting.

The coroner from Holmes County, a contemporary of

Urso's with slicked-back hair and a deeply furrowed fore-head, knelt beside Kaitlyn. Latex gloves covered his hands. Gingerly, he turned her chin and inspected her head.

I said, "He sure got here fast."

Grandmère nodded. "He was having dinner with Chief Urso."

Umberto Urso, whose sheer size dwarfed the already teensy cottage, stood in profile beside the cobblestone fire-place. A glow from the waning fire made his uniform seem more gold than brown. Beneath his broad-brimmed hat, his dark hair was mussed, as if he had been scratching it trying to figure out what happened.

Rebecca sat tucked into Ipo. Goldilocks in the presence of Papa Bear couldn't have appeared more vulnerable. Ipo had slung his meaty arm around Rebecca's shoulders, but by the look of his trembling chin, he needed consoling, too. Did Urso truly think kindhearted Ipo could kill someone? Why wasn't anyone speaking?

"Yep," the coroner broke the silence. "Some kind of wooden baton, I think."

"Baton?" I whispered to my grandmother.

"He thinks Ipo struck Kaitlyn's neck with a weapon," Grandmère answered. "Can you believe it?" She shook her head. "Apparently Kaitlyn fell backward from the blow and hit her head on the table. But they cannot find a weapon, and Ipo is not offering any clues."

I scanned the room. Six-inch cylinder candles, standing on the pass-through counter to the kitchenette, burned with intensity. The light from a pair of tapers created shadows on the fixings for a cheese tray, which included a wedge of Manchego, Brie, the Chevrot I had suggested, three wood-handled knives, crackers, and a jar of honey. A crystal bowl holding mixed nuts and another containing winter grapes sat on the nearby dining table. Two champagne flutes stood empty beside an unopened bottle of champagne, which rested in an ice bucket.

Earlier in the day, Rebecca had recited the menu for her romantic meal.

I glanced at her. Her lips were swollen. So were Ipo's. There was no doubt in my mind that they had done *it*— kissed. What an ending to such a promising evening.

I started to open my mouth to call to Urso when he cut a look in my direction and glared at me. I recoiled. What had I done to warrant such displeasure other than snag a front-row seat? He held my gaze with an unspoken warning: *Back off.* I glowered to let him know that I wouldn't budge, not when Rebecca could be in trouble. She was like my little sister. No way was I obeying him because he had a better bully look than I did. I folded my arms and raised my chin ever so slightly. *Take that!*

"Deputy Rodham," Urso barked.

The gangly young policeman with a roosterlike hairdo stepped forward from the shadows, his narrow shoulders squared.

"Secure this scene. ASAP. And close that front door."

Rodham saluted and fetched a roll of yellow crime-scene tape from a satchel. "Move back, folks." He pressed open the lower half of the Dutch door, which forced me to shuffle aside, then secured and shut the whole door after him.

But I wasn't done listening yet. He headed left, so I veered right and found a spot near a Bieber tilt-turn window, cracked open enough to ventilate but not refrigerate. Grandmère nestled in beside me.

"What can you see, *chérie*?"

"Urso is crouching beside the coroner. He's whispering something."

"What?"

"I don't know."

The coroner responded with a hushed word to Urso. Oh, to be Superwoman and have supersonic hearing.

"Thanks." Urso rose to his incredible height and faced Rebecca and Ipo, his back to me.

From where I stood, it was like watching a play. Shadows created by the varying light in the room danced on each of the players' faces.

Rebecca and Ipo sank deeper into the couch, both probably wishing they had worn red clothing and could blend into the background.

"Mr. Ho, you come from Hawaii," Urso said.

"Yes."

I stiffened. Where was Urso going with this line of questioning? What significance did it have? Why was he being so hard-hearted? On any other day, he would have called Ipo by his first name.

"Oh, there is your grandfather," Grandmère said. "He will want to know everything. I will return." She scuttled away.

A cold draft filled her spot, and then a body did. Sylvie. *Lucky me.* She was wearing a skintight purple sweaterdress and reeked of patchouli. I wondered if all her Under Wraps items smelled the same. If they did, I would run from the store the moment I entered. Not that I *would* enter. I had steered clear since it opened.

"Fill me in," Sylvie said, breathless with curiosity.

"Shhh."

"Don't you hush—"

I gave her a sterner than stern look. Without asking, she wedged herself in beside me so that she could peer through the opening.

"Oof," I whispered.

"Shhh," she said with a snicker.

Urso continued. "Tell me about your luau jobs, Mr. Ho."

"I was a fire dancer." An edge crept into Ipo's normally gentle tone.

"Fire dancer."

"Yes." Ipo's face pinched with concern. He seemed as baffled as I was by the questions.

Rebecca caught sight of me, and her eyes filled with such pleading that my heart wrenched. I held up a finger to give her hope. For what, I couldn't be sure—for a miracle answer, a suspect other than Ipo, something. And soon.

"Tell me about the wooden batons used in your ceremonies," Urso said.

Ipo fidgeted.

"What are they called again?" Urso snapped his fingers, but I would bet dimes to dollars he knew the name. During high school, when most teens suffered wanderlust, Urso had devoured the entire set of James Michener books. He had looked so dorky carrying huge thick tomes to school when the rest of us were trying to read the thinnest books possible.

"Kala'au rods," Ipo said.

"That's it. Kala'au rods. Hardwood, right? About nine inches long." Urso sounded somber. He fisted his hand, as if gripping one of the rods. "You've got a pair of them, don't you?"

Ipo said, "They're stored in a cabinet at home."

"I'd like to see them."

"I didn't do this," Ipo said, his voice ripe with intensity.

"He didn't!" Rebecca echoed. "We never saw this . . . this Clydesdale woman. Not here, I mean. We saw her in the shop but not here. I don't know why she came to my house. We were outside." She slurped in air and started to cough.

Ipo patted Rebecca's back and clutched her tighter.

"Outside?" Urso said.

"Yes, Chief," Ipo answered. "We were outside—"

"—smooching," Rebecca cried. "We smooched for a very long time."

Urso pivoted to the right, biting down on his lower lip. To keep from laughing? He ran his fingers along the brim of his hat, then turned back to Rebecca and Ipo. "How long were you, um, kissing?"

"How should I know?" Rebecca shifted on the sofa. "It was our first time. I was nervous."

"So nervous she couldn't stop giggling," Ipo admitted.

"Urso, she's telling the truth," I blurted.

Urso whirled around. When he spotted me by the Bieber window, he snarled. Not out loud, mind you, but I didn't miss the extrasensory thrust of his anger. In a seething stage whisper, he said, "Don't get involved this time, Charlotte."

He was referring, of course, to the other times I had inserted myself into an investigation. But how could I not? He was attacking Rebecca.

"She's Amish," I said. "She wouldn't lie."

"Are you sure?" Sylvie whispered.

I stomped my foot to drive her away from me. "U-ey, you can't possibly think Ipo did this."

Urso whirled away, and I instantly regretted using his nickname. As the saying goes: *Loose lips sink ships*. But since grade school I had called him U-ey—for the double *U* in his name: Umberto Urso. By the way he raked his hand down his neck, I could tell he wouldn't give me another second of his time. Shoot.

Sylvie nudged me. "Do you think Ipo whacked Kaitlyn with one of those whatchamacallits?"

"Hush!"

"He had motive, from what I've heard."

"What motive?" I glowered at her.

"Kaitlyn was in my shop earlier having a facial and talking about her empire. Ooh, did I tell you? I've added a facial room in the back of Under Wraps. I found this glorious woman with great hands. Doesn't my skin look better?" Sylvie turned her chin, lifting it to remove any glimmer of loose skin. "Mind you, women want more than a dress when they come to a boutique. They want to leave looking smashing. I've created a one-stop shop."

"Stay on topic, Sylvie."

"Right-o." She toyed with one of her gaudy purple dangle earrings. "As Kaitlyn left the shop, she said she was heading to Ipo's farm to have it out with him. It seems he's hired a lawyer to block her purchase of the Burrell farm."

"Block it?"

"On the grounds of unfair competition or something, but it sounds like motive to me." Sylvie punctuated her revelation with a curt nod.

"Miss Bessette." From behind me, Deputy Rodham cleared his squeaky throat. "I'm going to have to ask you and your friend to move."

I whirled around and froze, my mouth agape. Over Rodham's shoulder, I spied someone lurking in the shadows. A man in a trench coat. He looked like he was assessing the crowd.

"Miss Bessette," Deputy Rodham said, an officious edge to his voice.

"Not now," I snapped.

That caught the lurker's attention. He jerked his head in my direction. I couldn't make out his features before he hightailed it away.

CHAPTER

Curious behavior has often lured me to be impulsive. A man running from a crime scene definitely fell into the category of curious behavior.

I raced through the throng clogging the path leading to Rebecca's cottage saying, "Excuse me. Sorry. Let me through."

Sylvie ordered me to stay put, but I ignored her. I didn't want to lose the lurker. Who was he? Had he attacked Kaitlyn when Rebecca and Ipo were outside kissing? Or was he a Peeping Tom? Maybe he had been hanging around for a while. Maybe he could tell Urso what had happened at the cottage and exonerate Ipo.

I tore after him, north on Cherry Orchard and along sidewalks illuminated by streetlamps. As I drew closer, I could make out more of his shape. In a word: sloppy. Raggedy knit ski hat, baggy pants beneath his coat, work boots. He wasn't as tall as Deputy Rodham. He was more like the size of Matthew or Jordan or Lois's husband, the Cube. He passed Fromagerie Bessette, the Country Kitchen, and Under Wraps.

At the west entrance to the Village Green, my breathing grew ragged, but I wouldn't give up. I was gaining on him. When he cut around a couple pushing a baby carriage, he glanced over his shoulder and his mouth gaped open. My guess, he was surprised to see me on his tail. I recognized him. He worked for Ipo at the honeybee farm.

"Oscar," I yelled.

He didn't slow.

"Oscar Carson!"

He dashed into the Winter Wonderland. I ran faster, my lungs heaving, thighs burning. I definitely needed more exercise. Maybe a regimen. Twenty minutes of aerobics when I woke up, followed by twenty of stretching. No, that sounded much too difficult. Cobwebs usually clouded my brain until my first cup of coffee or tea. Maybe I could exercise after work. Or I could double up on yoga and walk the dog and cat an extra mile.

"Oscar!"

I had only met him a couple of times. He didn't make good eye contact. I'd heard he was slightly challenged. Ipo had hired him at the farm to clean out storage bins.

Oscar zigzagged left and right, weaving between the white tents. I sprinted after him, the twinkling lights and luscious scents of cocoa and fresh-baked goodies in Winter Wonderland distracting.

Focus, Charlotte.

I drew to within fifteen feet of him. Ten feet. Five.

Oscar veered around a corner. I followed and pulled up short as he charged into the ice sculpture of the knight on the horse. Splinters of ice spurted upward. The knight's lance shattered into pieces. Oscar slipped and skated forward. His feet shot into the forelegs of the horse. The sculpture buckled. The horse's head wavered. Oscar scrambled to get out of the way, but his hands got caught in the folds of his trench coat, and he lost purchase on the slushy grass. He hit the ground with a thud and flung his arms in front of his face to prepare for the inevitable.

The horse's head plunged. Its chin gored the ground inches from Oscar's hips.

Oscar screeched.

"What the heck?" The sculptor, none other than Tyanne's philandering husband Theo, arrived with a hot dog in his hand. He hurled the hot dog aside and stamped toward Oscar. A defensive linebacker in college, Theo hadn't lost any of his bulk nor, it appeared, any of his rage. Red faced, he grabbed Oscar by the collar and whipped him to a standing position. "What's going on?"

Oscar said, "Accident." Head lowered, he looked half a foot shorter than Theo, though if he stood tall, he would have been roughly the same height.

"All my work. My precious work. You . . . you . . ." Theo hurled Oscar to the ground, but rather than kick the man, he slammed his toe into an open metal box that held his ice-sculpting tools. The box rattled like thunder. Theo swiveled his head and shook a fist at me. "This was your fault."

"No, it wasn't," I said, knees knocking. Oscar was the one who had opted to run into ice sculpture territory. Why couldn't he have nailed the sculpture by our peace-loving hardware store owner? Mr. Nakamura would have uttered some blessing and re-created his artwork without a word of reproach.

Theo moved toward me, fist pumping. "You hired my Tyanne!"

How nimbly he changed gears, I mused. He wasn't angry at me for ruining his sculpture; he was railing at me for hiring his wife—the wife he had cheated on. I wondered if medication for a rapidly fluctuating temperament might be in his future.

"Fire her," he demanded.

A crowd emerged from between the surrounding tents. I peered among them for Matthew. He had to be in the area. I could hear the twins' chorale group practicing the Beatles' "She Loves You." Was Matthew aware that I was about to be ripped limb from limb? Would he save me?

Feeling bolstered by the crowd, I employed the tone I used for the twins whenever I had to mediate an argument and said, "I'll do nothing of the sort. Tyanne is free to do as she pleases. End of discussion." Oscar started to worm away from the scene, but I rested the toe of my boot on his arm. "Uh-uh, you stay put." I regarded Theo. "I'm sorry about the ice sculpture. Grandmère ordered extra blocks of ice just in case anything untoward happened. You're obviously very talented. You can carve your masterpiece again."

My apology redirected Theo back to the real reason for his anger. He raised his heel, I assumed to crush Oscar's pale face, but he stopped, foot in mid-air, and his eyes went wide.

"Problem?" a man said from behind me.

I turned toward the welcome sound.

Jordan, arms casually hanging by his sides, strolled toward Theo. He carried a sparkly white bag in one hand and looked relaxed, but something about his steady gaze and his loping walk reminded me of a panther ready to attack.

Theo must have picked up on the feral energy, too. He lowered his foot, took a step back, dusted off his parka with the edge of his hand, then thrust an index finger at Oscar. "You're lucky, you bozo." He eyeballed Jordan one last time, then grabbed his tool kit and stormed out of sight.

The crowd dispersed, discussions about the altercation rising in pitch as the folks departed, but soon the quiet of night settled around Jordan, Oscar, and me. Only the faint humming of the chorale filled the air.

I smiled at Jordan. "Thank you."

"No thanks needed. Someone in the crowd would have jumped in if you hadn't been assertive."

I wasn't so sure.

Jordan glanced at my toe, which was still pinning Oscar's arm. I felt my face redden. What kind of beast was I? I removed my foot and said, "Stay."

Oscar squirmed to a sitting position.

"What do you want with him?" Jordan asked.

"I want to interrogate him."

"You don't look like you need me for that. I'll mosey along."

"No, please." I grabbed Jordan's wrist, the one holding the sparkly bag.

"Why? Because you want some of my candy?" He wriggled the bag, which came from the Igloo Ice Cream Parlor. "I've got chocolate bonbons stuffed with peanut butter cream. I bought them for Jacky, but I'm sure she'll share."

"I don't want candy." I mean, I did. I often do. A girl doesn't live on cheese alone, although I do my best. As my grandfather says, *There are so many choices, so little time.* "Stay, please?" I explained about Kaitlyn's death and how Urso was honing in on Ipo as a suspect and the fact that I'd caught Oscar lingering at Rebecca's cottage.

Jordan's face turned grave. "Question away, but don't expect to get much from him. You know he's—" Jordan tapped his head.

Challenged or not, Oscar was going to answer me. I crouched beside him and held him with my gaze. "Did you kill Kaitlyn Clydesdale?" I was no district attorney. Subtlety was not my forte.

"We're talking somebody's life here," Oscar said.

His indirect response jarred me, but I continued. "You ran from Rebecca Zook's cottage."

"Do you think you were born with a monopoly on the truth?" he replied.

Again, his response struck me as odd. So did his speech pattern. It wasn't jagged. It sounded almost rehearsed.

"Oscar . . ."

His gaze roved—to the right and left, up and down. When he did focus on my face, he blinked rapidly. Was he purposely making his eyes flutter? I clapped my hands inches in front of his face. He looked at me—directly at me. His pupils didn't waver. Not a whit. I recalled a boy in seventh grade who would fake seizures if he hadn't done his homework. Old Miss Magilicutty, our apple-faced teacher, would buy the con every time and cart the boy to the nurse's office.

A cloud lifted from my brain. I said, "You're acting, Oscar. Those responses you just gave me are from the play *Twelve Angry Men*." As a teen, I had been cast as the judge in the high school play—the only woman in an otherwise all-male cast. Grandmère had rallied on my behalf.

Oscar said, "The burden of proof is on the prosecution."

"I'm right." I jabbed a finger at him. "You're spouting Juror Number Eight's lines. Why?"

Jordan deliberately cleared his throat.

Oscar cut a look in Jordan's direction and shuddered. "Wh-wh-who are you?" He wasn't asking Jordan's identity. He had met him around town.

"Your worst nightmare, if you don't start answering the lady's questions." Jordan grabbed Oscar by the elbow and hoisted him to his feet. "Are you going to talk? No more pretense."

Oscar shivered in his shoes, but not because the temperature hovered in the upper thirties. I rose, too, my gaze trained on Jordan as the question Meredith had posed to me earlier in the day scudded through my mind. Who was Jordan really? He had such command over people. Was he merely a cheese farmer, or was there something in his mysterious past that should frighten me?

Oscar lowered his eyelids, as if he was considering his options, and then his eyes blinked open. "Yeah, okay." He brushed off the front of his trench coat, all pretense gone. "I worked for Kaitlyn."

I said, "You mean you worked for Ipo."

"And Kaitlyn Clydesdale."

Adrenaline ping-ponged through my veins. Now we were getting somewhere. "What precisely did you do for her?"

"About ten months ago, she hired me to check out neighboring properties." Now that he was talking freely, he allowed a New Jersey accent to color his tone. "So's I got a job at Quail Ridge Honeybee Farm to fit into the community."

"Were you checking them out to rob them?" I asked.

"Nah. We were searching out a good buy."

"Are you a detective?"

"Sorta."

"A corporate spy?" Jordan said.

"That's more like it." Oscar steepled his hands. "See, I told Kaitlyn about the Burrell farm. They were having problems making payments. Based on my intel, Kaitlyn made a bid for the place."

"Why was Kaitlyn looking to invest in Providence?" I asked.

"Why not? There's a lot of growth here, what with all the tourism and people leaving the big cities for charming little towns. Kaitlyn is . . . was"—he gulped—"she was an opportunist."

I frowned. Something wasn't ringing true with Oscar's story. "Why were you at Rebecca's cottage? Did you kill Kaitlyn Clydesdale?"

"Me? No!" He gulped, peeked at Jordan, and returned my gaze. "Do you know Georgia Plachette? Kaitlyn's gal. Real pretty with dark curly hair."

She was Kaitlyn's CFO, the young woman with the bad cold who had reminded me of a wet poodle.

Oscar's cheeks flushed. "I like her, and, see, she wouldn't go for no liar. So's I decided to come clean with her about my so-called duties, but first I had to quit working for Clydesdale Enterprises and be who I really am."

"And who is that?"

"An actor," Jordan said.

Oscar tapped his nose and pointed at Jordan.

"Kaitlyn saw you in a play," Jordan added.

"Man, you're good." Oscar looked at me. "See, she checked me out, found out I was in debt. Big debt. She made me an offer I couldn't refuse." He stubbed his toe into the ground. "I was going to tell Georgia everything, but first I had to quit. I saw Kaitlyn at the pub around six. She had these shopping bags, and—"

"Wait a second," I cut in. "Sylvie said Kaitlyn left for Ipo's house after she'd had a facial at Under Wraps."

"Since when does Sylvie do facials?" Jordan asked.

"She doesn't do them. She hired a woman." I fluttered a

hand. "That's not the point." I zeroed in on Oscar. "You're lying. Kaitlyn didn't go to Timothy O'Shea's Irish Pub."

"Yes, she did," Oscar blurted. "I was at the bar. She was talking to Tim, himself. She said she wanted to meet with Ipo. Tim was the one who told her Ipo was on his way to Rebecca's. Kaitlyn asked Tim for directions. I hung out for about fifteen minutes, then set out after her. When I got to the cottage, there were shadows moving about inside. I figured I'd talk to her when she came out, so's I took a walk to that park for kids, the one with the climbing rocks and tunnels."

Cherry Orchard Park, near my grandparents' house, not far from Rebecca's.

I said, "It was dark. Why did you go there?"

"I told you. I took a walk. To clear my head. I didn't intend to play there. Sheesh." Oscar folded his arms across his chest.

"Why should I believe you?"

"I heard giggles. Lots of giggles."

My body began to vibrate with hope. I grasped Jordan's hands. "He heard Rebecca and Ipo. He corroborated their alibis." I did a victory dance. "I've got to tell Urso." I stood on tiptoe, kissed Jordan's cheek, and sprinted south.

CHAPTER

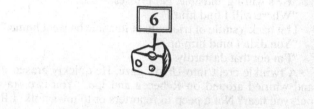

"You what?" Urso stood on the stoop of Rebecca's cottage and glowered at me. His broad-brimmed hat cast a shadow over his face and made his eyes look especially ominous. "I can't believe you sometimes."

Rebecca and Ipo stood at the Dutch door, the top half open once again. Light haloed their heads as they strained to hear our conversation. The crowd had dispersed.

"You are going to be the death of me, Charlotte Bessette," Urso said, sounding like an old coot. "What were you thinking, chasing after him?"

"Can't you get past that?" I said. "He corroborated that Rebecca and Ipo were in the park."

"They told me they were outside. I assumed the yard."

Rebecca shouted, "Outside in the park. You never let me finish, Chief."

Urso cut a steely look at her and then an even steelier one at me. "I'll question Oscar Carson, and we'll see what he says when he's not under duress."

"Oh, yeah, like I could influence him," I said, knowing

I had. I had held him in place with my toe. Having Jordan
looming beside me hadn't hurt, either.

Rebecca applauded.

"Hush, Miss Zook." Urso eyed me. "Did you at least
leave him in one piece?"

"He's willing and able. No bruises."

"Where will I find him?"

I bit back a smile of triumph. "I imagine he went home."

"You didn't bind him up?"

"I'm not that dastardly."

A twinkle crept into Urso's gaze. He quickly erased it
and whirled around on Rebecca and Ipo. "You two stay
put, you hear? Not a peep to reporters or to townsfolk. I'll
return."

"Do either of them need a lawyer?" I asked.

Urso stabbed a finger at me. I threw my hands up in
mock-defense. He didn't say a word and marched away.

* * *

The next morning started with a bang. Literally. Even
though I heard something akin to a poltergeist in my kitchen,
I dared to enter. I found Amy raging from cupboard to cupboard, slamming indiscriminately while muttering, "Stupid,
stupid, stupid."

Sometimes she was so like my grandmother it was
scary. Negative energy zinged out of her.

Our poor Briard pup, his eyes as wide as saucers, scooted
beneath the kitchen dining table and sought shelter by
Clair's legs. Rags, who was used to Amy's occasional out-
bursts, nestled into his rattan bed and placed a paw over his
exposed ear.

I glanced at Clair, who was working on a needlepoint
project for art class, and said, "What's wrong with your
sister?"

Clair tucked her hair behind her ears. "She's mad at
Tommy for not paying attention to her last night."

"Thomas," Amy cried. "I call him Thomas now. He told
me I had to. And, oh, he paid attention, all right," she went

on, her voice squeaky with outrage. "He squirted me with ice-cold water."

Clair stifled a laugh. "It could have been worse. He could have pelted you with ice chips."

I knew better than to get into this argument. I opened the refrigerator and retrieved gluten-free pancake mix. I had made it at midnight to settle my nerves. "Will flapjacks with crème fraîche and chocolate chips help your mood?"

Amy scowled at me. "Nothing will help me today. Nothing. He's so . . . so . . ."

"Stupid," Clair said.

Amy whirled on her. "He's not stupid."

"Last night you swore you would never like him again."

"And I won't." Amy sizzled with anger. "Never." She stormed from the kitchen and stomped up the stairs. The door to her bedroom slammed with a thwack.

* * *

An hour later, when I arrived at The Cheese Shop, I found Rebecca in a similar mood, for entirely different, more grown-up reasons.

She charged me like a freight train with no brakes. "You've got to do something." She tugged on the cuff of my red turtleneck sweater. "Something!"

"Where's Matthew?" I asked.

"I don't know. Maybe he's downstairs admiring the framing in the cellar. Please, do something."

"About what?"

The shop was empty of customers. I allowed her to pull me into the kitchen at the rear of the shop where she was preparing a gift basket. An assortment of cheeses sat on the granite counter, including a bloomy rind Brillat-Savarin, a washed-rind Taleggio, and a Mimolette, which was a perfect cheese for grating, with a unique tangerine color and heavenly hazelnut flavor. The basket already contained a jar of Ipo's Quail Ridge Honey, a box of gourmet crackers, and a bag of dried cranberries. Wheels of ribbon and a pair of scissors lay to the side.

Rebecca released me. "Urso went to Ipo's after he met with that horrible Oscar Carson."

"O-ka-a-ay." I pushed up the sleeves of my sweater and started wrapping the cheese selections in our special paper.

"He wanted to see those luau sticks that he'd asked Ipo about, but Ipo couldn't find the sticks. They weren't where he stored them in his house. Somebody stole them."

"Why would someone steal them?" To each selection of cheese, I added an identifying sticker that informed the customer of the name of the cheese, its country of origin, and the type of milk used: *cow, sheep, goat*.

"I don't know. Neither does Ipo." Rebecca worried her hands in front of her. "Please, please help him."

"What can I do?"

"Find the real killer. You're the smartest person I know. You can do it."

"How?"

"I don't know."

I shot her a concerned look. Usually she gave me a play-by-play of the steps I needed to take to solve a crime—steps she had gleaned from TV repeats of *NCIS*, *Murder, She Wrote*, and *Law & Order*. "How long were you at Cherry Orchard Park?" I asked, deciding that the first step in any investigation was establishing a timetable of events—not that I would be investigating, but I liked to be prepared.

"At least forty-five minutes." Rebecca picked up the scissors and a strand of ribbon and curled the heck out of it.

"Did you know Kaitlyn was coming over to talk to Ipo?"

"We didn't have a clue." Rebecca started in on another unsuspecting strand of ribbon. Curl, curl, curl. She ended up with the tightest corkscrew twist I had ever seen.

"So whoever killed her was impulsive," I said. "He—"

"—or she," Rebecca cut in.

"—or *she* couldn't be sure you wouldn't be there. Maybe he . . . or she . . . simply wanted to chat with Kaitlyn, but things got out of hand."

"What about Barton Burrell?" Rebecca shook the scissors at me. "What if he didn't want to sell his farm?"

I calmly removed the scissors from her hand and set them at the far end of the counter. "Then he would have opted out of his contract."

She crossed her arms and tucked her hands beneath her armpits. "What if he couldn't?"

"Any contract can be broken. It might have cost him, but he could have broken it. Besides, I saw Barton at Lois's Lavender and Lace doing chores right before Kaitlyn died."

"No, you didn't. You went to yoga class. There was plenty of time for Barton to have gone to the pub and overheard where Kaitlyn was headed. He could have run to my place, seen Ipo and me leave, and realized his opportunity. He waited for her inside, argued with her, and wham." She slammed a fist into her palm and begged me with her eyes to conjure up a better scenario.

"Charlotte?" Matthew called. He strode past the kitchen, reading from a sheaf of papers. Seconds later, he reappeared and peeked in. "Aha, there you are."

"I thought you were in the cellar," I said.

"A while ago. Hey, Tyanne came in looking for you."

I tensed. Did she want to discuss the destruction of her husband's ice sculpture? Thomas and Amy's budding friendship? What would I say?

"You hired her, remember?"

Of course, I did. The last twenty-four hours had sped by in a blur.

"I sent her to our Winter Wonderland tent to help Pépère," Matthew went on. "Hope that's all right. Do you have a sec to review some vendor contracts?"

"Sure, I—"

"Matthew." Rebecca pushed me aside and made a beeline for my cousin. "You're brilliant. Don't you think Barton Burrell could have killed Kaitlyn Clydesdale?"

So much for me being the smartest person she knew.

Rebecca explained her theory.

"Nah, Barton is harmless," Matthew said. "In fact, he might be one of the nicest guys in town."

"Nice guys commit murder," Rebecca said.

"Not usually."

Rebecca poked me. "Charlotte, you told me once that Barton loves his cattle farm more than life itself." She had a mind like a steel trap. "If he were going to lose it . . ." She looked to Matthew for support.

Matthew tubed the sheaf of papers and slipped them under his arm. "Sure, Barton loves his farm. Why shouldn't he? It belonged to three generations of Burrells. But I promise you, he would never hurt a fly. Back in school, he didn't go out for any contact sports. Ride a horse? You bet. Rope a steer? He won contests. But kill somebody?" Matthew shook his head. "Barton did not do this."

"Neither did Ipo," Rebecca said.

"I didn't say he did." Matthew stepped into the kitchen and put his hand on Rebecca's shoulder. "Hang in there. Justice will prevail." He plucked the papers from under his arm and waved them at me. "When you've got time."

As he left, Rebecca stamped her foot, clearly frustrated. "What about that Oscar Carson? He could have killed Miss Clydesdale."

"He's your alibi," I said.

"But what if he's actually establishing us as *his* alibi? What if Oscar didn't hear us giggling? What if he made up overhearing us to give himself an alibi?"

I hadn't considered that because I was so delighted that his testimony would help Rebecca and Ipo.

"You didn't grill him that hard," Rebecca went on. "What if Oscar broke into Ipo's and stole those kala'au rods? I'll bet he knew about them. He lives on the property. He could have gone in and out in a flash." She darted out of the kitchen. "He was an actor, right?" she said, calling over her shoulder. "Is Oscar Carson his real name or is it a stage name?"

"Where are you going?"

"The office. I want to do a Google search."

I started to chuckle but bit my lip. This was not a laughing matter. My eager assistant was serious. I hurried after her, taking a quick moment to peek around the shop. No customers.

The office was toasty. The fax machine, copier, and computer were all switched on, adding to the warmth.

"What if he has a criminal record?" Rebecca asked as she nudged Rags out of the office chair and plunked herself onto the seat. After opening a Google search page, she tap-danced her fingers across the computer keyboard.

"Hold on there, Nancy Drew." I gripped her upper arm.

She wrenched free and continued typing. "He's an actor. An actor could fake every bit of what he said."

She had a point. Oscar admitted that he wanted to quit working for Clydesdale Enterprises. Maybe Kaitlyn wouldn't let him out of his contract. Maybe he became so incensed that he slugged her. But where had he gotten one of Ipo's kala'au rods? Ipo said they were stowed at his house. No, something didn't jibe with the scenario I was fashioning. The killer had brought the weapon to the cottage. That indicated premeditated murder.

Rebecca's search revealed hundreds of Oscar Carsons from which to choose. She inserted a plus sign and the word *actor* on the search line. The listings narrowed to three. Each Oscar had a different middle initial, which I assumed the actors' union required to distinguish one actor from the other. There couldn't be three George Clooneys, right? Rebecca clicked on the first entry. A picture of an ancient-looking man materialized. "Rats, not ours," she muttered. She opened the second Oscar Carson record, the one with an *I* as its middle initial. The actor looked like a hoot of a character, with a big bulbous nose and thick black glasses and a sloppy grin. "Not this one either."

Upon opening the third listing, a movie database site came into view.

"Gotcha." Rebecca zoomed in. Oscar stared out from his headshot photograph with intense, soul-searching eyes. "Zowie, get a load of him. Who'd have guessed a hunk

lived beneath all the baggy clothing and scruffy beard?"
Accompanying photos showed Oscar escorting at least a
dozen beautiful women to events. Each photo blazed with
flashbulb glare. "Phooey. No criminal record for him that I
can see." Rebecca closed the window and swiveled to face
me. "What about Creep Chef?"

"What about him?"

"Maybe he killed Kaitlyn."

"Why?" I sputtered.

"I don't know. What if he has a criminal record?" She
started to type his name into the search field.

"Uh-uh. No way." I pinned her wrists and hitched my
head toward the door. "Back to work."

She wriggled free. "C'mon, Charlotte."

"No. We're done in here. You are not going to bring
up Chip's history on the Internet, got me?" I had no desire
to see how many beautiful women Chip had escorted in
France—not that he had—but knowing how much Chip
loved the limelight, his living a glamorous nightlife was not
beyond possibility. "Besides, he had every reason to keep
Kaitlyn alive. She was going to make his dreams come
true." As much as I wanted Chip out of my life, I couldn't
forget his delight when he had told me about the restaurant
he would one day own.

Chimes at the front of the store jangled.

"Customers," I said, relieved. "Let's go."

Rebecca harrumphed as she hurried ahead of me. She
stopped short of the cheese counter and whispered, "Speak
of the devil."

I faltered. Was a day going to pass without seeing my ex-
fiancé? How could I encourage him to leave town ASAP?
He swaggered into Fromagerie Bessette, grinning like a
drunken cowboy who'd prevailed in a shoot-out. Okay,
maybe I was embellishing, giving him attributes that didn't
fit. Could you blame me? I didn't want to like him and
didn't want to feel the least attracted to him.

"Hey, Charlotte." Chip sauntered toward the cheese
counter. "Looking good. I like you in red."

I fingered the collar of my sweater, which suddenly felt as tight as a tourniquet. Dang. I could only hope my cheeks hadn't turned the same color as my sweater.

Rebecca leaned in. "He sure seems cheerful for someone whose benefactor just died."

"I heard that." Chip's mouth turned down, his gaze grim. "I am sorry. It's a shame, isn't it? But accidents happen. It was an accident, right? That's what Lois Smith told me."

"Urso isn't sure," I said.

"He thinks one of Ipo's luau sticks was deliberately used as a weapon," Rebecca added.

"Wow, I didn't realize that." Chip fidgeted. "Look, I'm sorry she's dead, and I'm sorry to hear about Ipo's problems, and I don't want to seem heartless, but"—he brandished a pair of tickets—"do you want to go to a Bluejackets hockey game with me, Charlotte? Lois's husband, Ainsley, gave them to me."

"Can't."

"How do you know? I didn't tell you when they were for."

"I just can't."

"Oho, I get it." He pocketed the tickets and viewed the cheeses displayed in the case. "How about giving me a taste of that Wisconsin Colby?"

Whenever a customer requested a taste of a cheese, I complied. I didn't want anyone to complain that he didn't like it after buying a quarter- or half-pound. That would be bad for business.

I removed the Colby from the case and, using an OXO wire cheese slicer, shaved off a thin piece. I placed it on a square of cheese paper and offered it to Chip. As he reached for it, his fingers grazed mine. On purpose? I snatched my hand back.

He plopped the morsel into his mouth and groaned with delight. "Oh, yeah, cut me a good-sized wedge of that. I love American cheeses. I'll take some of these, as well." He plucked two boxes of seed crackers off the shelf by the annex and set them on the counter by the register, then pulled his wallet from his pocket. The sight jolted me. It

was the same wallet he had carried in high school, with a peeling *Winner* sticker stuck to the cracked brown leather.

He saw where I was looking and winked. "Good memories, huh? Hey, I heard you're dating some new guy. A farmer."

"A cheese maker. His name's Jordan." Thinking of Jordan made me feel stronger, more assured, but I wasn't about to discuss him with my ex. I completed Chip's order and stowed it in a gold bag. "I guess you'll be heading back to France."

"Why?"

"Your contract will be null and void with Kaitlyn Clydesdale's death."

"I hope not. I'm discussing the issue with Georgia Plachette, the CFO, in a half hour."

Rebecca purposely cleared her throat. I knew what she was trying to do; she wanted me to view Chip as a suspect.

I glowered at her to back off and handed Chip his purchase and change. "Good luck."

"Hope you mean that. If Georgia comes through, I'll be sticking around." He tipped an imaginary hat and strode out of the shop.

A minute later, Georgia traipsed in, head lowered, gaze fixed on the floor. Why did I get the feeling that she had seen Chip inside and had waited in the shadows, pretending to be invisible until he'd left? Her face was puffy; her nose redder than before. Had she been crying? Was she mourning the death of her boss? Her outfit of funereal black did nothing for her pale complexion, though she looked quite put together. Leather gloves matched her platform high-heeled shoes and purse. Her makeup looked fresh, and she had tamed her previously matted curls into attractive locks.

Rebecca nudged me with her elbow and whispered, "She might know who Kaitlyn's enemies were. And remember how Sylvie said Kaitlyn wanted to take over Providence? What did that mean? Was she planning to buy more property? Ask Miss Plachette."

"Excuse me." Georgia sneezed and dabbed at her nose

with a tissue. "I heard you're having a cheese tasting. I need something to distract me. Am I too early?"

"A wee bit. It's tomorrow," I said, bemoaning my lack of foresight. What had I been thinking scheduling a tasting right before we opened our tent at Winter Wonderland?

"Oh, sorry." Georgia turned to leave.

Rebecca prodded me again. "Ask her."

"Before you go, Miss Plachette—" I cut my sentence short. How could I ask her about Kaitlyn Clydesdale's enemies and her real estate intentions without sounding inappropriate?

Georgia swiveled around. "What?" she said curtly, then jammed her lips together. "Sorry. It's just . . ." She fluttered her hand, the tissue waving like a white flag. "Poor Kaitlyn. She'd expected so much from this trip."

What a perfect opening. I nearly cheered. I edged my way around the cheese counter to draw nearer to her. "Um, exactly what expectations did she have?"

"She wanted to expand her Do-Gooder programs, and she wanted to reconnect with old friends."

Rats. Not the answers I'd hoped for. *Be direct,* I could hear my grandmother say.

"Why did she want to purchase the Burrell place?" I asked.

Rebecca clapped her hands silently.

Georgia cocked her head. "So she could build a honeybee farm."

"Was she planning to buy more property?" I asked.

"I can't say."

Rebecca stepped toward her. "Can't say or *won't* say?"

Georgia winced. "Kaitlyn wanted to give back to the town she used to call home. She—"

The front door whisked open. Cool air flooded the shop. A tourist flipped off her fur-hooded parka and cried, "Oh, my!" She made a quick U-turn, as if she had forgotten something, and ran headlong into Urso.

Like a gentleman, Urso stepped out of her way and held the door open for her. She flew outside.

Urso spun around as the door swung shut, and a gloom in his eyes made me wary. He didn't make a beeline for me, so perhaps my grilling Georgia Plachette wasn't the cause of his turmoil, but I didn't want to take any chances. I ended the conversation with a polite nod.

Rebecca, on the other hand, abandoned caution and bolted forward. "Ipo is not guilty."

"Good morning to you, too, Miss Zook," Urso said. Despite his snappy retort, his hangdog face didn't brighten. Had he and Jacky broken up, as I had feared at the yoga studio? He slogged toward the counter.

"Barton Burrell." Rebecca shadowed him. "What do we know about him?"

"How about a sandwich, Charlotte?" Urso said. "The Country Kitchen is full-up."

More than happy to placate him, I returned to my position behind the cheese counter and grabbed a torpedo-shaped sandwich from the refrigerator. Urso's favorite sandwich was Jarlsburg with maple-infused ham on sourdough. The savory flavor of the cheese blended perfectly with the salty sweetness of the meat. I set the sandwich on the cutting board and sliced it in half, at an angle.

"Barton Burrell," Rebecca repeated, undaunted. "Charlotte said he was doing handyman stuff at Lavender and Lace around the time of the murder, but he could have left with plenty of time to kill Kaitlyn Clydesdale."

Urso fixed her with a glare. "I questioned him. He has a solid alibi. His wife verified it."

"His wife?" Rebecca swished her ponytail over her shoulder.

"They were home watching television."

"Oh, please." Rebecca addressed Urso like he was an underling.

As she continued to harangue him, citing weak alibis and how TiVo was changing the face of investigations, I recalled the moment when Kaitlyn had come into The Cheese Shop that first day. Her phone had rung. She'd talked to someone like a minion, too. She cut off the caller with a

curt, "I'll ruin you," and then slapped on a phony smile. Had the caller been one of her employees? Oscar Carson, perhaps? Had her threat caused him to want her dead?

"You're wrong, Chief." Rebecca waggled a finger. "Barton Burrell could be guilty, alibi or not."

Urso growled. I finished wrapping his sandwich, inserted it into a gold bag, and handed it to him, free of charge.

"Maybe Octavia Tibble knows more about the sale of his farm," Rebecca went on. "Maybe Kaitlyn Clydesdale was trying to pull a fast one, and Mr. Burrell came to my place, and he lost control, and—"

Urso raised his free hand in surrender, thanked me for the sandwich, and strode from the shop . . . before I could tell him about the phone call Kaitlyn received.

I glowered at Rebecca. "Why do you incite him that way?"

"Because he's stubborn!"

I explained my theory about the conversation between Kaitlyn and her anonymous caller. "I'll bet whoever called wanted her dead."

A woman gasped. I spun around, having forgotten Georgia was in the shop. She had moved to the Camembert display on the barrel in the center of the store.

"What's wrong?" I said. "Do you know who Kaitlyn was talking to that day?"

Worming one hand into the other, Georgia moved toward the counter. Her lower lip trembled. Finally she said, "It could have been any of a number of people. Plenty wanted Kaitlyn dead. She could be quite exacting."

"Did you want her to die?" Rebecca eyed Georgia with cold suspicion.

Georgia stopped wringing her hands and shot Rebecca a withering glare. "Of course not. She and I were"—she licked her upper lip—"the best of friends."

"Where were you last night?" Rebecca had no shame.

Me? I felt like crawling under the tasting counter at Rebecca's brashness.

"I was at Timothy O'Shea's Irish Pub playing darts." Georgia cocked a hip and tilted her head, a pose a teenager

could perfect—a pose that looked weak for a woman in her late twenties. "Lots of people saw me. I told Chief Urso. He came by the inn and interrogated me last night. Question him if you don't believe me." She pointed to the street. Urso was out of sight.

An awkward silence filled the shop.

"Ask her, Charlotte," Rebecca said.

"Ask her what?"

"The question that's on the tip of your tongue."

Perhaps I was slow, but I felt a step behind in this game of twenty questions. I didn't have a question on the tip of my tongue or anywhere else.

Rebecca faced Georgia. "Who else might have wanted Kaitlyn Clydesdale dead?"

Georgia counted a list on her gloved fingertips. "Her spy, her developer, and don't forget her lover."

"Are they three different men or all the same man?"

"Three."

"Who is the lover?" I asked.

Georgia shrugged. "I don't know. Kaitlyn could be very discreet."

Visions of Chip in bed with Kaitlyn Clydesdale sprang to mind, except he was twenty years her junior. On the other hand, she had offered him a big role in her enterprise. Would he have offered himself up as a boy-toy for the chance to own his own restaurant?

"And then there's Ipo Ho." Georgia raised one lip in an Elvis sneer. "He's very cute. Kaitlyn liked them cute."

"He's innocent!" Rebecca cried.

"Is he?" Without purchasing a thing, Georgia pivoted and strutted out of the shop, and I had to wonder whether the whole intent for her appearance at my store had been to upset my sweet assistant.

Breathing high in her chest, Rebecca scurried to the office and I followed. She braced her palms on the desk, shoulders heaving. Rags weaved figure eights around her ankles and mewed loudly. I nudged him away with my toe and petted Rebecca's arm.

"No matter what," I said, "the way Kaitlyn died will be considered involuntary manslaughter." I hoped I sounded reassuring. "Remember, the coroner said it was the bump on her head from the coffee table that killed her. It could have been an accident, which would mean no malice aforethought."

"The killer didn't report it, didn't stick around. That can't be argued as no malice aforethought, and you know it." Rebecca broke away from the counter and jabbed her index finger at me. "You think Ipo did it, don't you?"

Truth be told, Ipo was as passive a man as I had ever met. I couldn't see him hitting Kaitlyn. And if he had, wouldn't Rebecca have witnessed the event? She didn't go outside to smooch by herself. She wasn't twelve, for heaven's sake.

"You do," she cried before I could answer. "You're trying to console me by making me think Ipo will get a shorter prison sentence. Well, he shouldn't get any prison sentence, do you hear me? He didn't do it. I was with him. Every minute." She thumped her chest. "Besides, I couldn't love a man who committed this crime or any horrible act. Could you?"

Her words coldcocked me. Had Jordan ever committed a horrible act? Could I love him if he had?

"You've got to beg Octavia Tibble for details about the sale of the Burrell farm," Rebecca said. "There's a story there. I can feel it in my bones."

CHAPTER

I was pretty sure what Rebecca felt *in her bones* was a drop in the temperature, now hovering at below freezing. The gentle snowstorm that had been predicted had passed north of us, but a nippy wind had taken its place. What I craved was a warm fire, a good book, and a cup of tea, but I would have to wait. The remainder of the day beckoned. Bundled in my camel coat, red scarf, and matching gloves, I braved the afternoon chill and headed to the Le Petit Fromagerie tent.

For three hours, while Tyanne and I decorated and moved stock, I couldn't help thinking about Ipo. How could I bail the love of Rebecca's life out of a jam? Ipo was innocent until proven guilty, right? Except Urso didn't seem to be focused on anyone else as a suspect—at least, not to my untrained ears.

By the time Tyanne and I had finished our tasks, I decided the best course of action was to follow through on my promise to Rebecca. I would discuss the sale of the Burrell farm with Octavia Tibble and find out if something had gone awry with the contract.

* * *

Octavia wore two professional hats. She spent half of her time as the owner and sole operator of Tibble Realty and the other half as our town librarian. Bracing against the wind, I headed to our quaint library to track her down. The moment I entered the Victorian building, which was built the same year as the town and painted the color of ripe lemons, I felt an instant sense of peace and harmony.

I followed the sound of young laughter and found Octavia in the children's section, decked out in a plumed feather turban, purple brocade robes, and brocade slippers, prancing in front of a dozen three- and four-year-olds. She was reading from a glittery book, and as she turned a page, the plumed feather fell forward—intentionally, I was pretty sure. She blew it off her face, and the children roared again with laughter.

I smiled to myself. As a child, how many hours had I spent entertained by the clever librarian who read stories of adventure in far-off lands? Oh, to be that child again, at a time when cruelty and death were no part of my daily life.

When the reading ended and the children started to toddle out, I said to Octavia, "Purple looks good with your coloring." She had the richest, creamiest café au lait skin I'd ever seen.

"Why, thank you." She removed her turban and swooped her beaded black braids over her shoulder.

"I see you had the kids in stitches, yet again."

She chuckled. "You know me. Always in for the fun of it." She brandished *The Fortune-Tellers* by Lloyd Alexander. "This author is incredible, and the artwork is exquisite. It might be a little young for the twins, but you never know." She had recently turned the twins on to reading the original Nancy Drew series. After setting *The Fortune-Tellers* on the checkout table, she said, "To what do I owe the privilege of your company?"

"It's about the Clydesdale murder."

Octavia fanned her chest. "Lord, isn't it horrible? Wooden batons to the throat."

"That's not proven yet. It's just a theory."

"Ipo couldn't find them, I hear."

"It's a rumor." I sounded like one of Rebecca's TV lawyers. Next thing I knew, I would be attending an online law school.

Octavia said, "You know, I was thinking—"

"Bye-bye, Mrs. Tibble." A little girl with golden locks danced on tiptoe and wiggled her fingers. "Want to see me twirl before we leave?"

The man holding the girl's hand spun her like a jewel-box ballerina. Around and around and around.

Octavia regarded him. "Is she your grandchild, Luigi?"

Luigi nodded. "She's my youngest daughter's child."

If Octavia hadn't said Luigi's name, I almost wouldn't have recognized him. Luigi Bozzuto, the restaurateur who owned La Bella Ristorante and was dating Delilah, was usually devilishly handsome, but he looked worse for wear, as if he had run a hundred miles without drinking a sip of water. Bags folded beneath his aging eyes. His skin sagged with fatigue.

"What a pistol," Octavia said. "Why haven't I seen her in here before?"

"They're visiting from Wellington."

"One of my favorite libraries is in Wellington." Octavia bent at the waist to speak directly to the little girl. "Do you go to the library near your home? Do you love to read?"

"Yep. Watch me pirouette by myself." The girl released Luigi's hand and did another spin, arms wide, chin upturned.

"Oh, yeah, she's a pistol." Octavia rose to her full height and squeezed Luigi's arm. "Hope you can keep up."

"I can as long as I don't drink shots. I feel like somebody slipped me a Mickey Finn." He chuckled. "I'm getting old."

That explained his dreary look. I had rarely known Luigi to have more than one glass of wine. His daughter was a flibbertigibbet who could bend an ear. Perhaps entertaining her and her family had driven him to over-imbibe.

As Luigi ushered his granddaughter out, I couldn't help but wonder what Delilah was thinking by dating him. He was old enough to be her father. Actually, he was older than her father, Pops, who was a prime force at the Country Kitchen. Sure, Luigi was charming and a talented restaurateur, but he was too old for someone as vibrant as Delilah. On the other hand, could I wish her spinsterhood? Since returning to town, defeated by the fickleness of Broadway, Delilah hadn't found anyone to date in Providence. Urso, the first love of her life, was captivated by Jacky. I didn't want Delilah moving away because she was forlorn.

"Charlotte, follow me." Octavia guided me to the added-on sunroom at the rear of the library. Sun had broken through the clouds outside and, despite the cool weather, warmed the room via solar panels.

Octavia indicated a teensy stool beside a squat table. Readers occupied all the comfy chairs nestled beside the windows. I sat first, feeling a bit like Gulliver in the land of Lilliputians.

"What do you want to ask me?" Octavia said.

I told her about Rebecca's belief that Barton Burrell might have killed Kaitlyn. "She thinks he's lying about his alibi. She's certain there's something more to his business deal with Kaitlyn. Did you broker the sale?"

"I did."

"Did he want to cancel the deal?"

"Yes."

Rebecca was on the right track. I said, "And did he?"

"He couldn't." Octavia set her turban on the table and took a considerable amount of time twisting it until the feather was flopping away from her.

"Because Kaitlyn had a clause that favored her, is that right?"

Octavia cocked her thumb and forefinger at me like a gun. "Good guess."

It wasn't actually a guess. Our contract with the former owner of our building contained a similar clause.

"The contract was rock solid," Octavia said. "That CFO

of Clydesdale Enterprises made us go over it line by line. Everything was in order. All the inspections were done and completed to Clydesdale Enterprises' satisfaction. Barton could not back out."

"Not even if he paid a penalty?"

She shook her head. "The only one who could alter the scenario was Kaitlyn."

"Why did Barton change his mind about selling? I'm guessing that he needs the money. He's been doing odd jobs at Lavender and Lace."

Octavia chewed the inside of her lip, obviously reluctant to answer.

I shifted in my chair. "I get it. You can't tell me because of Realtor/client privilege."

"Yes . . . and no." Octavia beckoned me to lean forward and whispered, "The Burrells have had a rough go this past year."

"The cattle farm is suffering."

"Not only that. Emma . . ." Octavia rubbed her thighs, obviously needing time to mull over the moral issue of revealing secrets to me. Finally she said, "You know Barton and Emma have been married for ten years."

I had attended the late summer wedding. They had rented Harvest Moon Ranch for the occasion. Emma had waltzed beneath the arbors looking like a fashion plate in her tiered white gown.

Octavia continued. "They have three sons, but Emma really wants a daughter."

"Is she pregnant?" Having three children could put a strain on a pocketbook, but having a fourth could break the bank.

"They've tried a few times. Each time, Emma . . . miscarried."

"Oh, my!" I slapped my hand over my mouth and said through spread fingers, "I'm so sorry." I couldn't imagine suffering a miscarriage, let alone multiple ones. Nobody deserved that fate. Especially Emma. She was a good-hearted woman. She campaigned vociferously for organic

farm choices and had served as a Cub Scout den mother for all three boys, which took grit. "That gives her all the more reason to sell. She could leave Providence and the sad memories behind her."

"Except it's also the reason she wants to stay. This is their home. This is where they both grew up. Emma is convinced she must have her daughter in Providence." Octavia rested her hands in her lap. "You said they provided Chief Urso with alibis."

"They told U-ey that they were watching TV."

"Well, then."

"Rebecca thinks their alibis ring false."

"People do watch television, Charlotte."

"What if Emma thought her only way out of the binding contract was to get rid of Kaitlyn?"

Octavia clicked her burgundy fingernails on the tabletop. "No, I don't see Emma as a violent woman."

"What about Barton? A man protecting his family can be fierce. If he knew where to find Ipo's kala'au rods—"

Octavia coughed.

"You know something. Tell me."

Octavia sat straighter. "Mind you, I don't believe the Burrells are guilty for a second."

"Got that."

"But Barton and Ipo play cards every Thursday night at Ipo's house. He might have known where Ipo kept those instruments."

CHAPTER

8

In one fell swoop, dusk settled around the town like a theater backdrop. The skies grew dark purple. Polaris, the brightest star in Ursa Major, twinkled with persistence, offering a glimmer of hope to the hopeless. As a girl, I loved to walk at night and wish upon stars and predict my future. Sometimes I talked to my parents and felt sure they were listening up in heaven. On this evening, I did both.

So why, when I reentered Fromagerie Bessette, did my blithe spirit wane? Because Chip and Jordan were both there. Chip stood at the tasting counter, chatting it up with Lois and her husband Ainsley, while Jordan lingered near the jars of honey, glowering at the trio. Jordan inclined his head, signaling he wanted a private chat, but as much as I needed to get a handle on his past, I knew I couldn't dally. A flurry of customers filled the shop, as well.

Where were Rebecca, Tyanne, and Matthew? They couldn't all be downstairs checking out the cellar.

I headed for the rack of aprons at the rear of the store. "Grab a number, folks." I hadn't wanted to resort to a

number system in The Cheese Shop, but I had succumbed a few months ago. The crowds at the holidays had overwhelmed me.

Chip laughed heartily. "Good one, Ainsley!" He punched Ainsley on the arm and laughed again, louder than he needed to. Was he trying to show up Jordan? He was failing miserably. I had never enjoyed Chip's bluster, and he knew it.

"Hey, babe!" Chip cut me off near the arch to the annex. "Looking beautiful, as always." He pecked me on the cheek.

For a guy who had just lost his meal ticket, he seemed too primed and pumped. Concern prickled the back of my neck. Did he have something to do with Kaitlyn's death? *No, no, no.* Chip was impulsive. He had a temper, but he would never lash out. He would smolder like a heap of ashes and attack with verbal undercuts—a snipe here, a snipe there. It had taken years to rebuild my confidence after he left. I could never explain why I missed him and sobbed myself to sleep, and I had tried explaining—to two different therapists.

I swiped his moist kiss off my skin, snagged an apron, and moved to my position behind the cheese counter. "Who's got number"—I glanced at the wall behind me— "fifty-seven?"

"Me." Chip waved a tag in the air.

"You bought cheese earlier," I said, unable to curtail the miffed tone in my voice.

"And I shared it with the folks at the inn. Let's see, give me a wedge of that Point Reyes Farmstead blue. That's one of your favorites, isn't it? I remember something about it being so good because of the combination of the milk from the Holstein cows and the coastal fog and"—he wagged a finger—"something else."

"The salty Pacific breeze," I said.

"That's it." As I prepared his order, he sauntered back to Lois and Ainsley. "Hey, babe, we were talking about the game last night." He elbowed Ainsley. "Tell her."

Ainsley, a brick of a man, equal in height to Chip and

Jordan but squarer, raked his thinning red hair. "It was something, all right," he said, his soft voice a stark contrast to Chip's bravado. Ainsley had never been a loud man. He was thoughtful, Lois told me, preferring books to conversation. At times, I felt Lois hungered for more. Perhaps an evening out at the pub or a Sunday picnic at Kindred Creek.

Chip jabbed Ainsley again. "Tell her about Lukashenko. You said he had two goals."

Ainsley nodded.

"Wham-bam." Chip did a one-two punch. "Man, did I miss hockey when I was in France."

I slipped his wedge of cheese into a gold bag and gestured for him to come to the cash register.

As Chip paid, he continued. "I mean, yeah, France has got teams, but not like the Bluejackets. Hey, babe, remember the roar inside the Nationwide Arena? It scared you so much the first time that you leaped into my lap." He eyed me lustily. "Sure you don't want to go with me to a game?"

I raised my right eyebrow.

"Right, you said you can't because you've got to work at the faire." Chip thumped his head like a goof. "I forgot."

I heard someone groan and looked for the source. Jordan was retreating through the rear door of the shop. He gave me a two-finger salute as he disappeared, our signal for *catch you later*, and my pulse revved. If I ran, I could catch him by the iced-over co-op garden. And do what? Kiss him or grill him about the deceased cheese maker issue?

The door swung shut.

Move, run, talk to him, my heart urged, but I couldn't because Rebecca popped out from the kitchen doing something akin to a St. Vitus's dance. Was she ill? Her skin color looked good.

"Psst." She waved her hands wildly overhead.

"Fifty-eight," I said.

Lois tittered. "That's us, but I think your little assistant wants a word." She slipped her hand around her husband's elbow. "Ainsley, dear, let's take a look at the tea biscuits. I need something to go with the stew I prepared for dinner,

and I'm not up to baking tonight, don't you know. And Charlotte, when you get the chance, we'll want a quarter of a pound of the usual. It's so yummy with Ipo's honey." She tsked. "Poor boy."

As they moved away from the counter, Chip said, "Babe—"

"Not now!" I snapped.

Chip's mouth opened slightly, as if he wanted to say something more to me, but then he closed his mouth. He wasn't going to offer an apology for rehashing our past in front of my boyfriend. He never would.

"Psst," Rebecca repeated.

Silently Chip trudged from the shop. He lingered on the sidewalk for a brief moment before moving on. I didn't give him a second thought and gestured for Rebecca to join me at the counter.

While I cut a portion of Lois's favorite Rouge et Noir Brie, Rebecca whispered, "What did Octavia say?"

"Is that why you were doing a jig?"

"I'm so nervous I can barely breathe."

"Tend to the next customer." The line had grown to six deep. "We'll talk in a while."

"Uh-uh. Now. Scoop first." She folded her arms.

I kept mum and wrapped the Brie in our special paper and applied a label, but she didn't budge. Finally giving in, I filled her in about the Burrells' sad situation and the possibility that Barton might know where Ipo had stowed his kala'au rods.

"I can't believe it." A sound of glee burst from her mouth. "Barton Burrell might have killed Kaitlyn Clydesdale."

"No, siree." Lois stopped examining the boxes of tea biscuits on a display barrel and scooted toward the counter. "He did no such thing."

I swear Lois has elephant ears. More than once, she had inserted herself into a private conversation I was having on my porch at home, which abutted the gardens of Lois's bed-and-breakfast.

"Barton Burrell did not kill Kaitlyn Clydesdale." Lois

edged into her spot at the front of the line. "I won't believe it for a second. Mr. Burrell was at the inn that night until just about this time." She tapped her watch. "And, mind you, he was dog tired. He wouldn't have had the energy to swat a fly. Not to mention, I have never known that man to argue."

"Ipo doesn't argue, either," Rebecca cried.

Could a murderer go free based on public opinion? If judged by their peers, neither Barton nor Ipo would be declared guilty.

"If you ask me, that Arlo MacMillan has something to hide," Lois said.

I offered Lois a slice of Pecorino Romano. Though she preferred soft-centered cheeses, I was always trying to introduce her to something new. The Pecorino Romano was a firm cheese made from ewe's milk and tasted great shaved on top of pastas and such.

Lois downed the tidbit in one bite and licked her fingertips. "Mmm, nice. Buttery. I'll take a quarter pound of that, too."

I cut and wrapped the cheese and handed it to Rebecca.

"Go on about Arlo MacMillan," Rebecca said as she bagged Lois's purchases and moved to the register.

"That man." Lois sneered. "Just the other day he was snooping around the inn, asking folks if they'd seen Kaitlyn Clydesdale. It was right after she transferred to Violet's."

"Don't gossip, Lois." Ainsley laid crackers and a jar of honey by the register and handed Rebecca a credit card.

"Gossip is what makes the world go 'round, dear." Lois patted his arm. "As I was saying, there was Arlo, looking all creepy as he normally does."

Rebecca handed Ainsley a credit slip to sign. He scrawled a quick signature and attempted to pull Lois away from the counter.

"Don't manhandle me," she said.

But he persisted and won.

As he steered her toward the exit, Lois called over her

shoulder, "There was something between Arlo MacMillan and Kaitlyn Clydesdale. Mark my words."

Something between them? I flashed on Arlo racing from The Cheese Shop the moment Kaitlyn had shown up. He hadn't acted scared, but after he bumped her shoulder, he ran out looking like he had tasted a dirty penny. Moments later, Kaitlyn's cell phone chimed. Had Arlo called her? According to Georgia Plachette, Kaitlyn had dallied with a lover. Could the lover have been Arlo? No, I couldn't see dramatic Kaitlyn with passive-aggressive Arlo. So what was the connection that Lois had sensed?

Rebecca untied her apron and whipped it off.

I gripped her wrist. The apron dangled between us. "Where do you think you're going?"

"We've got to question Arlo MacMillan."

"Uh-uh, no way. Look at the line."

"Tyanne can watch the shop. Can't you, Tyanne?" Rebecca looked past me at Tyanne, who was emerging from the office carrying Rags.

"Sorry, Tyanne," I said, "but Rags stays in the office."

"I forgot, sugar. He's so darned sweet." She looked like she had been crying. Should I be worried?

She deposited the cat in the office, then quickly returned, a smile planted on her pretty face, and said, "Fifty-nine." A thickset man waved his number. "Mr. White," Tyanne said. "So good to see you, sir. What'll it be? How about a creamy Camembert?"

"Told you. She's totally capable on her own." Rebecca wrenched her wrist from my grasp. "And your grandfather will be here soon, too."

"Says who?"

"You know he sneaks in every day for a nip of cheese before dinner."

"I thought he'd stopped that habit."

Rebecca held a finger to her lips. "Don't rat him out to Grandmère. Promise?"

If my grandmother found out Pépère was nibbling foods

not included on his diet, he would be toast—French toast, sizzled to a crisp.

"Charlotte." Delilah whooshed into the shop, speeding past the line of customers with the fury of a tornado. Brisk air followed her inside. A shiver squiggled down my spine. She sashayed behind the counter and clutched my elbow. "That creepy guy is on the loose again."

"Who do you mean?" I cut a look from Rebecca, who sniffed because I had allowed my attention to be diverted, and back to Delilah, who seemed miffed beyond compare.

"Oscar what's-his-name," Delilah said. "You know who I mean. He wears that stupid hat and trench coat all the time. He's stalking the new gal in town. Starts with a G."

"Georgia Plachette."

"That's it."

I shook my head. For a former actress, Delilah sure couldn't remember last names well. Not that she had to. At the diner she called people *hon* and *sweetie* and got away with it. Nicknames, according to her father, made people feel at home.

"The creep is obsessed with her, I think," Delilah went on. "We should tell Urso. C'mon." She guided me toward the exit.

"Uh-uh." Rebecca scooted around the counter and blocked our path, hands on hips. "We're checking out Arlo MacMillan." She leveled me with a glare that sent shivers to my toes. How well my grandmother had trained her.

Delilah huffed.

Caught between two formidable goddesses, I said, "Arlo first."

Rebecca clapped with smug glee and started for the exit.

It was my turn to play defensive lineman. I darted to the front door of The Cheese Shop and blocked Rebecca, making full body contact. She bounced off me and staggered backward in the direction of one of The Cheese Shop barrels. I pursued her.

"What's wrong?" She attempted a defiant pose.

"You're not going. Not this time."

"Why not?"

"Because you like your job."

She frowned. "You're kidding. You'd fire me?"

I wouldn't. Not in a million years. But I also wanted to rein her in. I promised to report back as soon as possible. A teenager assigned to kitchen duty couldn't have looked more miserable.

On our way out of town, Delilah and I drove past the Winter Wonderland faire where ice sculptors were fine-tuning their ice blocks and vendors were making last-minute finishes to their tents. The lights on the tents and pine trees twinkled with magical delight.

"What a night!" With her head all the way out the passenger window, Delilah reminded me of a dog, her curls flapping like floppy ears. "This is what fairy tales are made of."

The sliver of sun that dared to make an appearance in the afternoon hadn't dried up the moisture in the air.

"Close the window," I said. "It's freezing in here."

"You think this is cold?" She chuckled. "Try getting around New York in a sleet storm."

As we headed north, I whizzed past a variety of roadside stores, including garden shops that wouldn't open their doors until April and a shed maker who also made playhouses. The twins had been begging for a pink and white mini-mansion. Matthew promised that when Meredith and he got married and moved into their own home, he would buy the girls the house. While growing up, I'd had something similar at my grandparents' house, but it was now painted ten layers of white and held a lawn mower and garden tools. A memory of kissing Chip in the shed swept through my mind. I stepped harder on the gas pedal as our view became mile after mile of farms and rough-hewn fences, each laced with barbed wire to keep livestock penned in. The wood glistened with crystallized particles of ice.

"Thinking about Chip?" Delilah said, a teasing bite to her question.

I glowered at her. How had she guessed?

"What was he doing at the store?" she asked.

"How did you know he was there?"

"He was carrying one of your tote bags."

I drummed the steering wheel.

"At some point you have to talk about him," Delilah said. "There's an elephant in the car. Is he stalking you like Oscar's stalking Georgia?"

"No. And Oscar's not stalking Georgia."

"Oh, yes, he is."

"He likes her."

"That doesn't give him the right to moon about. It doesn't give Chip the right, either."

I drummed the steering wheel harder.

"Georgia was at the diner," Delilah said. "She sat at the counter, drinking a root beer and mumbling to herself. She looked pretty torn up. When I asked her what was wrong, she said she didn't believe for a second that Oscar witnessed the giggling incident between Rebecca and Ipo. She said it would be just like him to make that up."

That piqued my attention. Oscar had said that he wanted to get to know Georgia better, meaning he didn't know her well, but her statement implied a deeper intimacy. What was the truth?

Delilah said, "Tell me, why are we in such a hurry to see Arlo?"

"He's been acting pretty suspicious." I related what Lois had told me.

"But Arlo's always shifty, so why the giddyup now?"

"Someone made a call to Kaitlyn Clydesdale when she was at The Cheese Shop. She was not happy and threatened the caller. She said, *'You'll do nothing of the kind. I'll ruin you.'*"

"And you think she was talking to Arlo."

"It's as good a guess as any." I turned on my bright headlights. With no streetlamps, the curves of the road were harder to navigate as dusk turned to dark. "She was buying the property next to his. Maybe she had designs on his place, too. Maybe that made him mad."

"Angry enough to kill?" Delilah tapped the car door with her fingernails. "You know, Arlo's great-grandfather was among the original settlers in Providence. He's lived here his whole life. Preserving one's heritage might be a strong motive for murder. On the other hand, how would Kaitlyn know that Arlo's homeland mattered to him?"

"She lived here years ago," I said.

Delilah thumped her thigh. "Whoa, didn't know that."

"She and Arlo were about the same age," I added. "Do you think he might have been having a relationship with her?"

"Not Arlo." Delilah frittered her hand. "No way. Have you taken a look at him lately? He's pasty and has that

perpetual sneer. And he's always wearing that dreadful oversized overcoat. For all we know, he's a flasher." She laughed heartily. "My, oh, my, did we have a lot of flashers in New York. I don't miss running around the lake in Central Park, I'm telling you. You know, Arlo's an enigma," she went on, changing the subject easily. "I remember him, years ago, bringing candy into the Country Kitchen and passing it around. He was sweet and not so"—she searched for a word—"odd."

I swerved around a cattle truck and nearly came nose-to-nose with an Econoline van. Braking, I fell in behind the truck. Delilah gripped the handle over the passenger window.

"Slow down," she said. "Arlo's not going anywhere."

I veered up the road that entered the property between the Burrells' place and Quail Ridge Honeybee Farm.

"Something went screwy with Arlo once his wife died." Delilah twisted in her seat to face me. "Do you think that's what happens when someone doesn't have a mate to help them through life?" Her voice caught.

I glanced over. "Are you okay?"

Her eyes glistened in the dark. She wasn't going to cry, was she? I didn't need a sobbing sidekick.

"Luigi loves you," I said.

"I know that." She paused. "Why did you feel the need to tell me?"

"Because your eyes were getting teary, and I thought—"

"I'm crying for Arlo, you nitwit. He's such a sad, lonely soul."

Who might very well be a killer.

*   *   *

A pair of posts carved with the surname MacMillan flanked the entrance to the MacMillan Chicken Farm. My tires crunched on the gravel driveway as I drove toward the rundown, ranch-style house. The car's headlights highlighted toys and rusty bikes lying on the dormant grass.

I couldn't see Kaitlyn Clydesdale setting foot on the

property, but I wouldn't rule out Arlo being her paramour. Lois said Kaitlyn had moved to Violet's Victoriana Inn. What if she had met her lover there? Would a taste of Violet's favorite double-cream cheese—Fromager d'Affinois— help me persuade her to reveal the truth? Maybe I would throw in a wedge of Caciotta al Tartufo—a semi-soft cow and sheep's cheese with the delicate flavor of truffles—and a bottle of a lusty Merlot. Violet had her vices.

I pulled to a stop in front of Arlo's house and put my hand on the door handle.

"This place gives me the creeps," Delilah said, her voice barely a whisper. "What a dump. Why doesn't Arlo keep it up? It's not like he doesn't have the money. I've seen him at the art gallery. He bids on pieces of art."

"Perhaps he bids but never buys." I often browsed shops to admire the beautiful wares, but I couldn't afford to purchase everything I set eyes on.

"Maybe that would explain why he only buys a seltzer water at the diner. He's flat-out cheap."

"Don't be quick to judge. He could be thrifty. He did have four children with his wife."

"Where do they live?"

"Got me." I hadn't seen Arlo accompanied by anyone since I graduated high school. "Maybe he prefers to live lean, like his chickens."

Delilah shot me a *yeah, right* look.

Taking a courageous breath, I exited the car, and despite the fact that the porch light was broken, headed to the front door. The muted cackle of chickens drifted from the weathered chicken house.

Delilah joined me, plumes of her warm breath clouding the chilly air. "What's the plan? Bang on the door and beg him to confess?"

"Something like that."

I pressed the doorbell, but like the porch light, it didn't work. I knocked and waited.

"Not home," Delilah said. "Let's go check out Oscar's story."

I grabbed her elbow to detain her and knocked again.

No one answered.

"Hear that?" I said, craning an ear to listen. Eerie music emanated from somewhere deep in the house. I recognized the theme from the movie *Psycho*. Grandmère had used the piece as background music in one of her dramatic plays.

Delilah shivered. "I'm heading back to the car."

" 'Fraidy cat."

"Sticks and stones."

A frisson of fear snaked up my back. "Wait." I held her in place. "What if Arlo knew something about the killer, and the killer found him first?" *With a knife, in a shower,* my vivid imagination added. "What if Arlo is lying injured inside?" So much for him being guilty in my mind. "I'm going in."

"Charlotte Bessette, you are not the appointed savior of everyone in Providence, Ohio, no matter what people say," Delilah said snarkily, then moaned. "Sorry, that was rude of me."

I had heard people talk. Solve one murder, I was lucky. Solve two, I was a snoop. Only recently had the *appointed savior* nickname surfaced. I had overheard someone whispering the words in The Cheese Shop. I rarely bought into gossip. "Rebecca's going to have my hide if I don't come back with info."

"Ooooh, she's so scary."

I glowered. "Truly, he might be hurt."

"Fine. One peek, but then we're out of here." Delilah tried the front doorknob. It didn't budge. She stole to the corner of the house and peered around it. "Got a flashlight?"

I scampered back to the car, fetched the flashlight from my glove compartment, and returned. I flared the light on the wood siding. "I see a window. I think it's ajar, but it's too high up."

"There are knotholes. I'll go first."

As girls, Delilah, Meredith, and I had spent many hours climbing trees, most particularly the two-hundred-year-old

oak on Meredith's family property. Delilah had been the best climber.

While I trained the flashlight beam on the wall, Delilah ascended. She forced open the window; it squeaked its resistance. Delilah peeked inside. "Oh, lord, I think there's a body on the floor. Toss me the flashlight."

I did. Poorly. It hit the lip beneath the window and caromed to the ground; the top popped off and the batteries flew out.

"Never mind. I'm going in." Delilah slithered through the opening.

Stuffing down any worry about what Urso would say if he found me breaking and entering yet again, I clambered up the side of the house, slithered over the windowsill, and dropped to the floor inside.

"Psst," Delilah said.

I spun around. Shadows and the musty smell of chicken feathers and dust filled the room. "Where's the body?"

"This way."

I hurried behind Delilah to a puffy shape. I tapped it with my toe. It gave ever so slightly. I bent down, and the scent of wet hay met my nostrils. "You goon. It's an old scarecrow."

"My mistake. I'm going to find a light switch."

As my eyes adjusted to the gloom, I made out a table in the center of the room. It was filled with a variety of shapes. And there was shelving everywhere. Racks and racks of shelving on every wall. The shelves looked packed, but with what?

Before I could find out, a guttural howl wracked the air.

The lights flipped on, and I saw Arlo leaping headlong at me. He was wearing chicken-decorated pajamas. In his hands he gripped a pair of karate-style nunchakus. The chain connecting them clacked with ferocity.

Delilah screamed and attacked him from behind.

"Whoa," I yelled. "Arlo, stop."

He kept coming. I tucked my head down to bear the brunt

of his rush. He hit me full force. The top of my head made contact with his solar plexus. The air popped out of him. The nunchakus flew from his hands and clattered on the wooden floor. Groaning, Arlo bent forward and clutched his knees.

Delilah, who had been attacked once when she lived in New York and swore she would never let someone get the better of her again, slung an arm around Arlo's neck. "Grab his hands," she ordered.

"Let him go," I said.

"Not until he calms down."

Arlo took multiple short breaths. "I'm okay now. I won't attack. I'm sorry. Uncle."

"Delilah, let him go."

She did.

"Arlo, why are you dressed in pajamas this early at night?" I said.

"I've been fighting a cold. I was in bed."

"Watching *Psycho*?"

He bobbed his head. "I didn't know it was you."

"Who'd you think it was?"

"Someone's after me. People have been following me. Watching, watching, watching."

"Whoa. No more Hitchcock for you," Delilah said.

"I've got the whole set."

I'll bet he did. And the whole set of a lot more things, if the contents of his living room were a telltale sign. Curios, trinkets, DVDs, and canned items filled the shelves. The floors swam with bikes and balls. It was a junk hoarder's paradise. I also spotted peculiar looking things that I was pretty sure were medieval weaponry, and another idea hit me. Arlo liked to collect weapons. Had he stolen Ipo's kala'au rods?

"What is all this, Arlo?" I swept my hand at the array of goods.

"A mess." Delilah left us to browse the room.

"Why are you inside my house?" Arlo folded his arms in front of his torso as if that might make him look brawnier. It didn't.

"We thought you might be hurt." I didn't add that we thought he might have been dead or Kaitlyn's lover or possibly a killer. There was no need to confuse him with the details.

Delilah held up three tubes of wrapping paper with wedding bells on it. "Arlo, why do you have these? And what about this?" She displayed a stuffed spotted giraffe, the freebie given only to tots from the children's store in town.

"I can explain."

"How about this?" Delilah nabbed a carton of seven-seed crackers. "Did you buy this?"

"No."

Delilah turned to me. "Are you missing inventory from the shop, Charlotte? As far as I know, you're the only one in town who sells these. There are hatbox-style cheese containers here, too. Not refrigerated. Ugh." She glowered at Arlo. "Did you filch all this stuff? Are you a kleptomaniac?"

I looked at Arlo, searching for a nicer word. "Are you a collector?"

His arms fell to his sides. He lowered his chin. "When my wife died, I had this . . . need . . . to fill the void."

"With things?" I said.

He kicked the nunchakus on the floor with disgust.

"Who are you afraid of, Arlo?"

"Huh?" He looked at me, rheumy eyed.

"You said you believed someone was following you. Who?" I thought of Oscar Carson. Delilah claimed he was stalking Georgia. What if Oscar was stalking Arlo on Kaitlyn's orders? She was dead, but that didn't mean Oscar didn't have a job to do. "And why?"

"Blackmail," he said.

"Kaitlyn Clydesdale was blackmailing you."

"Yes, yes, yes!" he blurted, as if prompted to confess on his deathbed.

On the night of the murder, had he gone to confront Kaitlyn? Had the confrontation gotten out of hand?

"For how much money?" I asked.

"I don't have any money. I'm broke. I've given everything

I have to my four girls. But do they and their kids come to visit Grandpa? No, they hate me!" His face drew into a pitiful pucker.

Delilah nudged me. "We're getting off track."

"Arlo," I said, wishing I could salve his obvious pain. "I'm sorry about your family, but I asked you a question about Kaitlyn. You said she was blackmailing you. For how much?" Peanuts might not be a good enough motive.

"She didn't want money," he snarled.

"What did she want?"

"My property."

I couldn't see Kaitlyn Clydesdale ever setting foot on the chicken farm. Had she wanted the property so she could expand the honeybee farm she was planning?

"Did you steal Ipo's kala'au rods?" I asked.

Arlo looked perplexed. "Why would I do something like that? Ipo's my friend."

At least Arlo had a modicum of honor. Or did he? I eyed the nunchakus again. They looked about the same size as the luau instruments. Had Urso and the coroner gotten the weapon of destruction wrong? Arlo glanced where I was looking and back at me. His gaze narrowed.

"Arlo, you were in The Cheese Shop the other day," I said. "You left hurriedly when Kaitlyn Clydesdale entered."

"Did not."

"Yes, you did. A few minutes later, someone called her. Was it you?"

"I don't have her number."

Delilah jabbed a finger at him. "She was blackmailing you."

"We never spoke on the telephone." He shifted feet.

"It's easy enough to check," Delilah went on. "Hand over your cell phone."

"I don't have to."

Delilah took a menacing step toward him.

Arlo sputtered, "I lost it."

"Oh, please." Delilah threw him a cynical look.

"It's true. I lost it yesterday while I was at the Village

Green. It must have fallen out of my overcoat. It's got a hole in the pocket."

"Did you check lost and found?" I asked. Grandmère had set up a booth at the north end of the faire, closest to the Providence Precinct.

Sheepishly, he shook his head.

I said, "Arlo, your story is sounding fishy. I think you were worried that Kaitlyn was going to tell people that you are a kleptomaniac. Did you hurt her before she could?"

"I threatened her, but I didn't kill her." His eyes flickered with desperation. "I need help. Mental help. I know that. I'm a thief, but I'm not a killer. Please, you've got to believe me." He caved in on himself. "Please," he whimpered. "I did lose my phone."

Pépère always said: *Never hit a man when he's down.*

"Arlo, I believe you." I crossed my fingers behind my back. A little white lie wouldn't hurt anything, right?

The man looked as happy as if I had bailed him out of a raging river.

"But you have to do one thing for me," I went on.

"Name it."

"Come with me and tell Chief Urso everything." The least I could do for Ipo Ho was give Urso the notion that there might be other suspects.

CHAPTER

10

After suggesting that Arlo change into something more appropriate than pajamas, Delilah and I escorted him to the Providence Precinct. Clad in black trousers, a sweater, and the peacoat that Delilah insisted he wear, he looked like a decent, upstanding citizen. We left him with the clerk and entered Urso's office.

Quickly I gave him a recap: how we went to Arlo's place for a chat; how we entered when we thought he might be injured; and what facts we had gleaned—Kaitlyn had blackmailed Arlo about his kleptomania and had barred Barton Burrell from backing out of the contract.

"Okay, stop right there." Urso strode around his tidy desk and stalked me like a hungry bear ready to pounce on fresh meat. "Charlotte, you have a lot of nerve—"

"We had to do something," I cut in, my voice weaker than I'd hoped. "Arlo was acting so sneaky. Lois said he was skulking around the B&B."

"Lots of folks in town are sneaky. Are you going to break into their homes, too?"

"We came up with answers," Delilah said, much more forcefully than I.

Urso cut her a harsh look. "Not a word from you, understood?"

Delilah wove her hands behind her back like a chastised student in the principal's office.

Urso regarded me again. I wished I could melt into the carpet and disappear. He sighed. "Explain about the blackmail."

I did. Because I wasn't completely sold on the idea that Arlo was innocent of attacking Kaitlyn Clydesdale, I added, "You've got to make sure he doesn't bolt until he's signed a statement."

"I do not need you telling me how to do my job," Urso said.

"I know. It's just—"

"Charlotte, what am I going to do with you?"

"Ipo is not guilty."

"Maybe, maybe not. I'm checking out all angles."

"Did you know that Kaitlyn Clydesdale had a lover?" I blurted, remembering an item I had forgotten to include in my previous rundown.

Urso worked his tongue inside his cheek, a telltale sign that meant he hadn't known. I squelched the urge to cheer. One-upmanship was not my style, but I didn't want him to bully me out of following my instincts.

"You could have gotten hurt," he conceded.

"Could have, but didn't." I nudged Delilah. "We'll leave now."

Urso raised a finger. "In the future, if you impede my investigation—"

"I won't." At least, I hoped I wouldn't. As I reached the door, I pivoted. "Oh, by the way, Delilah thinks Oscar Carson might be stalking Georgia Plachette."

* * *

I said good night to Delilah, but before heading off to Le Petit Fromagerie to double-check that everything was ready

for our grand opening tomorrow, I returned to The Cheese Shop to bring Rebecca up to date. I told her about our raid on Arlo's home, about Arlo's propensity for, shall we say, filching things he didn't need, and about our tête-à-tête with Urso.

Rebecca paced behind the cheese counter like a caged tigress. "It sounds to me like Arlo is guilty. Do you know why he isn't behind bars?" She didn't give me a beat to respond. "I'll tell you why. Because the chief is biased against Ipo."

I gaped. "Umberto Urso is the least biased person I know."

"He's going to lock Ipo up and throw away the key. You watch."

"No, he's not. I won't let him."

She halted and jutted a finger at me. "Cross your heart."

I obeyed. Far be it from me to annoy a tigress. "Hope to die," I added, although I prayed I didn't need to go that far.

Rebecca wrapped her arms around her chest. "Oh, Charlotte, what am I going to do?"

"You're going to close up shop and take one day at a time. Got me?" I pecked her on the cheek, then dashed off to the faire.

By eight P.M., though I was exhausted from multiple shifts and my side job of trespassing, I felt Le Petit Fromagerie was ready to open tomorrow evening, thanks to Tyanne's expert help. What a smart hire she was turning out to be.

"Let's call it a night," I said.

Tyanne agreed. As she fetched her purse from beneath the antique buffet table, the door flew open and Amy bolted into the tent.

"Hi, Aunt Charlotte. Hey, Mrs. Taylor. How's it going?"

"Fine, thanks." Tyanne set her purse on the table and started rifling through it.

"Hello, Mrs. Taylor." Clair traipsed in behind her sister. Her blonde hair crackled with electricity as she removed her turquoise knit cap. In her arms, she toted a book about

training a dog. She had taken to Rocket. She was the one who played ball with him, tugged rope with him, and combed the shaggy hair from his eyes.

"What are you girls doing here?" I asked.

"We just finished rehearsal," Amy said.

Matthew and Meredith entered the tent and waved a greeting. Matthew said, "Hey, cuz, did you hear? We've sold the most tickets ever for our Founder's Day celebration. Tomorrow tourists will be flooding the area."

"Daddy, I was talking," Amy said.

"Sorry, princess." Matthew steered Meredith toward the wine-tasting area on the buffet and straightened the stacks of tasting cups. "Please continue."

Amy whisked off her striped scarf and swung it like a lasso in the air. "Aunt Charlotte, do you want to hear about what happened at rehearsal tonight?" Her cheeks shone pink from the brisk weather; her chocolate brown eyes glistened with enthusiasm. "It was great. Really great. Grandmère listened."

"And guess who else?" Clair said in singsong fashion.

Amy glowered at her.

Clair tilted a head in Tyanne's direction. I winked that I understood. Tyanne's son Thomas must have made an appearance. When I had arrived at the faire earlier, I had seen Thomas and his sister watching their father ice sculpt a second knight on a horse.

"We sang lots of songs," Amy went on. "Want to hear one?" She burst into a chorus of *Let It Snow*. On key.

"Tommy blew her a kiss," Clair said.

Amy stopped singing. "His name is Thomas."

I glanced at Tyanne, who was applying lipstick while trying to stifle a smile. A teensy chortle escaped her mouth. If I wasn't careful, I would follow her down the path to outright laughter. I nudged her ankle with the toe of my shoe. She nudged me back.

"He was moony-eyed." Clair tapped her chin with a fingertip. "Or maybe he was feeling queasy because you make him sick."

Amy huffed and slogged away to inspect jars of jam on the decorated shelves. Clair trotted after while continuing her taunting.

At the same time, Sylvie pushed open the tent door. "Hello, my babies. Did you see Mumsie at the rehearsal?"

How could they have missed her? She was wearing a thickly quilted white outfit with shoulder pads so wide she could have been a hockey goalie . . . or the Pillsbury Doughboy.

The girls abandoned their tiff and sprinted to their mother. They threw their arms around her. Out of the corner of my eye, I saw Matthew and Meredith wince. Both had admitted to me that sharing the girls with the ex-wife was hard, especially when the ex-wife didn't deserve them. Since she had moved back to town, Sylvie had won the girls' affection, and she wasn't half-bad as a mother when she focused her full attention on them, but too many times she was *busy, busy, busy*—her words.

"What are you wearing, Sylvie?" I asked.

"Yes, do tell." Tyanne's pert nose curled up as if she had smelled something bad.

Sylvie missed the look. "Like it?" She freed herself of the twins and pirouetted.

"Not really," Tyanne whispered for my ears only.

"It's an original Gretchen Grunfeld."

"Never heard of her," I said.

"Tosh!" Sylvie said. "Everyone who is anyone has heard of Gretchen Grunfeld."

I guessed I wasn't anyone. And I was glad I wasn't.

"Are you cold, Sylvie?" Meredith asked.

"Must be," Tyanne said. "An Eskimo would sweat in that." That dig, Sylvie could hear.

She planted a hand on her quilted hip. "I'll have you know that this one-of-a-kind outfit is made of wicking material. It breathes." She bent forward with great effort to display the designer's tag at the neck.

As she did, I feared she might pop and fly around the room backward. I held my breath. She didn't. Rats.

"Girls, do you want Mumsie to buy you matching outfits?" She tweaked their chins and grabbed hold of their hands. "Let's see what I've got in my magical tent for my two beautiful daughters."

Nothing, I imagined. Her wares were for adult women.

"Wait," Matthew said. "We're taking the girls for ice cream."

"Too bad, love. I'm here now." As Sylvie and the twins reached the door, she turned. "By the by, Charlotte, it smells sort of musty in here. I'd spruce it up if I were you. A spritz of patchouli incense might do the trick."

In a cheese shop? Never. Not to mention that the faire was awash with other aromas. Cotton candy, cocoa, cookies, and pine trees. I did not want to add to the sensual overload.

"Incense is *trés chic* and oh so stylish." Sylvie flicked her acid-white hair over her shoulder. "A quality you lack at times."

My hands formed into fists.

As fast as a ninja, Tyanne pinned my arms to my sides. "Don't let her rile y'all."

Sylvie exited with the girls, and though she didn't laugh out loud, I could tell she was pleased with her gotcha moment. Her padded shoulders were jiggling.

Matthew huffed. "Another nice night, ruined."

"It's not ruined, sugar," Tyanne assured him. "You go get those girls back."

"She's right," I said. "Go."

Meredith rubbed Matthew's neck. "Remember what you told me, honey? No more kowtowing to Sylvie. We set our plan, and we keep it. If the girls happen to hear a debate—"

"A fight," Matthew corrected.

"Fine. A fight. Then so be it. We had plans. We stick to them."

"Be strong," Tyanne said. "Sylvie doesn't set the rules."

Meredith gave Matthew a shove. "Let's go, mister. Be a Daddy hero."

Matthew stood taller, which made me proud. He had

suffered enough. It was time to grow back the spine that
Sylvie had ripped out of him.

As they headed for the door, Meredith said over her
shoulder, "After going to the Igloo, we'll go home and see
to the puppy. We fed him before we came to the faire. You're
getting Rags at The Cheese Shop, right?"

"When I wind up my business here," I said. Taking care
of two animals was infinitely more challenging than one.

They departed, and I said to Tyanne, "You certainly
showed your mettle with Sylvie."

"Blame it on therapy. I had my second session today.
The doctor said: *Say what you feel; feel what you say.*"

"It's working."

She offered a smile that quickly dissolved. "It's all a
cover. I'm a mess, sugar, no two ways about it. I am not
adjusting well to being without Theo. And my kids are suffering something awful. Thomas is acting up. He flails at
things. It's like he can't control himself."

"Which is why you have to set rules."

"I had to give him three time-outs yesterday. Three."
She fanned herself. "I don't want him smacking his sister,
you know? So far, he's only hurt a lamp, but . . ." Her shoulders heaved. "Boys are so darned impulsive."

I patted her back. "Take a break. In fact, take off the rest
of the night. We're done here."

"Are you sure?"

"Find your kids and take them for ice cream. I hear the
double-deluxe strawberry mascarpone is great."

She bussed me on the cheek, fetched her purse, and sped
out the door like a Thoroughbred.

As I closed up, I found myself humming *Pretty Horses*,
a song my mother had sung to me.

Hush-a-bye don't you cry. Go to sleep-y little baby.
When you wake you shall have
All the pretty little horses.
Dapples and grays, pintos and bays
All the pretty little horses.

First, I checked the plug on the refrigerator. Next, I made sure the zippers on the tent windows were secure and the knife case locked. Lastly, I dropped to my knees to switch off the temporary fluorescent light strips that were plugged in behind the antique buffet counter.

As I started to stand, I heard a creak followed by a rasp. I peeked over the edge of the counter. In the dim light cast by the strands of twinkling lights outside the tent, I made out the shadow of a person. Inside the tent. The intruder was dressed in a black peacoat and trousers and wearing a face mask. He—I assumed it was a he; he looked too broad-shouldered to be a she—scooped something from one of the coolers and dropped it into a knapsack. I swallowed hard. He was robbing the shop? Would he hurt me?

Fearful of drawing attention to myself—loss of cheese was better than loss of life—I ducked lower, but my knee hit one of the boxes beneath the counter. I peeked to see if the intruder had heard me. He had. He ran at the counter. I was trapped, with nowhere to escape. My only option was to scream.

"Security!" My plea sounded muted, like the kind of non-shriek I had when waking out of a nightmare. Great. Right when I needed a cheerleader-sized voice, I had turned into a pipsqueak. "Security," I tried again, this time louder with more conviction.

The intruder cut around the buffet and dove at me. The attack was so forceful that I pitched forward. I hit the fake green grass floor with both palms, but from the narrow position behind the counter, I couldn't scramble to my feet. My one route of escape was through the legs of the table. I crawled as fast as I could, bumping my head and then my tailbone.

The attacker didn't pursue me. Didn't grasp my ankles. I heard footsteps slapping the fake grass floor, followed by the clackety-clack of the door. Had he fled?

I scooted from beneath the table and saw the tent was empty. I raced to the window. I didn't see any sign of the thief. He was fast, I had to give him that.

The door squealed open again.

Heart hammering, I turned, hands raised to defend myself.

Jordan drew to a halt, arms held high. A halo of light outlined his rugged frame. "It's just me. Are you okay? I heard you scream."

He had heard my pitiful appeal? Let's hear it for super-human hearing.

"I'm fine. A thief—"

"Where?"

"He ran that way." I pointed at the door.

Jordan sprinted out.

By the time I was able to switch on the lights inside the tent, Jordan returned, frowning. "I didn't see anyone running."

I sighed. "He probably decided it was safer to blend into the crowd."

"Who was it?" He gripped my arms. "Did you get a good look?"

"He was wearing a ski mask." I thought of Arlo, an ad-mitted thief. Before leaving his house, he could have tucked a ski mask in the pocket of his black peacoat. Had he es-caped police custody? Had Urso let him go? Granted, the intruder had looked bigger and broader than Arlo, but I had learned in the too-recent past that fear could warp all sense of dimension. I also pictured Oscar Carson, who I had pinned to the ground the other night. He was about the right size. I told Jordan.

He offered a wry grin. "It wasn't Oscar. I saw him out-side watching Mr. Nakamura put the finishing touches on his ice sculpture. Do you think it could have been random? There are a lot of tourists roaming about. What did he take?"

"Cheese. He rooted through the cooler."

The top of the cooler hung open. I peered inside. The cartons of cheese were jumbled. I couldn't tell what was missing.

"Maybe he wanted to increase his calcium intake."

"Very funny."

Jordan tucked a hair behind my ear, then traced his finger along my jaw. "Just making sure he didn't take off with your sense of humor, sweetheart." He wrapped his arms around me.

"Why would anyone risk robbing one of the tents?" I asked. "There are guards roaming the area, around the clock."

"He saw an opportunity and took it."

"I should tell Urso."

"I wouldn't bother him. He's got a lot on his plate. Inform security."

"Do you think he'll come back?"

Jordan chuckled. "I doubt it. You probably scared him more than he scared you."

That might have been true of a mouse, but I wasn't so sure about a thief.

Jordan drew me in tighter. "Look, whether you're ready to accept it or not, the world is changing. Providence is changing."

"Don't say that." I loved our town, loved the small-town feel, and the fact that most everybody knew and liked everybody else.

"It's expanding, and with growth . . ." Jordan let the sentence hang and kissed my forehead. "People are not as good as you believe them to be."

A shiver ran through me. Was Jordan one of those people? I pressed away from him. "Speaking of which, you told me something the other day."

He quirked a grin. "That I love and adore you?"

"That you were taught how to make cheese by a cheese maker named Jeremy Montgomery."

Jordan's face grew quiet.

"He died before you were born," I said.

His expression didn't change. He wasn't outraged. He was, in a word, calm. Deadly calm. I wanted to pound his chest. How could he be so composed when my insides were as squishy as an overripe cheese?

"Are you checking up on me?"

"Not me . . . Meredith . . ." I swallowed hard, felt my cheeks flush. "She asked how you learned to make cheese, so I told her, and she was intrigued and did a Google search, and . . ." No matter how hard I tried, I wouldn't be able to get out from under this kettle of glop.

"Do you trust me?" he asked, his voice throaty.

"I do. I want to. But I need to know everything about you. Everything." I drew in a deep breath and let it out. A spent balloon couldn't feel more limp. "I promise I won't tell anybody anything you reveal to me. I know you're worried about Jacky's husband coming after her." Jacky's husband had abused her. With Jordan's help, Jacky had moved from New Jersey and changed her identity.

"Jacky's husband will never come to Providence," Jordan said.

How could he be so sure?

Jordan ran his fingers down my arms and took hold of my hands. "I'll bet Meredith looked up the wrong Jeremy Montgomery. Have her try Jeremy K. Montgomery."

"K?"

"For Kenneth. I didn't lie. I was a teen when I learned to make cheese. J.K. was Jeremy's son."

At that moment, Jacky burst into the tent, her infant strapped to her chest in a BabyBjörn pack. "Jordan, thank God you're here." She looked pale, her lustrous brown hair windblown. "My car broke down. Cecily and I need a ride. She has a high fever. The doc is way the heck out on the Emerald Pastures farm."

Jordan looked at me for permission. I said, "Go."

He kissed me goodbye, then flew with Jacky and the baby into the night.

CHAPTER

Life can be fortuitous, or it can smack you upside the head with bad timing. The more I thought about how quickly Jordan had fled Le Petit Fromagerie, the more upset I got. I know, I know. I gave him permission to go, but I felt stretched as thin as taffy and I wanted answers. Real answers, not simply another clue. Was he worried that if he told me the truth, the whole truth, and nothing but the truth that I would blab? I wasn't that kind of person. That was Sylvie and a whole bunch of other people, but not me.

"Jordan Pace, you're going to tell me about your past or else," I muttered. *Or else* sounded so silly. Would I walk away from him? To what? When I was a senior in high school, I had threatened Chip with an *or else*. Either he attended OSU with me *or else*. He said he wouldn't, but at the last minute—thanks to a full scholarship—he switched. What if he hadn't? Would I have ended our relationship? Would I have taken an entirely different path in life?

Not eager to rehash my life's decisions, I closed up the tent, described the petty thief to security so they could be

on the alert, and hustled back to The Cheese Shop. I turned on lights as I went, first to the kitchen for a snack and then to the office.

Rags leaped from the office chair and bounded to my side. He nudged my calves with his head and did a little samba.

"No, I didn't forget you, fella. I'd planned to get here earlier, but life came at me fast." I sighed and recited a line from a Robert Burns' poem. "'The best-laid schemes o' mice an' men *gang aft agley.'*"

Rags meowed, as if in agreement.

I set my plate of green apple slices and Pace Hill Farm Gouda—a tribute to the task at hand—on the desk, nestled into the office chair, and patted my thigh. "Up!"

Rags hunkered down and sprang into my lap. Before he settled in, he stared at the Gouda. I broke off a teensy corner. He licked it from my fingers, padded in a circle until he found the right spot, and tucked himself into a coil.

"Let's see what we've got." After pairing a piece of cheese with apple and popping it into my mouth, I woke up my computer with a quick press of a key and clacked the keyboard with my fingertips. Using Google, I searched for Jeremy Montgomery, middle initial K for Kenneth. There were more than two hundred thousand possibilities, and none on the first page looked to be a perfect match. I moaned, wishing mysteries were easier to solve.

Jeremy Kostura was a ditch digger from Montgomery County. Jeremy L. Montgomery was an attorney at law. Duncan K. Montgomery had served in the Civil War. Jeremy G. Montgomery was a player on the K (for Kansas University) football squad.

Go team.

I added *Britain* to my search and the word *cheese*, but only the deceased Jeremy Montgomery's name came up. No sons were mentioned.

A heavy feeling of foreboding engulfed me. Was Jordan lying to protect me? His sister had been married to a bad man. What if Jordan had been associated with a bad man?

He said Jacky's husband would never find her. Was that because he was dead? How else could Jordan be sure that the man wouldn't come calling?

I banged my hand on the desktop. "Rats, rats, rats!"

Rags's head popped to attention.

"Sorry, fella. Not you." I sighed. How could I explain to my sweet pet that the words rats and Rags were not the same? I scruffed his ears to help him fall back to sleep and tried one more search, only this time I entered: *Kenneth Montgomery*, thinking perhaps this elusive cheese maker didn't use his first name.

As before, lots of possibilities emerged. An entry halfway down the third page of results caught my eye. J. Kenneth Montgomery was the name of a protagonist in a novel. Montgomery's occupation: *international spy*.

I leaned back in my chair, ideas exploding in my brain like fireworks. Had Jordan expected me to stumble upon this name? Was he trying to reveal that he was a spy?

Oh, please, Charlotte, be realistic. Jordan is no Jason Bourne. He's a cheese farmer. An affineur. A spy doesn't learn the art of affinage. There's got to be some other explanation.

But I couldn't fathom what it was.

* * *

The next morning, while I stood behind the cheese counter and laid out a selection of cheeses for the afternoon tasting class, I sorted through my feelings about last night's discovery. If Jordan was a spy, could I live with that? What if he had killed someone in the line of duty?

I called him on the telephone, but he didn't answer. He was probably making his morning rounds on the farm. There was always so much to do: milk the cows, check the temperatures on the cheese caves, and ensure that the apparatuses used to rotate the cheeses were in good operating order. I left a message for him to return my call and hung up.

To quell the pent-up anxiety peppering my system, I

went looking for my cousin. I needed someone sane to talk to, but Matthew wasn't in the wine annex. I glanced at Rebecca in the kitchen, who was hovering beside her boyfriend, Ipo, as he unloaded jars of honey from a box. Now was not the time to burden her with my troubles. But it was time to get to work.

"Rebecca, let's get a move on," I said.

She blew Ipo a kiss and joined me at the cheese counter. Standing together, we looked like a team—she in her ivory shawl-necked sweater and slim black trousers, I in my ecru V-neck and slate chinos.

"Perhaps we should start checking with each other regarding our wardrobe," I said. "I don't want anyone to think we have a uniform policy."

"Just good taste," she quipped.

"Grab that marble tray with the silver handles," I said. "Lay out a wedge of Tilsiter on it." The soft yellow, semi-hard cow's cheese with Prussian origins would look good against the black. "Let's add the Brebirousse D'Argental."

She cocked her head, not following.

"You know, the sheep's cheese with the orange rind and milky goodness. And add that Alabama Fromagerie Belle goat's cheese. Then let's set out a jar of raspberry jam and lay a couple of jewel-handled spreaders in the middle." I glanced behind me. "Do we have any of the Providence Patisserie sourdough bread?"

"Yes." She fetched a baguette.

"Perfect. Slice it thin and toss the slices into this basket." I placed a gold napkin into a shallow, square basket and flipped the corners of the napkin over the edges. Easy but elegant. "When the tasting is over, we're off to the tent. Tyanne is already there."

"I wouldn't miss it for—" Rebecca gasped and pointed. "What's he doing here?"

Urso lumbered into the shop, a deep crease forged between his eyebrows. He said, "Where's Ipo Ho?"

I looked toward the kitchen. Urso didn't wait for an invitation. He strode between the display barrels, around the

cheese counter, toward the rear of the shop, and into the kitchen.

Rebecca said, "Oh, no. He's going to arrest Ipo." She scuttled after him. I followed.

"Ipo Ho." Urso advanced.

Ipo backed into the doublewide refrigerator. If he wasn't guilty, he sure looked it.

Undaunted, Rebecca wiggled herself between the man she loved and the man who wanted to incarcerate him and tilted her chin upward. "Why are you here, Chief? What are you doing about Arlo MacMillan? Have you investigated him? Is he guilty?"

"Miss Zook, please step aside."

"I asked you a question."

"No, you asked me four."

"Getting technical, are we?"

Urso jammed his hands into his pockets, trying to look as casual as he could, but he didn't fool me. He was on to something. "I'm investigating everyone I think has motive at this point, okay? Arlo, included."

"Then why are you here?" Rebecca demanded. "You've got your work cut out for you, and you've already asked Ipo everything but his suit size."

"I have one more question for him."

"Like what?"

Urso prodded Rebecca to one side and addressed Ipo. "Where are your pu'ili sticks, Mr. Ho?"

"His what?" Rebecca looked blank.

Ipo gazed to the right, toward the kitchen's exit. Was he thinking about bolting? *Don't be a fool,* I silently urged him. As if picking up my message, he settled his shoulders and raised his head proudly. His guilty mien melted away. "Pu'ili sticks," he said to Rebecca. "They're luau instruments, too, about twenty inches long with one end uncut and the rest split into thin strips. They make a shaking-rattling sound when slapped against the body."

"I've seen those," Rebecca said.

Urso said, "You have?"

"In an episode of *Hawaii Five-O*. They were having this party, and—"

"Miss Zook, please be quiet. Where are they, Mr. Ho?"

Rebecca looked to me for help.

I moved closer. "Chief, I thought you said a kala'au rod was the weapon used to knock down Kaitlyn Clydesdale."

"We've changed our minds."

"You and who, the coroner?"

Urso gave a curt nod. "He found bamboo fibers lodged in Miss Clydesdale's neck. Bamboo fibers like those found in pu'ili sticks."

"A pu'ili stick is hardly strong enough to use as a weapon," I said.

Urso focused the brunt of his gaze on me. "Ipo could have had the stick in his hand and struck her with one end." He showed us the swift move. "Miss Clydesdale would have stumbled backward and hit her head." He eyed Ipo. "Is that what happened? Were you serenading Miss Zook?"

"No!" Rebecca mewled like a wounded cat.

Ipo wrapped his arm around her. "Shhh. It's all right." He addressed Urso. "Chief, you know I didn't do this, but if you want to see the sticks, I can show you. They should be in a storage box in my attic."

"You already showed me—"

"Not that storage box," Ipo said, his voice steady. "Another one. Half of the instruments belonged to my father's family. The other half to my mother's. Theirs was not an approved marriage. In their honor, I have never mixed any of their heritage. I have two separate storage boxes. My mother's—"

"Let's go." Urso headed out of the shop.

Ipo offered a supportive glance to Rebecca and followed Urso.

A thick silence hung in the air after their departure.

"C'mon," I said to Rebecca. "Back to work." I strode to the cheese counter and did a mental inventory of what I needed to reorder.

Rebecca trotted after me. "Charlotte." She clutched her

hands in front of herself, begging with more sincerity than any penitent. "Do something. He's not guilty."

"Charlotte!" Sylvie barged into the shop.

Prudence Hart hurried in behind her. Both wore horrid thigh-length coats, neither of which went well with the women's skin tone. Prudence's was speckled orange, Sylvie's oxblood red. How they ever convinced themselves that they were fashionistas was beyond me.

Sylvie said, "Wait'll you hear—"

"Don't listen to her, Charlotte," Prudence said.

"Charlotte," Rebecca whispered.

I petted her cheek. "Get back to work on the platters. I'll follow up with Urso. Promise. We'll figure this out."

Prudence stomped her foot. "She's been telling everybody that Georgia Plachette said Kaitlyn Clydesdale was not a nice person."

"But Georgia *is* telling people that," Sylvie said. "I heard her with my own ears."

I moaned. I had felt stretched as thin as taffy before, but now I felt like a frayed rubber band ready to snap. I whirled on Sylvie and Prudence and jabbed my finger. "Stop it. Both of you." I weaved past them to the cheese counter and resumed my slicing.

"Kaitlyn was a wonderful woman," Prudence said, heedless of my warning.

"You're only saying that because she came through with a donation to the historical museum." Sylvie folded her arms across her ample chest. "Money, money, money. Is that all you ever think about?"

I looked at her askance. Like she didn't?

"But Kaitlyn didn't come through." Prudence's face turned sour.

"She didn't?" I said.

"No, not for the museum or for the theater."

"Ha!" Sylvie spread her arms wide. "You see? She wasn't a nice woman."

"She died too soon," Prudence snapped.

"Oh, please. Why are you defending her?" Sylvie rubbed

her thumb and forefinger together like a moneylender. "Now you'll have to wheedle your precious cash from Georgia Plachette, and don't think that'll happen anytime soon, love. She's as tight as the Queen Mother."

"Psst." Rebecca tapped my forearm with the flat blade of her carving knife and leaned in for a private conversation. "Maybe we should check out Georgia. Maybe she'll benefit from Kaitlyn's death. You know, the CFO takes over or manages the estate or something like that? It could be worth a lot of money to her. Remember how cagey she was when you were questioning her the other day?"

"But how would she have known about Ipo's pu'ili sticks?" I sighed, wishing Kaitlyn Clydesdale had never come to town and life could return to normal, but then I mentally kicked myself for having such a selfish thought. The woman was dead. No matter how mean she had been, she hadn't deserved that fate.

"Please, Charlotte, question her." Rebecca's voice cracked. "Please."

I moaned and pressed a hand to my heart. Had I instilled in Rebecca a desire to become as gung-ho to solve crimes and crises as I was? I grabbed my fingers, steepled them, and I leaned back in the chair and regarded our situation.

Kaitlyn was a wonderful resource. Financier. And boss in the warming.

"I'm only saying that if we can come from both directions in the investigation," she said, "we've looked at other angles, too. Think of all you can make of us."

I moved to her posture. To her mind, I had...

"But Rebecca's plea came in and came true." Rebecca was upset now.

"All right, I'll ask."

"You are the best crime-solver in the house."

"I will ask her, but for pity's sake," I told her, "stop sounding so mean."

She threw her arms around me. "Thank you."

"Have you ever, will you ever, stop hugging?" I smiled, then realized...

CHAPTER

I found Georgia at Clydesdale Enterprises' temporary offices, located above the Café au Lait Coffee Shop. Kaitlyn hadn't gone to any expense to decorate the place. She had provided a couple of hardback chairs, a glass-top desk, and a file cabinet. Shelving on one wall held legal-sized boxes, a historical guide to Holmes County, and a feeble looking silk plant. A photograph naming Kaitlyn the Do-Gooder Woman of the Year hung on the opposite wall.

Georgia sat at the desk, typing on a laptop computer. She looked up when I entered and adjusted the shawl swaddling her shoulders. "May I help you?" Her face was puffy, her nose redder than before. Had she been crying? That was a bad combo with a cold.

"I wanted to see how you were feeling." I removed my scarf and gloves but kept on my winterberry red blazer. The temperature in the office was warm, but not warm enough to shed a layer.

"I'm fine." She sneezed three times in a row and reached for a pile of wadded-up tissues beside a to-go cup from Café

au Lait. Her hand stopped short. Her gaze flitted to a stack of papers on the other side of the computer. In a flash, she scooped the papers off the table, slipped them into a file folder, inserted the folder into a red briefcase beneath the desk, then snatched a tissue. A magician ripping the tablecloth from a table couldn't have been more deft.

The fleetness of her actions piqued my curiosity. Was she simply being organized or was she trying to keep me from seeing the papers, which in a brief glance looked like court documents? Was it a document ceding control of Clydesdale Enterprises to the CFO, as Rebecca had suggested?

Whoa, Charlotte. I reined myself in. Who was I to jump to conclusions? Except I did want a close-up and personal look at the papers she had hidden. ASAP.

Georgia dabbed her nose. "Why are you here?"

To snoop was probably not the best answer. Neither was *I'm the town's appointed savior, didn't you hear?*

"To check in on you." I stared at her coffee cup. "Want a refill?"

She sneezed again and quickly blew her nose. "No, that's okay." She sounded whiny and even more miserable than when we had first met, but why wouldn't she? Her boss had died. She had to be devastated. Unless, of course, she killed the boss.

"My treat," I said. "Drinking plenty of liquids while you're sick is important."

She offered a weak smile. "Okay, sure. It's orange oolong tea."

I set my scarf and gloves on the desk, hustled downstairs, and returned with two teas and six packets of honey. Georgia looked like she could use extra sweetness in her life. I handed her the goods and settled on a hardback chair with my cup of tea. Steam rose through the tiny sipping hole and glazed my face with moisture.

"So how are you doing?" I asked.

"Horrible. All the journalists calling. All the police questions." She sipped her tea and let out a teensy hum of enjoyment.

I allowed a comfortable silence to settle between us as if we were girlfriends sharing a cuppa. After a long moment, I said, "I didn't know Kaitlyn well, but people say she was a wonderful woman."

Georgia hesitated. She glanced at the commemorative Do-Gooder photograph and back at me. "She gave her all to everything."

"My grandmother adored her."

"Kaitlyn spoke highly of your grandmother, too."

I gazed through the glass-top desk, but I couldn't get a clear view of the briefcase below. Georgia's slouch ankle boots, which were as saggy as a Shar-Pei's skin, blocked my line of sight. I craned my head to spy beyond the leather, but I couldn't make out the words on the file folder. "How long had you known Kaitlyn?"

"A long time."

Again she had hesitated. What was up with that?

"Tell me about you." I set my cup of tea on the desk, rose a tad from my chair, and overemphasized tucking the tail of my blazer under my rear. While I did, I scooched my chair an inch to the left so I could get a better angle on the file folder. Squinting, I could read the word *Plachette* on the tab. There were two more words but I couldn't make them out. If only I had Supergirl's vision. "When did you first start working for Clydesdale Enterprises?"

"Five years ago."

"When did you become CFO?"

"Right away."

"You can't be much older than thirty."

She blushed. "Actually, I'm thirty-eight."

"No way." I scooched some more. She had to be thinking I had ants in my pants, but I didn't care. I had no shame. "I want the name of the skin products you use."

She bit back a hint of a smile, reminding me of somebody, but I couldn't put my finger on whom.

I eyed the file folder tab again. *Plachette: Georgia . . . something.* I needed to stare, but she would catch me if I did. I reached for my cup of tea and accidentally knocked

my gloves and scarf to the floor. "Clumsy me," I said. As my fingers grazed the cashmere, I got a clear view of the file folder tab. *Plachette: Georgia Clydesdale.*

Color me stupid. That was why she looked familiar. That was why she had hesitated when I had asked how long she had known Kaitlyn. She was Kaitlyn's daughter.

Snagging my things, I returned to a sitting position and studied Georgia. She had Kaitlyn's eyes and the same haughty cheekbones, but she was at least ten inches shorter and fifty pounds lighter. And her dark curly hair was a stark contrast to Kaitlyn's blonde straight coif. Did she dye and perm it?

"What's wrong?" Georgia said. "You're staring at me."

"You're Kaitlyn Clydesdale's daughter."

"I—" She pursed her lips.

"Why keep it a secret?"

Georgia squirmed.

"Because she didn't want people to know how old she was, right?" I said. "She wanted people to think she was in her fifties, and if they found out you were thirty-eight—"

"You're wrong. She feared she'd be accused of nepotism."

I gaped. "That doesn't make sense. She owned the company; she set the rules."

Georgia examined her chewed-to-the-nub fingernails. "She didn't think her associates would welcome the idea that they had to report numbers to her daughter. She—" Georgia sneezed and the shawl fell off her shoulders, revealing a skintight plunging neckline black dress. I had seen the same dress on a mannequin in the Under Wraps display window. How dare Sylvie convince the poor girl that it looked appropriate for mourning.

"Did you tell Chief Urso you were her daughter?"

"I've answered all his questions."

But what if Urso hadn't asked the right questions? I mused. He was a good cop, but a hard-hitting DA, he wasn't.

"Did he ask if you were Kaitlyn's daughter?"

"He didn't ask, but I did offer." She sat taller. "Satisfied?"

Why hadn't Urso told me? Because I wasn't one of his

deputies. Because I had no business whatsoever investigating. Except Rebecca had pleaded, and I had promised. I never reneged on a promise.

I glanced at the briefcase again. Could there be a lucrative will inside that would give Georgia sole proprietorship of the company? That would be a strong motive to kill her mother. How could I get a peek?

"I have a solid alibi," Georgia offered.

She had said the same thing at Fromagerie Bessette. Why did she feel the need to reiterate it? Perhaps guilt was rearing its mighty head.

"I was at the pub playing darts until closing. Plenty of people saw me."

"Then you have nothing to worry about, do you?"

Georgia pulled the shawl back over her shoulders. "My mother and I didn't get along at times."

"Most mothers and daughters don't." I'd had plenty of altercations with Grandmère during my teens and early twenties. At the ripe old age of twenty-eight I started to realize she was smarter than I had given her credit for.

"She could ruffle feathers with the best of them," Georgia added.

"I'll bet she could." I recalled Sylvie's tirade about Georgia lambasting Kaitlyn. "Did you like your mother?"

"Like her?" Georgia's chin quivered. "Of course, I did. I loved her."

"You were heard telling customers at Under Wraps that your mother wasn't a nice woman."

Her chin stopped trembling. "That's not what I said." Her voice took on that imperious tone that I had heard from Kaitlyn. "Who told you that?" Her nostrils flared like a bull's. "What I said was that she wasn't nice to employees."

"Meaning you."

"Meaning Chip Cooper, Oscar Carson, that hack developer she found in Columbus, and a ton of others."

I tapped the arm of my chair, unable to find a nice way to raise the next question. "Was she nice to her lover?"

"Sure, why not? Whoever the heck he might be."

"You don't know?"

"No clue. Isn't that the beauty of having a lover—secrecy? Look, my mother kept a tight rein on everybody. She—" Georgia nipped her upper lip with a tooth, as if trying to curb herself from saying anything more. She glanced at the door. Did she wish she could flee? She fingered her curls. I could see her mind whirring behind her deep brown eyes. "If you ask me, that Barton Burrell is the prime suspect."

"Why?"

"He wanted out of his contract, and now, with my mother dead, the contract is null and void. There was a clause in the contract that if something happened to my mother, the deal was canceled."

* * *

When I returned to The Cheese Shop, Rebecca was nowhere to be found. Matthew said she was worried because she hadn't heard from Ipo after he had left with Urso. She asked for a break to check on him. An hour later, even though she hadn't returned, we started our cheese and wine-tasting class.

Members of the class spilled out of the annex into The Cheese Shop. I had known we were going to have a crowd, but word of mouth had doubled the attendance. The hum of excitement was intoxicating.

I stood near the bar in the annex and held up one of the wooden platters that I had arranged with cheese and fruit. "Don't worry. Everyone will get to taste." Individuals beyond the archway popped up, trying to peep over the head of the person in front. "If you don't have a note card and pencil, wave your hand. Tyanne will come around."

Luckily, Tyanne had arrived early to work. She said she was so excited about the upcoming opening of Le Petit Fromagerie that she couldn't sit at home. She brandished a pack of cards overhead.

"I've got champagne." Matthew moved from person to

person, passing out shots of a luscious Schramsberg champagne from Napa Valley. Champagne was a fail-safe wine selection with cheese, he said. The flavor never intruded.

"On this platter," I went on, "we have Brie and Camembert from America, and their French counterparts." I twisted the platter in my hands. "Notice the mounds of winter red and green grapes. See how they provide a nice contrast to the white-rinded cheeses." The students weren't simply tasting cheese. They were trying to learn how to create a lovely presentation. "Now, in case you didn't know, cheeses made with unpasteurized—otherwise known as raw—milk cannot be sold in the United States unless they have been aged for at least sixty days."

I heard a chorus of: "I didn't know that."

"Why?" Tyanne asked, as I had prompted her to do during the hour before the class began.

"Because bacteria might grow. However, there are cheese lovers worldwide who might put up a stink if all cheeses were pasteurized."

"*Moi*, for one," Pépère said as he forged through the crowd with a basket of saltwater crackers. "Pasteurization takes away the full flavor of the cheese."

As customers tasted, I heard arguments start up. A couple of people loved the French Brie. A few others preferred the American one.

"Please, folks," I said. "The enjoyment of one cheese over another doesn't mean someone is wrong. It's all a matter of taste. Now, if you'll also pay attention to how I added nuts and scoops of honey and brown sugar to the platter. Why do you think I—?"

"Charlotte!" Rebecca's voice cut through the murmurs. She wedged between patrons, her face panic-stricken.

I set the platter down and hurried to her. "What's wrong?"

"It's Ipo."

"Is he hurt?"

She shook her head and placed a hand to her chest, gasping for breath. "His instruments. Those"—she snapped her fingers—"what do you call them?"

"Pu'ili sticks."

"They're missing."

"Missing?"

"As in *gone*."

I raised a reproachful eyebrow.

"Sorry," she said. "I know you know what *missing* means, I'm just so upset. And Chief Urso"—she hiccupped and gripped my wrists—"Urso arrested Ipo. I tried to tell the chief that Barton Burrell might have taken the pu'ili sticks, but he wouldn't listen to me."

CHAPTER

13

I left Matthew and Tyanne to finish up with the tasting in the annex, and Rebecca and I hightailed it to the Providence Precinct. We rushed into the old Victorian house, bypassed the flock of tourists gathering around the Tourist Information Center that had taken up residence in a nook of the foyer, and approached the new receptionist—a cherub-faced redhead.

She set the bear claw pastry she had been savoring to one side, wiped her fingers with a paper towel, and said, "Oops. Caught me in the act."

How could she resist? Providence Patisserie donated sweet rolls on a daily basis.

"We need to see the chief," I said.

"You just missed him. He went to All Booked Up."

The bookstore was one of my favorite spots in town. Often I slipped in to buy a book, and before I knew it, found myself nestled in one of the many chairs with a stack of recommended titles on my lap, reading while listening to strains of Beethoven or Mozart.

"Let's go." Rebecca grabbed my hand and hauled me at a clip out of the building, down the street, and around the corner.

When we arrived at the bookstore, she pushed me through the door first. Like a klutz, I tripped over the checkerboard carpet. I regained my balance, smoothed the lapel of my blazer, and scanned the store, searching for Urso among the teeming crowd threading through the rows of bookshelves.

Rebecca trotted in and plowed past me, hand to her forehead like an Old West tracker. In seconds, I feared she might drop to the carpet to listen for hoofbeats.

"Where's the fire?" Octavia Tibble plucked my elbow.

I spun around and bit back a smile. No longer was my friend clad in her fortune-teller costume. This time she wore what could only be described as an arctic explorer outfit. In her arms she held a pile of children's books. At the top of the pile was *The Polar Express.*

I tapped the book. "I didn't know you dressed up to purchase books, too."

"Very funny. I'm actually here on business to broker a deal. Did you know the bookshop is for sale?"

"Who's the buyer?"

"Me . . . I hope." She thumped her chest with pride. "I've always wanted to own a bookstore. If I close the sale, I'm giving up real estate forever." She leaned in. "Confidentially, I hate sellers and buyers calling me at odd hours of the night. They're never happy."

"Speaking of which," I said, "I heard the deal between Clydesdale Enterprises and Barton Burrell is null and void."

Octavia bobbed her head. "There was a death clause in the fine print. I'd missed it." She glanced past me. "Oh, there's the store owner. Sorry. I've got to go."

As she hurried off, Rebecca returned, out of breath. "Follow me. I see Urso."

Urso stood in profile by the end cap of the mystery/thriller section, chatting with someone—a younger man in

a stylish suit. I could only make out the edge of the young man's face.

"Go, go, go," Rebecca said.

"We shouldn't interrupt."

"Do you see mouths moving? No, you do not. Go." She pushed me like a feisty steam engine trying to force a car off the tracks.

I tried to hold ground, but her will was stronger than mine. I stumbled into Urso with an *oof.*

He whipped around and barked, "What?"

"A fine way to greet friends," Rebecca said.

"You're not my friends when you barge into me like a pair of hoodlums."

"Sorry to bother you, U-ey," I said, my voice choked with embarrassment, "but we wanted to discuss your plans for Ipo."

Urso ran a hand down his neck, his exasperation obvious.

"You know he didn't do it, U-ey," I continued.

"Charlotte, just because you've helped solve two murder cases in as many years does not make you our number one crime fighter."

"I—"

"Don't talk. You either, Miss Zook." He jabbed a finger in her direction. "I'm doing my job. I've done my investigative work. I've dotted all the *I*s and crossed the *T*s in the murder book."

A murder book was a chronological order of all the facts related to a case, including forensic information and witness lists. Urso had shown me his last one.

"I'm only missing a murder weapon," Urso went on. "A murder weapon that happens to belong to one Ipo Ho. When I find that murder weapon—"

"Excuse me," I said, "but wouldn't it be considered involuntary manslaughter and not murder?"

Urso snarled. "Oh, no. Don't tell me Miss Zook has convinced you to watch TV crime shows now."

"No, I—"

"Crime shows do not have all the answers."

I bridled. "I happen to know a thing or two about the law."

"Do you? Where'd you get your information? Google?"

Heat crept up my chest and into my neck. Despite the anger or humiliation or whatever it was that I was feeling, I wouldn't be put off. I said, "You can't be certain that the weapon is a pu'ili stick."

"The coroner is pretty certain."

"Pretty certain. That sounds iffy."

"You don't have motive," Rebecca added.

"Mr. Ho didn't want Kaitlyn Clydesdale to compete with his business," Urso said. "He'd filed an official complaint. With her death, the deal to buy the Burrell Farm is officially off. That's motive enough."

"But he has an alibi," Rebecca said. "Me."

"Look, I know you love him, Miss Zook, but love is not an alibi."

"What about Barton Burrell?" she said.

"What about him?"

I said, "Barton Burrell didn't want to sell, Chief. He has as much motive as Ipo. You have to let Ipo out on bail."

"I don't *have* to do anything, Charlotte, thank you very much. If you don't mind, I'm conducting business. I'm interviewing a new deputy while showing him the town." Urso gestured at the young man who was thumbing through a bestselling thriller.

The young man looked up and my breath caught in my chest. He reminded me so much of Chip at that age— buoyant, aspiring. His eyes were as light as Chip's, too, and his nose equally noble.

I forced my gaze back to Urso. "Is Deputy Rodham quitting?"

"No. I'm trying to beef up our force. We need more men."

"Or women," Rebecca said.

"I'm interviewing women, as well," Urso said, his tone defensive. "In the past few months we've had a spike in theft and vandalism."

I thought of the thief who had raided our Winter Wonderland tent. I had told security. Should I have brought the incident to Urso's attention, as well? *Let it go, Charlotte. Theft of cheese is not related to the matter at hand.*

"If that's all," Urso said.

Deflated, I started to turn away, then remembered something else I had forgotten to tell Urso and spun back. "Somebody called Kaitlyn when she was in The Cheese Shop," I blurted. "Whoever it was made her furious. She threatened the caller."

"It wasn't Ipo," Rebecca said.

"Fine. I'll check it out." Urso gestured. "Now scoot."

"*Scoot?* Did you say *scoot*? Why . . ." Rebecca folded her arms. "Uh-uh. This is a public place. We're not budging."

Bolstered by her defiance, I lifted my chin. "She's right. We can stay if we want."

Urso growled.

I growled back. He was being slack, and that wasn't like him. I started to wonder again what was going on in his life. Had Jacky dumped him? Was he taking out his frustration on the world? On Ipo?

* * *

Needing to calm down before opening Le Petit Fromagerie to the public, I sent Rebecca back to the shop, and I headed to my grandparents' house to hold a pity party. I didn't need a long one, just one lengthy enough to cool off.

I entered through the kitchen and pulled to a stop at the heavenly scent of cinnamon, chocolate, and vanilla. The women of Providence had been baking. A pretty white platter filled with a variety of home-baked cookies was perched on the counter. A gaggle of women sat clustered around the Shaker-style square table. Each wore a turquoise-studded cowboy hat, including my grandmother.

They sang in a united chorus, "Hi, Charlotte," then continued stuffing envelopes with colorful leaflets of some kind.

My grandmother split from the group and scuttled to

me, her arms open wide for a hug. I went into them and drew in her strength for a moment, then pecked her cheek and snatched a cream-cheese Hershey's Kiss cookie from the platter on the counter. Hershey's Kisses and I had a longtime love affair. As the owner of a gourmet cheese shop, I knew that I should prefer something more elegant like Scharffen Berger chocolate, but Kisses had been my mother's favorite candy. How could I resist?

"*Chérie*, such a delight." Grandmère took a cheese and jam button cookie for herself and nibbled the edges. "Why are you not at work?"

"I needed a breather."

"You do too much. You should arrange for personal time."

"That's why I'm taking a breather."

She aimed her forefinger at my nose. "You want to talk about something. I can tell, but I cannot right now. We are so busy."

"What are you up to?" I gestured at the group of women.

"In honor of Kaitlyn, we have created a local chapter for the Do-Gooders."

That explained the cowboy hats.

"We will carry on her work. It is good for the soul." Grandmère winked. "Of course, our first project will be to persuade the organization to support our local theater makeover, as Kaitlyn had planned." She plucked a flyer from the table and brandished it like a banner. In glimpses, I saw photographs taken at the Providence Playhouse that included Grandmère's latest plays, *No Exit with Poe* and *The Ballet of Hairspray*, as well as rehearsal photos for the upcoming *Chicago*. "To raise money, we are working on bringing the cast of *Glee* to do a one-night performance. The show is set in Ohio. It is perfect, *non*?"

I nodded. "Speaking of Kaitlyn, did you know her CFO is her daughter?"

Grandmère laid a hand on her chest. "I had no idea. What a horrible ordeal for the poor girl."

Woman, I thought. A woman who was older than I, but I didn't press the point.

"I didn't think you liked Georgia, Bernadette," one of the Do-Gooders said.

"Why don't you like her?" I asked. My grandmother was rarely wrong about people.

Grandmère fluttered her hand. "It is not mine to say. Gossip is never fruitful." She addressed her group. "We must let Miss Plachette know our plans to form a Do-Gooder group in her mother's honor."

The women nodded their agreement.

"She'll be thrilled," I said, though I didn't believe it for a minute. My last impression of Georgia was of a woman who couldn't wait to split Providence. Had she killed her mother in hopes of taking control of the company? How much was it worth? "Grandmère, what do you know about Clydesdale Enterprises?"

"Nothing."

"Didn't Kaitlyn share anything with you about her reason to return to Providence?"

"She intended to start a honeybee farm."

"Did she tell you anything else? I mean, you seemed to be such buddies."

"Truly, *chérie*, she was quite private. Perhaps your grandfather might know something. He has been at the Country Kitchen every day this week. You know how gossip abounds at the diner."

"Gossip that isn't fruitful?" I said.

She slapped my arm playfully. "Go see him. He is in the dining room with the twins, building an aquarium."

A moan escaped my mouth. I couldn't help it. I couldn't imagine taking care of Rags, Rocket, the twins, and fish, too.

"C'est rien," Grandmère said, reading my mind. "The fish will live here. The girls will visit."

I breathed a sigh of relief and pushed through the swinging door. The scent of wood stain hung in the air. My

grandfather and the twins circled the dining table. Tools cluttered the oak-finished sideboard against the wall.

Amy, wearing a smock smudged with paint, broke from the project and ran to my side. "Aunt Charlotte." She grabbed my hand as if she hadn't seen me in days, not simply a few hours. How I wished I could bottle her energy and enthusiasm. "Come see what we're making." She pulled me toward the empty mahogany-trimmed aquarium, which sat upon a plastic mat atop the table.

"Isn't it beautiful?" Clair said. Unlike Amy, her smock was spot-free. Her hair was pulled into a clip and fell in wisps around her sweet face. "You can touch it. The wood is dry, right, Pépère?"

"*Oui.*" Pépère peered over a pair of thick-lensed glasses perched on his nose. "We are starting with the basics. Plants and neon tetra."

"I love tetras!" Amy held up a plastic bag, which was partially filled with water. Inside, shiny iridescent fish finned about. "They're so pretty."

"Tetra fish are found in blackwater and clear-water streams in Brazil, Colombia, and Peru," Clair said, sounding like a well-read expert. "They are peaceful fish and do well in aquariums."

"Why are you here?" Pépère asked as he poured a bag of colorful rocks into the bottom of the aquarium.

I told him about my encounter with Urso at All Booked Up.

"He cannot arrest Ipo, can he?" Pépère said. "Not without these . . . what did you call them?"

"Pu'ili sticks."

"Without even one instrument in his possession? It is not right."

Amy stamped her foot. "Chief Urso is horrible."

"No, he's not," I said. "He's doing his job."

"But he's doing it wrong," she wailed.

Was he? What if Ipo did mean to harm Kaitlyn Clydesdale? Except Rebecca swore that he never left her side that

night. Who else would have known about the pu'ili sticks and where to find them?

"How is Rebecca doing?" Clair asked, her face growing more serious by the nanosecond. Whenever Rebecca visited the house, she played board games with the girls. They adored her.

"She's coping."

Pépère caught my cautious tone. *"Ne t'inquiète pas, chérie."* How could he expect me not to worry? "She will rebound."

"I'm not so sure. Losing a first love can have such an impact." I thought of my first love, Chip, but pushed him from my mind. Now was definitely not the time for me to rehash my past.

"She'll only lose him if he's guilty," Clair said.

I brushed her bangs off her forehead, not as certain as she was that our legal system worked to perfection. "Let's hope so."

"Girls, spread the pebbles," Pépère said. "Make them level."

As Amy and Clair set to work, Pépère wiped his hands on the apron he wore over his shirt and trousers and took a seat in one of the burgundy and gold striped dining chairs. "Pu'ili sticks, eh? I cannot say that I have ever seen those. What a versatile plant bamboo is, *non*? It is used in so many ways. Gardens, aquariums." He lifted a bag of bamboo that would serve as the tetras' undersea world. "What else is made of bamboo, *mes filles*?"

"Basketry," Clair said.

"And jewelry!" Amy thumped the table with her palm.

"Oui," Pépère said. "You know, Charlotte, I heard talk at the Country Kitchen earlier. I cannot remember who said it—perhaps that deputy candidate of Urso's—he was saying how the marks on Kaitlyn Clydesdale's neck were not consistent"—he scruffed his chin—"yes, that is the word he used. They were not consistent with a bruise that would have been made by a smooth rod."

"How so?"

"They were separated. Would a pu'ili stick make this kind of bruise?"

"Possibly. The bands of the bamboo would jut out and not hit the skin flush. There would be spaces in between, so the bruises wouldn't be one mass."

He hummed and rubbed his chin again. "What else could make such a bruise and leave fibers?"

"A hatbox-style cheese container could," Amy said.

"Could not," Clair countered.

"Could so. It's got bands on it."

"It's made of wood."

"Not all of them." Amy took on the same righteous tone that my grandmother did whenever she argued. "Some are made from bamboo."

"They're not hard enough," Clair countered.

"Are, too. Tell her, Aunt Charlotte."

"I'm sorry, sweetheart. I'm afraid Clair is—" I stopped myself as an image flickered at the edges of my mind.

"What is it?" Pépère asked.

"On the night of Kaitlyn's death, Rebecca took a round of Emerald Isles goat cheese to add to her cheese platter."

"That particular cheese is cased in just such a bamboo container," Pépère said.

"See?" Amy turned to Clair, who blew air up her bangs in frustration. They fluttered then settled down.

I wracked my brain, trying to remember if I had seen either the cheese or the box when I had scanned Rebecca's cottage that night from my position beyond the Dutch door. I recalled the makings of the cheese platter on the pass-through counter. Rebecca had laid out a wedge of Manchego, Rouge et Noir Brie, and Chevrot, as well as crackers, cheese knives, and a jar of honey. But I couldn't remember seeing the goat cheese. I said, "The Emerald Isles box wasn't there after Kaitlyn died. I would stake my reputation on it."

Pépère said, "But, *chérie,* Ipo could not have knocked Kaitlyn over with a box of cheese."

"What if the box was filled with rocks?" Amy asked.

"That's a silly question," Clair said.

"Rebecca says there are no silly questions." Amy huffed. "Besides, Ipo is strong. Have you seen his muscles?"

"But Rebecca was there," Clair protested, "and she said he didn't do it."

"That is enough, *mes filles*. No more talk." Pépère nudged the girls' shoulders. "Back to our project."

As they set to work, I thought of Arlo again. What if Kaitlyn's promise to reveal his secret had sent him over the edge? What if he had lied about not stealing Ipo's pu'ili sticks? Arlo played cards with Ipo. He might have known where Ipo stowed the luau instruments. He could have gone to Rebecca's, fought with Kaitlyn, and whacked her with one of the pu'ili sticks. As Kaitlyn fell and struck her head on the coffee table, Arlo could have noticed the cheese platter and, unable to restrain his kleptomaniac compulsion, taken the goat cheese. He had a stash of filched hatbox-style cheese containers in his home.

CHAPTER

14

Perched on one of the dining chairs at my grandparents'
table, I whipped my cell phone from my purse and dialed
Urso to tell him my renewed suspicions about Arlo. Urso
didn't answer his phone—no big surprise. He probably saw
my number on his caller ID and opted to ignore me, the
toad. I dialed a second time, listened to three cheery rings
and an annoying beep, hung up and dialed again. I could be
a pest when provoked.

Grandmère pushed open the dining room door and
peeked in. "Charlotte, my ladies are leaving, and I am putting together a snack for the girls before they go to their
chorale rehearsal. Are you hungry? I am cooking Parmesan
zucchini circles. *Votre favori.*"

My mouth watered instantly. At about the twins' age,
I had gone through a cycle where I had wanted zucchini
every day for a month—probably because it was growing
rampant in my grandparents' garden. My grandmother
couldn't brew a decent pot of coffee, but she could cook up
a storm—in a variety of styles. Back then, she had made

stuffed, baked, and barbecued zucchini for me. She had incorporated it into bread, pasta, salads, and even hamburgers. I couldn't remember the last time she had made circles—succulent pieces of zucchini dipped in a Parmesan batter and fried to a golden brown. Major comfort food. Exactly what I needed when irritated with our dear, sweet, dedicated chief of police.

I said, "I'd love some, thanks! Can you hurry?"

"Five minutes." She disappeared into the kitchen. The door swung shut.

Pépère said, "Girls, remove the aerator from the box and place the pieces on the table."

As the twins obeyed, I entered Urso's number on speed dial and pressed Send again. And again and again. I muttered under my breath. He was adding a second deputy to his roster. He could certainly spare a moment to answer my call. If I'd had the time, I would have tracked him down to tell him to take a long walk off a short pier, but I only had fifteen minutes, tops, before I had promised to open Le Petit Fromagerie at the faire. When Urso didn't answer after my twelfth attempt, I stabbed End on my cell phone.

"What's wrong, Aunt Charlotte?" Clair rested a supportive hand on my shoulder.

"Nothing. I'm just mad at a friend."

"At Chief Urso?" Amy said.

How did she know? I hadn't spoken his name aloud during any of my phone call attempts.

"Amy, hand me the screwdriver," Pépère said.

She plucked it from a wicker basket and held it out to him, handle first.

"Why are you mad at Chief Urso?" Clair asked.

"Because Aunt Charlotte wants to tell him that some cheese boxes are made from bamboo," Amy said. "Right?"

"Girls, fetch me a cloth." Pépère gestured at the stack of cloths on the buffet.

As they scuttled to do his bidding, he lasered me with a look. I got the message. It was time to end this conversation. For the girls' sakes. I set the cell phone on the dining

table and twirled it in a huff. Watching it spin, I thought of Kaitlyn Clydesdale and the telephone call that had incensed her. Was the call crucial to the case? Had Urso followed up?

I picked up the phone and dialed Urso one more time. If he could link the telephone call to Arlo and connect Arlo to the missing goat cheese, he might be able to weave this murder mystery to an end.

As I waited through three more rings, Pépère laid his hand over mine. "Let it go, *chérie*."

"This time I'm leaving a message."

"Do not burn the bridge." He held up his hands. "I am only saying."

The girls trotted to him and, giggling, flapped their white cloths at me like surrender flags.

I covered the mouthpiece and mock-snarled, "Very funny."

They giggled louder. Pépère snatched the cloths, warned them with a stern finger, and started to polish pieces of the aerator to a shine.

I listened to Urso's greeting message. After the beep, I forced my voice to be light and deliberately charming. "Urso, it's me, Charlotte. I was wondering—did you happen to follow up on the mysterious phone call to Kaitlyn Clydesdale? I have a tidbit of a thought to offer. Call me."

When I hung up, Pépère said, "A *tidbit of a thought*?"

I shrugged. Fine, perhaps I had sounded phony. Urso would have to deal with it.

Amy said, "Didn't Chief Urso already pull up telephone records?"

"Of course, he did," Clair said. "That's one of the first things the police do."

I gaped. "Where did you two learn something like that?"

"On TV," they said in unison.

"*CSI*," Clair added.

"Uh-uh." Amy shook her head. "It was *Murder, She Wrote*."

"Oh, no, no, no," I said. "Don't tell me Rebecca gave you her list of favorite mystery shows."

"It wasn't Rebecca," Amy said.

"It was Mum," Clair chimed in.

Oh, my. Matthew needed to have a talk with Sylvie. The twins were too young to be watching adult detective shows. They were also too young to be listening to me theorizing with my grandfather about murder. I would have to monitor my own behavior, as well. *Monkey see, monkey do.*

The door to the kitchen swept open. Grandmère glided through carrying a tray filled with glasses of water, paper napkins, plates, three little bowls filled with dipping sauces, and a colorful serving dish mounded with fried circles of goodness. The zesty aroma made my mouth water.

"Girls, wash your hands," Grandmère said. As the twins skipped from the room, she set the tray on the dining table. Using tongs, she transferred some zucchini circles to a plate. "So, *chérie*." She handed the plate to me. "Did you and your grandfather solve the problems of the world?"

Making sure the girls weren't within earshot, I filled her in on Ipo, the pu'ili sticks, the missing goat cheese, and the angry telephone call between Kaitlyn and the mysterious caller.

Grandmère pulled a chair away from the table and sat down. "What if someone wanted to frame Arlo?"

"Like who, and why?" I dipped a zucchini circle into the peach jam sauce, plunked it into my mouth, and licked my fingertips. Heaven.

"Georgia Plachette. If she is Kaitlyn's daughter, as you say, she had much wealth to gain." She looked at both my grandfather and me, but Pépère kept mute.

"How would she have known about Ipo's luau instruments?" I asked.

"Word gets around." Grandmère handed me a napkin.

"She has an alibi on the night of Kaitlyn's death," I said. "She was playing darts at the pub."

"Did you question everyone at the pub to corroborate? No, I think not. And are you sure she did not take a short break, short enough to run a few blocks and have it out with her mother?" Grandmère held up a finger. "I believe—"

The doorbell jangled its merry dingety-ding.

Grandmère looked at Pépère. "*Mon ami*, are we expecting anyone?"

"Maybe Urso picked up my message and decided to seize my phone and declare me a public nuisance." I chuckled.

"What are you talking about?" Grandmère said.

"*De rien.* It's nothing." Prepared for a head-to-head with our illustrious chief of police, I strode to the door and opened it. I was more than surprised to find Chip standing there.

"Hey, babe." A porch light cast a hazy glow over him. A dusky orange and gray sky served as his backdrop. He whipped his wool cap from his head and clutched it in front of him. That was when I spotted the flowers; he was carrying a fistful of daisies.

As swift as lightning, my flight instinct kicked in. I wanted to run. Not hear. Not see. Chip had brought flowers. Was he wooing me? And why, for heaven's sake, did he look so disarmingly handsome in his zippered suede jacket, black turtleneck, and jeans? I had to remind myself that we weren't good together. At the end of our relationship, we were snarling like cats and dogs. Not to mention, I was in love with Jordan.

"I stopped by Fromagerie Bessette," Chip said, apparently not picking up on my distress. "Rebecca told me you'd be here. Can we talk?"

"I've got to leave for the faire."

"I'll escort you."

"No."

"It'll only take a minute."

"Chip, look, I can't." No flowers. No date. No future. I wanted him to stop pursuing me.

"Charlotte, please, I—" Chip's eyes widened. He was looking past me, over my shoulder.

I could feel my grandfather move in behind me, breathing through his nose like an enraged bull. I could only imagine his perturbed glare. He had never liked Chip. He

said Chip's standards in the kitchen were too low. I deserved someone who took more care, someone who didn't cut corners. When I had first met Jordan at a cooking class at La Bella Ristorante, I had noticed how precise he was at slicing vegetables. Not prissy. Exact. Where in the heck was he? Why hadn't he returned my call? I needed to grill him about my Internet search.

"Barre, toi," Pépère said, then repeated in English, "get lost." He nudged me to one side and took a confident step forward.

Chip steeled his jaw. Through clenched teeth, he said, "I just want a minute of your time, Charlotte. Don't go all weak on me and hide behind your grandfather."

There it was. A snipe. Other snipes—years old— peppered my mind. He had said I wasn't smart. He had called me untalented and provincial. He was wrong, wrong, wrong, of course, but old tapes were hard to erase.

"Barre, toi, or I'll boot you down those steps." My grandfather might have been in his seventies, but he was strong from lifting wheels of cheese all his life. And I was sure he thought he had righteousness on his side.

Chip didn't budge. "It's about the hockey game."

"She does not give a whit about going to a hockey game with you. *Barre, toi.* One, two, three . . ."

"I don't want to ask her to a hockey game," Chip said, then added something about a hat trick.

"What?" I said.

"Never mind." He flopped his cap onto his head and then blustered down the path, scuffing his heel every third or fourth step.

"Temper, temper," Pépère said as he closed the door and bolted it.

"Pépère, he came to tell me something."

"Bah! He tricks. He fools." He turned to me and clutched my arms. *"Chérie,* he is not worth your heartache. You are better off with Jordan. He is a man who knows the world. A man who knows what is right and what is wrong."

"Pépère—"

"No! Let me finish." He released me but held my gaze. "Jordan is a man who knows how to love and love fully. I have seen much of life. I know these things. This man, this Chip—what kind of a name is that for a man? He is not for you. He is selfish and vain, but I am sorry if—"

I put my fingers to his lips. "Shhh. I know, Pépère. You can relax. You are watching out for me, and I appreciate it." I kissed his cheek and shooed him to my grandmother.

As I watched them embrace, a frizzle of uneasiness ran through me. Was Jordan the man for me? Would he still be, once I learned his full story?

CHAPTER

Clair and Amy insisted on holding my hands and skipping to Winter Wonderland. My grandparents scuttled behind us, Pépère still muttering about Chip's sudden appearance and Grandmère telling him to hush. I wished she could tell my mind to hush, as well. Seeing my ex-fiancé with flowers in his hand had thrown me off-kilter. What I wouldn't give for a week of simple, carefree thoughts and a heart-to-heart chat with Jordan.

I tugged on the girls to pick up their pace. We had decided to walk as a family—they to their rehearsal and me to the opening of Le Petit Fromagerie.

Dusk was rapidly settling into darkness, but as we drew near to the faire, the sky grew brighter. A glow emanated from the twinkling lights outlining the white tents and the clock tower.

"Isn't it magnificent?" Clair said.

I didn't respond. I couldn't catch my breath enough to speak. When, oh, when could I fit more aerobic exercise into my daily routine?

"Look at the crowd." Amy gaped. "Yipes."

People meandered between the tents like a river. Whenever someone stopped to peer inside a tent, the people-river dynamic shifted.

I grumbled, unable to scoot up the right side of the crowd with the twins in tow.

"Relax, *chérie*," Pépère said. "Remember you have others who work with you. They will see to the opening."

"Follow me. I will make a path." Grandmère, who had added a star-studded patriotic sweater to her eclectic Do-Gooder ensemble, broke free of my grandfather and forged ahead. "Move everyone. The mayor is coming through. Move, please. *Merci.*" Give the woman a flag, and she could lead a parade—any parade.

Once we pushed ahead of the throng, Amy broke free of my hold and started to twirl. "I love the faire." She spread her arms wide. The ends of her striped scarf eddied out of control.

"Whoa, twinkle toes." I reined her in so she wouldn't accost some unsuspecting soul.

"Aren't the smells yummy?" she said. "Cloves and sugar and pine."

"Where's Le Petit Fromagerie?" Clair asked.

"Not far from your recital stage," I said.

"Hello-o-o!" Meredith, wearing a canary yellow parka over a heather sweater and chic gray slacks, swooped between the girls. They latched onto her with glee.

"Glad you found us," I said. She had offered to be the twins' guardian for the evening. Their mother was seeing to business at her Under Wraps tent, and my grandparents had a brief faire-planning meeting to attend.

"Your parka is pretty," Amy said.

"Thank you." Meredith fingered the stand-up collar. "I thought the color would make it easy for you girls to spot me, should we get separated." She assessed me. "Charlotte, you look stressed. What's wrong?"

"I'm running behind." I didn't have time to tell her about Chip's surprise visit.

Clair did a hop-skip. "Look, there's a sign pointing to Le Petit Fromagerie. See it, Amy?"

Grandmère had come up with the brilliant idea of adding arrow directionals at the faire. They looked like old European signs, each stacked atop the other. *The Igloo Ice Cream Parlor, ten paces. Sew Inspired Quilts, twenty paces.* Nothing was farther than a hundred paces, though there were rows and rows of tents, and if someone wasn't careful, he or she could get lost. I had gotten turned around a couple of times earlier in the week when bringing items to the tent.

"Oh, look! There's Thomas and Tisha!" Amy released Meredith's hand and tore ahead.

Clair scurried after her.

The two quickly blended into a group of adults and children who were admiring the nearly finished knight on a horse ice sculpture. If only I had thought to dress them in yellow jackets as well, I mused.

Apart from the crowd, I caught sight of the sculpture's artist, Tyanne's burly husband, Theo. He was standing beside a sizzling-hot young woman who was toying with the tails of her ruby red scarf. Was she the lover Theo was leaving Tyanne for? With no regard for privacy, Theo pulled the Lolita-esque woman to him and kissed her intimately.

"Remember when we were that age?" Meredith slipped her arm through mine. "We had so many secrets."

"I never had a lover."

"What are you talking about?"

I glanced at her and saw she wasn't looking anywhere near Theo and his girlfriend. With dreamy eyes, Meredith was watching the twins, who stood among the crowd, whispering to each other.

I smiled. "Yes, we had secrets. And we were always getting into trouble. At your insistence."

She poked me. "You mean *your* insistence, don't you? 'Let's climb this tree, explore that barn, sneak into Mrs. Jones's garden and steal some carrots.'"

I pulled on my earlobe. "Funny, I remember it the other way around."

"Do you?" Meredith winked at me. "Hmm, I do love carrots."

"You mean you enjoy bossing me around."

"That, too. Catch you later." She bussed my cheek and hurried to join the girls.

As I headed to work, I couldn't help thinking about secrets and lovers, and wondering about Kaitlyn Clydesdale again. Would her paramour come forward now that Kaitlyn was dead, or was he content to remain anonymous? Was he remaining anonymous for a reason? Was the man married? What if Kaitlyn had wanted to proclaim her love to the world, but her lover had lashed out to keep her silent?

* * *

When I reached Le Petit Fromagerie, the crowd was curving out the door. Tyanne had beaten me to the opening, thanks to Chip's untimely visit. She manned the cheese counter, her cheeks flushed the same pink as her sweater, her blonde hair scooped into a sparkly pink clip. Using a cheese slicer, she slivered off tastings of cheese to one customer at a time. Wine and cheese tasting selection lists and a dozen gold pencils perched on the counter alongside the stack of souvenir plates, which had already dwindled by half.

"Sorry I'm late," I said as I joined her. "What a slew of people."

"You're telling me. Over thirty in our first fifteen minutes, sugar."

"A good showing."

"Matthew went outside to manage the line. Did you see him?"

I hadn't.

"I'm sure he'll be back in a flash." Tyanne greeted our next customer by name and handed him a slice. "You're going to adore this Zamorano. Don't you just love the texture?"

As the man mumbled his agreement, a woman bellowed, "Out of my way." Sylvie, wearing a zebra print fleece co-

coon that looked like an ugly sleeping bag, hopped into the store, banging into customers with abandon as she headed to the front of the line. *"Ciao*, Charlotte."

I struggled not to laugh. How did she expect to get around without feet? "What are you wearing?"

"A Snugglee-Bugg." She jumped in a circle. "Isn't it darling? Perfect for cool weather."

"To be worn inside on a couch."

"Tosh! I couldn't very well invite everyone to my home to see it modeled, could I?" She plucked a souvenir plate from the pile and waved it. "Thought I'd slip in and grab mine before they're all gone. Stop by my tent. You might win a garter."

Just what I needed.

As she bounded toward the exit, I said, "Sylvie, wait." I cut around the cheese counter and nudged her to a corner of the tent. "You're always good for gossip."

"I am, indeed." She grinned like the Cheshire cat.

How it pained me to flatter her, but I continued. "Do you know who Kaitlyn Clydesdale was having an affair with?"

Her mouth dropped open. Her fleece paw flew to her chest. Had I stumped her?

"Georgia Plachette said Kaitlyn was in a relationship," I explained.

"Ooh, that vixen is a blabbermouth!"

Black kettles calling each other names did a kick line in my mind. I said, "Georgia didn't know the lover's identity. Just that it was so."

"I'll do some digging and come up with answers." Sylvie leaped once, then swiveled back. "By the way, Charlotte, that V-neck thing you're wearing is not flattering."

That *thing* was an ecru cashmere sweater that had cost me a pretty penny and looked perfect beneath my red blazer.

"You don't have the bosoms for it," she added. "In the future, try a Peter Pan collar. Ta-ta!"

As she bounced toward the exit, bumping into people on her way, I prayed she would do a face-plant. She didn't. Life wasn't always fair.

When I returned to my position behind the cheese counter, Tyanne sidled up to me. "Sugar, I forgot to tell you, the tasting at the shop was a hit. All because of me, don't you think?" She blew on her fingernails and polished them on her sweater, then chuckled. "L-O-L. Just kidding, but Matthew did say it was a financial windfall. Why hasn't he returned?"

"He's probably buying a hot chocolate. He's like a little kid when it comes to cocoa." The Country Kitchen made the most luscious chocolaty goodness and topped it with a dollop of whipped cream that was infused with sugar crystals.

"Say, speaking of kids, did you see mine outside?"

"I did. They're watching the ice sculpting."

"You mean watching their snake of a father," Tyanne said quietly so customers wouldn't hear. "You saw *her*, didn't you? Miss Ohio-in-her-dreams."

"Gee, hmmm, I can't recall," I said, sounding like a reluctant witness.

Tyanne chuffed. "It's okay to admit it. I'm so over him." She sliced another tasting of cheese and offered it to our next customer. "Here you go, enjoy. By the way, Charlotte, so far, the Zamorano is the favorite. The Vacherin Fribourg comes in a close second. And the Mount Eden chardonnay seems to be the most popular wine, despite the cold weather." She lowered her voice. "Though I tasted the zinfandel and loved it. That's okay, isn't it? It was only a sip. I don't think I've had a whole glass of wine in over a year. We were trying to get pregnant again." She bit her lip. "Maybe that's what sent my Theo searching. A woman wanting to procreate on a time schedule is so not-sexy."

"Tyanne, I'm sure—"

"Don't, sugar." She flicked the air with her hand. "Don't try to make me feel better. I'm fine, really. We've decided to divorce."

I observed the crowd of customers. None were listening to us, all of them too busy tasting and marking their lists or browsing the items in the tent.

"Our marriage was over years ago," Tyanne went on. "I

was just too hooked on the idea of marriage to admit it. Now, with a job and being good at something again—and I am; I love cheese!—I'm ready to soar. Thank you, thank you, thank you for believing in me." She embraced me for a brief second, then pushed away with a teensy pat to my arm. "Sorry. No public display of affection. That's what Theo always says."

From what I had observed a moment ago, good old Theo had changed his tune, but far be it from me to zap Tyanne's glow by mentioning that I had seen her husband canoodling with some lusty dame.

"By the way, mum's the word about the d-i-v-o-r-c-e," Tyanne went on. "We haven't told the kids, yet. My sister Lizzie is moving to Providence to help out. You'll like her a ton. She's so funny and warm. My other sisters, Selby and Linda Jo, can't make it, but you'd like them, too. They wish I'd out-and-out kill Theo for cheating and be done with it." She laughed. "Can you imagine? Did you hear of that book: *I'd Kill to be a Widow*? Too funny."

Tyanne turned away and offered a bright smile and a souvenir plate to the next customer, but I couldn't let go of what she had said. Had Kaitlyn's lover's wife attacked Kaitlyn? How did the missing container of goat cheese at Rebecca's cottage play into that scenario?

"Yoo-hoo, excuse me." Rebecca waltzed into the tent, wheeling a cooler on a pull cart. Strands of hair straggled around her face and stuck to her lipstick. "Let me through, please. Yoo-hoo, Charlotte, I have more cheese." She cut through the crowd, removed the cooler from the cart, and set it on the green grass carpet. As she unpacked wedges of cheese and plunked them on the staging table behind us, she said, "Did you have a clue we'd have so many people?"

I sidled to her and whispered, out of earshot of our guests, "Got a question."

"Ipo's fine. Except Urso's starving him. He's withering away to nothing."

"I doubt that." It would take weeks for brawny Ipo to wither away.

"Urso's a pill," Rebecca added.

"Forget him. There's something off between Jacky and him, I think." Maybe Jacky wanted another baby. Perhaps, like Tyanne said, a woman on a time clock wasn't sexy. Urso could be letting his frustration spill over into his work, and that was why he hadn't answered any of my earlier telephone calls. "Back to my question. The goat cheese."

"What goat cheese?"

"The round of Emerald Isles goat cheese you took home for the evening with Ipo. The night Kaitlyn, um, died. I didn't see it among the fixings you'd set on the pass-through counter. Where was it?"

"I don't know. On the platter still wrapped? Maybe in the kitchen? I started putting the platter together, but then I got so flustered because"—Rebecca turned three shades of crimson—"because Ipo wanted to take our . . . um . . . walk. I didn't even open the champagne. He clutched my hand all the way to the park. I remember thinking the moonless night was so dark but romantic. And then everything happened so fast. He kissed me. And I kissed him back and, oh—" She fluttered her fingers in front of her face. "I will not cry. I will not. Why does it matter?"

I explained.

"You mean the cheese is gone, as in someone stole it?" Rebecca sucked in a breath. "I'll bet it was that Arlo. That puts him in my house. Do you think he's the murderer?"

"Not so fast."

"Do you remember that day Miss Clydesdale came into the shop? Arlo was standing by the Camembert and goat cheese display with that customer . . . you know the one." She snapped her fingers. "Remember the dad with all the children in heavy winter coats? Big buttons on the coats. You made sandwiches. Urso came in and bought his usual. Oh, look, there he is."

"The dad?"

"Urso, the pill."

I caught sight of him through one of the tent windows, introducing the new deputy-hopeful to locals. Seeing the

young man made me think again of Chip standing on my grandparents' porch, hat and flowers in hand. I was a wimp to have allowed my grandfather to scare him off. I should have confronted Chip and told him to stop pursuing me. On the other hand, he had claimed he'd come to tell me something. If that were so, why had he brought flowers? Should I have given him the chance to explain?

"Tell Urso about the missing cheese," Rebecca said.

"Now?"

"No time like the present." She prodded me.

Before she had pushed me two steps, a jaunty guy with shaggy hair sauntered into the tent. "Hey, Rebecca! Got a sec?"

"Fiddlesticks." Rebecca uttered a teensy growl. "When did he get back in town?"

"Who is he?" I asked. He looked familiar—charming, with spirited, aware eyes.

"Don't you remember Quigley?" Her tone was as tart as a cheese that had gone bad.

The man zipped through the throng saying, "I'm not cutting in line, folks, promise."

Rebecca met him at the end of the counter and thrust a finger at his chest. "Stop right there! You're mean. And spiteful. And manipulative."

He smirked. "I am not."

"You took advantage of me when my armor was off."

"The phrase is 'when your armor was down.'"

Rebecca sputtered. "Ooh, you make me so mad."

"May I quote you?" he gibed.

When Quigley offered a lopsided grin, it all came back to me. He was the reporter. A year or so ago, Rebecca had fallen for him hard until she found out he was dating other women. Lots of them. With money.

"You're so cute when you get angry." Quigley smoothed the lapel of his plaid blazer. "Beautiful, in fact."

"O-o-oh," Rebecca repeated, longer and shriller. She raised her arm, palm flat. Tension vibrated through her muscles. I could tell she wanted to slap him, but she held

back. I was proud of her for showing restraint. I wasn't sure
what our customers would do if a fracas broke out. "Leave
before I clobber you."

"Gimme a quote." Quigley held up a tape recorder.
"Just one."

"Not on your life."

"Not even to save your boyfriend?"

"He's innocent."

"The police have evidence," Quigley said.

"Ipo doesn't know where those pu'ili sticks disappeared
to. He hasn't seen them in years."

"What pu'ili sticks?"

Rebecca yelped. "You tricked me."

"I did nothing of the sort." He switched off his tape
recorder.

"Racaille," Rebecca said, adopting one of Pépère's favorite words—French for rascal.

"I've been called worse. See ya." Chuckling, Quigley
sauntered from the tent like a cocky duck, tilting to and fro.

Rebecca grumbled. "I wouldn't put it past him to have
framed Ipo."

"To gain what?" I asked. "You?"

"He's a Lothario. That's what your grandmother called
him. He's only interested in a woman if it benefits him.
Good thing I never kissed him."

She harrumphed and set back to work. In the ensuing
calm, I started thinking about Kaitlyn's Lothario. Had he
been after more than sex? Property, perhaps? Or a return of
property acquired by blackmail?

CHAPTER

16

The evening sped by so fast, I felt like I had purchased a
ticket on a bullet train. I had hoped that Jordan would stop
by the Le Petit Fromagerie tent, but he hadn't. I'd also hoped
Urso would seek me out, but he hadn't either, the skunk.

As I strolled home, tighter than an over-wound yo-yo, I
remembered I had set my cell phone to vibrate. I fetched it
from my purse and saw that Jordan had called. He had left
a message around ten thirty. He said he'd been busy helping
Urso's mother with a calamity at Two Plug Nickels Farm.
In a charming put-on twang, he added that he was tuckered
out and hitting the hay. Before signing off, he whispered
that he adored me. Though I cherished hearing his voice,
something about his words fell flat. I didn't want to question him on the telephone; I needed to talk in person. But it
was an inappropriate hour for me to show up on his doorstep. Our discussion would have to wait until morning.

When I arrived home, I spotted a light on in the bedroom
next to mine. The twins must have fallen asleep reading
and forgotten to turn off their bedstand lamp. I tiptoed into

the house through the kitchen, flicked on the swagged chandelier over the kitchen dining table, and spotted Rags and Rocket nestled together in Rocket's dark brown wicker bed. The vision tickled me. A few months ago, I never would have thought the two could resolve their differences, let alone be best pals.

As I crept up the stairs, a few treads creaked beneath my footsteps, which reminded me that I needed to accomplish something on my home improvement to-do list soon. *One to-do item a month* had become a new mantra.

I reached the landing and heard Matthew speaking to the twins.

"No more questions," he said.

"Please, Daddy, one," Clair cried.

Questions about what? Egged on by a voice in my head that sounded curiously like Rebecca's, I stole to the door and pressed my ear to it.

"Yes, sweetheart?" Matthew said, the exasperation in his voice palpable.

"Will we be wearing flowers in our hair?" Clair asked.

Aha. They were talking about the wedding. Had he given them a specific date? Something more concrete than Meredith's nebulous *autumn*?

"Yes, if you want. Flowers, tiaras, you name it," Matthew said. "Now, I know you're keyed up from rehearsal, but it's time for sleep."

"Daddy, wait," Amy said. I heard a thump and then bare feet padding across the area rug. "Mum said . . ." She went silent.

"It's okay," Matthew said. "You can tell me what she said. I can only imagine."

Me, too.

"Mum said you and Miss Meredith don't have a future together, and we shouldn't count on a wedding. Please, Daddy, please," Amy went on, her voice filled with passion. "Please have a future."

Her words stung the pit of my soul. Tears sprang forth like a fountain. Not for Amy. Not for Clair, either. Matthew

and Meredith were going to be together for life. Sylvie's prediction would not come true. But I ached because of my own fears. Did I have a future with Jordan? Would we be able to resolve our differences? Without knowing the truth about him, I couldn't even contemplate it.

* * *

When I woke the next morning, my pillow was still damp from my tears. I hustled into my cheery bathroom—one of my recent to-do projects that had turned out right. To the shower and the backsplash behind the sink, I had added a strip of white tiles, which had been hand-painted with sprigs of herbs. White lace curtains trimmed with pale green ribbon finished off the face-lift. Baby steps, Pépère said, were key to finishing home-makeover projects. If I made reasonable goals, I might finish the list, which numbered in the hundreds, in three years.

"Now to tackle you, Charlotte," I whispered while assessing the damage that crying through the night had done to my face.

First, I applied warm tea bags to my swollen eyes. Next, I massaged in dollops of face cream and added a dab of blush to my cheeks. I finished off my personal makeover with a jewel-necked turquoise sweater, tan trousers, a silk matka tweed jacket that tied it all together, and my most comfortable loafers. The ensemble boosted my overall mood. After downing a sinful breakfast of sourdough toast tiered with raspberry jam, slivers of Bosc pears, and warm Brie, I took a brisk walk with Rocket and Rags, and by seven a.m., I felt almost normal. Almost.

Before heading to work, I left yet another message for Urso.

* * *

A couple of hours later, I was glad I had taken the effort to put myself together. I was standing in The Cheese Shop's kitchen, setting baked apple slices on a set of pepperoni quiches, when Jordan entered through the rear door.

No warning, no call. Granted, I probably had flour dust all over my face, but at least the rest of me looked decent enough.

"Morning," he said, looking like a hero out of a romance novel—distressed leather jacket, white henley shirt tucked into jeans, tousled dark hair, smoldering eyes, and a denim knapsack slung over one shoulder. Something inside me went *snap*, in a good way. "Hungry?" He tapped the knapsack. "Thought we could catch a bite."

"You bet." I would never turn down a meal with him. I brushed off whatever flour might be clinging to my face and tucked my hair behind my ears, a tingling sensation of anticipation coursing through me.

Tyanne, who had arrived early to work and had turned out to be quite deft with pie shells, whispered, "You look great, sugar. Go on." She shooed me to leave.

Jordan headed toward the rear exit, and I balked. "Where are you going?" I said. "It's colder than a polar bear's toenails outside."

"I thought we'd have our meal in the hothouse." He grinned. "Need a jacket?"

The moment I had arrived at the shop, I had removed my tweed jacket; it hung on the coat rack. But I shook my head. The co-op vegetable garden behind the shop was dormant and uninviting, but the town's communal hothouse was a toasty seventy-two degrees. Tomatoes and herbs thrived in the steady warmth.

We slipped out the door and into the cold.

As we entered the hut, the scent of basil tickled my nose. But all my senses heightened when Jordan set the knapsack on a potting table, drew me into his arms, and kissed me like a romantic hero should—deeply and intimately. Heaven. Minutes passed before we came up for air.

When we did, he eyed his satchel. "I whipped up some fortification." From the knapsack, he withdrew two brown restaurant to-go-style boxes. He popped the lid off one and beckoned the aromas to waft into the air.

I drew in the luscious aroma of brown sugar pancakes

topped with melted Gouda and figs, and my stomach did a happy dance.

"I've brought warm syrup, too," Jordan said.

"Yum."

Jordan fetched a forest green fleece blanket, napkins, and utensils from his knapsack, and arranged our picnic on the floor. He had even thought to bring a thermos of French Roast coffee. We nestled onto the blanket and dug into our breakfast, the flavors bursting in my mouth. When I finished my last bite, the need to discuss my Internet search findings reared its ugly head. I had to have answers. I urged myself to speak but words wouldn't come. My throat felt clogged with emotional cotton.

"I got your phone call," Jordan said, breaking the poignant silence. "You sounded worried. Is it about Chip? I heard he came to your grandparents' house. He and your grandfather fought."

"Where did you learn that?"

"Your grandmother told Urso's mother, who told me."

"Ahhh." My grandmother might not like idle gossip, but she could dish it. "Words. It was nothing."

"That guy isn't right, Charlotte. He puts me on edge."

"You barely know him."

"And you? How well do you know him?"

"I was engaged to him."

"But he's been gone for how long? People change."

"He's—"

Jordan tapped my leg to quiet me. "He came here with Kaitlyn Clydesdale and now she's dead. He could be the killer, Charlotte."

"Oh, please. Chip, a killer? He's—"

"—hot for you, and hotheaded, to boot. He took on your grandfather. Sweetheart, even you know that's just plain stupid." Jordan traced a line up my sleeve to the tip of my chin. Shivers ran through me. He leaned forward and kissed me gently. "You're like a magnet right now. Even if Chip's not the guy to fear, how about the looter that came into your tent the other night?"

"He didn't want to hurt me, either."

Jordan frowned. "Don't be naïve; you're a perfect target."

"What does that mean?"

"You're pretty and a wee bit cocky. Get up." Jordan slid the coffee and our breakfasts to a spot beneath a stand of hothouse tomatoes, hopped to his feet, and stretched out his arms. "Show me what you've got."

"What do you mean?"

"Show me your defensive moves. You've been taking classes with Meredith."

"Not for a while." Our weekly self-defense classes ended in November.

"You shouldn't get rusty." He beckoned with both hands. "C'mon. Up!"

Eager to show how scrappy I was, I scrambled to a stand, and without warning, rushed him. He grabbed me by the arms, whisked me like a broom, and landed me on the green fleece blanket. Gently. But I was down.

"Sheesh." I fingered the hair at the nape of my neck, wishing I could wipe the self-satisfied grin off his face. "Guess I wasn't ready."

He offered a hand and pulled me up. "Ready now?"

"Absolutely." I would show him. "Reach for my shoulder."

He did. As I had been taught, I blocked him with my forearm. He groped for my other shoulder. I mirrored the block. While I gloated over my quick reflexes, he took hold of the first shoulder, whipped me around, and pinned my wrist up between my shoulder blades.

"Uncle!" I said.

He spun me around and stared at me gravely. "As I thought. Brash with no oomph."

I scowled. Good thing Meredith hadn't seen the display. She would have teased me for weeks.

"I'm going to teach you a few more moves," Jordan said.

A flutter of desire zipped through me. How I wished we would continue the lesson in my Victorian home. In my bedroom. Once he answered my questions.

"The natural effect of real aggression," he went on, cooling my flames, "causes what some call an adrenaline dump. That means high volumes of adrenaline shoot through the attacker. You've got to be able to bring the guy down. Got me?"

I nodded.

"Let's say the jerk tries to strangle you. Let me show you what you do." He asked my permission, then gripped my neck.

Even though his touch was tender, my stomach constricted. It sickened me to think how I might react in a real situation. Thick-voiced, I said, "I poke your eyes."

"Try."

I reached over his arm and thrust upward with two fingers, but he jerked his head back and grabbed my wrist.

"Not good enough." He didn't let go. "What else can you jab?"

"I don't know."

"Think."

"I can't." My heart pounded double-time. "Let me go."

He did. "C'mon, what's open? What's within reach?"

"The hollow of your neck."

"Exactly. Right below the Adam's apple. Do it now. Be precise."

Slowly, I set my fingers in the hollow of his neck.

"That's it. Except, in real life, you go for it with all your might. Shock your attacker. He'll release his hands. And then what do you do?"

"Run."

"Good. Now for lesson two."

A rush of my own adrenaline zinged through me. Enough of the kissing and self-defense lessons. I pushed him away and blurted, "Are these spy moves?"

He stiffened. "What are you talking about?"

"You're a spy." There. It was out. No more pussyfooting around.

His mouth quirked up, creating a huge dimple down his cheek. "What kind of spy?"

"Espionage."

"Oh, right. Hyah-hyah." He chopped the air. "Shaken not stirred and all that rot." He laughed. "Where'd you get that crazy idea?"

"You're so private."

"Cheese farmers are allowed to be private."

I swallowed hard. *Ask him.* "You said Jeremy Kenneth Montgomery is the name of the man who taught you to make cheese."

"That's right."

"J. Kenneth Montgomery is the name of a spy in a novel."

Jordan frowned. "I'm not following."

"Jeremy Kenneth Montgomery doesn't exist. He's not on the Internet. I think you had me look up this Montgomery guy because you knew I'd come upon this character. You wanted me to catch on."

"Catch on to what?"

"That you're a spy. That's why you're so cryptic. That's why you moved to Providence. To hide out between missions."

Jordan burst into laughter.

I whacked his arm with my palm. "Stop it and answer my question."

He sobered and folded my hands into his. "Contrary to popular belief, not everyone lives on the Internet, Charlotte. I'm private; you said so yourself. Trust me. I am not a spy."

"Were you ever a spy?"

"I was in the army for a stint."

"Then why are you living under an alias? Are you in the Witness Security Program?" I'd had the same notion when I first met Jordan. He had come out of nowhere.

He released my hands and let his arms fall to his sides. Casual, and yet he looked primed. "You can't tell anyone what I'm about to reveal."

"If I do, you'll have to kill me?"

"No." He leveled me with a somber look. "Someone might kill *me.*"

My heart plunged like a cannonball. "I won't tell a soul. Not Matthew or my grandparents or Rebecca."

"Or Urso." He waited for my nod. "Yes, I'm in the Witness Security Program."

I gulped. I had read books about people in WITSEC. Not all of them had been upstanding citizens, but most were trying to reform their lives. Was that what Jordan was doing? I searched his eyes for the answer but found none.

"Do you have a handler?"

"A marshal to whom I report? Yes."

"Is Jacky part of this?"

"In a roundabout way."

Was that what had been bothering Urso? Jacky could be as tight-lipped as Jordan.

I said, "Can you at least tell me why you had to disappear?"

Jordan licked his lips. "I owned a restaurant in upstate New York. I saw something I shouldn't have."

"A murder."

A quick nod. "The government moved me, gave me a cover. Because I had learned to make cheese—truly, I did learn to make cheese—the government decided that was as good a cover as any. I was told I could never have contact with my sister again. I agreed. She was happily married at the time, or so I thought. When her husband hurt her—he beat her and their story made it into the newspapers and onto the Internet—I was worried sick."

"Was he your business partner?"

"No, nothing like that. These were two totally separate incidents. He's a defense attorney with some very bad clients." Jordan squeezed my hands. "I don't want to tell you anything else, okay? The less you know, the better."

I nodded.

"Jacky had no children, no ties to her community. Our parents were dead. I asked that she be able to join me in the program. WITSEC agreed." He kissed my forehead and held me close. "I'm sorry I didn't tell you until now. I couldn't be sure. Of anyone. The trial comes up in a year."

"So you ran a restaurant," I whispered. "That explains why you're so good with a carving knife."

"It also explains why I have such a healthy appetite. And I'm not talking about food." He pulled me to him and kissed me firmly.

When we broke apart, I said, "One last question."

"Anything."

"Have you ever killed anyone?"

The silence was so thick I could have used one of those carving knives to cut it.

Finally Jordan said, "In self-defense." His face turned darkly still. "Does that end it for us?"

CHAPTER

I stood, riveted in the middle of the hothouse, an imaginary vise trying to squeeze the breath out of my chest, but I fought it. After my recent altercation at the old Ziegler Winery, I understood having to make the decision to kill or be killed. I couldn't fault Jordan for his actions. Not in the least.

"No," I said finally. "It doesn't end it for us. But I want to know everything."

He enfolded me in his arms and whispered, "Can I tell you over a late dinner?"

"Not tonight. I've got the faire and the twins' recital."

"Then tomorrow when the faire closes."

"My grandmother's having her Founder's Day celebration. I invited you, right?"

He nodded. "Monday night then, and you'd better say yes. I'm not waiting a week for this conversation, and I can't have it now. I've got to swing by the faire, and then I've got meetings at the farm."

I answered yes, and we kissed again.

"Trust me, Charlotte," he said before parting.

I said I would.

By the time I returned to The Cheese Shop, a horde of teenagers had invaded the place. They chatted and gossiped while waiting to order sandwiches. On Saturdays, to draw a younger crowd, I made sure to offer spicier, less fussy sandwiches like pepperoni and Swiss or salami and a sharp Cheddar. No arugula mushrooms or gooey things, as the twins liked to call them, though they enjoyed all of those *gooey things*.

"Hi, Miss Bessette," a couple of girls yelled.

I waved, then tossed the remains of our mid-morning picnic into the trash and ambled to the counter to help Tyanne.

"Charlotte, sugar, guess what?" Tyanne said as she wrapped up a sandwich for one of the teens. "Bozz says I have a facility for numbers and the Internet."

"Is he here?" I had to admit I had missed seeing my Internet guru's cute mug.

"He's in the office updating our web page. He came in early to teach me how to do the newsletter and the books. Isn't it great? When he starts college, I can be your maven!"

I loved her enthusiasm.

"Hey, Miss B." Bozz sauntered from the office, hands jammed into his droopy jeans, a sheepish grin on his face. He jerked a thumb over his shoulder. "What's that search you've got going? Who's Jeremy Montgomery?"

A quiver of worry shimmied up my back. Had I left the computer on all night? Bozz was smarter than a whip. Could he figure out what I had been doing? Would he rat out Jordan? I needed to be more careful what I left open for view in the office.

"It's nothing," I lied.

"Yeah, okay." He scratched his head.

I changed the subject. "Nice of you to show up once in a while, by the way."

"It's hard to make time on school days."

I patted his shoulder. "I know."

"Hey, did I tell you? Philby got into Providence Liberal Arts College, too." Philby was his brainy girlfriend. "We're hoping to study marketing and get our MBAs so we can manage the family business someday." The Bozzuto family owned the Bozzuto Winery, which for generations had made delicious white wines and had recently branched out by adding natural sodas to their line.

"Big plans."

"Yeah, and once I'm wealthy, I might even run for mayor. Watch out, Grandmère."

Bozz was one of those kids who wanted to stay in Providence forever. Small towns needed young people like him.

Tyanne said, "Sugar, I have to get a move on."

She was due at Le Petit Fromagerie for the first shift. Rebecca would join her at noon. Matthew and I would helm what I expected to be the busier traffic from late afternoon until dusk. Then we would leave to attend the recital, and Bozz and Philby would man the store until close.

"Can you handle the crowd here?" Tyanne asked.

"Not a problem, but where's Rebecca?" I spotted Matthew at the bar in the annex, writing on a chalkboard.

"Got me."

"I'll take over for Mrs. T." Bozz slung on an apron and addressed the teens by name as they ordered sandwiches.

Tyanne waved goodbye then trotted off. I followed her to the front door and peered out. It wasn't like Rebecca not to call in if she was running late. And she was awfully late. Though I didn't see any sign of her, I urged myself not to worry. Maybe she had made a detour on the way over and gone to the precinct to tell Urso about the missing goat cheese. Maybe she thought that tidbit would ensure Ipo's quick release.

I started to turn around when I spied Georgia Plachette slinking between a delivery truck and an SUV. She halted and crouched down. Dressed like she was on a reconnaissance mission, she trained a pair of binoculars on the Country Kitchen across the street. I cupped my hands around my eyes to block the morning glare and glimpsed Barton

Burrell and his wife, Emma, sitting with Octavia at one of the booths by the window. Was Georgia sleuthing like me? Did she think Barton was guilty of murder? Did she believe he had killed her mother to thwart the sale of his property? Perhaps she had something more nefarious in mind.

Try as I might, I couldn't shake my reaction to her at the Clydesdale Enterprises office yesterday. She was hiding something. Not simply the fact that Kaitlyn was her mother. Something else. She said her alibi for the night of her mother's death was flawless. What if, like my grandmother intimated, Georgia had figured out some way to fool the people at the pub into thinking she was there?

A flash of red caught my attention. Rebecca, wearing a fire-engine red raincoat, stormed toward The Cheese Shop, swatting her palm with a rolled-up newspaper. She wasn't trying to nail a bug. She barged into the shop.

"What's wrong?" I said.

"Look!" She flailed the newspaper.

I snatched it from her and unfurled it. On the front page, the reporter, Quigley, had posted a picture of Rebecca angrily pointing a finger.

"I was at the precinct, waiting to talk to Chief Urso, when I saw that." Rebecca flicked the newspaper with a fingertip. "Quigley must have been wearing some sneaky camera device in his lapel. How dare he!" She stabbed the headline: *Luau Sticks Implicate Hawaiian.* "I didn't say that."

I scanned the article. "He doesn't say Ipo is guilty."

"He might as well have. Ooh, I'm so mad at Chief Urso, I could spit."

My mouth fell open. "At Urso?"

"He's not doing his job. He's being lazy."

"Rebecca, calm down. Urso is always fair." Well, almost always. But now was not the time to fan the flames.

"Bah!" Rebecca said, sounding like my grandfather as she stomped to the rear of the store and shrugged out of her raincoat. If she had been a cartoon character, steam would have billowed from her ears.

Minutes later, as the teens filed out, our local animal rescuer scuttled in.

"Morning, Charlotte, Rebecca, Bozz." In her hooded coffee brown winter coat, I was struck by how much Tallulah Barker reminded me of an Ewok from *Star Wars*. Not only was she cuddly and squat, but she spoke in a high-pitched, garbled voice. I was surprised to see her without any dogs or cats in tow. She was always trying to place one in a good home.

She pitched off her hood and shook out her frizzy curls.

"New hairstyle, Tallulah?" I asked. How many times had she tried a new hairdo over her sixty-plus years? I had seen at least a dozen.

She peered from beneath her longish bangs. "What do you think?" It came out more like *whatdoyouthink?*

"It suits you."

"I think it makes me look like a Cocker Spaniel." She pulled her hair into two floppy ears.

I bit back a smile. Yes, from a certain angle, she also resembled a Spaniel, which was a much more apt and flattering description than an Ewok.

"That's what I get for going to a cut-rate barber instead of a stylist," she said. "Silly me, trying to save a dime. I'll take the usual plus an eighth of a pound of that Salame Toscano. I love the peppery flavor." She scanned the shop. "Wow, is it ever quiet in here. There are swarms of people milling about the faire." Typically brief at conversation— Tallulah reserved most of her chatter for her animals—she slipped one of the shop's wicker baskets over her arm and headed toward the jars of honey and preserves.

I edged behind the cheese counter and said, "Thanks, Bozz. Take a break. I'll need you when Rebecca leaves."

"Cool." He shuffled toward the office.

I glanced at Rebecca, who was angrily cutting four slices of Chabichou—Tallulah's regular order. Chabichou—the pasteurized version—was a dense, slender cylinder of sweet mild cheese. So why was Rebecca sawing it? I considered

removing the knife from my lovable assistant's hand but decided to let her work through her rage. Neither Quigley nor Urso were within range. The cheese would survive.

The front door chimes jangled. Delilah hurried in. "Alert. I need some Tom Cruise cheese, fast." She meant Tomme Crayeuse, one of my favorite cheeses with citrus overtones. It was a semisoft cheese with a chalky center. "Got some? I need at least two pounds. We're trying out a new breakfast sandwich, and it's a major hit."

"Good morning to you, too," I said.

"Oh, sorry. Good morning. Beautiful day. Hurry."

"What else is in the sandwich?" I fetched a wheel of the cheese—*tomme* means wheel—set it on the counter, and prepared the order.

"Scrambled eggs and green onions, two slices of TC, three grinds of the peppermill, and a dash of Tabasco. Simple yet zesty." Delilah plucked at the red ruffled skirt of her waitress costume. "I took a sample to Urso, to see if I could get the inside scoop on the case. He was with that new deputy. A cutie, if you ask me. Dangerous, but in a good way."

"Uh-oh. Luigi, watch out," I teased.

Delilah fluttered her fingers, dismissing me. "Luigi doesn't have a thing to worry about. The new kid's way too young for me."

And Luigi was on the near side of old. I kept mum.

"By the way, did you know that those luau thingies are missing?" Delilah continued.

"The pu'ili sticks," Rebecca cried. "Yes!"

"I asked Urso if he'd thought to look at Arlo's house for them. Urso said he had, but they weren't there."

"He'd better check out Barton Burrell's house," Rebecca said, then eyed me. "I know, I know. I sound like a broken record, but Barton's got motive. You said so yourself."

I glanced through the front window. Georgia had disappeared and Barton and his wife weren't in the diner. Had Georgia decided to tail Barton? If she believed he had hurt her mother, might she do something rash?

"Can you hurry up, Charlotte?" Delilah tapped her foot.

I threw her an acid look. I was slicing and wrapping as fast as I could, and she knew it.

Tallulah approached the register, her basket filled with black sesame crackers and an assortment of jams.

"Yum. It looks like you're having a party, Mrs. Barker," Rebecca said.

"I like to snack. Oh, I almost forgot." She reached into her oversized purse and pulled out two small brown paper bags. "I brought treats for the sweets." Tallulah spoiled Rags and Rocket with homemade kibble.

Rebecca took the bags and set them on a shelf beneath the register, then started ringing up Tallulah's items. I rounded the counter with Delilah's order.

Delilah grabbed the packaged cheese out of my hand and said, "Don't need a tote, thanks. Put it on the diner's tab." And she dashed out.

"That girl never slows down." Tallulah sidled to the tasting counter and plucked a piece of straw yellow Piave Vecchio from the daily platter. She slipped it into her mouth and purred like one of her cats. "Mmmm. It tastes like Parmesan."

"And Asiago," I said. "It's made in Northern Italy."

"I love it. By the way, Rebecca, if your Ipo needs another person to corroborate his alibi, I can step up."

Rebecca's eyes widened with hope. "You can?"

"How?" I said.

"The two of them weren't, you know, hush-hush." Tallulah winked, then chortled, the sound reminding me of a tiger chuffing.

Rebecca turned hot pink. "You heard us, too?"

"You betcha." Tallulah lived next door to Cherry Orchard Park.

"How did you know it was us?"

"Your laughter is very distinctive, my dear. Like crystal chimes. And I almost forgot." Tallulah tapped the side of her head. "Should I tell Chief Urso that I saw a person run past the park that night?"

"You saw someone?" Rebecca nearly shouted.

"Man or woman?" I asked.

"Not sure. It was too dark. It was a rather tallish shape, running at a clip. Whoever it was made a heck of a noise."

With Tallulah being so short, *tallish* would describe almost anyone other than my grandmother.

Using her hands, she outlined the runner, then erased it in the air. "No, that's not right. I can't draw worth a lick."

I wondered if it could have been Georgia Plachette wearing those platform shoes she favored.

"What time was it?" Rebecca said.

"Half past the hour. I was taking four of the pups out for their duty call. Whoever it was held something like a bat."

"Was it a pu'ili stick?" Rebecca asked, breathless.

Tallulah raised a shoulder and let it drop. "How would I know? It was dark, honey. Didn't I say that already?"

"It doesn't matter." Rebecca grabbed my hands and guided me in a ring-around-the-rosy dance. "He's innocent. Ipo's innocent. I told you, I told you," she sang.

I broke free and gazed at Tallulah. "Why haven't you mentioned this to Urso?"

"I didn't want to intrude."

"Coming forward with information is never intruding."

"Point taken." She paid for her purchases. "I'll go to the precinct now."

As she shuffled out with one of our gold totes swinging on her forearm, Amy and Clair sprinted in. With all the people coming and going, it felt like a revolving door had been installed in the shop.

"Aren't we pretty?" Amy spun in a circle. Her red choir robe fluted out like a toreador's cape.

Clair copied her. "Don't we look like professional singers?" Her eyes glittered with pride.

"Very. Where's Meredith?" The girls had gone on a morning shopping spree with her.

"She had to run."

"Did she sew the hems of the robes?" I asked. I had planned to take a break and return to the house to finish the job.

"No, Mum did," Amy said.

"How did she get them?" I had left the robes in the laundry room by my Singer sewing machine and knew I had locked the house after the girls departed with Meredith.

"Um . . . She let herself in." Clair nibbled on her lower lip.

"How? She doesn't have a key."

"Um . . . She made a copy of mine," Clair said. "She was there when we got home."

"She was what?" I moaned. Sylvie and I would have to have a chat about privacy.

"Uh-oh," Rebecca said.

"Clair told her not to," Amy added quickly, always ready to defend her younger-by-a-minute sister. "But you know Mum."

I did. I was intrigued that the girls were catching on, too.

"By the way, she has some gossip for you," Amy went on. "She said it had something to do with seeing that Miss Platch . . . Platt . . . Plate—"

"Plachette?" I said.

"That's the one. Mum saw Miss Plachette in the diner talking with an older couple."

To Sylvie, that could be anyone over forty.

"They were talking about a contract. Mum said they were dressed nicely, but they looked like they were after something."

That gave me pause. Were they attorneys, hired to help Georgia deal with her mother's will? Or were they real estate people, interested in following through with the purchase of the Burrell farm and Arlo's property and whatever other property they could garner?

Amy slipped a sliver of cheese from the platter on the tasting counter, held it to her nose, and inhaled. "What's this? Smells yummy."

"Guess," I said, realizing I had forgotten to set out a nameplate.

She plopped it into her mouth. "Mmm. Savory, slightly crystallized. Piave, from Italy."

"Good job."

Amy would make a fine cheese monger one day, if she chose the career.

"Aunt Charlotte," Clair said. "We left Ragsie playing with Rocket in the backyard. That's okay, isn't it?" She looked tentative, as if she couldn't bear to be told she had done two things wrong in a day. "He'll use the dog door to get back inside."

"It's fine," I said, though I didn't know Rags had gotten the hang of the dog door. Maybe having the Briard pup around wasn't such a bad thing. A creature probably wouldn't attack Rags with Rocket around, but my fence was short, and almost anything could encroach. Rags, being the scaredy cat that he was, could get spooked. However, not being cooped up in The Cheese Shop office all day might be good for him. I would have to weigh the options.

"Can we go across the street for some hot chocolate?" Amy said.

"Ask Daddy." Clair hitched her head toward the annex, where Matthew was buffing the wine-tasting counter.

"No. Aunt Charlotte can decide. We'll come to the tent afterward," Amy pleaded. "Promise."

Saturdays weren't easy for a working parent—I wasn't theirs but they lived under my roof. I had arranged for the girls to help Tyanne at Le Petit Fromagerie during lunch. They would hand out the souvenir plates. Afterward, they would head to the library to finish their homework, and then meet up with Meredith for a quick dinner before their chorale debut.

"Okay, as long as you stay together," I said.

They darted out of the shop, hand in hand.

Moments later, Grandmère scurried in. "Emergency!"

I sighed. Was everything going to be a crisis today?

"Your grandfather is making his famous pizza for our theater rehearsal. You know, the hot pepper one."

"Mrs. O'Leary's," Rebecca said. "Named for the woman whose barn caught on fire."

Pépère loved giving clever names to his creations. Mrs.

O'Leary's pizza was deliciously piquant, with three kinds of peppers, red pepper flakes, garlic, onion, mounds of pork sausage, and Lioni Smoked Mozzarella that was laced with hickory and cherrywood overtones. A beer chaser was needed after every bite of pizza.

Grandmère clucked. "Because we are in rehearsals for *Chicago*, he thought it would be fun to give our actors a Chicago-themed pizza. He is adorable, *non*?"

"*Oui*," I said. "Rebecca, would you fill the order?"

Grandmère gazed at Rebecca and her face turned grave. "How are you, *chérie*?"

"Better," Rebecca said, "now that we have a new witness."

"Who?"

Before Rebecca could say Tallulah Barker, Urso pushed open the door and bellowed, "Where's Jordan?"

CHAPTER

18

To say my stomach felt like it had jumped on a roller coaster and was doing a loop-de-loop was an understatement. Panic zipped through me. Had Urso found out about Jordan's past? Had Bozz put two and two together and spilled the beans? Could anyone be trusted with a secret?

I steadied myself by gripping the cheese counter, and in what I was proud to call a level tone, said, "Why do you need Jordan?"

Urso marched across the hardwood floor, offering a quick nod to my grandmother as he passed. "He might have witnessed a crime."

Eager to contain the conversation, hoping I could control the damage with a private tête-à-tête, I cut around the counter and clenched Urso's elbow. "Follow me," I said, pulling him toward the rear exit.

"Where—?"

"Just follow."

"I will not follow." He jerked to a stop by the archway

leading to the annex and wrenched free. "I've got pressing business."

"U-ey, now is not the time or place to discuss this."

"Discuss what? All I asked is whether or not you knew where Jordan was."

"You don't have to shout," I said.

"I'm not shouting."

"You are, too."

From behind the cheese counter, Rebecca yelled over both of us, "Did you talk to Tallulah Barker, Chief?"

Urso turned toward her, his eyes beady, his nostrils flared. "Should I have?"

"She saw someone charging down the street the night Kaitlyn Clydesdale died." Rebecca hefted a wheel of Lioni Smoked Mozzarella onto the cutting board. It landed with a thud. "And she also said she could corroborate—"

"Look, Miss Zook—"

"No, you look, Chief." Rebecca's voice crescendoed as she lifted a knife and brandished it overhead. "If Tallulah Barker says she saw someone running away from my cottage, it's important."

"I'll get to that," Urso said, his voice matching hers. "I promise. But right now, I need to find Jordan Pace. He's not answering his telephone."

"What's going on?" Matthew crossed under the archway from the annex, wine bottle and corkscrew in his hands. "Why is everyone yelling?"

"No one's yelling," Rebecca shouted.

Matthew smirked. My grandmother seemed mortified. Rebecca set the knife down on the counter and folded her hands into her chest as if in supplication.

Urso said, "Someone stole some ice sculpting tools from the faire. Theo Taylor remembered Jordan passing through the area. He might have seen the thief."

Tension melted from my shoulders. Urso wasn't there to haul Jordan to jail for some crime from the past. I had to stop overreacting. On the other hand, our charming town

was, yet again, the scene of a crime. Minor—not death—but a crime nonetheless.

"Urso, the other night a thief stole cheese from our tent," I said. "He attacked me, but he ran off."

Urso spun to face me. "And you're just telling me now?"

"I informed security."

"Someone stole a box of goat cheese from my house, as well." Rebecca resumed preparing Grandmère's order. "I wanted to talk to you about that, Chief."

"What is Providence coming to?" Grandmère said.

"Oh, man." Urso removed his broad-brimmed hat, scrubbed his hair with his hands, and wedged his hat back on his head. "One crime at a time. This one first."

Matthew said, "I'll help you track down Jordan, Chief. Charlotte, any idea where he could be?"

"He said he had meetings scheduled at the farm."

Matthew handed me the wine and corkscrew and clapped Urso on the shoulder. "Let's go."

"I'll accompany you." Grandmère turned on her heel.

"I don't think that's necessary, Bernadette," Urso said.

"*Oui, il est nécessaire.*" She swatted the air. "It is not open for discussion. I am mayor of this fine town. I am going, no argument." Like a steam engine, she plowed after Matthew and Urso toward the exit.

"By the way, Bernadette, I've hired another deputy," Urso said over his shoulder. "With your approval."

"*Absolument.*"

Rebecca flitted after them. "Grandmère. Your cheese." She held out a gold tote bag. "And Chief, don't forget to talk to Tallulah Barker."

"I won't."

My grandmother slipped the bag into her crocheted purse and patted Rebecca's cheek. "If he says he will not, he will not. *Bon courage.*"

I smiled. In the past year my grandmother had done a one-eighty regarding Urso, forgiving him completely for thinking she could have killed someone. Deep down, I felt she wanted to see me end up with Urso and not Jordan.

Urso whipped open the door and let Matthew and Grandmère pass through first. As he started to lumber out, Chip entered, chin tucked in as if bracing against the cold, one hand holding his zippered suede jacket closed. The two butted shoulders. Chip gave Urso a hearty shove, then looked up and recoiled.

Urso grunted his disapproval but pressed on.

"What do you want, Chip?" I said, at my wit's end from the recent frenetic pace in the shop.

"Yeah, what do you want?" Rebecca echoed.

Chip drew up short, his gaze as hangdog as a scolded puppy's. He withdrew a plastic-wrapped bouquet of daisies from inside his jacket and offered them to me. "Your favorites."

They weren't my favorites anymore, I thought nastily, irritated that he was bringing me flowers, yet again. When would he leave town and take with him all the reminders of our past together? With Kaitlyn Clydesdale dead, he couldn't have any more business here.

I snatched the flowers and, grumbling thanks beneath my breath, retreated to the counter. I set the daisies as well as the wine and corkscrew that Matthew had handed me beside the cash register, and began wiping down the cutting board and knives with a wet towel. Each swipe felt angry yet justified. Rebecca joined me and grabbed another wet towel. Together, we presented a united front.

Chip sidled to the display barrel in the center of the shop and lifted a package of sourdough crackers. As he examined the box from all angles, he said, "About last night."

"What about it?" I said.

"I came over to tell you something." He replaced the crackers, picked up a jar of apple jelly, and put it back. He looked fidgety. His cheek twitched. "Ainsley Smith lied about where he was on the night of the murder. He wasn't at the hockey game."

"How do you know that?" I stopped wiping the counter.

Like a wary stray dog, Chip edged closer. "Remember when Ainsley, Lois, and I were in The Cheese Shop the

other day? We were talking hockey. Well, Ainsley didn't mention Lukashenko's hat trick."

"What's a hat trick?" Rebecca asked.

"A single player making three goals in one game," I explained. "It's a big deal."

Rebecca glanced at me. "Mr. Smith said that Luka-what's-his-name had two goals."

Chip clicked his tongue. "That's what I'm telling you."

"Maybe it was an oversight." I resumed wiping.

"No way," Chip said. "Anybody who had witnessed it would have bragged about it. It doesn't happen every day. Ainsley wasn't at that game, babe. He was making up an alibi for that night."

I frowned. Why was Chip so eager to turn in Lois's husband? Did he think his good-citizen act would ingratiate himself to me? Jordan didn't trust Chip. Should I? "Why tell me? Tell Urso."

"I'm telling you because you were the one who heard Ainsley. You were a witness to the lie. He should have given us a play-by-play. 'Lukashenko did this. Lukashenko did that.'" Chip grew animated. He pranced in a circle, arms held overhead. "'Lukashenko scored!'"

"Tell Urso," I repeated.

Chip stopped his victory dance. "Like he'll listen to me."

"Why won't he?"

"He's riding me, like old times. Didn't you see him on the way out of here? He bumped into me on purpose."

I could've sworn it was Chip who had done the bumping, but maybe I had imagined it. Urso had never liked Chip. They had been warriors on the field; warriors for the same girl—me. I had expected Urso to have moved past their history by now. What did he care whether Chip was back in town, unless Chip had made a move on Jacky? Perhaps that was why Urso and Jacky seemed at odds.

"What's he giving you a hard time about?" I said.

Chip worked his tongue against his cheek. "He asked me where I was when Kaitlyn was killed."

"He's asking everybody."

"I was with Luigi at the pub." He slipped onto one of the ladder-back chairs at the tasting counter and batted the salamis, which were hanging on a goosenecked hook. The salamis swung to and fro. "Lots of people saw me. Georgia Plachette, for one. She was playing darts. She had a set-to with Luigi."

I wadded up the wet towel, plopped it on the counter, and gazed hard at him. Why had he felt the need to tell me his alibi? Warning signals flared in my overextended brain. Was Chip having an affair with Georgia? Had corroborating her whereabouts been his real intention in telling me the story? Indict Ainsley and clear Georgia?

Stop it, Charlotte. Jealousy does not become you!

But I wasn't jealous, was I? I wanted to solve this crime and clear Ipo. I had made Rebecca a promise. If Urso wasn't looking in the right direction, I was there to guide him, right? On the other hand, Georgia's alibi sounded solid. Dozens of people would have seen her at the pub.

I refocused on Chip, wishing he would disappear. From town. From my life. "What was your deal with Kaitlyn?"

"What do you mean?"

"Your contract. What were the stipulations?"

His jaw tensed. He blew an angry stream of air through his nose. "I see how it is."

"How what is?"

"I had no motive to kill her, if that's what you're implying."

"I'm not—"

"Sure, you are." He slipped off the chair and started to pace in front of the counter. "Look, I only prospered with her alive. If you don't believe me—" He jammed a hand inside his jacket and pulled a folded set of papers from a pocket. He snapped the papers in the air. "Would you like to review my contract? Huh?"

"Stop that."

"Sheesh, Charlotte." He hurled the papers on top of the

flowers and wine that were sitting beside the register, then made a U-turn and stomped toward the exit. At the door, he pivoted. "I thought you knew me better than that."

As the door slammed, Rebecca swooped up the contract and scanned it. "He's telling the truth. Like the Burrells, his contract is null and void now that Kaitlyn Clydesdale is dead."

What law school did she attend? I thought snarkily, but bit back the comment because Chip's contract wasn't what was worrying me. Neither was his angry outburst. I had witnessed him blow before. He would calm down. But seeing him passionate enough to track me down—not only at my grandparents' house but at The Cheese Shop, as well— made me think again of his objective. He had wanted me to focus my suspicions on Ainsley Smith. Ainsley hadn't attended that hockey game, or if he had, he hadn't stayed for the whole thing. So where had he gone?

A notion zipped into my mind. What if Ainsley had been Kaitlyn's lover? He was married. What if Kaitlyn had wanted to proclaim her love to the world, as I had reasoned before? Ainsley could have become angry. He might have followed her to Rebecca's. He could have lashed out as a warning to keep quiet. And the rest was history.

CHAPTER

While working through my theory, I resumed swabbing the cheese counter with a vengeance, though nothing needed swabbing, not in the entire shop. Every wedge of cheese was in its place. The barrels looked neat and appealing. We had a cleaning service come in every week to vacuum up any fleck of dust. The rime at the base of the plastic covering over the basement door had been whisked away.

Rebecca snapped her fingers in front of my face. "Yoo-hoo, Charlotte." She set Chip's contract by the register and swooped up the daisies. "I can see the wheels turning in your head." She moved to the kitchen, plunked the flowers into an amber vase, and added water. "What are you thinking?"

"That Ainsley Smith might be hiding something."

"I agree." She returned with the vase. "Chief Urso has to question him."

"Except Urso is looking for Jordan and a thief."

"Then it's up to us." Rebecca set the flowers aside,

snatched the towel out of my hands, and launched it into a laundry bin near the kitchen. "Let's go."

I held out a palm to stop her. "Uh-uh. Not you. Me. Alone."

"But—"

"You have to go to Le Petit Fromagerie and relieve Tyanne."

"Send Bozz."

"He's got the afternoon shift here at The Cheese Shop."

She stamped her foot.

I smirked. "Oh, yeah, that works for the twins, too." I toted the wine bottle and corkscrew that Matthew had left to the annex. Over my shoulder, I said, "Look, I know Lois and Ainsley. Neither will react well to us ganging up on them. Let me do this my way."

"But Mr. Smith could be a murderer."

"If he did kill Kaitlyn, it was an accident. In the heat of passion."

"It's not in the heat of passion if he willfully took a weapon with him." Rebecca grabbed the vase of daisies, and we crossed paths as I returned to the shop. "People don't walk around with pu'ili sticks tucked in their pockets. They just don't." She set the vase of daisies on the display shelf against the wall, shifting bottles of aged balsamic vinegar to make room for it, and looked for my approval. I hated to admit it, but the cheery flowers did give the shop an instant face-lift.

"When do you think Ainsley could have stolen the pu'ili sticks?" I removed my apron. "He didn't play poker with Ipo and Barton and the others, did he?"

"Not to my knowledge, but maybe he did some handy-man work for Ipo. I could ask."

"No."

"I can do it without Mr. Smith even knowing." Rebecca lifted her chin proudly. "I've been studying interrogation techniques."

"You've been what?"

"There's this TV show that has a site on the Internet. I've learned all about interrogation and spy equipment."

Oh, my, I thought, surprised by what she was learning on television and online.

"Please, Charlotte? Let me grill him."

Grill him. Spare me. "No. You're going to the tent. Now."

Her lower lip puckered. "Whatever you do, be subtle. Don't ask direct questions. Compliment him, if you need to. It'll take him off his guard. He'll trust you."

"Go."

"You flip out the fishing line and let the fish swallow the bait." She mimed her instruction, reeling back as if she had caught a fifteen-foot marlin. "Then tug."

I prodded her. "I've got this. Promise."

She dug in her heels. "Ooh, and if for any reason you need to break into the inn, take along some sunglasses. If you snap off the ends"—more demonstration—"you can use the arm of the glasses like a pick, but if Urso were to catch you, he wouldn't know you were breaking and entering. You'd merely have broken sunglasses. Cool, huh?"

Why couldn't she get hooked on family-friendly shows? "Go," I repeated.

As she scurried out of the shop, I considered making a plaque to honor the event: *Rebecca obeyed Charlotte,* inscribed with a date. I kept gold paper and glitter pens that I used to make signs for the shop in a drawer in the office.

"Bozz!" I called.

He didn't answer.

"Bozz?" I dashed to the office and saw a Post-it note stuck to the computer screen: *Philby called. Had to go. Hope it's okay.*

No, it wasn't okay. I couldn't leave the shop unattended. What was I going to do now? Rebecca would never forgive me if I let the opportunity to question Ainsley Smith slip away.

The front door chimes jingled. I hurried into the shop, spotted my grandfather, and nearly applauded.

"Bon soir, chérie." He toddled to the counter, a look of concern pinching his forehead. "Have you seen your *grand-mère*? I sent her for cheese, but she didn't return. I have got hungry actors, and you know what that means."

I explained that Grandmère had fetched the cheese, but she had run off to help Urso.

"I knew something was up." He shook his pudgy finger. "She is getting too old for this life as mayor."

"She isn't old. Shakespeare said, 'April hath put a spirit of youth in everything.'"

"Now you are quoting Shakespeare, too?" he grumbled. "So like your *grandmère*. I suppose I must return to the theater empty-handed." He snatched a piece of cheese from the platter on the tasting counter and slipped it into his mouth. "Ah, Piave. One of my favorites. *Merci. Au revoir.*"

"Wait. Could you . . . Would you manage the shop for an hour? Please, Pépère. It's not busy. The actors can run lines without you. Hunger will make them focus, no? I have an errand."

"An errand?" He raised one eyebrow. *"Ma petite-fille.* You think you are as sly as your *grandmère*, but you lack years of practice."

"Perhaps I do," I said, but I wasn't dim-witted. I fetched a heart-shaped cheese called Rivers Edge Chèvre Old Flame from the display case. It was a silky, bloomy-rind goat cheese—a specialty offered only in February—and just to my grandfather's liking. I sliced off a sliver and offered it to him. He reached, and I snatched it back. "Uh-uh, not unless you watch the shop for me."

"Diablesse. You know I can't refuse. Fine, fine. I will stay." He slipped the cheese into his mouth and his face lit up with delight.

Ah, if all men could be so enticed.

* * *

Ainsley Smith sat in one of the wicker porch chairs at the front of Lavender and Lace. A plaid blanket lay across his lap. The Shih Tzu, Agatha, sat on top of the blanket.

As I strolled up the front path, Agatha yipped a greeting. Ainsley glanced at me, but pretending he hadn't seen me, spanked out the creases of the newspaper he held in his hands and zeroed in on the headlines.

I snickered. Did he honestly think I hadn't seen him look?

Agatha shimmied, padded in a circle, and settled back down.

I climbed the steps and said, "Hello, Mr. Smith," offering him due respect.

"Charlotte." He peered at me, this time clearing his throat. "Didn't see you there." A jackrabbit being stalked by a wolf couldn't have looked more wary. Had Chip alerted him? No, he wouldn't have done that.

I kneaded my hands together, ruing the fact that I had run out of Fromagerie Bessette without donning gloves. Real smart. At least I had slipped on my coat. "Brisk, isn't it?"

"I'm dressed for it." He wore a heavy peacoat, corduroy trousers, leather gloves, and Timberland boots. Wisps of his thinning red hair poked out from beneath a lavender knit cap, no doubt one of Lois's many creations. How she loved the color lavender.

"Got a moment to chat?" I said.

He squirmed.

I took that as a yes and plunked down into the chair opposite him. The rattan squeaked beneath my weight. The chill in the air cut through my coat and up the legs of my trousers, but I wasn't about to ask if we could go inside. I wanted him on edge with no time to regroup. "I heard some news. Gossip, probably."

He folded his paper and tucked it between his thigh and the side of the chair. "Hungry?" he asked. The front door was open a crack, and the flavorful aroma of pot roast wafted through the screen door, but he wasn't inviting me for lunch. He lifted a pretty floral plate from the table beside him and offered me a frosted cookie. His hand shook ever so slightly.

"No, thanks," I said.

"So what's your news?" He popped a cookie into his mouth and fed a crumb to Agatha, who licked his fingers in thanks.

"It's about that hockey game."

He swallowed the cookie and replaced the plate on the table. "Which one?"

"That Bluejackets game you went to on the night of Kaitlyn Clydesdale's death. You were talking about it at the shop. Lois gave you the tickets as a birthday present."

He stroked his chin, as if culling the memory from a distant place in his mind. "Oh, yeah, I remember. We played the Kings."

"That's the one. Did you stay for the whole game?"

"Sure did." He folded his arms across his chest. "I don't go often. I've got to relish every minute when I get the chance."

"I know what you mean. I'm that way at an OSU football game." I pumped my arm overhead. "Go Buckeyes." I made the warbling sound that had become a standard cheer at games.

Ainsley chuckled and his shoulders relaxed. He was getting into my rhythm. Rebecca would have been proud of me.

"So what's the gossip?" he asked.

"It was about their star. Luka . . . Luka . . ."

"Lukashenko."

"That's the guy's name." I smacked my thigh in agreement. "I heard Lukashenko achieved a hat trick that night. That must have been great to see."

"It was."

"Except I don't remember you mentioning the hat trick when you were in The Cheese Shop yesterday. You told us he'd scored two goals."

Ainsley blanched but quickly recovered. "My mistake."

"So, you did see it. How did it play out? Did he score in each period?"

"Um, gee . . ." He tapped his head with a knobby finger. "The old noggin's not as good as it used to be."

"Maybe you missed seeing one."

His eyes drew to narrow slits.

"Perhaps you were someplace else," I went on, throwing him a bone. "Maybe you were buying food at the concession stand."

He bobbed his head. "That was it. I ate my way through the game. The hot dogs at the arena are the best."

"Slathered in beans and cheese."

"And onions," he added.

"You need a fork to eat them." The thought made my mouth water. My grandfather had tried to duplicate the recipe, but his beans were always missing something. I had suggested extra molasses and maybe a dash of white pepper. "Except"—I shook a finger—"there are television screens by every concession stand. You should have seen the play. Fans would have been going wild."

Ainsley grew quiet. He glanced at the screen door and back at me. In a thin voice he said, "I wasn't at the game, but you know that, don't you?"

"Where were you?"

Silence.

"Were you with Kaitlyn Clydesdale?" I said.

"What? No."

"You knew her."

"Of course, I did. She stayed here for one night, but she moved on to Violet's Victoriana Inn." His gaze shifted up to the porch ceiling and down again. He was lying.

"Years ago," I said, "she lived in Providence. Did you know her back in high school?"

"I don't recall." He sounded like a well-prepared witness.

"I see." I slid forward in my chair, as if I were planning to get to my feet. "Maybe I should talk to Violet to get the scoop. I'll bet she knew who Kaitlyn Clydesdale's gentlemen callers were."

"What do you want, money?" Ainsley blurted. "Do you

have compromising photos? Huh, do you? I'll pay whatever you ask."

"I don't want your money, Ainsley."

"If you don't want money"—he screwed up his mouth—"then what do you want?"

"I want the truth. I believe you were having an affair with Kaitlyn Clydesdale."

The man exhaled like a harpoon had punctured him. "It's not what you think."

"Tell me what it was," I said, sitting taller, feeling my oats.

"You have to promise not to tell Lois." He glanced again at the screen door.

I followed his gaze, seeing no sign of his wife or any of the inn's guests, for that matter. I said, "Where is Lois?"

"In the kitchen, making pot roast using your grandmother's recipe."

Grandmère, who had inherited the recipe from her grandmother, had raffled off the recipe at a fund-raiser. The dish asked for extra bay leaves, a handful of cloves, and ten grinds of the peppermill. It was the kind of food that went down easily in the winter and worked like a heating element from the inside out.

"Promise you won't tell Lois," Ainsley repeated.

"It's not mine to tell."

He drew in a deep breath. "Whatever you've heard, you don't know the half of it." He plucked Agatha from his lap, wadded the blanket into a ball, and rose from his chair. Agatha leaped back onto the chair and nestled on the cushion as Ainsley ambled down the porch steps. He crooked a finger for me to follow. I shook my head. I wasn't stupid. I wasn't going to follow him to a shadowy spot behind the inn, not after Rebecca had reminded me that he might be capable of extreme violence.

I remained in my seat. "We can talk here, sir."

"But Lois might—"

I remained steadfast.

"Fine, whatever. She shouldn't be out anytime soon. She

recently brought me the cookies." He returned, scooped up the dog, and slumped into his chair. The wicker hissed.

"Kaitlyn Clydesdale," I repeated.

He started to rub the dog with intensity. Agatha yipped and leaped off his lap. She nosed the screen door open and scurried inside.

"Were you her lover?" I said as the door clacked shut.

"Lover? Bah!" Ainsley snarled. "I was her pawn."

A stream of arctic air swirled around the porch. I shivered and slipped my hands into my coat pockets. "Explain."

"Lois and I . . ." He massaged his temples. "With couples our age, things get tired after too many years together. When Kaitlyn showed up, she reminded me of the good times we'd had back in school. She made me feel young and frisky. I couldn't resist her bigger-than-life charms. After a couple of rolls in the hay, however, I realized she wasn't that into me. Know what I mean?" He shifted uncomfortably in the chair. "She had an ulterior motive. I just didn't get it at first. When I wanted to end the affair, she said she was going to blab to Lois. I pleaded with her to keep our secret. She said it would cost me."

"She wanted cash?"

"Worse. She'd only keep the secret if I granted her a portion of the raw land I owned north of town." He jabbed his forefinger at me. "That's when I caught on."

"Caught on to what?"

"She'd planned to blackmail me all along."

There was that word again. *Blackmail.* Who else had Kaitlyn threatened?

"Such a lowly word, isn't it?" He plucked pills of wool off the wadded-up blanket. "I agreed to give her the land, but she died that night, and, well . . ." He waved his hand in a circle.

"Pretty convenient timing," I said.

"Oh, lord, I didn't kill her!" He shook his head along with his denial, but there was something he wasn't telling me. His eyes began to blink rapidly.

"You saw her that night."

"No, not that night." His gaze flitted upward again. How many lies did the man think he could get away with? He would fail a lie detector test, for sure. "I met with her earlier that day."

"Where?"

"At Violet's Victoriana Inn. She was downright vicious," Ainsley continued. "She said, agreement or no agreement, she was going to tell Lois about us because"—he heaved—"because she thought all women should know when their husbands cheat."

It sounded to me like Kaitlyn had experienced a bitter breakup.

"I told her if she did, that would constitute an end to our agreement about the land. Kaitlyn laughed, and—"

"Hey, Ainsley!" A neighbor, who was walking his Malamute on a leash, waved from the sidewalk. "How's business?"

"Good, Fred. Good." Ainsley shot a sociable hand into the air, but his gaze was flat. When the neighbor passed by, Ainsley continued. "Kaitlyn laughed and said she would give me until morning to tell Lois myself, and then she dashed off to a Do-Gooder meeting. Can you believe that? The hypocrite! She was no Do-Gooder, I'll tell you." He slapped his palm on the arm of the chair. "She was going to ruin my life, but she wanted everyone to believe she was a saint. Bah!"

I let his diatribe settle like dust, then said, "It sounds like you could've killed her right then and there."

Ainsley folded his hands together and pointed at me with his index fingers. "I wanted to, but—"

"Hey, Mr. Smith." A gangly man in his thirties trotted up the path to the inn with a female companion. The woman stomped up the stairs first and removed her knit hat. The man held the screen door open for her. As they entered the inn, he said, "Good weather for Eskimos, huh?" The woman tittered, like the guy was the funniest man in the universe. They let the screen door slam behind them.

Ainsley opened his hands, palms up. "I swear I didn't kill her."

"What did you do after meeting with her?"

"I came home, but I couldn't drum up the courage to tell Lois myself, so I went for a walk with Agatha."

"For how long?"

He gripped the arms of his chair, looking like a man on the *Titanic* who believed a deck chair would save him. "Two hours, maybe three."

"Where to?"

"To the property I own, north of town."

"What did you do when it grew dark? You didn't go to the game." I knew I sounded like a coldhearted, cross-examining attorney, but I needed answers.

"I couldn't. I felt sick to my stomach, so I walked some more, okay?" He shot to his feet and stomped to the screen door. He peered inside, then pivoted and marched to the railing. "I was a Boy Scout, back in the day. I got a number of badges in camping and trailblazing. The stars offer up as much light as any flashlight, if you know how to use them."

"Any witnesses?"

"Agatha was with me," he said over his shoulder. "But the pup hasn't learned to people-speak yet. She's no Lassie."

"Didn't Lois notice that Agatha was missing?"

"Agatha is like a wild child. She'll chase squirrels and disappear for hours on end. Lois thinks it's cute. I needed someone to talk to. The dog was as good as anything."

"Did anyone pass you on the road?"

"No one I knew. I saw an Amish man, but he wouldn't remember me. They drive with blinders on, don't you know." He smacked the railing again.

"What did you do when you came home?"

"Kept as quiet as a clam. Lois was scrubbing pots. The guests were in the dining room, polishing off their dinner." He hung his head and swung it from side to side. "I couldn't tell her about the affair."

"Even though Kaitlyn Clydesdale was going to."

"I planned to tell her in the morning. I needed the courage." He raised his hand as if on the witness stand. "I never went near your friend's cottage, I swear."

I joined Ainsley at the railing, an idea nipping at the edge of my mind. Cool air snaked around my ankles and sent a shiver up my legs. "You said your property is north of town. Is it near the Burrells' property?"

"It abuts it."

I recalled a conversation with Sylvie outside Rebecca's cottage on the night of the incident. Sylvie had said Kaitlyn had come into Under Wraps and talked about her empire. At the time, I hadn't given it much thought, too distracted by Sylvie's claim that Ipo had motive to hurt Kaitlyn. Now, I wondered. The word *empire* was unusual. I said, "Did Kaitlyn ever talk about wanting to build an empire in Providence? It seems she wanted to acquire more than yours and the Burrells' properties. She was after Arlo's, as well."

Ainsley scratched his chin. "She never specifically said the word *empire* to me, but she was power hungry, that's for sure." He sighed. "I'm not sorry that she's dead."

A woman uttered a teensy sob. I swiveled toward the sound. Lois stood beyond the screen door, her hand over her mouth. Agatha, parked at Lois's feet, growled between sharp teeth. So much for not being Lassie. The scamp must have tugged her mistress to the door to hear the conversation.

Ainsley darted to the screen door and whipped it open. He reached for his wife. "Lois, darling."

She swatted him. "Don't *darling* me." She slurped back tears. "How could you? With Kaitlyn Clydesdale, of all people?" She peered at me, her eyes shooting missiles. "I told you that woman was trouble, didn't I?"

"She was blackmailing me," Ainsley said.

"After you gave in to her wiles."

"I was weak." He held his hands out, as if being powerless was a good enough excuse for cheating.

"Then I'll be strong." Lois drew tall. "Pack up, mister."

"You don't mean it."

"Oh, yes, I do." She gestured, for emphasis.

Ainsley dropped to one knee. "But I love you." He snatched Lois's hand in his.

"Too late." Lois flicked his hand away. Agatha yipped her support. "We're through."

"But—"

"Move out." Lois jabbed a finger. "Go to your mother's. She thinks you walk on water."

Ainsley flinched as if she had slapped him, then scrambled to his feet and slinked into the great room. Through the archway, I saw him reach for the prized hockey stick hanging on the wall.

"Oh, no, you don't." Lois stormed in after him. "Stop right there. You'll take none of those things, you two-timer."

"I was just going to set things right."

"My foot!"

He jammed his hands in his pockets and ogled Lois with hangdog eyes. "Please, darling, don't kick me out. We can fix this."

Lois crossed her arms, looking as immovable as one of the ice sculptures at the Winter Wonderland faire.

Ainsley cut me a stony look, obviously blaming me for his current situation, then shuffled down the hallway toward his room behind the kitchen.

When he disappeared, Lois sank onto an ottoman, lifted Agatha onto her lap, and scratched the dog's ears. "What have I done?" she muttered. "Oh, what have I done?"

She continued murmuring, seemingly unaware that I was standing at the front door, and I had to wonder, by her quick decision to boot out her husband, whether she had already known about his affair with Kaitlyn.

Had that knowledge driven her to do something rash?

CHAPTER

20

I trudged back to work, no wiser. On the way, I felt horrible for even considering that Lois could be guilty. Though she had been quite brusque with her husband, I didn't believe, in my heart of hearts, that she could have lashed out at Kaitlyn—or anyone, for that matter—and left her to die.

When I entered Fromagerie Bessette, I found Bozz shadowboxing with his reflection in the glass that fronted the cheese counter. He stopped mid-punch, dropped his hands to his sides, and said, "Hey, Miss B. Sorry about skipping out earlier. I had no idea you needed me."

"No worries. Where's my grandfather?"

Bozz slung a thumb over his shoulder. "He just left. If you ask me, he sounded a bit like the Mad Hatter. He was mumbling, 'I'm late, I'm late, I'm late.'"

"You mean he sounded like the White Rabbit."

Bozz looked perplexed.

"In *Alice in Wonderland*," I said. "The White Rabbit is the one who's late. He wore spectacles." I drew an outline

of an imaginary pair of glasses. "He was doing the queen's bidding."

"Whatever. Anyway, Pépère was perspiring."

Worry cut through me. It was my fault that my grandfather was late bringing food to starving actors. If only he weren't always on the go. A while back, Matthew and I had wanted to send our grandparents on a vacation, but to date, we hadn't convinced them to go anywhere. Oh, sure, they took occasional day trips to other Ohio hot spots like the German Village in Columbus or the zoo and botanical garden in Cincinnati, and my grandfather had joined Matthew and me on a tour of American cheese farms, but none of those trips counted as a vacation. Recently I had suggested they take a trip to France, but they had pooh-poohed me. They did not have a love affair with their native land.

I said, "Bozz, can you watch the shop for a while longer? I want to help Pépère distribute his pizzas at the theater. I'm sure you can handle the crowd."

He scanned the store—which was empty—and winked. "Don't think that'll be a problem. Everyone's at the faire. What time should I close up?"

"Five thirty is fine. Put a sign in the door steering customers to the Le Petit Fromagerie tent, then head on over for the night shift."

"Gotcha."

* * *

I needn't have worried about my grandfather. When I arrived at the Providence Playhouse theater, I found him on stage scuttling around a long buffet table, tending to actresses, many of whom wore work shirts or robes slung over racy, very lacy getups. The *Chicago* costumes weren't nearly ready this early in the rehearsal process, but Grandmère liked her actors to dress in character at the first opportunity.

Crew people, who always ate first at the Playhouse, sat on the floor in front of a giant neon ROXIE HART sign.

Most had polished off their meals. A few of the cast had climbed onto the raised platform located at the rear of the stage, which would hold the five-piece combo during the show.

"Do you need anything?" Pépère asked a pair of actresses who were dressed like sexy prison inmates. "Are there enough beverages? Is everyone happy?"

How could they not be content? The peppery aroma of Pépère's pizzas filled the air.

He spotted me and waved for me to join him. "*Chérie*. Welcome. How do you like our flashy sign? It has been donated from a touring Broadway company." He plucked a wedge of pizza from a platter and bit off the tip. Melted cheese and bits of pork sausage dripped between his fingers. He slurped it into his mouth. "Have some." He encouraged me with his elbow.

I fetched a paper plate and viewed the selections of cheese and salads that Pépère had also provided, but chose the pizza. The aroma was the lure. One bite and I moaned my pleasure. Hints of hickory, cherrywood, and garlic popped in my mouth. "Oh, wow," I said. "You've outdone yourself."

"Extra garlic; that is the key."

We ate the rest of our pizza in silence.

When we finished, he said, "How did your *errand* go?" His eyes twinkled with mock-judgment. "You were snooping, I assume."

"I don't snoop."

He chortled. "It is your nature, as it is your *grandmère's*. Did I ever tell you about the time she investigated a crime at the Harvest Moon Ranch? She—"

"Etienne." The stage manager, a spark plug of a woman, hustled down the aisle of the theater toward the stage. "We have a minor lighting problem. Can I borrow you for a second?"

"But of course."

"Wait." I tugged on my grandfather's sleeve. "What did Grandmère do?"

"It matters not. But I remember she said one must possess all the pieces of the puzzle and then adjust one's thinking when it came to clues." He tapped his forehead.

"Adjust one's thinking? What does that mean?"

"I do not know. She quoted Hercule Poirot. 'It is the brain, the little gray cells on which one must rely. One must seek the truth within—not without.' She solved the crime that afternoon."

As Pépère toddled down the stairs and hurried with the stage manager to the lighting booth at the rear of the theater, I wandered back to the buffet while contemplating Hercule Poirot's advice. Did I possess all the information—all the clues—I needed to solve the puzzle of Kaitlyn's death? What was I missing?

"It can't be true!" a svelte actress yelled. She was standing in the wings, conversing with a shorter, perkier actress wearing a red silk teddy.

"It is. Now, keep your voice down." Miss Perky looked around to see if people were listening in. They weren't.

Except me, of course. What rumor could have made the svelte actress so upset?

Miss Perky adjusted the length of a garter on her garter belt. "*Chicago*, the musical, is based on the play of the same name. The reporter, Maurine Dallas Watkins, wrote about real-life murderesses. The character of Billy Flynn is based on two actual lawyers."

"I'll bet those lawyers didn't tap-dance," the svelte actress said.

"Probably not."

"So why does *our* Billy have to tap-dance?"

I grinned. So that was what had disturbed the svelte one. Big deal.

"Because his whole court case relies on his tapping out the points to the jury," Miss Perky explained.

I started to move away, but stopped when I heard Miss Perky add, "Barton would have been so much better in the role. You know what the gossip is about Barton, don't you? He was having an affair with that woman."

"Where'd you hear that?" the svelte one asked.

"At that clothing store."

At Under Wraps? If Sylvie had picked up some big scoop, why hadn't she pranced into The Cheese Shop and lauded it over me?

The svelte actress cut a look over her shoulder at me. Had I talked out loud?

Miss Perky flitted her fingers, as if to say, *Forget about her. She's no one.*

I sidled away from the gossiping girls, but I couldn't shake what my grandfather had said about adjusting my thinking. I had always connected Barton to Kaitlyn because of the sticky terms of their real estate contract. What if Barton had been Kaitlyn's lover? What if she had lured him the same way she had lured Ainsley Smith? But to what end? She already had a real estate contract with Barton. She didn't need to blackmail him for a piece of property. Was it possible, despite their age difference, that they had been truly in love?

* * *

Around four o'clock, I entered our Winter Wonderland tent, which was bustling with customers. Rebecca and Matthew stood at the counter, handing out slices of our three cheese selections. To my surprise, Tyanne had returned, as well. She held a tray of plastic stemware, each glass filled with about two ounces of wine. Her cheeks were flushed as crimson as her sweater.

I shrugged out of my coat and tweed jacket, folded them, set them with other coats on the lowest shelf of the baker's rack, and sidled behind the counter.

Matthew eyed his wristwatch and then me. "About time you showed up."

"I'm not late." I tweaked the collar of his tan pin-striped shirt, which looked stylish beneath the shop's chocolate brown apron. "Were you able to help Urso track down Jordan?"

"Yes. They're on the hunt for the thief."

"And Grandmère?"

"Is sticking to them like glue."

I slipped an apron from beneath the counter and put it on over my jewel-necked sweater. "Why is Tyanne here?"

"She said she needed to keep busy. Theo has the kids. I'm teaching her all about wine. Watch this." Matthew cleared his throat. "Tyanne, tell the folks about the Sin Zin."

Like a TV display model, Tyanne flourished her hand in front of a plastic glass, and in an announcer-sized voice, said, "Sin Zin. It's zesty with a hint of vanilla and berries." Customers flocked to her for a glass.

Matthew beamed like a proud professor. "Isn't she a natural?"

I nodded. Was there anything Tyanne couldn't do? Except possibly keep her marriage together—a marriage she had emotionally left years ago, I reminded myself.

Rebecca edged closer to me and whispered, "What happened with Ainsley Smith?"

I explained in two sentences.

Matthew gave me a reproving look. Sotto voce, he said, "Don't you think you're taking this investigation thing too far? We have a police force."

"Of three," I said.

"Three's better than two."

"Are you kidding? We have three people working for us at The Cheese Shop, not to mention Pépère and Bozz on occasion, and we can barely make do. Urso and his crew can't oversee an entire town. We should have a formidable force by now."

"That requires"—Matthew rubbed his fingers together—"cash."

Rebecca said, "Charlotte, I almost forgot, there's a guy—"

"Ix-nay on the investigation alk-tay," I said.

Meredith, pretty in an emerald jacket, biscuit-colored silk blouse, and brown slacks, sauntered into the tent and waved.

I sliced my finger across my neck, indicating that we should end the conversation. Meredith would give me

what-for if she knew that I was nosing around. After last year's run-in with a criminal, suffice it to say, she was overly protective of me—hence the self-defense lessons.

Apologizing to the crowd, Meredith scooted around them and headed for us. She cozied up to Matthew and planted a kiss on his cheek, then frowned at me. "Oh, no. Not again. What are you investigating now?"

"I'm not."

"You are, too." She jutted a finger. "Your eyes are shiny and hyper-alert. Fess up."

I sighed. So much for thinking I could keep anything from my pal. "I was telling Matthew that I won't sit idle while Urso incarcerates Ipo." I ogled my cousin. "You, yourself, said he wasn't guilty."

"I've been known to be wrong about people," Matthew said.

"Hell-o-o-o!" Sylvie, wearing a quasi-antebellum outfit with big flowing skirts and a strapless black bustier top, sashayed into the tent. She looked tartish, at best. The black lace fan she fluttered didn't help. A few customers pointed and whispered.

Meredith said, "Does she have a clue how ridiculous she looks?"

"I doubt it." How dare Sylvie have the gall to give me advice about my wardrobe. I reveled in the fact that her shoulders looked covered in goose bumps.

Sylvie waltzed to the counter and posed. "How do you like the new trend? I'm calling it Punk-Southern."

Meredith bit back a laugh and elbowed me. I nudged her to hush.

Sylvie whacked Matthew playfully with her fan and held out a lace-gloved hand to him. "Let's go, love. Time to hear our girlie-girls sing."

"The recital isn't for two hours, Sylvie, and I'm attending with Meredith." Matthew grabbed Meredith's hand. He must have squeezed it too hard because she winced.

"Tosh." Sylvie pouted. "Whatever happened to parental unity?"

Matthew kept his voice low. "It vanished the day you walked out of our lives."

Sylvie visibly jolted, and Matthew smirked, which warmed me to my toes. He couldn't have made that comment a year ago. He had rebounded in the confidence department, thanks to Meredith's love.

"You're holding that against me?" Sylvie huffed.

"Why shouldn't I?"

"I didn't rove, I didn't stray. I quite simply took a breather."

Matthew said, "Sylvie, the way you rewrite history amazes me." He turned to me and waggled his thumb between us. "You and I . . . we married Peter Pan and Tinkerbell."

"Except Chip and I never married," I reminded him.

"Minor detail." Matthew pecked Meredith on the cheek and returned to his duties at the counter. "Next." Customers in line moved forward.

Sylvie huffed at Matthew's dismissal and started for the door. A few feet short, she turned back. "Oh, Charlotte." She hurried back to me, the skirt of her ensemble swinging like a bell, and pulled me toward the side of the tent. She cupped a hand around her mouth. "I found out with whom Kaitlyn Clydesdale was having an affair."

I tilted an ear, ready for her to corroborate the gossip I had heard at the theater.

"Ainsley Smith," she confided.

"I know."

"You know?" Sylvie sputtered. "Why did you ask me to do your bidding then? My time is precious."

"I recently found out," I said.

Sylvie rolled a bare shoulder back in triumph. "Oho! I"—supreme emphasis on the *I*—"discovered it yesterday."

"Why didn't you tell me then?" I said, employing the same tone she had used on me.

"Because gossip is tastier if it takes longer to learn."

Wish I'd thought up that line. Rats. "What about Barton Burrell?" I said.

Sylvie tapped her fan against her palm. "What about him?"

"He was having an affair with her, too."

Sylvie sniffed. "Where did you learn that?"

"You mean you haven't heard it?"

"No, and if I haven't, it's probably not true."

The actresses at the theater said they had picked up the tidbit at the clothing store. Had they meant Prudence's Le Chic Boutique? I said, "Sylvie, you do not own the market on gossip."

"Oh, yes, I do, Charlotte, and when you figure that out, you'll be oh so much smarter. Ta-ta." Sylvie gathered the train of her skirt in a bundle and trotted out. Scarlett O'Hara couldn't have made a more dramatically smug exit.

"Charlotte, we're running out of Zamorano," Rebecca said.

"I'll handle it." I fetched a new hunk of cheese from the ice chest and set it on the prep table behind the cheese counter. "Why don't you take a break."

As she wiped her hands on a towel, she said, "Well, well, lookie who's still roaming about."

"Who?"

"That creep." She jerked her chin toward the northern-most tent window where Oscar Carson was pacing back and forth outside. "He came in earlier, asking when you would arrive, and I said I wasn't sure, so he said he'd wait out there." She grinned. "He must not have seen you slip in."

Wondering what Oscar could possibly want to tell me, and spurred on by my grandfather's insistence that I *adjust my thinking*, I said, "I'll be right back."

"What about my break?"

"In a minute." Quickly I wove a path through the crowd; however, by the time I reached the spot outside the tent where Oscar had been pacing, he was gone. I spun in a cir-cle and caught sight of him walking down an aisle with Georgia. She had her arm looped over his shoulders; her face was turned toward him; she was speaking into his ear. I was tempted to follow and listen in, but before I moved a

step, Georgia swiveled her head, locked eyes with me, and smirked. A shiver of suspicion spiraled down my back. What was her story? Why the smug look?

I had no time to mull over the answer because at that same moment Barton Burrell, with his three sons in tow, was striding purposefully between the tents. They looked like a posse in search of a criminal. I tracked the direction Barton was headed and spied his wife, Emma, who fidgeted near the knight on a horse ice sculpture. Though she stood tall, her shoulders nearly even with the horse's, Emma looked withdrawn and sullen. The heavy drape of her coal black coat didn't help the image. She clung to a bottle of soda and her mouth was moving, as if she was talking to herself.

Barton arrived beside her, his face a solemn grimace, and seized the soda from her hand. He tossed it into a nearby trash can, then returned to Emma and pulled her into a fierce hug. Emma burst into tears. The boys clutched their parents in a ring of love.

My heart broke at the sight. Had Emma heard about Barton's affair with Kaitlyn and gone off to contemplate her options, or had she gone off to grieve the child she had miscarried? Either way, the family appeared devastated.

CHAPTER

At five thirty, Rebecca left the tent to visit Ipo. Matthew and Meredith departed a few minutes after her. At six o'clock, Tyanne and I left the shop in the capable hands of Bozz and Philby.

Outside, the scents of hot pretzels and roasted nuts rose up to meet us. My stomach panged big time. Since my quickie slice of pizza at the theater, I hadn't eaten more than a nibble of Zamorano cheese.

"We've got an hour to get a bite of dinner before the recital starts," I said. "Are you hungry?"

"Sure am, sugar. Good ol' comfort food would do."

"Charlotte and Tyanne," Delilah called. She and Freckles looked like happy-go-lucky children, skipping toward us, each carrying a wand of fluffy cotton candy. The glow of the tent's lights danced on their faces. "We've decided we need a spur-of-the-moment night out."

"There's so much electricity in the air," Freckles said.

Delilah bobbed her head in agreement.

"My sweet hubby is escorting our daughters around the

faire, so I'm a free woman." Freckles did a gleeful hop-skip. "Are you game?"

"What we are is starved," I said. Even the sight of their cotton candy made my mouth water. "But we don't have much time. We've got to attend the recital in an hour."

Delilah grabbed our hands. "Let's get a move on, then."

"Have you spoken to Jacky?" I asked. "How's baby Cecily?"

"They came into the diner," Delilah said. "Cecily's fine. Colicky but fine."

"Is Jacky going to join us?"

"Her babysitter stood her up. She's trying to find another."

The noise at Timothy O'Shea's Irish Pub was deafening. Beyond the long antique bar, a pair of electric violinists played a Clancy Brothers' tune. Many in the large crowd—which, thanks to the Winter Wonderland event, was double the normal size for February—clapped in time. Others watched the variety of sporting events playing silently on televisions that hung over the bar.

Waitresses wearing jeans, plaid shirts, and red scarves at their necks, meandered through the throng. One patted Freckles's shoulder and said, "I've held a table for you over there."

Freckles herded us toward a wooden booth, which had been set with a reserved sign.

After removing our hats, gloves, and coats, we clambered into the oak banquette. Freckles and Tyanne settled opposite Delilah and me.

Freckles said, "By the way, I saw Matthew heading over to secure some seats for the recital. Meredith was on one side of him and Sylvie was on the other. He didn't look pleased."

Oh, no, I thought. Sylvie must have lain in wait for Matthew to leave the tent. What a plotter.

"That woman," Tyanne said. "She opens her mouth and out comes nastiness."

"No kidding," Freckles said. "My, oh, my. A customer

was in Sew Inspired Quilt Shoppe yesterday. You know who I mean, that curly-haired woman who is now running Clydesdale Enterprises."

"Georgia Plachette," I said.

"She needed some lace to repair her black gloves," Freckles went on. "Anyway, Sylvie was there, too, and she had the gall to walk right up to Georgia and tell her lace was passé. Can you believe it?"

I couldn't, not after seeing Sylvie's Punk-Southern look today.

Freckles giggled. "Hollywood should do a TV show with Sylvie as a personal taste expert. That would be a hoot. British trailer park chic."

"There she is," Delilah said.

"Who, Sylvie?" I turned.

"No." Delilah tweaked my arm. "That Georgia woman, talking to Prudence."

Tyanne snuffled. "Prudence looks like she's had a nip too many, don't you think?"

Prudence Hart, hard to miss in her mustard yellow suit and teetering on stiletto heels, was hugging Georgia. The whole scenario looked awkward. In my lifetime, I had never seen Prudence hug a soul. What was she doing? If I had to guess, I would bet Georgia had bestowed some Do-Gooder funds on Prudence's pet project. Locked in Prudence's uncomfortable embrace, Georgia looked ill at ease. Her nose and eyes were puffy, and her black sheath bunched around her thighs. Like an antsy riveter, she rat-a-tatted her clunky five-inch platforms on the hardwood floor. Prudence finally released her and Georgia regrouped.

At the table with Georgia was an elderly couple. Was this the twosome Sylvie had mentioned to the twins? Without needing to draw nearer, I could tell Georgia and the woman were related—her grandmother, perhaps. They had the same curly hair, the same prominent chin.

From the right, Oscar Carson approached Georgia's table. In his hands he carried a tray filled with glasses and

a pitcher of beer. While he set the beverages down, Prudence bid the group goodbye and sauntered to a table with her zipper-thin friend who ran the garden club. Georgia offered Oscar a sly smile, which again set off alarm bells in my head. What was their story? Oscar seemed to have won her approval. Had he won her heart, as well? Was that why she had smirked at me earlier? Had she viewed me as competition? *Puh-leese.*

With his mouth moving, Oscar slid onto a chair beside the gray-haired man who I assumed was Georgia's grandfather. The man laughed heartily at whatever Oscar said. His eyes crinkled like Georgia's. All thoughts of the elderly couple being *after something*, as Sylvie had intimated, flew from my mind. They were there to support Georgia in her time of need. But was she in need, or was she looking to inherit a vast sum?

"Charlotte." Delilah tugged on my sweater sleeve and handed me a menu. "Time to order."

Our waitress tapped a pencil on her pad. Not to keep rhythm with the music. Time meant money to her.

"Oh, right, just a sec." I scanned the menu.

The pub was known for its selection of more than one hundred and fifty beers. We all ordered flights of beers—three choices poured in miniature beer steins. I asked for the potato skins, but was informed that they had sold out. The goat cheese mushrooms had gone quickly, as well. So I opted for my third favorite item on the appetizer menu, bite-sized morsels of ciabatta with ricotta cheese and sardines. Tyanne echoed the choice. Delilah and Freckles decided to split the mac-and-cheese mini-tureen appetizer, and our waitress sashayed away.

"Hey." Tyanne pointed. "Look who's out of jail."

Ipo and Rebecca strolled through the front door and paused near the hostess's podium. Both wore heavy coats and matching blue scarves. Rebecca held her head high, as if daring anyone to indict her beloved. Ipo looked nervous. His gaze darted from patron to patron.

"I think Urso's got a soft spot for our local honey maker," Delilah said.

"Why do you say that?" Freckles asked.

"He let him go on bail."

Either that or Urso had come up with evidence that exonerated Ipo. I felt the urgent need to talk to Urso. Where in the heck was he? Had he and Jordan tracked down the thief? Did he now suspect the thief of killing Kaitlyn?

Our waitress returned with our flights of beer and placed them in rows in front of us. Each set included a Pilsner, a Porter, and a micro-brewed beer. I tasted the Pilsner first. It was light, creamy, and refreshing.

"Say, what's the scoop with Lois and Ainsley?" Delilah knuckled the table. "When he came into the diner a bit ago, I spotted a pile of luggage stacked in the rear of his truck. Is he moving?"

I confided that Ainsley had had an affair with Kaitlyn Clydesdale and Lois found out.

Delilah snorted. "Talk about the least likely person in Providence to have an affair. I mean, the Cube's not exactly Rhett Butler in the looks department."

"Looks aren't the only reason someone strays," Tyanne said with authority, not an ounce of self-pity on her face.

"Do you think Ainsley killed Kaitlyn to keep the affair quiet?" Freckles asked.

"Maybe. Maybe not," I said.

"Aha!" Delilah shot a finger at me. "I knew you were involved. Spill the details. How did you find out about the affair? And don't tell me Sylvie told you."

I related my chat with Ainsley.

"He claims he was walking his dog?" Delilah scoffed. "That's not a very reliable alibi."

"Who else do you suspect?" Freckles leaned forward on her elbows, all ears.

I said, "Barton Burrell."

"No way." Freckles shook her head.

"No stinking way," Tyanne said. "He's the sweetest man."

"He might have had an affair with Kaitlyn, too." I added that he didn't want to sell his property. "She might have lured him into an affair to blackmail him."

Delilah said, "First Arlo, then Ainsley, and now Barton."

Freckles's jaw dropped open. "Kaitlyn was blackmailing Arlo?"

"He's a klepto," Delilah said.

"Hoo-boy, not good." Tyanne whistled.

"That explains why he hangs around the shop all the time," Freckles said. "Just last week I had to shoo him out. He never buys a thing, but now that you mention it, sleeves of buttons have gone missing."

"And this, my friends, is how rumors get started," I said.

"Except sometimes," Delilah said, "rumors contain a nugget of truth."

We went mum as our waitress returned with our appetizers. The six slices of ciabatta, topped with ricotta and sardines, were set in a pinwheel pattern on the silver-gray stoneware plate and set off by a fresh sprig of basil. I popped a morsel into my mouth. The ciabatta was crispy. The ricotta-and-sardines combination had a nice salty tang; the underlying flavor of olive oil was just right.

Freckles took a bite from her half of the mini-tureen of mac-and-cheese and hummed. "Mmm. Havarti, Parmesan, and Fontina cheeses. Delish!" She pushed the stoneware tureen to Delilah.

"One bite, that's it?" Delilah said. "That's all you're going to eat?"

"I'm watching my figure."

"And I'm not?" Delilah laughed. "Who am I kidding? I'm not when I've got this to eat." She pulled the tureen closer and started to devour the contents. Between bites, she said, "Back to the Kaitlyn Clydesdale mystery. What's with that Oscar guy?" She gestured with her thumb. "One day he's stalking Georgia Plachette; the next he's chummy with her."

Oscar was still sitting with Georgia and her grandparents,

but he wasn't paying an iota of attention to them. He was scanning the room. Why had he gone off with Georgia at the tent when, according to Rebecca, he had wanted to talk to me?

"He seems pretty suspicious," Freckles said. "He's big and he's got beady eyes. But then so does Arlo. He's downright creepy."

"And Barton Burrell is not," Tyanne said, matter-of-factly.

"Speaking of which"—Delilah pushed the mini-tureen away from her—"I saw Georgia spying on Barton earlier."

"I saw her, too." I revealed Georgia's semi-secret identity.

Freckles said, "She doesn't look a thing like Kaitlyn Clydesdale. Does she stand to inherit everything?"

"I'm not sure," I said. "But she has an ironclad alibi. She was here at the pub until the wee hours of the morning, playing darts. Chip verified it."

"That doesn't mean she didn't hire somebody to kill her mother," Tyanne said.

I gawked at her, wondering if she was channeling Rebecca. "This is Providence."

"Providence is in flux," Delilah said.

"She's right. We're in flux," Tyanne echoed.

"Flux?" Freckles huffed. "Is that what you call it? You know me, my business is all about attracting tourists, and I was in support of the addition of a college. But lately we've been getting more than studious types and tourists in search of a good deal. All sorts of riffraff are coming to town." She clapped her hand over her mouth, then removed it and whispered, "Will you listen to me? I'm starting to sound like Prudence Hart. Did I actually say *riffraff*? Heavens."

Delilah chortled.

I didn't. I flashed on the thief that had assaulted me in the tent and the other thief who had stolen ice sculpting tools, which spurred me to consider what Jordan and I had discussed. Was there anything we could do to thwart what was happening to our gentle town? Were we being overrun by riffraff? Perhaps I should suggest that Grandmère put on

the show *Brigadoon* next year. Maybe the musical would remind townsfolk that we lived in a magical place, and everyone who lived here had to do his or her part to preserve the town's innocence.

Dream on, Charlotte. One theater show would not turn the tide. Change has to be organic.

"Lose the frown," Freckles said. "Providence is fine. We're still the safest town in America. Promise."

Delilah elbowed me. "Take a gander at who just entered the pub. You have to admit he's a handsome devil."

Chip, dressed in his zippered suede jacket, striped buttoned-down shirt, and jeans, lingered by the front door, chatting with the hostess. A hint of a five-o'clock shadow outlined his jaw. His wavy hair looked windblown. The Marlboro Man couldn't have looked any better.

"Feeling any of the old passion for him?" Delilah asked.

"No."

"Don't snap at me."

Had I snapped? Yes, I probably had.

"He is awfully good looking," Freckles said.

"He's average," I said, knowing I was lying.

Tyanne clucked. "Sugar, there is nothing average about him. If he were an actor, he'd win *People* Magazine's: Most Beautiful Person award."

Chip split from the hostess and sauntered to Georgia's table. He put his hand on the back of her chair and she looked up, her eyes glistening with interest. She introduced him to the older couple and offered him the extra chair. He didn't sit. Oscar, who looked miffed at Chip's arrival, deftly wiped the scowl off his face, then stood up and clapped Chip on the shoulder as if they were old friends. He said something. Chip buffed Oscar's arm with his knuckles. Oscar bandied with a one-two jab, pulling his punches and reminding me of Bozz when he was shadowboxing. Chip countered playfully. Oscar attempted another jab at Chip's face, but Chip raised both hands to protect his jaw. At the same time, as sly as the corporate spy he claimed to be, Oscar ducked and rifled through Chip's pockets. He

came up with Chip's iPhone and danced backward in a celebratory way. Chip tried to snatch the cell phone back. In the process, he spotted me. Quickly he backed away from Oscar, made some excuse to Georgia, and strode toward me.

"Here he comes," Delilah said.

"I'm not blind."

"You're snapping again."

For good reason. Chip wasn't carrying flowers, but he looked like a man on a mission. I steeled myself. I would tell him, once and for all, that he didn't have a chance with me. With his dream of being a restaurateur squelched by Kaitlyn Clydesdale's untimely demise, it was time for him to leave Providence. I nudged Delilah to scoot out of the booth. She did, and I followed. I was almost at a full stand when Chip arrived.

"Ladies," Chip said.

Freckles tittered. I glowered at her.

"Can we talk, Charlotte?" He ran his thumb along my shoulder. "Alone?"

"Chip, I—" Why was my mouth stone-dry?

"It'll only take a minute."

"No," I managed to say. *Superb, Charlotte. Clever. Forthright. Not!*

"Fine, I'll tell you here." He hooked a finger into the loop of his jeans. "I'm moving back to France."

Relief, mixed with something else I couldn't identify, swept over me.

"Georgia has power of attorney for Kaitlyn," Chip went on. "She won't honor the contract. She's being a b—" He mashed his lips together. "A businesswoman. She's not interested in having me around."

Why didn't I believe him? She had looked way more than interested.

"I—" Chip's gaze darted to the left.

I followed his stare and saw Jordan marching past the hostess who was pointing in our direction. Jordan ground his teeth as he walked. Chip stepped toward him. The two

faced off as if they were players on the ice, waiting for a referee to blow a whistle and drop the puck.

"What's your problem?" Chip raised his chin.

"Are you bothering the lady?" Jordan demanded.

"I was telling her my plans for the future. What's it to you?"

"You know what it is."

I didn't. My pulse started to race. Would Jordan spell it out? And not in Morse code. I was no good at deciphering code. Especially when hyperventilating. He had said that he adored me. Did he love me? Would he say it in front of everyone? Now that I knew the truth about him, I could shout *I love you* back. The anticipation made me tingly all over. But he didn't utter a word.

While he glowered menacingly at Chip, I caught sight of Oscar waggling Chip's cell phone. I thumped my chest and mimed: *Me?* He nodded. Did he have someone waiting at the other end of the line that he wanted me to talk to? Not now, for heaven's sake.

I mouthed: *No.*

Oscar shook the phone harder.

Chip glanced over his shoulder. Oscar, like a copycat, peeked over his own. At Georgia? She glimpsed up from the table. Her mouth drew into a thin line of disapproval.

Oscar glanced at me, his gaze full of fear, and a new thought occurred to me. The other night when I had tackled him, he had told me that he had been working for Kaitlyn. Was that a lie? Had he been working for Georgia all along? Was his declaration of love for her a ruse? Tyanne had suggested a murder-for-hire scenario. Had Georgia paid Oscar to kill her mother? But then why would he want to talk to me? And why now? He waggled Chip's cell phone with more vigor. I was missing something, but what?

I peeked at Georgia, whose eyes burned with unbridled fury. Had Oscar borrowed Chip's cell phone another time? Had he used the telephone's camera to snap an incriminating picture of Georgia, perhaps, on the night of the murder? Or had Chip taken the photograph and Oscar had stumbled upon it?

*Be real, Charlotte. Oscar's trying to get a rise out of
you or out of Georgia.*

"Charlotte, sweetheart, what's wrong?" Jordan cut around
Chip and brushed my cheek with the back of his hand.

At the same time, the music in the pub ceased. The quiet
was unsettling.

I shivered. "Nothing."

"Something has you spooked."

I couldn't tell him about Oscar. Not in front of Chip,
who might run and blab to Georgia to get in her good
graces.

"Nothing," I repeated.

"You're lying," Chip said.

I whipped my gaze to my ex-fiancé. "You don't know
me. You don't know anything about me. When I say nothing has me spooked, nothing has me spooked."

He threw his hands up, palms forward. "Alert, alert! I'm
not the enemy."

"Had me fooled," Jordan said.

I shot him a sharp look. Chip chortled, as if he had won
round one.

I lasered my gaze back at him. "I'm sorry things haven't
worked out for you here, Chip. Good luck in all your future endeavors." A game-show host couldn't have sounded
more disingenuous. I thrust out my hand. Chip took hold and
ran his thumb along the curve. I snatched my hand back.
"Goodbye."

Chip flinched but he didn't make a peep. What could he
say? Jordan, smart man, also kept mute.

As Chip skulked away, I scanned the room for Oscar,
but he had disappeared. Before I could make excuses to
Jordan so I could track down Oscar, the antique entry door
that the pub had purchased from a defunct Irish castle
crashed open.

Quigley, the shaggy-haired reporter, barged in. "Rebe-
e-e-cca!"

Visions of a drunken Stanley Kowalski in *A Streetcar
Named Desire* boogied through my mind. Quigley wasn't

buff like Stanley, and he was wearing a rumpled linen jacket, not a tattered undershirt, but he was wild-eyed and looked highly unpredictable. He headed toward Rebecca and Ipo, who had taken seats at a small round table.

Ipo tried to leap to a stand, but a foot tangled in his chair. He and the chair slammed to the floor.

I raced to intervene, with Jordan at my heels, but Rebecca was swift. She bolted from the table, cut around the fallen Ipo, and smacked Quigley hard across the face.

CHAPTER

22

"Ouch!" Quigley scanned the pub, checking to see if anyone saw the slap. Everyone had. Jaws hung open. Quigley glanced at Rebecca, hurt filling his gaze. "Why'd you do that?"

"You . . . you . . ." Rebecca hauled back a second time.

I grabbed her arm in midair. "Cool it, Babe Ruth."

After a long, edgy moment, Rebecca whispered, "I'm good, Charlotte. Let me go."

I did. Instantly she swung again, the little snip.

Jordan, in a quicker-than-lightning move, pinned her arms to the side. "Chill, Rebecca. He's not worth a lawsuit."

Rebecca squirmed, her feet tap-dancing in front of Jordan's, but he didn't release her.

"I'd never sue her." Quigley sniffled. "I love her."

The word *love* burbled through the crowd.

"Out of the way, folks." Tim, the owner of the pub, his red hair and beard matching the burnt red plaid of his shirt, lumbered through the throng. In his hand, he carried a pitcher of ice water. If a fight got out of hand, Tim wouldn't think

twice. He would douse the participants. Water required fewer stitches than a baseball bat, he had once told me.

"Darling." Quigley dropped to the floor on one knee, emitting a grunt as he landed. He wobbled for a second, then licked his lips and said, "Will you marry me?" Fumes of alcohol drifted our way.

"For heaven's sake." Rebecca wriggled free of Jordan. He let her, I was pretty sure. She folded her arms across her chest. "No."

"Why?" Quigley teetered.

"Because she's marrying me." Ipo broke through the pack, face flushed, chest heaving with emotion.

"We're engaged," Rebecca announced, and for the first time I noticed a ring on her finger—a narrow band of gold etched with hearts. When had she received that? Why hadn't she told me? Could that have been why Ipo had looked so nervous entering the pub earlier? I could only imagine his proposal at the precinct, kneeling behind bars.

Rebecca curled into Ipo. He slung his arm around her slender back.

Quigley scrambled to his feet and tugged on the hem of his linen jacket. "But he's a murderer."

"No, he's not." Rebecca resumed her combative stance. "Take it back."

"But the luau thingies—"

"Someone took them, don't you get it?" Rebecca poked Quigley's chest. "He was robbed, and he's being set up." She whirled in a circle, pointing at everyone who had gathered around. "Ipo is innocent, do you hear me? If one of you knows something, you've got to speak up. Go to the police. It's your civic duty. And now, if you'll excuse us, we're leaving." She grabbed Ipo's hand, and as regally as she could muster, forced people to clear a path as she marched her dearly beloved out of the pub.

As the door swung shut, Quigley grazed his hair with his hands. "I don't get it. I thought she had the hots for me."

I shook my head. Apparently Chip wasn't the only man missing signals on this chilly evening.

Jordan bypassed me and patted Quigley on the back. "Hey, buddy, let's get some coffee into you."

As Jordan guided Quigley to the bar, Tim twirled a finger in the air. In an instant, Irish music resumed and members of the lookie-loo crowd returned to their tables or stools.

"Sugar." Tyanne tapped my elbow. "Come on back to the table. Food's getting cold."

As much as I wanted to assist Jordan, I had to admit that he would have better luck getting Quigley sober by himself than with me tagging along.

I returned to the booth with my friends and polished off the rest of my ciabatta appetizer. "Has anybody heard back from Jacky?"

Delilah jiggled her cell phone. "She just called. She found a sitter, but she dumped us for a date with the big guy."

I was tickled to learn Jacky and Urso might be working out whatever their issue was. I was also delighted that Urso was no longer scouring Providence for a thief. I hadn't had the chance to ask Jordan if they had tracked him down, but I didn't think either man would have given up until they had.

Licking my fingers clean, I glanced around the pub. Georgia and the elderly couple had departed, their meals virtually untouched. Oscar wasn't anywhere to be seen, either. What had he been trying to show me? Had his signal to me incited Georgia to disappear? Was there something on Chip's iPhone that would refute Georgia's alibi? Maybe Chip had a picture of her slipping out of the pub on the night of Kaitlyn's death. A time stamp on the photo could be mighty incriminating. So would a confirmation from an eyewitness. I decided now was as good a time as any to investigate, and rose to my feet.

"Back in a sec," I told my friends. I traipsed to the bar and caught up with Tim ducking under the bar's hatch door. "Hey, bartender."

Tim rose to his full six-foot height. "Hello, darlin'." Tim may have been born in America, but he loved to put on an

Irish brogue. It was good for tourists, he said. He hitched his head. "Looks like Jordan has come to the rescue again."

A few stools away, Jordan sat with Quigley, a steaming cup of coffee in front of each of them. The sight of him nursing Quigley back to sober-dom made me proud. He didn't know Quigley at all, and yet there he was, being a friend.

"Jordan's got a way about him, don't you think?" Tim said.

I cut a look back at him and tilted my head. Had he and Jordan known each other before Jordan moved to town? They had bonded right off the bat. If Jordan had been a restaurateur, the two knowing each other previously wasn't outside the realm of possibility.

If? Stop it, Charlotte. You do not want to question Jordan's story any more. Look at him. He was dealing with Quigley like a restaurant owner would. My fluttery nerves settled down, and I concentrated again on Tim.

"Got a question," I said.

Tim slung the white towel over his shoulder and spanked the bar. "Fire away, darlin'."

"Georgia Plachette said she was here playing darts on the night of Kaitlyn Clydesdale's death."

"Indeed, she was. She's an eagle eye, that one."

"Did she ever leave?"

Tim cocked an eyebrow. "I told Chief Urso all of this. Why're you asking?"

"Humor me."

Tim laughed heartily. "You are one for the books, Miz Bessette, you are. A snoop, like my mother, if ever I knew one. I couldn't slip anything past my mom." He tweaked his beard with his thumb and forefinger. "Okay, let me see. Georgia stopped throwing darts to go to the restroom once or twice."

"That's it? She didn't leave the pub?"

"Takes a world of tries to hit the bull's-eye. She was going for a record. She hit it nine times. The gang was

counting." He gestured to the crowd and leaned forward on his forearms. "Poor lass couldn't get the tenth. Some of the guys were giving her guff about that, to be sure. Your pal Chip and Luigi, as well as a few others. Luigi got into an argument with her."

"That's what Chip said."

Tim shook a finger. "Not wise. The poor sot was critiquing her form. She had a bit of an arc to the throw." He showed me the action. "Luigi said she was cheating. She sniped. He carped back. He'd had—" Tim rocked his fingers, indicating Luigi had downed a drink or two.

I flashed on Luigi at the library with his granddaughter the other day. He had looked worse for wear and had admitted that he had drunk shots the night before.

"He's a bit of a lightweight when it comes to alcohol." Tim chuckled. "Say, what's this I hear about Barton Burrell being a suspect?"

"Who told you that?"

"That delicious Tyanne." He gazed longingly over my shoulder. "While Rebecca was talking to Quigley."

I swiveled and caught Tyanne making eyes at Tim from where she sat in the booth. She coyly looked away, and I had to laugh. Something about February always stirred up romance. Perhaps St. Valentine's Day truly had a way of uniting hearts, and Tyanne's, for all intents and purposes, was available.

A clatter resounded at the end of the bar. Quigley pushed his coffee aside. He lumbered off his stool and headed my way. "Hey, you!"

Jordan tried to stop him, but Quigley eluded him.

"I heard you, O'Shea!" Quigley growled.

I felt somewhat gratified he wasn't prepared to attack me.

Tim glanced over his shoulder and thumbed his chest. "Me?"

"Yeah, I'm talking to you." Quigley sneered. "Who else around here is named O'Shea?"

"I can think of a dozen," Tim quipped, not flustered in the least. "I've got six brothers and they've all got wives and a ton of kids."

"Don't be a smart aleck. You don't know the half of it."

Half of what? I wondered, not sure I wanted to know.

"Barton Burrell is a saint. Don't go spouting bad things about him, hear me?" Quigley moved closer and banged his palm on the bar. "Barton Burrell is one of the best. He takes that wife of his back and forth. Never thinks twice."

"Back and forth where?" I asked.

"To the hospital. Week in, week out. I saw them the other night. You know"—he snapped his fingers but they didn't quite click—"that night what's-her-name died. She looked white as snow."

"Kaitlyn Clydesdale?"

"No. Emma Burrell." Quigley brandished a finger. "You know how people look when headlights of oncoming cars hit the—" He fluttered his fingers and drew them apart, at a loss for a word.

"Windshield," I said. Back in college, I was a master at charades.

"Yeah. I was driving the other direction. The lights made her look so pale." He tapped the side of his head. "A journalist notices things like this, see? Rebecca doesn't appreciate me. She goes for that . . . that hula dancer. Sheesh. I can hula." He jiggled his hips and nearly toppled over.

"Whoa, buddy." Jordan wrapped an arm around Quigley. "Let's get you home. The coffee isn't working its magic quickly enough." He cast a glance over his shoulder at me. "I'm afraid I'll miss the recital."

Recital? In the to-do, I had nearly forgotten. Yipes. I glanced at my watch. I was late, yet again. "Tyanne!"

I thanked Tim for his input and raced to the faire, my mind reeling with ideas. Why would Barton say Emma and he had been watching television the night Kaitlyn died? Why wouldn't he tell the truth about taking his wife to the hospital? That would provide a perfect alibi.

CHAPTER

23

While we were in the pub, a light snow had started to fall outside. Now, a thin layer decorated the ground. Flakes dusted my face as Tyanne and I sprinted through the Winter Wonderland tents. I dialed Urso to tell him about the new information on the Burrells. When he didn't answer, I followed with a call to the precinct. The clerk said she wasn't sure she could reach him. He was indisposed. *Indisposed*, I wanted to shout; he was with Jacky. If I wished, the clerk said she would patch me through to one of the deputies, both of whom were on non-urgent calls.

"Sugar, hear that?" Tyanne said. "The recital's starting. We might better get a move on."

The lilting strains of a piano sonata that my grandmother had written to herald the start of the recital filtered through the faire's speakers.

Not wanting to arrive late to the songfest, I left a message for Urso or one of his deputies to call me, and dashed ahead.

The recital "hall" was housed in an oversized tent with

a gaping entrance and white poles that held up the center peak. Rows of polished wooden benches, set in graceful arcs, faced a stage that was thirty feet wide. On the stage there was a three-tiered semicircle where the girls would stand. A combo band, consisting of an electric piano, guitar, and drums, was wedged into a tiny spot on the right of the stage.

Dusting snowflakes off my face, I hurried to the buffet that was set up against the tent wall. Tyanne followed. Grandmère trundled around the table, setting out napkins, forks, and shimmery blue paper plates. Pépère poured plastic cups of his spiced cider and set them in lines.

I pecked my grandmother hello. "The song you wrote is lovely, and the food looks yummy, Grandmère." I reached for a cider, but she thwacked my hand.

"Shoo. No eating or drinking until after."

"Spoilsport."

She clucked her delight.

The table was laden with a variety of dishes. Fromagerie Bessette had supplied the pepperoni-apple quiches. Providence Patisserie had provided breads and pastries. Other locals had made casseroles and an assortment of appetizers.

"By the way," I said, "did you catch the thief?"

"No, but Urso said not to worry. He has an idea who it is." She touched my cheek. "You're perspiring, *chérie*. Are you all right?"

"Tyanne and I ran the whole way here." I spotted a sign in front of a Crock-Pot that read: *Tyanne's Creole Casserole*, and I turned to her. "When did you have time?"

"This morning." She twirled a finger. "Slow cookers make everything so easy. Plop the items in and switch on the heat. It's my mama's recipe."

I gave her a knowing look. She had arrived at The Cheese Shop before eight, which meant she had to have made the casserole at the crack of dawn. "You're not sleeping, are you?"

She shook her head. "I will soon."

I drank in the scent of sausages, onions, and spices, and my stomach grumbled. Silly, I know. After eating the

ciabatta appetizer at the pub, I shouldn't have been hungry in the least, but tasty aromas always stirred my taste buds.

"Oh, there are my kids." Tyanne waved to her children. "Thomas. Tisha. Mama's—" She halted and dropped her arm to her side when her husband emerged through the tent opening with his Lolita-esque girlfriend.

"Are you going to be okay?" I asked.

"Fine, sugar." Like a steel magnolia, Tyanne shook off any sign of distress and pasted on a big smile. "My little darlings need me to be a good role model. Don't you agree?" She squeezed my arm for support, whispered, "Thanks," and then she zigzagged through the crowd toward her children.

I admired how resilient she was. Theo would have to watch out for himself in divorce court.

"Charlotte!" Matthew called. He sat at the center of the third row of benches, flanked by Meredith and Sylvie. Their coats were piled on the bench beyond Meredith.

Sylvie, still clad in her ridiculous antebellum outfit, said, "I've saved you a seat right next to me, Charlotte."

Oh, lucky day.

I scooted down the aisle. As I settled into my spot, Sylvie handed me a program. I read the list of songs that the girls would be singing and recognized many from my youth. "Meredith, did you see?" I leaned around Sylvie and pointed at a title on the program.

Meredith snickered. "Hope they can make it all the way through." She was referring to an incident from our past.

Matthew made a face, letting me know that he remembered the event. When Meredith and I were slightly older than the twins, we had sung in the Winter Wonderland chorus. Meredith was notorious for making me laugh at the most inconvenient times. For one rousing rendition of "Swing Low, Sweet Chariot"—a song the twins were going to sing—I had been given a solo. During my moment in the sun, Meredith, who was standing beside me, repeatedly cleared her throat, pretending she had a frog in it—imitating me, of course. I could have clocked her. Luckily neither of

the twins had solos. I could only imagine what precocious Amy would have done to Clair—or vice versa.

I chuckled to myself and continued reading.

"By the way, what are you wearing, Charlotte?" Sylvie plucked the sleeve of my tweed jacket. "How *tres passé*."

"Actually, I purchased it recently." I wasn't lying. I had found the jacket at a secondhand store in Columbus that specialized in businesswomen's attire. I liked the neutral tone, the wing collar, and the one-button front.

"What is fashion coming to?" Sylvie sniffed. "You and Prudence Hart have a lot to learn. Speaking of Prudence, she's so mad at your grandmother about starting a Do-Gooder chapter without inviting her. I don't think I'll ever hear the end—"

"Shhh. The recital is starting."

A dozen girls in scarlet robes trotted onto the stage and formed two lines.

"There are our babies, Matthew. Amy! Clair!" Sylvie rose from the bench and waved her arms like she was guiding in a 747 airplane.

Matthew looked like he wanted to disappear into the fake green grass flooring.

The conductor, none other than my friend Octavia, strode in front of the chorale. She swept back the folds of her chorale robe and, facing the audience, took a brief bow. Then she pivoted, brushed her cornrow braids over her shoulder, and struck a baton on the music stand. The musicians began and the chorus launched into a breezy version of "Let It Snow" followed by "Big Rock Candy Mountain," "She Loves You," and "Swing Low, Sweet Chariot."

In between the fourth and fifth songs, Sylvie said, "Like I was saying, Prudence is so mad—"

I flicked her hoopskirt. "Sylvie, please. Wait until the songfest is over."

"I'm simply saying that your grandmother had better watch her backside. You never know when someone like Prudence might thwack her with one of those . . . those"—she flicked her finger toward the stage—"batons."

I followed to where she pointed and a shiver wriggled up the back of my neck as Octavia raised one hand overhead to hold the girls in a vocal pause. In her other hand, she poised the baton, ready for the downbeat. The image made me think of the weapon that was used to fell Kaitlyn Clydesdale. Had she seen the attack coming or had she been taken by surprise? Had she arrived at Rebecca's cottage to argue with Ipo, only to find that someone had followed her? Whoever it was had arrived with the pu'ili stick in hand. Was it Arlo, trying to keep her from telling the world about his kleptomania? Or Oscar, who had wanted to be released from his employment contract? Or her daughter, Georgia, who stood to inherit cash and possibly control of Clydesdale Enterprises? I wouldn't rule out Barton Burrell either, despite Quigley's assertion that Barton had not one but two alibis that might stand up in court. Barton's real estate contract bound him to sell, and Emma wanted to nullify it. And then there was the rumored affair—

"O-o-o-oh." The chorus of girls held a long note, drawing me back to the moment at hand, and then they broke into a bubbly version of "She'll Be Coming 'Round the Mountain."

As they headed into the second verse, Sylvie whispered, "You know, I was a great singer when I was young. I started a band. We called it Spicy Chicks."

I whispered, "Shhh."

"When the Spice Girls stole the name and became famous, I was ready to wreak bloody havoc on them. I was so jealous."

Another theory about Kaitlyn's death invaded my thoughts. Was jealousy the reason for the attack? I didn't believe Lois had hurt Kaitlyn. Though she was upset now, she had a backbone of iron. She wouldn't have let Ainsley's momentary fling with Kaitlyn drive her to violence. Had some other wife lashed out? Emma Burrell, perhaps?

The girls finished singing, and Octavia turned to the crowd.

"For our finale . . ." Octavia spread her arms and beck-

oned us all to stand and join in the singing of "America, the Beautiful," one of my all-time favorite songs. The lyric about amber waves of grain perfectly depicted the hills of Ohio in autumn.

When the song ended, the audience cheered. The applause died out and folks started to filter from the benches toward the buffet.

Sylvie trailed me like a shadow, chattering about her failed musical career. Matthew and Meredith followed.

"Sylvie Bessette!" Prudence plowed into the tent.

Everyone turned to stare.

"Aha. There you are." Prudence charged through the crowd, her arms pumping like pistons. "How dare you."

Matthew moaned. "What did you do now, Sylvie?"

"Nothing," Sylvie replied, but I saw amusement in her eyes. She had done something, all right. On purpose.

"You have crossed the line." Prudence reached the buffet, plucked a handful of canapés, and without an ounce of hesitation, hurled.

Canapés pelted Sylvie in the face and chest. One slipped down her lacy cleavage.

Sylvie plucked it out, dropped it on the ground, then winked at me. Before I could stop her, she grabbed a pepperoni-apple quiche and raced at Prudence. With the precision of a slapstick clown, Sylvie planted the quiche in Prudence's face. For extra effect, she twisted it a quarter-turn.

My grandfather looked shocked. Grandmère couldn't hide her glee. I gave her a stern look. She flitted a wrist, pooh-poohing me.

"Why you—" Prudence scooped the quiche custard off her face and flung the goop to the ground. "I'll have you know that my dress shop is not under investigation for infestation."

Oh, my. Rumors heaped upon more rumors.

"Whoever would have suggested such a thing?" Sylvie countered.

"I know it was you," Prudence yelled.

"Liar!"

"Slut!" Prudence grasped Sylvie's bodice and yanked.

Sylvie thwacked Prudence's hands with her lace fan and snapped her jaw as if she meant to bite.

"Enough. Stop it, both of you." I grabbed Sylvie's shoulders and, tugging with all my might, pried her away.

Matthew and Meredith reined in Prudence.

"I'll take you to court, Sylvie Bessette," Prudence said, struggling to get free.

"Not before I see your dreadful boutique fold, you cow." Sylvie broke free of me, swooped her antebellum skirt into a bundle, and skulked out of the tent without a goodbye.

Amy and Clair and the rest of the singers raced toward us, mouths agape.

"Where's Mum going?" Clair said. Her eyes glistened with tears.

"What happened?" Amy looked to Matthew for an answer.

He took the high road and kept quiet.

* * *

A short while later, after helping my grandparents clean up the mess, Matthew, Meredith, and I steered the twins out of the tent and into the cool night. Snow had stopped falling and the temperature had risen a smidge, turning the pretty layer of white into mush. The twins, intent on making squishy sounds in the wetness, quickly forgot about their mother. As they played, they chattered with excitement about the songfest.

"Did you hear the redhead miss the high note?" Amy said.

"Did you see Thomas smiling at Amy?" Clair asked.

"Did you notice Mrs. Tibble mouthing each and every word?" they said in unison.

The aroma of warm liquor and the tinkle of happy laughter drew my attention. Ahead, Delilah hovered beside the La Bella Ristorante concession cart—a cute red box on wheels, fitted with gas burners, a stainless-steel serving

station, and a flagpole brandishing an Italian flag. Luigi and one of his sous chefs were assembling Italian *dulce* crepes. A hand-scrawled sign gave the filling ingredients: ricotta cheese and Grand Marnier. A crowd of tourists and towns-folk stood nearby, transfixed as Luigi poured the liqueur into a skillet and set the skillet on a burner.

But my gaze was drawn to a spot beyond them, by the ice sculpture of the giant tooth. Urso and Jacky were having what looked like an intense conversation. Plumes of warm breath clouded the air in front of Jacky's mouth. A frown creased her pretty face. She poked Urso's black Patagonia jacket with her finger to make a point.

"Matthew, girls. I'll see you at home. I need to chat with Urso." I kissed the twins and gave them a mock-stern look. "Make sure you brush your teeth for two minutes."

"Yeah, yeah, yeah," they sang à la the Beatles and, gig-gling, ran ahead of Meredith and their father.

As I drew nearer to Urso and Jacky, I could hear passion in Jacky's tone.

". . . not your property, understand?" She gave his chest a final slap, then turned on her heel and dashed away.

Was Urso being too territorial? Was that the problem festering between them? Only last year, Jacky had confided that one of the major problems in her marriage had been that her husband had demanded to know where she was at all times. Every relationship needed breathing space.

Pretending I had heard none of their conversation, I put on a game face and nabbed Urso before he could run off. He was still our chief of police, and he had a murder to solve.

"What's up?" His eyes looked strained, his jaw tight. "I was planning on returning your call."

I told him about Barton Burrell's new alibi. "Quigley said Barton was taking Emma to the hospital. It was a regular occurrence. I know she lost more than one child to a miscarriage. Perhaps she was pregnant again and some-thing happened."

"Why lie?" Urso said.

"Exactly. Something's up with—"

"Whoa!" A roar and applause exploded from the crowd around Delilah and Luigi.

I glanced over my shoulder. Flames flared from the skillet. The sight triggered something in my mind, but I couldn't for the life of me figure out what.

Adjust your thinking, my grandfather had said, and I tried, but nothing registered.

And then, like a vision, through the flames I caught sight of Barton Burrell hurrying after Emma. I didn't see their three boys anywhere. Barton grabbed his wife's arm and spun her around. She mouthed easily understood words— *You lied*—and raised her hand to smack him. He gripped her wrist, then his gaze turned sad. In slow motion, he released her, and as if he was working hard to harness his anger, stormed away.

Emma staggered backward. She looked ready to fall.

I raced to catch her.

CHAPTER

24

I slung an arm around Emma. The dormant grass between the tents was soggy from melted snow, and moisture would soak through her wool coat and corduroy slacks in seconds, but I didn't think she could remain standing. She was vibrating with anxiety. I guided her to the ground.

"Wait. Have her sit on this, Charlotte." Urso removed his jacket and placed it directly beneath Emma. She gave him a look of thanks. He pivoted and eyed the people circling us. "Show's over, folks. Give the lady room." As the crowd dispersed, he knelt on one knee beside us. "Do you want some water, Mrs. Burrell?"

She nodded. Urso rose to his feet and strode off.

"What's going on, Emma?" I said, keeping my tone gentle and unthreatening. "Why did Barton stomp away?"

"Angry."

Got that. "Why?" I said.

"Kids," Emma muttered.

"What about the kids?" Getting one-word answers was frustrating. I stroked her hair. "C'mon, you can talk to me."

"Girls."

"You have boys."

She sucked in a breath. "Almost had girls."

I took hold of her hand. She gripped my fingers like a vise as her eyes searched mine for something. Support? Redemption?

Urso returned with a bottle of water, uncapped it, and passed it to me.

I pressed it into Emma's hands. "Drink." She did, but not enough. I said, "Sip more if you can."

She drank hungrily, then coughed hard. When the coughing subsided, she whispered, "I started the argument."

"Why?"

She shrugged. "So difficult . . . Anniversary."

"It's your anniversary?"

She shook her head sharply. "A baby. We lost a baby."

Now I was getting the picture. "You miscarried a year ago."

"I get so angry. And I"—she covered her mouth with the back of her hand—"I—"

"Urso!" Delilah squealed. "Quick!"

A whoosh split the calm. The throng around the La Bella Ristorante cart screamed.

The Italian flag on the concession cart had caught on fire. Huge licks of flame rose from the skillet. Heat tumbled through the air. A spit of fire flew sideways and fell to the ground.

Urso bolted to the cart. "Back up! Everyone! Delilah, fetch a fire extinguisher."

Extinguishers were located every fifty to one hundred feet throughout the faire. Ten years ago a fire on Founder's Day had destroyed a quarter of the tents. No people were hurt, only merchandise, but Grandmère vowed it would never happen again. She had summoned extra city funds to pay for safety precautions.

I turned back to Emma, who looked dazed with fear. The reflection of fire danced in her hazel eyes. "C'mon, Emma, on your feet."

She resisted and whispered, "Barton lied."

"On your feet," I repeated. "It's not safe here."

"He lied."

"I heard you. And I know he lied. You weren't home that night watching TV. Please get up."

"Coming through, Charlotte." Delilah raced past me with a pair of fire extinguishers and gave them to Urso and Luigi.

"That night . . ." Emma allowed me to hoist her to a stand. She was heavier than she looked. Sturdy bones, my grandmother would say. " . . . the night Kaitlyn Clydesdale died, Barton and I were driving."

Even though the crisis was contained, I struggled to move her away from the commotion to a quieter spot in between a cluster of tents. I said, "You were going to the hospital."

She shook her head.

"Where were you going?"

"To a rehab clinic."

I gaped at her. "Do you have an addiction?"

"It's complicated."

Earlier, when Barton and his sons had found her, he had removed a soda bottle from her hands. Had it been filled with liquor or laced with pills? Had she separated from them a second time and found another source to nurse her habit, thus reigniting Barton's wrath?

I said, "You and Barton lied to Chief Urso because you didn't want people to know you had an addiction."

"Don't talk to her, Emma!" Barton hustled toward us, the front of his overcoat flapping open. He reminded me of a hawk ready to descend upon its quarry. He snatched Emma from my grasp and looked down his nose at me. "You have no right to snoop around our lives."

I faced him. "Why did you lie to Chief Urso?"

"What did you tell her?" he demanded of his wife.

I said, "You went back and forth to a rehab facility with regularity."

"No," Emma whispered.

She could deny it, but I knew what she had said.

"That's a lie," Barton yelled.

"You thought people in town would suspect Emma had an addiction." I kept my gaze fixed on him. "You were worried about your reputation."

"No, Charlotte," Emma said, this time more firmly. "I don't have an addiction."

I shot her a look. "But you said you were at the rehab facility that night."

"Only that night. Every other week we were going to the hospital for checkups."

"Useless checkups," Barton grumbled. His shoulders sagged.

"That night, it was the anniversary of"—Emma sucked back a sob—"of our last baby miscarrying. I couldn't handle it. I took pills. A lot of pills. I needed my stomach pumped. We went to the rehab facility because we knew they'd keep it private." She sighed. "Yes, Barton was worried that people would think the worst." She eyed him. "You did."

Barton pulled Emma closer and kissed the side of her forehead. "I'm sorry."

She mouthed: *Me, too.* "Where are the boys?"

"With your mother." Barton glowered at me. "If you say a word, Charlotte . . ."

"I'm not the nightly news, Barton, but unless you tell Chief Urso the truth, you could be a suspect in Kaitlyn Clydesdale's death. Watching television with your wife is not a good alibi, no matter what you think. And you need a good alibi. Word is that you didn't want to sell your property. You wanted out of the contract, but Kaitlyn wouldn't let you renege."

"How do you know that?"

"There are also rumors that you were having an affair with her."

"What? No frigging way!" He released his wife and smacked his gloved hands together. "I'll bet she started that rumor herself, dang it. Kaitlyn was a horrible woman. She

preyed on us. At times I thought of killing her. I imagined ways I would do it."

"An actor's mind is a creative sinkhole," Emma said. "Luckily, he's a farmer by day."

"Kaitlyn knew every facet of our lives," Barton went on.

"Did she blackmail you to coerce you to proceed with the deal?"

"No, she didn't have to. She knew what we owed. With three boys and medical insurance and the cost of keeping the farm, she knew we were strapped. But I wouldn't have put it past her to blackmail some of the more stubborn folk who didn't want to sell. Our property was the lynchpin."

"For what?"

"I'm not sure. I heard her telling Chip Cooper that she was after Urso's parents' property, too."

I gaped. Could that have been the *property* that Jacky and Urso had been arguing about? Did their argument have nothing to do with their relationship? Perhaps Kaitlyn had wanted to own the entire north section of town. I recalled Lois saying that Kaitlyn owned cattle farms, sheep farms, wineries, and more. It was the *more* that worried me now. Visions of combining lush green landscapes weren't scudding across my mind; visions of megastores and strip malls popping up on the north side of town were. According to Lois, Kaitlyn hated for things to be *behind the times.* Had she planned to update Providence by destroying the very thing that made Providence a desirable place to raise a family? I wasn't concerned about competition for The Cheese Shop. A megastore wouldn't carry many gourmet delights nor offer tastings, but a megastore might carry books and clothing and cause places like All Booked Up and The Spotted Giraffe to lose sales.

Emma said, "And now her CFO is after the properties."

"Georgia Plachette?"

"She's evil."

"Shhh, honey." Barton wrapped his arm around his wife's shoulders again. "We don't want to malign an innocent."

"She's not innocent," Emma hissed. "She's a shark. She looks so vulnerable with that curly hair and that pixie smile, but she's wicked." She shot an earnest look at me. "She's been stalking us, Charlotte. Trying to get dirt on us. She said things to my children. To my children! And to my doctor. And my hairdresser. She said we weren't honorable because we wanted out of our contract. You should question her, Charlotte. I wouldn't put it past her to have hired someone to off her mother."

The words hit me like a flat-ironed pan. Had Tyanne been right about that angle?

"If you're going to question her, do it quickly," Emma added. "I think she's getting ready to leave town. I saw her entering Violet's Victoriana Inn at a clip."

I thought of Oscar shaking his phone to me in the pub and his look back at Georgia. I could have sworn he had been the frightened one. Was Georgia afraid of Oscar because he could pin a murder on her? Had she hired him to do it?

I raced back to the crepe cart to invite Urso to join me for a chat with Georgia before she hightailed it out of town, but he wasn't there. I cornered Delilah, whose nose was smudged with soot. She smelled like fire-extinguisher foam.

"Where's Urso?" I said.

"On an urgent mission." Delilah smirked. "Starts with a J and ends with a Y—Jacky," she added, as if I hadn't guessed. "She stopped by the cart, crooked a finger, and he was off in a flash. Why do you need him?"

I didn't have time to explain.

CHAPTER

25

In her brochures, Violet called her Victoriana Inn a state-of-the-art bed-and-breakfast. In my humble opinion, the terms were mutually exclusive. While Lois had decked out the Lavender and Lace B&B in cushy couches, exquisite old carpets, and lace curtains, Violet had streamlined her inn using spartan furniture, no carpeting, and sleek blinds. Lois lured customers with home-cooked meals; Violet's chef offered spa food that would make even a vegetable-loving rabbit lose weight. From the rear of Lavender and Lace, guests could take long walks into the hills. At the back of Violet's Victoriana Inn, there was a gym filled with stair steppers, treadmills, and weight machines. If I were on vacation, I would opt for Lavender and Lace every time.

But Violet's Victoriana Inn didn't lack for clientele. The parking lot was filled with BMWs, Mercedes, Lexuses, and other high-end automobiles. The great room swarmed with well-dressed people talking about their days' adventures.

Violet, wearing a white jogging suit that was one size too small for her chunky shape, danced behind the reception

desk, keeping time with the jazzy music being piped through the overhead speakers. Her marshmallow-colored pigtails flopped in syncopated rhythm. "Hi, Charlotte. Can't stop. On a diet." Violet's weight swung like a pendulum. Up thirty pounds, down thirty pounds.

"I'm looking for Georgia Plachette."

"At this time of night?" She huffed and puffed.

"It's not even nine yet."

"That's late in Providence."

"Please, Violet."

She grabbed a white towel from beneath the check-in counter and wiped the sheen of perspiration from above her fleshy lips. "It's so sad what Georgia is going through. Did you know she's Kaitlyn Clydesdale's daughter?"

I nodded. I didn't add that I suspected Georgia might have put a hit on her mother. Too much information. "Is she here?"

"Funny you should ask. I just called her room to say her guests had arrived." She wiggled her fingers at the elderly woman and gentleman who had been at the pub with Georgia. They sat on a stiff-backed bench that was situated between two perfectly trimmed and potted ficus trees. "Georgia's packing. She's heading off with them soon."

"Are they her grandparents?" I asked, to verify my assessment.

"Sure are. Sweet couple. I hear they're going back to California to have a burial at sea." She wrinkled her nose. "Me, I'm all about ritual. A person should have a real funeral service and be buried in a casket in a cemetery. This whole ashes-to-ashes thing gives me the heebie-jeebies."

Cremation didn't bother me. My parents had specified in their wills that they wanted whoever survived them to bury their remains at the top of Kindred Hill. My grandparents had asked that an oak be planted on top of their ashes. From the center of town, I could see the thirty-year-old oak tree, and I drew strength from it.

I said, "Do you think I could visit Georgia in her room?"

Violet reached for the telephone.

I tapped her wrist. "Please don't call her. We're friends. I simply want to make sure she's got everything she needs before she leaves town. She's in room . . ." I let my voice trail off.

"You know I can't tell you that."

"I'll help you get a date with the guy who runs Café au Lait." Only last week, I had noticed Violet making eyes at the guy in The Cheese Shop. She usually liked soft-centered cheeses, but she had inched toward the brick cheese section where he was standing and had started chatting about *terroir*—like she knew anything about how cheese drew its flavors from the earth.

"Room two thirteen," Violet whispered.

Easy as bringing a cheese to room temperature.

* * *

A minute later, I rapped on Georgia's door and mumbled, "Peanut butter watermelon," a trick I had learned from Grandmère when she directed crowd scenes on stage. The words slurred together and sounded like a whole slew of other words.

Georgia, clad in yet another revealing black sheath and clunky five-inch heels, opened the door. The instant she saw me, she slapped a hand on her narrow hip and frowned. "You're not housekeeping."

"Didn't say I was."

She grumbled. "What do you want at this time of night?"

"May I come in? I thought I would get a chance to chat with you at the pub, but you left so quickly."

Her gaze darted to the sleek satin bed. A suitcase piled with black clothing lay on top. Pairs of platform shoes were lined up at the foot. Her red briefcase stood on the zebra-striped area rug beside one of the bed's legs. Files poked from the opening. Something drew my gaze back to the suitcase. A toiletry kit sat on the back flap of the suitcase. An iPhone was perched on top of that. It looked like Chip's. Had Georgia wrested it away from Oscar?

"Leaving town with your grandparents?" I asked.

"How'd you know who they were?"

"I'm psychic." I winked, trying to keep things light.

She huffed. "That Violet. She can't keep a secret."

"You look like your grandmother. You have the same eyes, the same pretty chin."

Reflexively, Georgia's hand moved toward her face. She stopped short and sneezed. Clearly exasperated with me, she traipsed to the bureau, her five-inchers clip-clopping as she reached the hardwood floor, and grabbed a tissue from a box. "Dang cold." She blew her nose.

Without invitation, I moseyed into the room. My fingers itched to get hold of the cell phone. "I hear you're returning to California. Violet said you're planning a burial at sea."

Georgia muttered, "Violet," and rasped a series of dry coughs.

"Brandy would soothe your throat."

"Yeah, like Violet would have something as decadent as brandy in this place. There's no wine, no beer. Nothing. I can order chamomile tea, but I'm tea'd out. What I need is a good cough syrup."

I pulled an herbal cough drop from my purse and handed it to her. A peace pipe couldn't have been more warmly received. She peeled off the paper, slipped the lozenge into her mouth, and murmured her relief.

Treading softly, I said, "I saw you sitting with Oscar Carson at the pub."

"Oscar." She sighed as she worked the lozenge to the inside of her cheek. "He didn't really work for Ipo Ho. He—" She started coughing again.

I patted her back, but she waved me off, raced to the bathroom, and kicked the door closed. I heard the clatter of a glass, followed by water gushing into the sink. I glanced at the cell phone and didn't hesitate. I needed to learn what Oscar had seen on it. As I reached for it, it rang.

"Drat." Georgia opened the bathroom door a couple of inches and waved her arm. "Could you hand that to me?"

I picked up the iPhone. The readout read: *Nana*, which

meant the phone wasn't Chip's. Both of his grandmothers had died years ago. I offered it to Georgia.

Without a thank-you, she closed the door, and I heard her mumble, "Yes, Nana. In a sec, I told you."

I peeked at the briefcase beside the bed. No time like the present. If Georgia had a clear-cut motive to kill her mother—like a will ceding her a sizeable estate or making her the sole owner of Clydesdale Enterprises—Urso deserved to know about it. I started with the file bearing her full name on the label. In it, I found a contract for employment, which included a starting salary that was measly at best. No language stated that she would receive bonuses for a job well done. In addition, the file included a copy of Georgia's graduation certificate from the University of Southern California. Post-its had been attached to both documents, with handwritten notes saying Kaitlyn had reviewed and approved them. I didn't detect a hint of favoritism, as Georgia had implied in our previous meeting at the Clydesdale Enterprises office.

The second file contained a list of the company's holdings, which included several strip malls across the country. As I feared, a megastore was the anchor at each. Kaitlyn hadn't been interested in returning to Providence and soaking up the local flavor. She had intended to change the landscape for profit. How many locals had known? How many of those people would have wished Kaitlyn a speedy and not-so-fond farewell?

The third file held plat maps of Providence properties. I flipped through them, looking for a document or will granting Georgia millions buried within them, but found nothing.

As the door handle to the bathroom turned, guilty heat gushed through my veins. I couldn't let her catch me snooping. As I raced to restore order to the briefcase, Georgia's cell phone jangled a second time.

From within the bathroom, Georgia said, "Now what?"

Using those few precious seconds, I stuffed the files into

her briefcase. I was rising to full height when Georgia stepped out carrying a pair of scissors. She pointed them at me, her face pinched with what could only be described as intense pain.

I gulped. Did she mean to run me through? Where had she left her cell phone? I would have preferred it to the scissors. I raised my hands, palms toward her in a placating gesture. "You're upset."

"I'm sick."

Okay, I could go with that. Twisted, perhaps.

"Are you spying on me?" Brandishing the scissors, she indicated the briefcase.

I cursed silently. One of the files was jutting up—a dead giveaway. Rebecca would be appalled at my shabby sleuthing skills. "Um . . . I was interested in what Clydesdale Enterprises was up to."

She edged toward me.

Though my pulse raced, I would lie, lie, lie if it would save my hide. "Rumor has it that your mother was trying to buy parcels along the northern route out of town. I wanted to see which—"

"Buy? Are you kidding me?"

I ogled the scissors. "Um, why don't you put those down so we can talk?"

Georgia glimpsed at the shears and back at me, then sneezed. The intense expression on her face faded. Had she been trying to hold in the sneeze? Her mouth turned up in a wry smile. She flipped the scissors around in her hand and offered them to me, butt first. "I was hoping you could trim a lock at the back of my head. I can't reach it." She spun around and pointed. "See it? Dead center. Curls are tough for even the best hairdressers."

I felt myself blush with relief. She didn't want to kill me. She wanted a helping hand. Trying to keep the conversation going, I said, "You seemed surprised when I said your mother wanted to buy property north of town."

Without looking at me, she said, "It was the word *buy*

that got me. She wasn't trying to buy anything. She was blackmailing people for the parcels."

"Really?" I said innocently. I could act as dumb as the best of 'em. I snipped off the offending inch-long curl and held it out to her.

Georgia took the lock and strode to the bureau. She checked out the back of her hair in the mirror and nodded with satisfaction. She held out a hand for the return of the scissors. I was a bit reluctant, needless to say, but I granted her wish. She set the scissors on the shiny silver runner that ran the length of the bureau and gazed again at me. "Townsfolk didn't want to sell," she said. "Many were savvy to my mother's wiles. So she resorted to her true nature. She got dirt on people and *voilá*." Her mouth pursed with distaste.

"I thought you said you liked your mother."

She sniffed, but this time it wasn't from her illness. "Truth? I feel like I can trust you."

I felt a smidge guilty for having raided her files, but not guilty enough to dissuade her from continuing.

"I hated her. No, that's much too gentle a word. I despised her. She didn't approve of anything I did. Who I dated. Where I lived."

I thought of the Post-its in Georgia's personnel folder. What kind of contempt had she suffered from her mother throughout her lifetime?

"I got over it," Georgia went on, "because I didn't approve of her either. I didn't like the way she did business or of the way she treated people. She was vicious."

And yet Chip said Georgia had been acting with similar heinous intent. So did the Burrells. She had been stalking them and ruining their reputation. Was she playing me?

"Why did you work for her?" I asked.

"When I graduated college, I needed a job. Nobody was hiring." She worried her hands together. "I thought I could put in a year and find another job, but I couldn't. It took fifteen years." She muttered something about a weak economy. "The day before my mother died, I learned that a

realty firm specializing in purchasing hotels wanted to hire me. I asked to quit, but my mother wouldn't let me." Georgia tilted her head, eyeing me like an apprehensive puppy. "Please don't think I would've killed her over a contract. Mother was tough, but in time, I could've persuaded her to release me."

"Not everyone could have."

"True."

"Like Oscar, for instance."

"Good old delusional Oscar." Georgia wrapped a curl around a finger.

"Do you know where he is?"

"Home, I expect, sleeping off a few too many beers." She released the curl. "Did you see him at the pub prancing around with Chip's iPhone? Men!"

Did she like him? There was a sparkle in her eye. However, despite her more relaxed demeanor, I couldn't erase the vision of Oscar looking fearfully at her at the pub. "Why did he want Chip's cell phone?"

Georgia coughed out a nasal laugh. "He made Chip a bet that he could win the heart of anyone Chip had in his little black book. Chip didn't want to give him the phone, but Oscar"—she clopped the floor with her heel—"let's just say he can be quite persistent."

"Do you know he's in love with you?"

"Yes." She sighed. "He was going to talk to my mother that night to beg out of his contract so he could ask me on a date. She was dead before he could."

"Do you think he killed her?"

"Oscar?" She shook her head. Her mane of curls bounced with abandon. "Not a chance."

"Are you sure? He's an actor. Did you know that?"

She gaped. Apparently she didn't know.

"That would make him a good liar," I said.

Georgia offered a dismissive wave of her hand. "He didn't kill my mother. He's much too passive."

"When he was playing with Chip's cell phone, he looked at you oddly. Like he was scared."

Her mouth twisted up on one side. "He'd better be scared. I told him if he called one of those women, he was toast."

Aha! So she did like him.

But that didn't solve my quandary. Oscar had wanted out of his contract. What if he met with Kaitlyn? What if she laughed in his face? What if rage, fueled by his love for Georgia, made him lash out?

CHAPTER

26

I spent another few minutes with Georgia. Although she wouldn't buy into my theory that Oscar might be guilty, as a favor to me and to our illustrious police force, she promised not to depart Providence until noon tomorrow. She assured me that as long as she was around, Oscar wouldn't leave town. I had to give her credit for believing in the power of her female allure.

As I drove home, headlights glaring through the windshield, wipers whisking icy rain off the glass, a chill gripped my body. A short while later, in the warmth of my kitchen, with my Briard and Ragdoll for companionship—the rest of the household was quiet—I settled at the table with a soothing cup of Cinnamon Stick tea and dialed Urso to update him on my findings. The clerk at the precinct answered. She explained that Urso and both of his deputies were dealing with another round of emergencies. Urso and the new-hire deputy were roping off a flooding road; the other deputy was aiding a stranded driver whose engine had erupted.

Frustrated that Urso and I had yet to complete a conversation in the past few days, I trudged upstairs. Rocket and Rags followed. I didn't tell them no. I needed company.

In the privacy of my room, I nestled on my bed and hit the first number on my speed dial. Jordan answered after one ring.

"Hey, gorgeous."

Hearing his throaty voice sent a rapture of good vibes through me. I didn't care that he hadn't said what I had hoped he would say at the pub when he and Chip had faced off. I was simply happy that we had gotten over the hump of his secret past, and I loved him. That was all there was to it. He would say he loved me, in time.

I asked him about Quigley.

"He'll sleep it off. How was the recital?"

I told him about Sylvie and Prudence's spat. He laughed.

"I miss you, sweetheart," he said. "We need a night. Or two. Or six."

More yummy feelings swirled through me. I murmured, "Soon." I didn't tell him about Emma Burrell's collapse or my meeting with Georgia. I didn't want our conversation to end with a warning to be careful. I whispered, "Soon," again and sent kisses through the receiver.

After washing my face and brushing my teeth, I cuddled beneath my duvet, read three delicious chapters of a new Domestic Diva Mystery, and finally, unable to keep my eyes open any longer, drifted to sleep.

* * *

The next morning, while coffee was brewing and a San Simon cheese frittata cooked on the stovetop, I trotted to the porch to fetch the newspaper. Bracing myself for the crisp morning air—more inclement weather was imminent, promising a sturdy wind and the possibility of a wintry mix—I swung open the door. Hundreds of icicles had formed after last night's rain and hung from the eaves. I ducked beneath a huge one and headed down the steps but stopped short when I spotted luggage sitting on the veranda

at Lavender and Lace. Seeing one of the suitcases whip-lashed me back to memory lane, to the first day of fresh-man year at OSU. Chip had appeared in the doorway of my dorm room, brown leather satchel in his hand, camera at the ready, dimple etched in his cheek. He snapped a picture of me and whisked me into his arms. "I transferred because of you, babe," he said. In record time, our relationship had zoomed to the next level. And now he was leaving. For good. I felt relieved and sad, all at the same time. I didn't love him anymore. I never would. Years ago, I had torn up the mental picture of us as a lifelong couple. Matthew was right. I had been engaged to Peter Pan—the boy who wouldn't grow up.

I considered going over and offering Chip a formal goodbye, but I halted when a silhouette in the shadows on the side of the inn caught my attention. Lois's husband, Ainsley, moved from window to window, popping up then hunkering down, reminding me of a meerkat needing an all-clear signal from the pack. The hackles on the back of my neck rose. When Lois had booted Ainsley out, he had tried to pilfer his prized hockey stick from the wall in the great room, though he had claimed he was merely adjusting its alignment. Did he hope to steal it now?

Lois burst from the tornado shelter. Dressed in a laven-der snowsuit and wielding a broom, she charged her hus-band. "You!" Her emergence from below made me recall a reference about the Furies in *The Iliad* by Homer. The Furies were: "Those who beneath the earth punish whoso-ever has sworn a false oath."

Was I wrong to suspect Oscar of killing Kaitlyn Clydes-dale? Was Ainsley, Kaitlyn's former lover, the real culprit? Had he lied to me about his whereabouts on the night she died? He only had a dog as his witness.

Lois yelled, "I told you to leave, don't you know."

"Lois, darling."

"Go! Get! I do not want to set eyes on you again, you lying, detestable womanizer." She flailed the broom.

Ainsley, fleet for someone so wide, hightailed it down

the street. Occasionally he slipped on icy patches but quickly righted himself. Had he been equally speedy and agile stealing into Ipo's place and taking his pu'ili sticks? Had he been the broad-shouldered thief running from my tent after filching a carton of cheese?

I paused and thought again of Oscar waggling Chip's iPhone. What if he hadn't been signaling me about a list of Chip's conquests? I returned to my previous notion. What if Chip had a photograph on his cell phone? Chip was always taking pictures. Without knowing the significance, he might have snapped a picture of Ainsley hiding the pu'ili sticks on the night of the murder.

No, he couldn't have. Chip had been at the pub with Luigi. But something—some piece of evidence—was on his cell phone. As Rebecca would say, I felt it in my bones.

I glanced toward the kitchen. The frittata was cooking on low; it wouldn't burn, and I needed to view Chip's phone. Now.

I scooted down the steps of my home, the nippy wind cutting through my silk honey-colored sweater and cotton trousers, and raced along the slippery sidewalk. My loafers skidded as I darted up the path to the inn. "Lois, is Chip here?"

She huffed. "Did you see that no-good husband of mine lurking around here? The gall." Her eyes grew watery. "I gave him my best years. The best, don't you know. You'd do right to stay single. All men are worthless." She turned on her heel and barged into the bed-and-breakfast, my question unanswered.

"Where's Chip?" I repeated, shivering, wishing I had grabbed a jacket before racing out of the house.

"He's gone out for one last sightseeing tour," she said through the screened door. "He said he'd be back in a while."

"Tell him I need to speak with him."

Church bells gonged, jarring me to act. I had to track down Oscar and get the scoop. Before I could, I had to finish serving up breakfast. I retrieved the morning newspaper,

sprinted back to my kitchen, and popped the frittata under the broiler. Three minutes later, as I was dishing the frittata onto plates, Matthew entered, rubbing sleep from his eyes.

"Mmm. Smells good. Let me guess." He placed his hands on the counter and peeked beneath the cabinets. "You used San Simon, a cow's cheese from Spain. Melts nicely and pairs well with sausage and spices."

"Cheater. You read the cheese label."

"Did not."

"You've trapped it beneath your hands."

He chortled and revealed his ruse.

I scooted around the counter with the plates.

"Why are you rushing?" he asked.

"Got someplace to be."

"Where?"

"Someplace." I set the plates on the table, yelled, "Girls, breakfast," and then hurried to the foyer. Rocket and Rags jogged after me, their claws clicking as they scurried around corners.

Matthew trailed the pack. "Where's the fire?"

"No fire. Just an errand."

"An errand. Uh-huh, and I'm competing on *Dancing with the Stars*." At the age of twelve, Matthew had taken ballroom dancing lessons, and on occasion, I caught him doing the cha-cha with one of the twins in the kitchen, but he wasn't what I would call dance savvy. "Tell me the truth," he said. "Who are you investigating now?"

I couldn't lie to Matthew. I simply couldn't. "I think Oscar Carson might know who killed Kaitlyn Clydesdale."

Matthew bayed like a hound. "Snoop Doggy Dogg."

Rocket echoed him. Rags yowled.

"Hush, you guys," I said.

Matthew frowned. "Have you let Urso in on your theories?"

"I've left messages." Myriad messages.

"And . . . ?"

"It's Sunday." I shrugged into my camel coat, looped a multicolored scarf around my neck, slung my purse over my

shoulder, and donned a pair of brown gloves. "Not everyone is up at the crack of sunrise like us."

"I'm tagging along."

"No, you and the girls are going with Meredith to church."

"It's not safe for you—"

"Oscar is not the killer."

"How can you be sure?" Matthew gripped my shoulders, his gaze filled with concern. "And don't tell me gut instinct."

A knock rattled the door. Expecting Chip, I opened quickly.

Rebecca faced me wearing no jacket, no hat, and no gloves. She was shivering. Her lips were nearly blue.

Fear spiked inside me. "What's wrong?"

"He . . . we . . ." She rushed inside. "I stayed the night at Ipo's."

"Oka-a-a-ay." I closed the door.

"He didn't . . . We didn't"—she stammered—"we wanted to, but we didn't." She tapped her legs nervously with her fingertips.

"Matthew, get Rebecca a cup of coffee, please." I forced her to don a nubby sweater I kept hanging on a hook by the door, then smashed a matching knit hat on her head—anything for warmth.

"We smooched again." Rebecca blushed. "We smooched a lot, and then he . . . I . . ."

I gestured the letter T. We were approaching the moment of *too much information*.

"What?" she said. "All I was going to say was I fell asleep. On the couch. By myself."

"Here we go." Matthew returned with a cat-shaped mug. Steam rose from the mouth of the cup. He handed it to Rebecca.

As she took a sip of warm liquid, she ogled me from head to toe. "Are you going someplace?"

"You bet she is," Matthew said with a smirk. "She's off to pry again."

"Oh, no, you don't." Rebecca's angst vanished in a poof. "Not without me." She set the coffee mug on the antique foyer table, grabbed my winter white parka for extra warmth, and whisked open the door. "Where are we going?"

"Back to Ipo's," Matthew said.

"Why?" Rebecca cried.

I kissed my cousin's cheek. "Thanks a bunch."

"Anytime." He grinned. "Anytime."

* * *

On the way to Quail Ridge Honeybee Farm, I explained to Rebecca that we weren't going to visit Ipo but rather to visit Oscar. Atypically, Rebecca kept mute, probably wondering whether going anywhere near Ipo's was her best move, but far be it from her to beg out of an investigation.

The wind, which had doubled in intensity since I left the house, kicked around fallen branches on the road north out of town. Horses in fields huddled together.

As I turned onto the road leading to Ipo's farm, Rebecca yelled, "Watch out!"

A hailstorm of eddying dirt and dust looked ready to attack. I swerved left. "Thanks."

"That's why I'm here." She tittered, definitely tense.

Rows of dormant fruit trees defined the perimeter of Quail Ridge Honeybee Farm. Small, weathered wooden pallet hives were stacked in rows in front of the trees. A state-of-the-art honeybee feeding facility stood to the left of Ipo's ranch-style house.

"What if Ipo sees me?" Rebecca said as we drove along the gravel road. "He'll think I'm throwing myself at him."

I cut her a look of admonishment. "Ipo has way too much respect for you to think that."

"Will he hate me? I ran out."

"You were overwhelmed."

She clapped her hands, the gloves muting the sound but not her enthusiasm. "Ooh, I like that. Overwhelmed. That's so much better than chicken."

"You are not a chicken if you're not ready."

She chewed on her lower lip. "I think I need to be married to be ready. Is that totally geeky?"

I shook my head. "It's refreshing."

Oscar's bungalow was located behind the ranch-style house. Rime coated the windows and eaves. A Dodge pickup was stationed in front, nose facing the porch.

I parked my white Escort beside the pickup and twisted in my seat. "Now, let's focus. I'm going inside to talk to Oscar. I want you to stay in the car and call Urso."

"Roger."

I offered my cell phone, but she fetched hers from her purse and shook it.

Adrenaline warming me like no sweater or coat could, I scrambled out of the car and dashed up the rickety stairs to the front door. Leaves kicked up around my ankles. As I was about to knock, I heard a squeak. I turned toward the noise. Rebecca was creeping out of the Escort. She mouthed an apology for the squeaky door and then stole around the side of the bungalow. What in the heck was she up to?

Dang. So much for expecting her to follow orders. When would I learn?

I rapped on the door and it inched open. No lights were on. I didn't detect the aroma of breakfast either. Remaining on the porch, I yelled, "Oscar? Are you there?"

A horse whinnied, but Oscar didn't answer.

Thinking a gust of wind might accidentally have jostled the door, I pushed it open farther, and whispered, "Oscar?"

In the path of daylight that swathed the hardwood floor, I caught sight of a pair of boots, toes to the ground. Legs in jeans jutted from the boots. A man lay facedown on the shabby area rug. It was Oscar. I recognized the pale blue shirt he had worn to the pub last night.

"Oscar!" I raced to him.

His back rose with breath, but he wasn't stirring. Blood dripped from his head. A busted floor lamp rested on its side beside Oscar's head. A leather wallet lay open beyond

the lampshade. Had someone robbed Oscar—the thief who Urso and Jordan had failed to capture? Was he still in the house? I scanned the dim room but didn't see movement. If the thief were there, he was as silent as a gravedigger.

"Rebecca!" I yelled. Had she reached Urso? She didn't answer. I tore to the door and said, "Rebecca, where are you? Oscar's hurt." I didn't see any sign of her.

I dashed back to Oscar, knelt beside him, and checked his pulse. Weak. I stabbed 911 into my cell phone.

A creature screeched. A ferret shot from beneath the worn green couch and flew across the backs of my calves. I yelped and clambered to my feet, heart pumping. Accidentally, I dropped the cell phone.

At the same time someone charged from the kitchenette wearing a ski mask and dark clothing. He . . . She . . . It grabbed me by the throat.

My self-defense refresher course with Jordan came back to me in a flash. Hands free, I rounded my right arm over my attacker's and jabbed the ski mask where the hollow of the attacker's neck should be. He—definitely a he—released his hands.

I tried to knee him in the groin, but my knee tangled in the folds of my camel coat and I missed my mark; I hit hard muscle. The intruder growled, cupped a hand around my head, and hurled me into the wall, face-first.

A loafer flew off my foot. My forehead slammed against wood. I moaned.

To my surprise, the attacker didn't rush me. He fled through the front door.

A moment passed before I could catch my breath and sprint after him. Wearing only one shoe, I hobbled. The icy cold from the hardwood floor bit through my sock. By the time I reached the porch, the attacker was gone. I remembered hearing a horse whinny. Had the attacker taken off on horseback? I didn't see tracks. There were no ruts, no footprints. The wind had wiped the area clean.

"Rebecca! Where the heck are you?" Dread clogged my throat. *Please, please, let her be okay.*

"I'm here!" She trotted around the corner, cell phone cupped in her hand, finger tapping in a message.

"Did you see him?" I rubbed my shoeless foot on my pant leg to warm my toes.

"Who?"

"The person who bolted out of the house."

"No! I went to Ipo's to see if he was awake. He wasn't there."

At the same time, I heard a vroom. I spun to my left. A Jeep hurtled down the gravel road and skidded to a stop.

Rebecca slapped her cell phone shut and pocketed it. "Oh, goodie, the chief got my first text message."

Urso bounded from the Wrangler. "What's going on? Charlotte, you're hurt."

"There was an intruder." I pointed at the bungalow. "We fought. I'll have a headache. Oscar's lying on the floor. His pulse is weak."

Urso rushed past me into the house. I followed, retrieving my wayward loafer on the way. Rebecca trotted behind me.

Urso knelt beside Oscar, who hadn't budged a muscle. While he checked Oscar's pulse, he wedged a cell phone to his ear. As Urso called his deputy, I remembered my cell phone and snatched it up. The readout read: *Call ended.* Urso shared what little he knew, then said, "No, he's not rousing. Knocked-out cold. Yeah, call an ambulance. Hurry." He sat back on his heels and put his hand on Oscar's shoulder. "Help is on the way, pal. Hang in there." He glanced at me. "What did the attacker look like, Charlotte?"

I described the mask and the clothing. I told him he reminded me of the thief that had attacked me at our tent at the faire.

Urso frowned. "Do you think it was the same person?"

"Could have been. He was taller than me and broader."

"Are you sure it was a man?"

An image of Georgia Plachette leapt into my mind. Wearing platform shoes, she might have been taller than me but not wider. But I was pretty certain the attacker was

male. And why would Georgia want to hurt me, I wondered, until I realized that the attacker hadn't been there to hurt *me*. He . . . or she . . . had come for Oscar.

I said, "Whoever it was smelled of horses and hay."

"Horses and hay?" Urso said. "That could be anyone from locals with farms to tourists who take Amish buggy rides."

Rebecca said, "Could it have been Barton Burrell? He's got lots of horses on his property."

I flashed on Emma Burrell, who was a tall, big-boned woman. Had Oscar seen something on Chip's cell phone that could incriminate her?

Urso rubbed a hand down the side of his neck. "Why did you come here?"

I explained about Oscar shaking that darned cell phone at me at the pub. "I was certain he saw something incriminating on the telephone—a photo or something. Does Oscar have a cell phone on him now?"

Urso rifled through Oscar's pockets. He came up with a BlackBerry phone.

"That's not Chip's," I said. "His is an iPhone. Is there another one?"

He searched again. A moment later, he said, "No. Why didn't you ask Chip about it?"

"I tried. He wasn't at the inn. Coming to Oscar's was more expeditious."

"And you couldn't have waited for me to join you?"

"It's Sunday. I didn't want—"

"You didn't think, that's what you didn't do," Urso barked. "Darn it, Charlotte, you are not a professional."

Rebecca cleared her throat.

Urso pinned her with a look. "Not a peep out of you, Miss Zook, unless you want me to plunk you in jail for trespassing."

"But, I—"

"Not a peep!"

She gulped.

Urso returned his stern gaze to me. "You are not trained

to put yourself in situations like this, do you hear me?" He jabbed a finger, realized what he was doing, and holstered it in his fist. "At least we know the attacker wasn't Ipo. I just saw him at church."

"You did? Hallelujah!" Rebecca said. "Praise be to—"

The screech of tires hushed her. Doors slammed. Footsteps pounded the porch steps. Urso's deputies stampeded into the room, guns drawn.

Urso scrambled to his feet and moved in front of Rebecca and me. "Okay, hotshots. Guns down. All clear. Where's the ambulance?"

"On its way," they said in unison.

CHAPTER

27

Before taking Oscar to the hospital, the emergency medical technician tended to the wound on my forehead and told me to take it easy. When I returned to The Cheese Shop, my grandfather was much more demanding. He ordered me to lie on the mini-sofa in the office and stay there. If not for the sweet potato–nutmeg quiche that he promised me if I was a good patient, I would have bolted. Within minutes, I fell asleep.

Around noon, I woke from my nap and struggled to a sitting position. The aroma of the quiche tantalized my senses; my mouth watered in anticipation.

"Lie back down," Pépère said.

"But I'm raring to go. I'm not dizzy." He was making way too big a deal of things. I had a cut on my head—a nick and, okay, a bump. "C'mon, let me up."

"Un moment."

"Ow!" I moaned. The antiseptic solution he was applying to my forehead for the fifth time stung like a you-know-what.

"You've got to be more careful," Pépère said.

"I know. Lesson learned. Now, let me up."

"You need a bandage."

"Is it bleeding? No, it's not. Let me up."

"You cannot go walking into suspects' houses alone, *chèrie*." Grandmère waited in the doorway, her voice crackling with authority. How long had she been standing there?

"I wasn't alone. I was with Rebecca."

My grandmother gave me the evil eye.

Agreeing with her, Rags yowled and paced at my feet like a sentry. Rocket yipped from his position on a tiger-striped pillow in the corner. He looked at me with hangdog eyes, as if admitting it was a weak response, but I should forgive him because he was only a puppy. Upon hearing of the incident at Oscar's, the twins had insisted the pets be brought to Fromagerie Bessette to comfort me. As much as I loved our menagerie, what I wanted was love without the communal judgment. And air to breathe. The tiny office was super cramped. At least my grandmother had convinced the twins to remain in the wine annex.

"Oscar wasn't a suspect," I added, trying to defend my actions.

"Everyone is a suspect." Rebecca reentered the office carrying the nineteenth or twentieth bag of ice. I had lost count at fourteen. She skirted the desk and handed the bag to me. "Apply for twenty minutes."

"Yes, doctor." I winced when I placed the ice on the wound. *A bump, my foot.* The bruise felt about the size of a doorknob. On a giant's house.

"*Chérie*, I'll get you that slice of quiche now." Pépère kissed my cheek and traipsed out of the office.

"I'm hot on your trail," I said, struggling to sit.

"Not without our help," my grandmother admonished. "Rebecca, some assistance please."

They each clutched one of my elbows and helped me rise.

Resembling a teetering three-legged-race team, we squished through the door. Over my shoulder, I gave a word

of warning to Rags and Rocket. "Behave." Both looked at me with mournful eyes as if wondering how I could ever think they would do otherwise.

"Are you sure you don't know who it was that attacked you?" Rebecca asked.

"For the last time, I'm positive." I tried to break free of my captors.

They clinched me more tightly.

"You said he smelled like horses," Grandmère said.

"Hay," Rebecca countered.

"Both," Grandmère said. "And he was wearing dark clothing."

"And taller than you," Rebecca added.

"Taller than any of us," I said. "And he was wearing a mask."

"What was his eye color?" my grandmother asked.

I moaned. "Just because I slept doesn't mean I don't remember you asking me all of these questions before."

"Close your eyes and try to remember."

"Oh, please, Grandmère."

"Try. Adjust your thinking."

There was that phrase again. What wasn't I adjusting? I was looking outside the box. Everyone was a suspect. Heck, if I didn't know better, I would even suspect myself. I closed my eyes for a nanosecond and reopened them. "I can't see a thing. Not a darned thing. Now, release me." I wrested free, exasperated and exhausted. Keeping the ice pack on my forehead and using one hand to plead my case, I said, "It's a blur."

My grandmother itched to grab hold of me again, but I backed away.

"Could it have been Arlo MacMillan?" she asked.

"Or Barton Burrell?" Rebecca said.

"For all I know, the intruder was a thief who had nothing whatsoever to do with Kaitlyn's death. Look, I'm not psychic. Stop badgering me."

I trudged into the shop, self-doubt squeezing the air out

of me. Were Oscar's attacker and the thief at the tent one and the same? Was he a tourist or a local? Could I travel, inn to inn or house to house, looking for someone who owned a ski mask? Maybe in my panic I had overestimated the height and size of him. Maybe the scent of horses and hay I had picked up had come from the properties around Oscar's house and not from the intruder. Everyone north of town owned horses.

"If only Oscar were lucid," Rebecca said.

Poor Oscar was lying in a coma on a hospital bed. The attacker had knocked him out cold. If I hadn't shown up, would Oscar be dead? If I hadn't used Jordan's self-defense technique, would I? The thought made my head throb.

As I reached the cheese counter, Amy raced from the wine annex and threw her arms around my waist. "Aunt Charlotte, you're awake."

Clair followed suit. She said, "Thomas, Tisha, and Frenchie came with us."

Tyanne's towheaded children were perched on the stools by the marble tasting counter, helping themselves to slices of Monterey Jack. Frenchie, Freckles's eldest daughter who was older than the twins by three years and usually the model of good behavior, stood beside them, flailing Thomas with her red braids.

"Stop it," Thomas cried.

Frenchie persisted.

Tisha said, "Mommy kicked us out of the tent. Frenchie and Thomas were sword fighting with icicles."

Thomas said, "Other kids were doing it, too."

"They were doing it outside, you goon." Tisha gave her brother a stern look, then turned her attention back to me. "Mommy told us to skedaddle."

Amy latched onto my sweater and drew me to her level. "Thomas is still being a pill to me," she whispered.

"I'm sure he'll change, in time."

"Ha! Never. Men."

My niece—a cynic at the tender age of nine. I smiled,

which sent another shooting pain to the knot on my forehead. So much for an ice pack dulling the ache. *Note to self: no more smiling for a decade.*

"*Chérie.*" Pépère flourished a rust-colored stoneware plate, set with a slice of sweet potato–nutmeg quiche, beneath my nose. "Come sit and have your treat."

"Matthew," my grandmother called to my cousin, who was polishing glasses behind the antique bar in the wine annex. "A glass of Pellegrino water for Charlotte."

I tossed the ice pack into the sink behind the counter and followed my grandfather and the heavenly scent to a mosaic café table. I nestled into a wrought iron chair and eyed the pale orange quiche appreciatively, then dove in. Pépère must have added extra nutmeg and maple syrup to his recipe. The luscious concoction melted in my mouth. I mumbled my thanks.

Neither Pépère nor Grandmère acknowledged me. They hovered on either side, hands folded in front of them, making me feel like a fish in a fishbowl. With a very bad lump on its head. Lucky me.

Matthew set a stemmed glass of sparkling water on the table and settled into the chair opposite me. "Do you have a headache?"

"I'll survive."

"Next time—"

"There won't be a next time," I promised.

"Thanks be to God," Grandmère said.

Pépère steepled his hands and said a French blessing of his own.

"Liar." Matthew chuckled. "Sure, there will. You're my sassy, headstrong cousin."

"I'm not headstrong."

Sylvie flounced into the annex and said, "Yes, you are." The sheer sleeveless dress she wore was better suited for the middle of July, but I didn't have the energy to tell her she had no common sense. "You're as headstrong as Matthew, Charlotte, hence that nasty bump. Bullheadedness runs in

the Bessette veins, doesn't it, love?" She peered at Matthew,
who flinched.

My grandmother clucked her tongue and elbowed
Pépère. Without a word, he ushered her into The Cheese
Shop. He preferred that Matthew handle his marriage is-
sues alone. Unfortunately, I was slow on my feet.

"You need to think before you leap, Charlotte," Sylvie
persisted.

"Who asked you?" I said, the words not nearly combative enough. If only I could master a tough New Jersey
accent. I couldn't. When I had tried to do one in a high
school play, I had sounded like a mixed-up urchin from
Ireland.

"And you're bossy," Sylvie continued, undaunted. She
flung her faux ocelot coat over the back of a chair and
fluffed her hair. "You push people around."

Matthew bounded to his feet. "Sylvie, this is a private
conversation."

"It's not private unless you're whispering."

"Leave."

"Matthew, I've got this." I clambered to my feet, ready
to have it out with his ex once and for all. "Sylvie, I do not
boss."

"Yes, you do. Listen to your tone."

Blood swelled in my head, but I fought off the dizziness.
"I delegate. There's a difference."

"Tosh! There's no difference. You're a general like your
grandmother. People talk."

"Okay, that's enough." Matthew scooped up Sylvie's
coat and thrust it into her arms. "Out! Now!" He muscled
his ex-wife toward the stone archway.

"Ooh, Matthew," she cooed. "I like it when you're so
manly."

"Can it." He released her. "Round up the girls and take
them and the animals back to Charlotte's house. And remember, be on your best behavior."

Sylvie huffed. "I'm always on my best behavior."

He snorted. "Might I remind you about the canapés smacking your face last night?"

Sylvie went silent. She mashed her lips together, as if she was pondering a comeback but couldn't come up with anything quite good enough. After a moment, she said, "Fiddle-dee-dee," like Scarlett O'Hara, and waltzed out of the annex into The Cheese Shop.

Matthew turned back to me. "She'll never change."

I thought of Amy's cynical words about Thomas. Was it possible that nobody changed? Would I? Could I?

I gazed at my cousin. "Matthew, am I bossy?"

"You're a woman who cares a tad too much, but you're never bossy."

I mumbled my thanks, then said, "I should get going. I've got to pack up the tent at Winter Wonderland."

"Don't bother. Pépère and I did that already. Tyanne's got the rest under control."

Tyanne. What a gem she had turned out to be. Our Winter Wonderland venture could have been a disaster without her.

Matthew chucked my chin and returned to the wine bar. "I've got some Bordeaux, 2005 Château Puygueraud, Côtes de Francs. Want a sip? Might help the headache."

He poured a thimbleful of wine into a glass. I sipped and savored.

"It's a flashy wine with hints of licorice and chocolate," he said. "It should go great with the dinner tonight, don't you think?"

"Tonight?"

"Grandmère's Founder's Day bash is right after the faire closes. Did you forget? How bad is that bump on your head? Or is old age creeping in?"

I glowered at him. "I'll always be younger than you."

Ignoring his laughter, I gathered my plate, glasses, and utensils and slogged into the kitchen. By the time I returned to The Cheese Shop, the place was bustling with customers, many clamoring for larger portions of the cheeses we had been offering at the faire. Jordan and Jacky and baby

Cecily waited among them. Jordan smiled at me and I attempted to smile back, though I was pretty sure I looked like I was grimacing. I strolled to the rack of aprons by the door.

Jordan made a beeline for me and ran his hand down my arm. "That's some bruise. Are you all right? I stopped by earlier, but you were asleep and your grandmother shooed me away."

"Your self-defense refresher course probably saved my life." I filled him in on what had happened.

He wrapped his arms around me and breathed warmly into my ear. My forehead smarted, but I didn't protest. A loving hug was worth the twinge.

After a long moment, he held me at arm's length. "You're going home to rest, right?"

"Soon," I lied. There was too much to do. I slipped a brown apron from a hook, looped it around my neck, and tied the strings in a bow at the arch of my back.

"How about a nice quiet dinner at my place later?" he said.

"Can't. Grandmère's party. You're coming, aren't you?" Maybe the hyper-electricity in the air that Freckles had talked about was making everyone forgetful.

"Don't worry, I'll be there." Jordan peered into my eyes. "In the meantime, because I know you won't go back to bed, take breaks. Regular breaks. A bop on the head can have lasting effects."

How would he know? How many brawls had he gotten into as a restaurateur? I snipped off the thought, not in the mood to rehash what was already solved. He was in the WITSEC program. He had witnessed something bad. He had killed somebody in self-defense. Soon he would enlighten me with details.

I strolled to my spot behind the cheese counter and called, "Forty-five."

Jacky waved a paper number in the air. "Me."

Jordan joined his sister at the front of the line.

"What'll it be?" I asked.

"Everything." Jacky toyed with her baby's feet, which dangled through the holes of the BabyBjörn pack. "That Minerva Amish butter cheese looks good."

"Great choice. It's creamy and melts well."

"And that Capriole O'Banon, too." Jacky peered into the case and read the label I had posted: *"A superb goat cheese. Named for the governor of Indiana.* How fascinating." She stood up. "What's it wrapped in?"

"Chestnut leaves soaked in Woodford Reserve Bourbon."

"We'll take some of each," Jordan said. He also ordered the last two prosciutto, pesto, and Provolone sandwiches in the case.

As I reached for the sandwiches, a previous debate started up again in my mind. About Arlo. Provolone was Arlo's favorite cheese, so why would he have stolen a box of Emerald Isles goat cheese from my tent or from Rebecca's cottage? Because he was a kleptomaniac; he couldn't help himself. Kaitlyn had known his secret and used it to get her way. But what if someone, like Oscar, had learned about Arlo's proclivity? What if Chip had taken a picture of Arlo in the act of stealing, and Oscar, upon seeing the picture, had decided to dun Arlo for money to keep Arlo's secret quiet? Would that have incensed Arlo? His chicken farm abutted Ipo's honeybee farm. In a matter of minutes, Arlo could have stolen to Oscar's bungalow, attacked Oscar—and subsequently me—and then sprinted back to his place. Except I wasn't sure Arlo was large enough to have been my attacker. Only minutes ago, I instinctively said the attacker was taller than Rebecca. She was at least three inches taller than Arlo. Besides, Arlo had confessed to Urso about his kleptomania. His secret was no longer a mystery.

No, someone else had attacked Oscar and me, but who?

Focus, Charlotte. You have customers waiting.

I slipped Jacky and Jordan's purchases into a gold bag, tied it with a grosgrain bow, and met them at the register.

While paying, Jordan said, "You look a little dazed, sweetheart. What's up?"

"Just thinking."

"On Mars?"

"Venus," I said.

"Try to stay grounded." He winked and another wave of sexy sensations streamed from my head to my toes. If I didn't have some intimate one-on-one time with him soon, I would burst. "I'm off to the farm," he said. "I'll catch up to you later."

As I started to rewrap the cheeses, Pépère ambled from the kitchen to the rear door. "Charlotte, I am going to Le Petit Fromagerie. Is there anything specifically you'd like me to do?"

I turned to blow him a kiss goodbye and froze in my spot, my gaze riveted on what he was doing. He was looping his apron on the hooked rack at the rear of the shop while nudging the rack to level. The move prompted a memory of Ainsley Smith nudging his hockey stick in the great room at Lavender and Lace. Not nudging. *Adjusting.* Had I missed a totally obvious clue? Ainsley had told Lois that he was setting the hockey stick right. Had there been some other motive for his action? Had he returned to the bed-and-breakfast, not to filch the hockey stick but to *set something right*, as in remove evidence?

I took the theory a step further. What if Urso and the coroner had been wrong about the pu'ili sticks being the murder weapons? Could a hockey stick leave ridged marks on a woman's neck? The stick wasn't made of bamboo, but perhaps shards of fiberglass resembled bamboo under a microscope.

"Aunt Charlotte," Amy called. "Frenchie wants to know if we can have some Camembert. I know it's expensive, but . . ."

The world turned strangely silent. I glanced at the kids and a quiver of excitement coursed through me as multiple ideas melted into one—Camembert, hockey sticks, my playful pets, and hyper-electricity.

Was the supercharged air causing people to act not only forgetfully but irrationally? Had Ainsley Smith snatched

the hockey stick from the wall of the bed-and-breakfast, tracked down Kaitlyn Clydesdale at Rebecca's, and argued with her? Had he flailed the stick at her? When the stick didn't hit its mark, had he, like Rags and Rocket, turned a hatbox-style cheese container—not of Camembert, but of goat cheese—into a hockey puck? Rebecca had brought a round of Emerald Isles goat cheese home to serve to Ipo. If Ainsley dropped the disk of cheese on the floor and swung hard, could he have propelled the cheese into Kaitlyn's throat with such force that she fell backward to her death?

The Emerald Isles goat cheese box was made of bamboo. While building the twins' aquarium, Pépère had suggested that the box could have left ribbed marks similar to what the coroner had found, but at the time I couldn't figure out how a hatbox-style container of goat cheese would have made contact with Kaitlyn's neck.

Now I had an idea.

CHAPTER

28

I was pretty sure that Urso wouldn't accept my theory. I needed evidence. When the crowd at Fromagerie Bessette thinned, I removed my apron, put on my camel coat, scarf, and gloves, and hurried to the office for my purse. Rags, who was nestled into the crook of Rocket's forearm on the tiger-striped pillow, looked up. His ears perked. Why in heavens hadn't Sylvie taken them home as Matthew had asked? Oooh, that woman.

"No treats," I said.

He mewled.

"All right. You win." I rummaged in the side drawer of the desk and pulled out the small brown bag of Tallulah Barker's homemade kibble. I set a handful of kibble on the floor. Rocket stirred and yipped. I said, "Sorry, pup. You'll eat what Rags eats." I replaced the bag then nabbed a Hershey's Kiss from my private stash. I pulled out the strip of

paper and unwrapped the foil. I plopped the candy into my mouth and hummed. Exactly the kind of fortification I needed.

I hooked my purse over my shoulder and turned toward the door.

"Boo!" Rebecca said.

"Yipes!" My heart beat triple time. "You surprised me."

Dressed in the nubby bisque-colored sweater I had given her earlier, she blended into the walls. She said, "Where are you going?"

"On an errand."

"My foot."

"To see Jordan."

"Uh-uh. You would have put on lipstick." She whistled and pointed. "Rocket, block the door."

To my stunned surprise, the traitor hurtled to his feet and obeyed. Maybe he was mad that I hadn't given him his own treats. Peering at me through his shaggy bangs, he didn't look very dangerous. I could take him.

Rebecca folded her arms and drummed her fingertips on the sleeve of the sweater. "Tell me the truth. I don't like it when you lie."

Neither did I. Lying left a bitter taste in my mouth. "I'm going to Lavender and Lace."

"To beg Chip not to leave?"

"Are you nuts? Whatever would make you think that? I don't want him to stay in Providence."

"You don't?"

"I'm in love with Jordan, or did you miss the signs?"

She screwed up her mouth. "Then why are you going to the bed-and-breakfast?"

"To fetch a hockey stick." I told her my theory.

She slapped her forehead with a palm. "You're right. It's as plain as day. I'm going with you."

"Not this time."

She stomped her foot. "Look, I told you a dozen times, I'm sorry about leaving you at Oscar's to look for Ipo. I'm

sorry that guy attacked you. Do you think it was Ainsley Smith?"

Ainsley would have been the right height.

"You have to take me along," Rebecca insisted. "He might be a killer."

"He's not there. Lois kicked him out."

"That doesn't mean he isn't skulking around."

I flashed on Lois chasing her husband with the broom and felt almost certain that he wouldn't return anytime soon, but Rebecca was not going to be dissuaded. She raced out of the office to the coat rack.

I followed.

She grabbed the winter white parka she had borrowed for our raid on Oscar's house and shrugged into it. "Your grandfather is here. He can watch the store. We'll tell him we're going to the precinct. He'll buy that."

Yet another lie. Was I becoming pathological?

Rebecca raced to the front door, snatched a burgundy-striped umbrella from the umbrella stand by the office door, and brandished it. "We'll take this for protection." She whipped open the front door.

"Rebecca, wait."

She didn't. She marched outside. Over her shoulder, she said, "I saw this episode of *The Avengers* where Emma Peel used an umbrella like a sword. It was so cool."

* * *

With Rebecca as my quasi-bodyguard, I hurried to the bed-and-breakfast. I trotted inside and nearly bumped into Lois, who was dusting her precious tea sets—Limoges, Dalton, Ucagco, Haviland. Each set was displayed on its own circular, marble-topped antique table. Agatha scampered at Lois's feet, barking at dust bunnies.

Lois nudged the Shih Tzu away and said in a lackluster voice, "Hello, girls." She plucked a piece of lint off of her lilac-colored jogging suit.

Rebecca said, "You sure look nice today, Mrs. Smith."

I cut my sweet assistant an odd look. We weren't there to bolster Lois's ego. On the other hand, we were going to drop a bomb on her. A compliment or two might not be a bad idea. She looked sullen and drawn.

Lois regarded Rebecca's umbrella. "I thought the storm was gone."

"Another is on its way. Better safe than sorry." Rebecca did a lunge, as if the umbrella were an épée. Agatha yipped her disapproval and hid behind Lois's legs.

"Hush, Aggie," Lois said. "She's only playing." The purple Plexiglas timer that hung on a chain around Lois's neck tweeted. "Excuse me." She bustled to the kitchen. Agatha trotted after her, glancing over her shoulder at us as to warn us not to follow.

But we did. The pipsqueak didn't scare me.

"It smells great in here," Rebecca said.

The sweet aroma of blueberry cinnamon scones hung in the air. The makings for cream-cheese icing sat on the granite counter.

"Where are all your guests?" I asked.

"At the faire, don't you know. The ice sculpting winner will be announced in about a half hour. It's all folderol, if you ask me." Lois pried open the oven door. Without pulling out the rack, she touched the top of a scone with a fingertip, then shook her head. The dough gave way; the treats weren't ready. She closed the oven door, reset the timer, and sauntered to the foyer. Without a word to us, she resumed dusting.

Her silence gnawed at my resolve. If it turned out her husband was a killer, would it break her heart? Was it already broken?

"Where's Mr. Smith?" Rebecca asked.

"Gone, gone, gone." Lois whisked the feather duster in rhythm. "I drove him away. Forever." A scowl formed the number eleven between her eyebrows. "Charlotte, you saw him run off."

I remembered how fleet he was. Fast enough to have beaten me to Oscar's. Fast enough to have disappeared

from Oscar's after attacking me before I could find my footing.

Lois plodded into the great room and dusted picture frames that looked freshly dusted. We followed. I glanced at the wall and my pulse went tick-a-tick. Ainsley's prized hockey stick, the one with three red stripes, still hung alongside the snowshoes and other decorative winter items. My fingers itched to take it to Urso.

"Oh, my, my, my." Lois crumpled into one of the Queen Anne chairs and wedged the duster beside her thighs.

I rushed to her side and took her hand. "Are you okay?"

Agatha bolted into Lois's lap.

"I love him, Charlotte. God help me, but I do." She massaged the pup's ears. "I would forgive him if he came back." Tears pooled in her eyes but they didn't fall. Not one. "That Kaitlyn Clydesdale. She was no good. She seduced him, don't you know. Whatever did she see in an old man like him? A moment of sport, that was all. He isn't to blame." Her shoulders heaved for a moment. Just a moment. Then she set Agatha on the floor and stood up ramrod straight. No self-pity for her.

Rebecca sidled to me and jerked her chin toward the wall. "There's the hockey stick," she whispered. "Ask for it."

"I can't."

"You've got to."

"Lois." I jammed my lips together. How could I convince her to let me take the hockey stick after what she had said? She wouldn't believe her husband was capable of an act of violence. He was a pawn. An innocent. *Oh, my,* was right.

"Chip is back from that sightseeing tour, if that's why you're here," Lois said.

"Ooh, did he go on one of the Amish ones?" Rebecca asked.

"No, he went on a tour of the town."

"I remember putting together dinners for the English," Rebecca continued. *English* was the term Amish ascribed

to anyone who didn't share the Amish faith. "That was probably the most fun I had as a girl, seeing outsiders enter our home."

"I would imagine," Lois said. "Well, I must get back to work." She smacked the duster against her hip. Particles of dust drifted to the floor. Agatha scampered to the vacuum sitting near the entrance to the great room and barked as if willing it to do its magic. "By the by, Charlotte, I told Chip you stopped in this morning, wanting to speak with him."

Rebecca's mouth quirked up on the right. "I knew it. You're holding out on me."

I waved her off. I had no desire to talk to Chip. Not now. I needed to get hold of that hockey stick.

Lois gestured with her duster. "I moved Chip's luggage into the sunroom over there." She shook her head and laughed wistfully. "Why do I persist in calling it the sunroom when the sun doesn't truly hit it? Ainsley named it that, the fool."

"I've got an idea," Rebecca whispered and winked at me. "Lois, would you mind fetching Chip for us?"

I gaped. Did she plan to steal the hockey stick when Lois left the room?

"No need," Lois said. "He'll be right down. A car is coming to take him to the airport."

"Rats," Rebecca mumbled.

I glanced at the sunroom and an idea came to me. Maybe, with Chip's help, I could convince Lois to hand over the hockey stick. I strolled into the sunroom, which was cheery despite the gray skies outside. Chip's luggage stood beside the lavender wicker sofa. An umbrella and his zippered suede jacket lay across the tote bag.

The sound of footsteps on the hardwood floor made me turn.

Chip, handsome in an ecru fisherman's knit sweater and jeans, sauntered in. He stopped inches from me, and a sly grin spread across his face. "Well, well, we meet again, babe. Having doubts about me leaving? Want me to stay?"

He ran a finger down my arm. "You know I would. I'd like to give us another try."

"No." I backed up. I wasn't having doubts. Not one, though for some stupid reason, a sense of loss coursed through me. He was truly leaving. Again. For good. It was for the best. I knew it; he knew it.

"How about one last kiss for old times' sake?" He leaned in.

I blocked him with my palm. "Chip, I need to take Ainsley's hockey stick to Urso."

"Why?" He grabbed his jacket and put it on.

"I think he used it to kill Kaitlyn Clydesdale." I told him about the affair.

Chip rakishly raised an eyebrow. "Good old dullard Ainsley and Kaitlyn? I can't see it."

I shared the news about Ainsley's weak alibi of walking the dog, his last plea to Kaitlyn, and Kaitlyn's blackmail scheme. "You were right. Ainsley didn't go to the hockey game. I think he followed Kaitlyn to Rebecca's cottage. He argued with her, lashed out, and resorted to using a hatbox-style cheese container like a hockey puck." I gave him the play-by-play I had envisioned in my mind.

"Wow." Chip zipped up his jacket. "It's hard to imagine. That would take some skill."

"Lois said Ainsley was an ace shot way back when."

"Okay, you've convinced me. I'll help you, but you have to promise me a kiss after I do." He didn't wait for me to respond. He strode ahead of me into the great room. "Hey, beautiful," he said, all charm and swagger. When Lois didn't respond, he crossed to her and repeated, "Hey, beautiful."

Lois looked up, her cheeks rosy, but she didn't stop sweeping her duster across the mirror above the fireplace.

"Cool it for a moment, Lois," Chip said.

"Can't."

"Sure you can. For me." He spun her around and tugged on her timer necklace to draw her to him. He held his hand out for the duster.

Like a woman under a spell, Lois relinquished it.

"Charlotte would like to take your husband's hockey stick and get it bronzed," Chip went on. "It'll be a real surprise to him when he returns."

"Do you think he'll return?" Lois sounded as fragile as one of her china tea sets.

"I'm sure of it. How could he leave someone as special as you?" Chip opened his arms, and Lois moved into them. She laid her head on his chest. "Special people deserve to be loved, right?" He winked at me, making sure that I had gotten his message. Though he had uttered the words to Lois, they were meant for me. He wanted me to reconsider taking him back into my life.

The scent of burning sugar penetrated the air and interrupted the tender moment.

Lois startled and checked her timer. "Oh, no, the scones." She scurried toward the kitchen.

Chip said, "What about the hockey stick?"

"Take it. What do I care?" Lois said over her shoulder.

"Rebecca, go with her," I said. "She's not herself."

"Will do. I'll meet you at the precinct." She darted after Lois.

Thankful I hadn't removed my gloves, I plucked the hockey stick from the wall and sprinted toward the foyer, pulling my cell phone from my purse as I ran.

"Wait up." Chip veered into the sunroom, grabbed his umbrella, and trotted after me. "Who are you calling?"

"Urso."

"You don't need to do that. I saw him at the diner. He was sitting down to a meal." He snatched the phone from my hand and dropped it into my coat pocket. "I'll go with you."

"But a car is coming to take you to the airport."

"It'll wait. I've got to see Urso's face when you tell him that *you*—not he—solved the case."

I sighed. Men and their egos.

CHAPTER

29

I was racing toward town, carrying what I thought was a murder weapon, and I had landed on a suspect with a clear-cut motive, yet my breathing was stilted, my body tense, and the bump on my forehead ached with a vengeance. Why, for heaven's sake? Not because the sky had grown dark and bloated with clouds, or because the wind had kicked up or an icy rain—the next wave of the predicted inclement weather—was starting to fall. I was born and raised in Ohio. I could deal with weather. No, I was edgy because my ex-fiancé was hustling beside me, grinning like he had won the lottery: *me*. I didn't have the time or the energy to boot him away.

"Let's plow through Winter Wonderland," Chip said, opening the umbrella and tilting it in my direction to cover my head. How gallant. "It's a shortcut to the diner."

At the north entrance to the Village Green, we skirted around a man offering horse-drawn hayrides. Chip, who had lived on a horse ranch for most of his young life, gave

the roan a pat on the nose. The roan snuffled a greeting and
jutted his head for more.

"Sorry, Chuckles, gotta go. Police business." Chip gestured for me to pass through the twinkling Winter Wonderland archway first.

As I did, the scent of horse and hay swam up my nostrils
and made me wobbly. I remembered the attacker's hands
on my throat at Oscar's. I could feel them pressing. Why
hadn't Ainsley wrung the life out of me? He was strong.
He could have finished the job before I had found the
chance to poke his Adam's apple. Had he held back because
he liked me?

"*Ciao*, Charlotte." Sylvie, dressed like a teenager in an
off-the-shoulder sweatshirt, torn jeans, and Uggs, pranced
toward me. In her arms, she lugged a cumbersome stack of
Under Wraps boxes while balancing a frilly umbrella overhead. "I'm closing up the tent and having a sale at the shop.
Why don't you stop by? You could use some wardrobe
advice."

Not from someone who dressed like a *Flashdance* extra,
I didn't.

Without waiting for my reply, she trotted past.

Chip nodded appreciatively. "She's hot."

"Keep off the grass. She's crazy."

"And you're not?" He chortled. "Don't worry about me.
I'm leaving town, remember? Unless you want me to change
my mind."

"No, I—"

"Wow, will you look at that?" Chip pointed.

Beyond Sylvie's retreating figure, a knot of people were
clustered beneath umbrellas, watching Theo put the final
touches on his knight on horseback ice sculpture. Nearby,
children fought with icicle swords. The adults in the crowd,
led by Theo's lusty girlfriend, began to chant, cheering
Theo to the finish. Theo's mouth quirked up with appreciation, and then after one last flourish with the ice saw, he
stepped away. The crowd went wild.

"Guess he's the winner," Chip said.

"Not until the judge says so." I gestured to a stoic man in a blue suit with a broad red ribbon across his chest. Sleet slipped over the brim of his hat and onto his clipboard. Mouth grim, he jotted notes.

Past the judge, I spied Tyanne hovering beneath the rim of a tent, sheltered from the rain. She stood frozen in her spot, a box of stemware from Le Petit Fromagerie in her arms. A pained expression consumed her face. I made a mental note to keep her busy at The Cheese Shop in the coming weeks so her sorrow over the demise of her marriage wouldn't drag her into a dark hole.

"Theo carved a good likeness of me, don't you think?" Chip thrust his chin upward for my assessment.

"You're far from a knight in shining armor."

"I try."

"And fail." I prodded him, and we zigzagged past the throng.

Seconds later, we neared the La Bella Ristorante concession cart, which looked a little worse for wear, thanks to last night's fire. However, a new Italian flag waved at the top of the flagpole. Luigi and one of his sous chefs were preparing brandy-laced crepes. Despite the icy rain, a crowd of hopeful gourmets stood beneath a makeshift awning. Barton Burrell, money in hand, waited with his family. His children looked eager to tear into a crepe. Emma appeared pale and even more withdrawn than she had seemed yesterday, if that were possible. Poor thing.

Luigi raised his hand. "Chip, hold on, son. Where are you going in such a hurry? Aren't you going to say goodbye to a pal? I got wind that you're leaving town."

"And I heard about the fire yesterday." Chip thwacked Luigi on the shoulder. "Way to go."

"I haven't been completely myself."

"Don't blame it on me. You're the one who bent your elbow one too many times. Be careful around that flame, or you'll go"—Chip gestured like a magician—"poof."

As if on cue, the contents in the crepe pan ignited. Seeing the blaze and feeling the waves of heat made me think *danger*. Was I wrong to have left Rebecca back at the inn? What if Ainsley returned? What if Lois or Rebecca blurted that Chip and I were taking the hockey stick to Urso? Ainsley might hurt them before coming after me. Granted, Rebecca had an umbrella, but it wasn't nearly the weapon she believed it to be.

"Chip, let's go." I explained my concern. "The sooner we get Urso on board, the sooner we get back to Lavender and Lace."

"This way, Charlotte. Too many distractions here." Chip grabbed my elbow and steered me down a familiar aisle, the one leading to Le Petit Fromagerie.

The lane felt cooler than the one we had just left. Though strands of lights outlining the tents were switched on, shops on both sides of the aisle were closed. Owners had packed up. Foot traffic was nonexistent. Other than the ice sculpture judging, the faire was officially over.

Chip said, "Let's exit by the pub and jog down the sidewalk."

With him holding on to my arm, I was forced to keep pace. "Speaking of the pub," I said, dodging icy spots of sleet. "Last night Oscar borrowed your phone. I think he saw something on it. Maybe a photo. He tried to get my attention. Did you take a picture of Ainsley without Ainsley knowing it?"

"Don't think so."

"Did you get the iPhone back from Oscar?"

Chip patted his jacket pocket.

"Let me have a peek." I wriggled free of his grasp and waved my hand.

"Not now."

"Yes, now. Maybe you got a picture of Ainsley hiding the round of Emerald Isles goat cheese or"—another idea struck me—"listening to Tim telling Kaitlyn where she might find Ipo."

"A photo of him listening to a conversation wouldn't be

incriminating. It would be impossible to know what he was hearing."

"Okay, fine. Let me have your phone anyway." I groped in his jacket pocket. My fingers hit something that felt like mittens.

Chip plucked my hand out and wheeled on me. "Stop it!"

I threw my hands up in surrender, hockey stick and all. "Sorry if I'm infringing on your space, but Urso's going to want to know how Ainsley knew where Kaitlyn would be. A picture of him in the pub would say more than a thousand words."

"That's a stretch."

"Oscar saw something on your phone. What if he called Ainsley and dunned him for money to keep quiet, and Ainsley tracked Oscar down at his bungalow?"

"Time out." Chip flattened his palm. "You told me Ainsley met with Kaitlyn earlier. He knew she was going to a Do-Gooder meeting. She probably gave him the rest of her agenda then."

"But Kaitlyn didn't know Ipo was at Rebecca's until she talked to Tim. Ainsley must have overheard them talking."

"Unless he waited outside the pub and followed her."

"But how would he know she was in the pub?"

"Maybe he trailed her from Under Wraps."

A snap-crackle cut through the air. A string of tiny white lights on the Le Petit Fromagerie tent blew. At the same time, a sizzle of electricity zapped the edges of my mind. I tried to tap the source, but I felt like I was trying to peel the waxy rind off a stubborn cheese. I said, "How did you know Kaitlyn went to Under Wraps?"

"Town gossip." Chip pivoted and jogged ahead.

Without the umbrella for cover, icy rain pelted me. I shielded my eyes with my hand and stared after my less-than-gallant knight.

As he ran, an image came to me—of the thief running from Le Petit Fromagerie. He had looked about the same size as Chip, and Chip was about the same size as my assailant at Oscar's.

I must have gasped because Chip galloped back. He held the umbrella over my head. "Babe, what's wrong?"

Fear peppered my insides. Were his eyes the eyes I had seen through the ski mask? Why would he have killed Kaitlyn Clydesdale? He had agreed to a contract with her. She was going to make his dreams come true. And yet—

A low, guttural rumble scudded through the heavy gray clouds overhead. I flashed on Oscar looking anxious when he had held up Chip's iPhone. Oscar hadn't been afraid of Georgia. He had been scared of Chip.

"Charlotte?"

A whiff of Chip's lemony cologne confirmed my suspicions. It was the same citrus aroma Chip always wore, so I should have known earlier that he was my attacker. But the night the thief had assaulted me in the tent, there had been so many conflicting scents—cotton candy and pine and cocoa. At Oscar's, my assailant had smelled like horses and hay and, I realized too late, lemon.

"You took the cheese," I blurted. "Someone robbed our tent. The thief stole a round of Emerald Isles goat cheese. It was you."

His eyes narrowed. "You're nuts."

"This morning, I stopped by the B&B. Lois said you were taking one last sightseeing tour of town, but you went on a hayride, didn't you?" Minutes ago, Chip had petted the roan at the entrance to the faire and called him by name. "To you, there's nothing more fun in life than a hayride."

"A hayride with you."

"You smell like horses and hay, Chip."

"So?"

"The guy who attacked me at Oscar's house smelled like horses and hay and lemon-scented cologne. You went on the hayride and then you went to Oscar's to get your cell phone back, and you—"

In a split second, Chip tossed the umbrella to the ground, grabbed me, whipped me around—hockey stick and all— and slapped his hand over my mouth.

I stomped down with my heel but missed his foot. I kicked back and only scraped his calf.

"Dang it, Charlotte. If you weren't so persistent." He lifted me off my feet and carried me, kicking, to Le Petit Fromagerie. A *Closed* sign hung on the door, but the latch was loose. He toed open the door and lugged me inside.

CHAPTER

As the tent door clicked closed, thunder rumbled overhead and dread flooded my veins. I tried to assure myself that Chip hadn't hurt me before, therefore he wouldn't hurt me now, but I wasn't very convincing. If only the ice-sculpting contest wasn't pulling the crowds away from this section of the faire.

Chip set me on my feet, snatched the hockey stick from me, and wielded it overhead. "Don't scream."

Throughout our relationship, I had known Chip had a temper, but I had never thought he was irrational. We fought; we made up. He oozed charm; I felt guilty. He had never laid a finger on me. If I disobeyed his order now and screamed, would he whack me with the stick? Talk about being conflicted, not to mention that I wasn't sure I could even whisper, let alone yell. My throat felt clogged with cotton.

"Whatever it is you think I did . . ." Chip let the sentence hang.

I didn't think; I knew. And he knew I knew. What I didn't know was why he had done it.

As my heart jackhammered in my chest, I scanned the tent for an escape. I couldn't crawl beneath the lower edges. They were weighted with metal pipes and lashed to stakes outside the tent. The windows were zippered shut. Sealed boxes of stemware and crates of wines stood stacked against one wall. Decorations that had adorned the walls were stowed in see-through containers. Cheeses were stored in ice chests. Cartons of souvenir plates sat piled on top of each other and strapped to a trolley for easy transport. Someone from The Cheese Shop was certain to return for the rest of the items, but how soon? Tyanne had been toting a box of stemware, which meant she was headed to Fromagerie Bessette, not to the tent.

"I'm innocent, babe. Tell me you believe me."

I gaped. He wanted absolution? Was that the way to keep him calm?

"Prove it." My voice sounded raspy, tight, but I couldn't make it any louder. Where was a megaphone when I needed one? "You have something fuzzy in your pocket besides your cell phone. Show me what it is." Ten bucks said it was a ski mask.

He didn't budge.

"The night Kaitlyn died, you claimed you were at the pub," I went on. "You watched Georgia playing darts."

"That's right. She scored nine bull's-eyes."

"Did you see each one?"

Chip tapped the hockey stick on the fake grass. As if keeping rhythm, rain pelted the tent's roof with an intense rat-a-tat.

"Here's what I think happened," I said, as the evening that Kaitlyn died played out in my mind. "Georgia announced she was going for ten bull's-eyes. When Kaitlyn came in and asked where Ipo was, you saw your opportunity. Georgia was in for the long haul; she wasn't going to quit. If you could find someone to corroborate your alibi,

you were gold. So you fortified Luigi's drinks." Back in college, to knock out the competition, Chip had done the same
thing to a guy who had hit on me. He had sneaked an extra
shot of vodka into each of the guy's rounds. "The morning
after Kaitlyn died, I saw Luigi at the library. He thought
someone had slipped him a Mickey Finn."

Chip jammed the hockey stick hard on the grass but
didn't say a word. His gaze turned glacier hard.

A chill crept into the tent. I fought hard not to shiver.
I needed to appear strong, in command. If only I could
scream. "When Luigi was sufficiently plowed"—my voice
was stronger, but not strong enough—"you sneaked into the
men's room, slid out the window, and raced to Lavender and
Lace. You grabbed the hockey stick and hurried to the cottage." Chip had always been fast. It was one of his greatest
assets when playing hockey. "Later, with Luigi three sheets
to the wind, you told him you were at the pub the whole
time. He confirmed your alibi. What I can't figure out is
why you killed Kaitlyn."

"I didn't kill her." Chip popped up the hockey stick and
caught it at the neck. Like a hockey enforcer, he spun the
stick around and glowered at me. I was the one person
standing between him and freedom.

I eyed the door. If I bolted for it, Chip might strike out.
If I continued talking, maybe he would see the error of his
ways. I tried to conjure up the spirit of one of Rebecca's TV
legal eagles, preferably one with the gift of persuasion.
"Kaitlyn was your ticket to Nirvana. She wasn't going to
renege on your contract."

"Exactly. Which gives me no reason to have killed her."

"She valued her contracts," I went on as I tried to figure
out Chip's motive. "She was standing pat on Barton's sale.
She wouldn't let Oscar quit. She wouldn't even let her
daughter walk away from her duties. So, if she wasn't going
to back out of your contract, why did you kill her?"

"I didn't. That's what I'm telling you."

I had never considered Chip a sociopath, but perhaps he
was. He didn't look one bit fazed by lying.

"You stole the cheese from the tent because"—I licked my parched lips—"you thought you needed to replace it at the scene of the crime. You had used a container as a hockey puck on Kaitlyn's neck and absconded with the evidence."

"No."

"But you never replaced the cheese at the cottage, did you? You changed your mind, because you realized if you replaced the cheese, Urso or one of his deputies might notice, and that would draw attention away from Ipo as a suspect."

"Ridiculous." Chip twisted the hockey stick, lost hold of it for a second, but quickly regained control. His eyes flickered.

"Tell me what Oscar saw on your phone. That's why you attacked him."

"He didn't see anything. Not one picture. Nada. He wanted to chat to his girlfriend, that was all."

Talking about Chip's cell phone made me remember mine. Chip had stuffed it in my pocket, not my purse. I started to remove my wet gloves.

"What are you doing?" he demanded.

"These are soaked. I need to warm my hands. I'm going to put them in my pockets. Do you mind?"

He shrugged.

I tucked the wet gloves under my armpit and slipped my hands into the pockets. With little movement, I was able to switch on my cell phone's mute button. Chip might hear the phone vibrate if someone called me, but he wouldn't hear me summon the first person on my speed dial—Jordan. I prayed for him to pick up. Maybe Jordan could tell what was happening by listening in.

To drown out Jordan's voice if he answered, I scuffed my loafers on the fake grass, like I was trying to warm myself up, except the scuffing wasn't loud enough. I needed to do something more.

In the angriest tone I could muster, I said, "I know what Oscar saw!" The American Theater Wing would never

award me a Tony for my overly dramatic performance, and Grandmère would have a hissy fit that I was telegraphing to the audience, but I could live with her disapproval. At least, I hoped I would live long enough to find out.

"Be quiet," Chip warned.

"Or what?"

He wheeled back with the hockey stick.

As he did, a notion hit me like a telephone book. Cell phones kept lists of the most recent telephone calls. I backed off with my tone but not my words. "Oscar saw a phone call from you to Kaitlyn the day she died."

"You're wrong."

"You called her the day she was in The Cheese Shop. She threatened to ruin you."

"Didn't happen."

"Then why are you holding me hostage?"

Chip stalked me. He tossed the stick from hand to hand. "So what if I called her? We were partners. I called her a bunch of times every day."

"She threatened to ruin you that day. Why?"

A heavy silence fell between us. Finally he said through gritted teeth, "Do you really want to know? Huh? Do you?"

"Yes."

He set the blade of the stick on the grass and flicked it with vengeance. "Kaitlyn lured me into her bizarre scheme with the promise that I would be a honeybee farmer, and in a year, I'd own my own restaurant. You saw the contract. That's what it said."

I hadn't read it, but I nodded to appease him.

"When I discovered that she didn't want a honeybee farm at all . . . when I discovered what she was truly up to, I lost it. You know how I am when I get shoved against the wall."

Yes, I did. He was one of the feistiest in a hockey brawl, hence the divot in his chin.

"I caught her in her office with plat maps spread out on her desk, as well as blackmail agreements signed by Arlo and others. Do you know why she was blackmailing them?"

"To get their property."

"Bingo." Chip tapped the hockey stick on the fake grass. "She wanted to own the whole upper north side."

"To build strip malls and megastores."

"Double bingo." Double tap. He growled like a caged animal. "She was going to raze the countryside. Tear down the trees. Widen the roads."

My biggest fears realized.

"I told her, 'No way.' I wasn't going to be part of destroying Providence. I wanted out, but she wouldn't budge. She said she needed someone with my pedigree to be the face of her project. *My* pedigree. I was to make statewide tours endorsing Clydesdale Enterprises. I was to be the face of honesty and integrity. Babe, I had no idea she'd use my heritage against me."

Lots of people in town were natives and had what people would call a Providencian pedigree, but Kaitlyn had selected Chip because he was as gullible as he was egotistical. Realizing the truth must have knocked him for a loop.

"That night I went to Rebecca's cottage and I pleaded with Kaitlyn. I told her my family name carried no weight in town, not since I walked out on you, but she wouldn't release me from my contract." He jammed the blade of the hockey stick into the grass again. "I knew I'd never win you back if I went along with her plan."

"Win me back?"

"I love you, Charlotte. I made a mistake. I never should have left."

"Hold it." Something wasn't ringing true. "After Kaitlyn died, you begged Georgia to honor your contract."

"In its original form. I would run the honeybee farm, and in a year I'd get my restaurant. No promoting. No endorsing. But good old Georgia"—he blew a long stream of air out of his mouth—"she said she would do exactly what her mother intended. She'd snatch the land and develop it. She's a—" He stopped himself. "She's a big-city witch eager to turn the rest of America into a parking lot. They were a real pair."

"So why didn't you kill Georgia, too?"

"I didn't kill Kaitlyn. It was an accident."

Semantics, I could hear a lawyer say. I said, "Back to Oscar."

Chip snarled. "I was an idiot. He said he wanted to call all the girls in my little black book, but he was onto me, same as you. He didn't think my alibi was solid."

Silly me, thinking I was the only one taking the investigation a step further. Did Urso know everything I did? He had said he had an idea who the thief was. Did he have an inkling that it was Chip? Was he trying, at this very moment, to drum up evidence? Where was he, or one of his deputies? Wasn't somebody missing me by now? Hadn't anybody seen the umbrella Chip dumped outside and wondered who had abandoned it? What I wouldn't give to have brought Rebecca along on this wayward side trip. Safety in numbers and all that.

I said, "Oscar took your phone, but you needed it back. He didn't give it to you that night, did he? The next morning, you went to his house wearing a ski mask, like the one in your pocket."

Chip looked ready to deny-deny, but he didn't.

"You attacked him because he'd seen more than your little black book. He'd seen your call list, hadn't he?" I went on. "And not simply one call to Kaitlyn. Like you said, there were dozens. But all the calls ended the minute you killed her."

"It was an accident." Chip whizzed the hockey stick in a figure eight. "Will you get that through your head?"

"You took Ainsley's hockey stick with you."

"To scare her."

"It's malice aforethought."

"She laughed at me. It was her fault I lost it. I was so angry. I swatted the pillows off of Rebecca's couch." Chip swiped the hockey stick; it swooshed through the fake grass. "That only made Kaitlyn laugh harder. To scare her, I knocked more things to the ground." Another swipe. Another swoosh. "When a box of cheese hit the floor and

started to roll, my days as a hockey player came back to me in a flash. I righted the cheese box, reeled back, and slapped that sucker." He acted out his story. "It soared into the air and hit Kaitlyn smack in the throat. Bam!" He paused. "I was never that good a shot."

People who had seen him play in his heyday would beg to differ.

"It wasn't on purpose. I was just so—"

"—mad. Got it." The bamboo fibers from the cheese box had lodged in Kaitlyn's skin. "Then what happened?" In case I lived to tell the story, I might as well get a full confession out of him. If I didn't, I hoped Jordan was listening in.

"It knocked the wind out of her, like the coroner said. Before I could grab her, she careened backward and struck her head." He stomped his foot on the grass. "Flesh striking wood sounds like one of those idiot comedy acts. You know, where the guy uses a hammer and splatters a melon."

"Why didn't you turn yourself in?"

"I panicked. I tossed the pillows back on the couch, picked up the container of cheese, and ran." He hung his head and swung it from side to side. "I've been dying inside ever since."

"No jury is going to believe that. You went to a hockey game. You toured the town. You pursued me with flowers."

"Dang it, Charlotte." Chip whipped the hockey stick up and held it like a crossbar in front of himself. "You always thought I hated Providence, but I didn't. I don't. It's my home. My parents might have moved away, but my heart has always been here."

I gaped at him. Was he for real? "You hightailed it to France."

"It was the wrong thing to do. I see that now. I want you back."

What Kool-Aid was he drinking to think I would ever want him?

"I was an imbecile," he said. "I've changed."

Oh, yeah, he'd changed, all right.

"I'll never hurt anyone again. I promise. You won't tell Urso, right?"

Yes, I would turn him in the first chance I got. I didn't say so out loud, but my eyes must have given me away because Chip's gaze grew steely. So much for true love.

"Uh-uh. Can't let you do that." He popped the stick up and sliced the air.

An icy breeze cut past my face. Nerve endings at the tip of my nose tingled. In a panic, I glanced around the tent again, looking for something that I could use to defend myself. The boxes of wineglasses looked too heavy to lift, and none were open. I wouldn't be able to break a wineglass to use as a sharp weapon. I needed to take my chances and run.

A thunderclap drowned out the sound of my scream. Bright light flashed through the window as I raced toward the door.

Chip blocked me and flailed the hockey stick.

I dodged a blow, dropped to all fours, and scrambled toward the buffet table that served as the cheese counter.

Chip pursued me. "I'm not going to jail, Charlotte. I won't."

Air whooshed above my back.

"I wouldn't last a day and you know it." He thrashed again. The stick seared the back of my thigh. I howled in pain.

I scrambled under the table and caught sight of the ice chest, lid open. Icicles jutted from inside—the icicles Tyanne must have confiscated from Thomas and Frenchie when they were having a duel. With the temperature remaining below thirty, the icicles had stayed sharp and firm. *Hallelujah!*

I seized one, swiveled on my knees, and jabbed it into Chip's thigh. He yowled.

Lungs heaving, I stabbed again. Harder, deeper.

Chip released the hockey stick and hopped on one leg. "You . . . You . . . How could you?"

The same way you could have, pal.

I latched on to the hockey stick, clambered from beneath the table, and wielded the stick overhead. "Back away."

Thunder cracked again, as if echoing my fury.

Chip crossed his arms in front of his face and retreated. His foot caught on the sticky fake grass, and he tumbled to the ground.

At the same time, the tent door flew open.

Urso rushed inside, water dripping off his hat and drawn gun. "What the heck?"

"She attacked me," Chip said, his voice mousy and put-on. Did he truly think Urso would buy his act?

"Stand down, Charlotte." Urso waved his free hand and his deputies jogged in behind him.

"He killed Kaitlyn," I said.

"I know."

The door squeaked a third time. Jordan, as drenched as Urso and the deputies, entered. In his hands, he held two cell phones. "Don't worry, sweetheart. We heard every word. I called the chief on my assistant's cell phone so he could listen in." He grinned. "Nice to see you on the defensive."

CHAPTER

31

Later that night, I sat curled into one of the armchairs in my grandparents' living room with a glass of white wine in my hand. Townsfolk circled the room as well, drinking and laughing, but I didn't hear a word they said. I was steeped in my own thoughts, which swarmed with doubt. Was it somehow my fault that Kaitlyn had died? If I had given Chip a clearer message when he'd arrived in town, would he have simply gone along with her plan with no thoughts about me . . . about us? I replayed those last moments with him. If I had agreed to keep things quiet, would he have tried to kill me? Once I had gained control of the hockey stick, he hadn't made a move for it.

Grandmère bustled into the room, clanging a cowbell. "Dinner is served, everyone. *Mangez!*"

As a herd of guests moved toward the dining room, Amy trotted to my chair. "Aunt Charlotte." She gripped my hand. "Come see."

"See what?"

"It's a surprise."

As I was rising to my feet, Grandmère said, "Wait, *mon amie*. A word with you first."

"That's not fair," Amy cried.

Grandmère pointed her finger. "Wait in the hall, please." Amy pouted. Grandmère started to count. "*Un, deux, trois . . .*"

"Okay, okay. I'll wait." Amy slogged out of the room. I could hear her impatient toe riveting the hardwood floor.

Grandmère gathered the skirt of her burgundy toile dress and perched on the arm of my chair. She smoothed the skirt over her knees and fluffed the hem around her leather boots. "We have had no time to speak all week. So many to-dos, so many upheavals, *non*?" She patted my hand. "We must discuss what happened to your parents."

"It's okay." I started to rise.

"No, it is not." Grandmère clutched my wrist and pulled me back down. Her skin was warm, soothing. "I want to set things right." She leaned forward and stared into my eyes like a mesmerizing fortune-teller. I couldn't look away. "What did Kaitlyn tell you about that day?"

"My cat . . . I'd forgotten about Sherbet," I whispered.

"Ah, yes, Sherbet. An adorable cat. Such pretty orange fur."

"Kaitlyn said Sherbet distracted Daddy and made him crash." I pulled my hand free of hers. "She said you blamed Sherbet. You had the cat put down, didn't you?"

"Oh, *chérie*, no, it is not as you say." Grandmère patted her chest with her palm. "It is not the truth."

"You removed all the pictures of Sherbet from our photo albums."

"Not because I blamed the cat. I . . ." She released my hand and ran a finger through my hair, separating the strands one by one, as she had when I was a girl. "You cried all the time. Every time you saw Sherbet, you cried. I believed she was, how do you say, a trigger for your memories. The crash itself and your mother pushing you from the fire. If Sherbet stayed with you, I was afraid you would continue to relive the event and blame yourself."

"What happened to Sherbet?"

"I gave her to Tallulah Barker."

And Tallulah never told me? The sly woman.

"Tallulah placed Sherbet in a good home. And when you were ready, she found you Rags."

I petted my grandmother's thigh. "Why don't you like Rags?"

"But I do."

I shook my head. "You can't fool me or him. He knows. You scoot out of his way. Your lip curls up at the sight of him."

Grandmère stopped toying with my hair and folded her hands. "The cat . . . he stirs up such sad memories for me, too. My son, your father. It is not right for a parent to outlive a child."

A silence fell between us. Finally, I said, "I want to know more about my parents, Grandmère. Everything. Not just what's in their memory box. Will you tell me? How they fell in love. What movies they liked. Everything."

"Of course." She rose. With her shoulders squared and her short gray hair secured off her face with sparkling combs, she reminded me of a regal dowager from a Jane Austen novel. "We will do it over picnic lunches. Many picnic lunches. Only the two of us."

"I'd like that." I stood and pecked her cheek. "By the way, I have one memory from that day. My mother yelled, 'Horses.'"

"You said the same back then."

"She must have seen one."

"Did you?" Grandmère tilted her head.

"How could I? I was too short to see over the seat. But I remember, as if it happened yesterday, hearing a high-pitched whinny." I pursed my lips, then continued. "Is it possible that Daddy had to brake for a runaway horse and Sherbet leaped from my arms and Daddy swerved into the tree?"

Grandmère smiled. "Entirely possible."

"Do you think I'm making it all up?"

"Who knows? Sometimes we have to rewrite history. To

protect our hearts." She stroked my cheek, then exited the living room.

I stared after her, not sure if she was referring to my life or hers. What horror had she seen in war-torn France? What events had she stowed at the far reaches of her mind?

Amy scampered in. "My turn, now?"

"You bet."

She grabbed my hand and ushered me to the dining room, which was crowded with guests. Chatter and the sound of glasses clinking together created a tympanic symphony.

Before I had moved a foot, Rebecca, wearing a formfitting floral dress, sashayed to my side and displayed her engagement ring, a lovely gold setting with baguettes pillared on the sides of a one-carat beauty. She had moved the smaller band of gold hearts to her right hand. Ipo, in a matching floral shirt, trailed her. He was grinning from ear to ear.

"Isn't it gorgeous?" Rebecca looked adoringly at Ipo. "It's Ipo's grandmother's. It's one-of-a-kind from Hawaii."

As if the ring were a magnet, other women in the room circled around us. Freckles and Delilah said, "It's lovely."

"There are all sorts of island blessings that go with it," Rebecca went on. "Ipo's trying to teach me Hawaiian."

A rarely used language in Ohio, I mused, but I wouldn't put a damper on her soaring spirits.

"*Aloha au iā 'oe* means I love you," Rebecca said, working hard at pronouncing all the syllables.

I said, "You're one lucky man, Ipo."

"Don't I know it."

Meredith swished through the kitchen door, carrying a pumpkin ricotta casserole dish that I loved—rich with pecans, eggs, and cloves. She offered a quick, "Very pretty," at the sight of Rebecca's ring, then glided to the dining table where Pépère was setting out the last of the potluck dinner, which consisted of chili and stew, lasagna that I'd made using my mother's recipe, three or four salads and side dishes, and baskets filled with fresh-baked breads

and Cheddar corn muffins. Candles in a silver scrolled candelabra in the middle of the dining table blazed with happy abandon.

Amy reappeared and tugged my hand. "Aunt Charlotte, is it my turn yet?"

I had almost forgotten I was being guided to a surprise. "Lead on."

Matthew, handsome in a gray pin-striped suit and soft gray shirt, stopped me. He popped the cork on a bottle of white wine and held up the label for display. "How about a fresh pour?" He laced his fingers around the stem of my glass. "This gewürztraminer is from the Bozzuto Winery. Delicate, fruity, a perfect aperitif."

"Daddy, I'm showing her something," Amy said.

He tugged gently on a lock of her hair. "In a sec, peanut. Adult business first. Remember what I told you."

She sighed. "Patience is a virtue."

"That's right."

"Guess I'm not virtuous," she mumbled.

Matthew chuckled. "So, my sweet cousin, how are you feeling?"

"Wrung out." The skin around the hamstring muscle where Chip had struck me had turned black and blue and ached like my forehead, but I was alive.

"Why don't you take a couple days off from the shop? Tyanne, Rebecca, and I have it covered."

"Work will be good for me. Busy hands."

"It's your call, but I think you should give yourself time. By the way, where's Jordan?"

"He'll be here soon. He said he had an errand to run."

Matthew pecked my cheek and continued to make the rounds to the other guests. I caught sight of Tyanne, who was leaning against the wall by the kitchen door and looking longingly at Theo, who stood at the far end of the table with his girlfriend. Sensitive to Tyanne's plight, Grandmère hadn't wanted Theo to come to the festivities, but the top three ice sculpture finishers were always included. If only he had placed fourth and not third. Tyanne heaved a sigh,

and I thought that she, like I, would have to give herself time. She might consider herself plucky, but life was coming at her fast.

"Now?" Amy asked, her voice peppered with annoyance.

"Yes, sweetheart."

She prodded me to the far side of the room. "Look." On the oak-finished sideboard stood an aquarium, complete with green bamboo, colorful stones, and a blue castle.

I bent over to get a closer look. The aerator bubbled merrily in the rear corner. Shimmery tetra swam in and around the castle. "It's fabulous."

"We haven't named the fish, yet."

"I have." Clair skipped up, her plaid skirt dancing around her thighs.

"I'm not calling them those names," Amy said. "They're stupid. Blitzen and Rudolph. Sheesh!"

"One has a red nose," Clair explained to me.

To my untrained eye, the four tetra looked exactly the same, but I wasn't one to discourage creative thinking. "Rudolph and Blitzen, it is."

"But they're reindeer names," Amy said.

"There are four fish. You get to name two and Clair gets to name two," I said judiciously.

"Okay." She bent forward to whisper in my ear. "I'll call mine Speedy and Tommy."

Clair giggled. "Wait until I tell Thomas." She ran toward the foyer.

Amy raced after her. "You wouldn't dare!"

"Oh, yes, I would."

"Hello, my babies." Sylvie flounced into the room balancing a foil-covered tray on one hand like a savvy waitress. She posed for a kiss, but the girls ignored her and skipped through the archway. "Well!"

Grandmère scuttled to my side. "*Mon dieu.* Sylvie wasn't invited. Why is she here?"

"I'll handle it." I marched to Sylvie, who had changed out of her *Flashdance* getup into an outfit appropriate for a sixties' disco. "Sylvie, I'm sorry, but you weren't invited."

"Oh, yes, I was. I got an invitation." She waved a pretty silver embossed card.

"Good try, but it was only a verbal invitation."

Caught in an outright lie, she blanched. "But"—she sputtered—"but I brought food. Bangers and mash." She peeled up a corner of the foil. The heavenly aroma of spicy sausages greeted me.

Pépère trundled to us. "Let her stay."

"But—"

"*Chérie,*" he whispered. "Keep your friends close and your enemies closer."

I knew the saying. A needlepoint my mother had made of the Sun-Tzu quote hung in my bedroom. But Pépère didn't fool me. He was a sucker for good sausage, and Sylvie knew it.

She smiled triumphantly. "There, you see? I've been invited. Verbally." If she could have stuck out her tongue and gotten away with it, she would have.

"Charlotte." Delilah scooted to our group, a spoon in one hand and wineglass in the other. "Matthew has an announcement to make." She tapped the wineglass with the spoon. "Matthew, you're on!"

Matthew stopped his wine pouring and looped an arm around Meredith's back. "I'm pleased to announce we've set a date."

"Congratulations," "About time," and "When?" filtered through the crowd.

"The first Saturday in October," Meredith said, her eyes glistening with joy.

Sylvie harrumphed. "I give it a year."

I glowered at her. "I give it a lifetime."

"Not everyone is meant to have a life partner," she said.

"Matthew is. It just wasn't you."

"Well, well." Sylvie gave me a look that bordered on respectful. "The vixen has come out to play."

I didn't rise to her jab. "I'm not a vixen, Sylvie. I'm truthful. If you want to spar, why don't you duke it out with Prudence?" Sylvie's latest rival chatted on the opposite side

of the room with a pack of town council members. "We don't have any canapés," I added, "but I'm sure you'll find some ammunition."

Sylvie turned pale. Valiantly, she slapped on a phony smile, sashayed to the dining table to set down her potluck contribution, and waltzed toward the foyer. I chuckled, happy that the canapé story would follow her for years.

As Sylvie disappeared into the foyer, Urso sauntered into the room, sans Jacky. Maybe she couldn't get a sitter. Or maybe I was right and they had broken up. He strolled to Delilah and me. "What's with Matthew's ex?"

Delilah raised her wineglass. "The M&Ms have set a wedding date. Our resident twit isn't happy."

"M&Ms, ha!" Urso chortled. "That's good. May I use that?"

"Be my guest." Delilah winked. "Oh, there's Luigi. *Ciao.*" She sashayed to him, her colorful skirt swaying seductively. She draped an arm around his neck. He kissed her in a way that might be more suitable in the boudoir.

I averted my eyes and caught Urso staring at me.

His face turned grim. "Charlotte, can I have a word?" He removed his broad-brimmed hat and jerked his chin toward the kitchen door.

Why did I have a bad feeling about what he wanted to say?

"Sure," I said, praying for nothing worse than a verbal slap to the wrists. I wouldn't hold up well in jail.

We moved into the kitchen where a foursome of Providence Do-Gooders were sitting at the table playing bridge. Turquoise-studded hats adorned each of their heads. When I'd arrived earlier, Grandmère boasted that the group had grown to thirty members. They were scouring our county, as well as the surrounding counties, for goodwill projects. In unison, they said, "Hello, Chief."

Urso returned the greeting. "Charlotte, are you warm enough to talk on the porch? The storm has passed."

I grabbed one of my grandfather's jackets from the mudroom beyond the kitchen and shrugged into it as we strolled

outside. The sleeves hung over my hands, making me look like Dopey in *Snow White and the Seven Dwarfs*. Perfect. I could only hope Urso wouldn't make the comparison.

I strolled across the patio and stopped at the edge of the grass. "Nice night." The air was brisk but refreshing. A shiver curled up my spine. "Look at the moon." A sliver of pale yellow hung in the black velvet sky, surrounded by shimmering, diamond-bright stars.

Urso touched my shoulder. I turned. In the soft light, his face looked as solemn as a judge's. "Let me cut to the chase," he said. "I'm not pleased with you."

"I know. I—"

"Number one, you shouldn't have gone to the inn with Rebecca." Urso tucked his hat beneath his arm, then ticked off points on his thick fingertips. "Number two, you shouldn't have walked down an abandoned alley."

I had hardly considered the Winter Wonderland aisles alleys. Or abandoned.

"Number three, you should've called me right away, and not—"

"Whoa." I held up a palm. "It's not like I didn't try to communicate, but you've been so busy."

"The next time you impede an investigation, I'm putting you—"

"Impede?" Heat flushed my neck and cheeks. I jammed my hands onto my hips, a clumsy move with the extra length of sleeves. "I did not impede."

"You allowed a suspect to trap you."

"You never told me Chip was a suspect."

"I didn't trust him within a lick of his life. I never have, in all the years I've known him."

"In the future, you might want to keep me in the loop."

Urso craned his neck forward, reminding me of a buzzard inspecting a worm. I stood taller. I wouldn't be cowed. Not by him. Not by anyone.

"Are you saying, in the future, you intend to nose around?" Urso asked.

"When I feel an injustice is being done, I'll do every-

thing I can to find a solution. Ipo Ho wasn't guilty, but you were so focused on him as your suspect that Rebecca was sick with worry." I shoved the jacket sleeve up my arm and thrust a finger at him. "Could you have figured out that a Camembert-style cheese container was used as a hockey puck without my input?"

He scrubbed his stubbly chin.

"No, you could not." I stabbed my finger for emphasis. "So don't tell me to—"

In one fell swoop, he grabbed my finger, pulled me to him, and kissed me. I didn't kiss back. At least I didn't think I did. How could I know? My body was vibrating with shock. A boiling heat brewed in my chest.

As fast as he zeroed in, Urso backed away. A stealth bomber couldn't have been sneakier. "I apologize," he said, a boyish flush suffusing his face. "I was just . . ." He whipped his hat from beneath his arm and beat it against his leg. "Earlier, when Jordan called, I was so worried for your safety that I couldn't imagine another day going by without telling you how I feel about you."

"But Jacky."

"We broke up. She said she felt like a surrogate for someone else. She was right. She doesn't know it's you. It's always been you."

"But—"

A man cleared his throat. I whirled around.

"Am I interrupting?" Jordan loped up the driveway, hands tucked into the pockets of his distressed leather jacket. The glow of lamps along the driveway lit the under-side of his chin and the planes of his cheeks. He looked in-credibly handsome.

I glanced between Urso and Jordan, and my heart kicked into overdrive. "We were discussing the case," I said.

"Ahhh." Jordan drew near, lips pursed.

Did he know? Had he seen? I needn't feel guilty. I hadn't instigated the kiss.

"I heard Georgia Plachette is clearing out tonight," he said to Urso. "She's broken off all contracts and hostile

negotiations. Oscar is leaving with her." Oscar had roused
from his coma at the same time Chip was holding me
hostage.

"Who told you that?" Urso asked.

Jordan chuckled. "Tim got it from Luigi, who learned it
from Arlo. I also heard that Barton and Emma Burrell are
selling after all."

I gaped. "But if Clydesdale Enterprises isn't buying
their place, who is?"

"Tallulah Barker. She wants to expand her animal rescue facility."

"Well, I'll be." Urso ran his fingers along the brim of his
hat. "Think I'll get some dinner and share the news with
the other folks." He winked at me, and I felt a flicker of
something skitter up the back of my neck. Attraction? *No,
no, double-no.*

As he disappeared into the house, the Providence Do-
Gooders offered another cheery, "Hello, Chief."

The door banged closed, and all I could hear were the
night creatures, which weren't many in the winter. Their
chirping waned. The evening grew silent.

I wrapped my arms around myself.

"Are you cold, sweetheart?" Jordan drew me into an
embrace.

"Not when you hold me." I craved the scent of him.

"You know, when Chip was in town, it made me realize
something. I never want to take you for granted."

A warmth shot through me. I felt heady with all the male
attention. "And now you're going to tell me you adore me?"
I teased.

"No." He paused. A long moment passed. "I love you,
Charlotte. I want to spend the rest of my life with you."

Had I heard right? My knees went weak.

"Do you think you can see past my, um, situation with
WITSEC? Will you—" He dropped to one knee, pulled a
small black box from his pocket, and popped it open. A
platinum diamond ring twinkled within the velvet folds.
"Will you marry me?"

RECITES

Cheese and Jam Button Cookie

   1 cup white sugar
   1 cup butter, softened
   1 3-ounce package cream cheese, softened
   ½ teaspoon salt
   ½ teaspoon vanilla extract
   1 egg yolk
   2 ¼ cups flour
   1 egg white
   1 cup favorite jam

In large bowl, combine sugar, butter, cheese, salt, extract, and yolk. Beat until smooth. Stir in flour. Chill the dough for 4-8 hours or overnight.

Preheat oven to 375 degrees.

Roll the dough into a long tube shape. Cut the dough in slices. Lay on cookie sheet 1 inch apart. Press with spoon. Brush with slightly beaten egg white and add a dollop of your favorite jam.

Bake for 7-10 minutes until golden brown.

* * *

Gluten-Free Cheese and Jam Button Cookie

> 1 cup white sugar
> 1 cup butter, softened
> 1 3-ounce package cream cheese, softened
> ½ teaspoon salt
> ½ teaspoon gluten-free vanilla extract or vanillin
> 1 egg yolk
> 1 ¼ cups sweet rice flour
> 1 cup tapioca starch OR potato starch
> 1 teaspoon xanthan gum
> 1 egg white
> 1 cup favorite jam

In large bowl, combine sugar, butter, cheese, salt, extract, and yolk. Beat until smooth. Stir in sweet rice flour, tapioca starch, and xanthan gum. Chill the dough for 4-8 hours or overnight.

Preheat oven to 375 degrees.

Roll the dough into a long tube shape. Cut the dough in slices. Lay on cookie sheet 1 inch apart. Press with spoon. Brush with slightly beaten egg white and add a dollop of your favorite jam.

Bake for 7-10 minutes until golden brown.

* * *

Grilled Breakfast Sandwich

by Delilah

(MAKES ONE SANDWICH)

> 2 eggs
> Dash of Tabasco
> 3 grinds of the peppermill
> 2 tablespoons butter
> 1 green onion, green ends only
> 2 slices white bread
> 2 slices (at least 1 ounce each*) Tomme Crayeuse cheese
> (may substitute cream cheese or Brie)

First prepare the eggs. Crack the eggs into a bowl; whisk to blend. Add a dash of Tabasco and three grinds of the peppermill.

Heat sauté pan on medium high. Grease the pan with ½ tablespoon butter. Chop the green onion ends. Drop the onion ends into the heated butter. Cook for one minute. Add the whisked eggs. Reduce heat to simmer. Stir the eggs until cooked through.

Heat griddle to 400 degrees.

Butter the outsides of each slice of bread using the remaining butter.

Slice the cheese and set aside.

Set the bread, butter side down, on the griddle. Top each side with half of the cheese. Mound the cooked eggs on one side of the bread with cheese. Set the other side of bread with cheese on top. Cook for two to three minutes until the bread on the griddle is a medium brown. Using a spatula, flip the sandwich and cook another two to three minutes.

*More cheese may be added, to your liking. After all, it is a grilled cheese sandwich.

Pancakes with Gouda and Figs

(SERVES 2)

Pancake Mix [Use grandmother's pancake mix recipe *
see below]
Eggs
Milk
Oil
4 ounces Gouda cheese, cut into 12-16 very thin slices
4-6 figs, stems removed, and then sliced

Make the pancake mix according to directions (below).

Warm the maple syrup by heating a pot filled with water. Set the syrup carafe into the boiling water. Turn off the heat.

Heat griddle to 400 degrees. Make 16 pancakes. After flipping the pancakes, top each with a piece of Gouda cheese. Cook until the underside of the pancake is desired color of golden brown.

Set the pancakes on two plates. Top with sliced figs. Drizzle with warm maple syrup.

* * *

Grandmother's Pancake Mix

1 ½ cups flour
3 ½ teaspoons baking powder
½ teaspoon salt
1 tablespoon sugar
1 ¼ cups milk
1 egg
4 tablespoons butter, melted

Mix together the milk, egg, salt, baking powder, sugar, and butter. Blend in the flour until smooth.

Heat a frying pan or griddle over medium heat. Pour about ¼ cup pancake mix, using large spoon or ladle, onto the griddle. Let pancake heat to warm brown and flip with a spatula. Brown the other side. Serve hot.

Note this recipe is not gluten-free. To make it gluten-free, substitute 1 ½ cups gluten-free flour of your choice and keep the rest of the ingredients the same.

* * *

San Simon Frittata

4 eggs
½ cup Parmesan cheese, shredded
½ teaspoon salt
½ teaspoon white pepper
1 tablespoon plus 2 teaspoons of olive oil
1 turkey sausage, about 4 ounces, diced
2 teaspoons rosemary
¼ cup red onion, diced
¼ cup scallions, diced
½ cup chopped Roma tomatoes
3 ounces San Simon cheese, sliced [may substitute other cow's milk cheese]

Preheat oven on broil.

Mix eggs and Parmesan cheese, salt, and pepper in a bowl and set aside.

In 8-inch skillet, sauté 1 tablespoon of oil. Toss in diced turkey sausage and rosemary. Sauté on medium high for 3-4 minutes. Drain.

Wipe skillet. Add 1 teaspoon of oil. Toss in onion and scallions. Sauté on medium high for 3-4 minutes until tender.

Add turkey sausage and egg mixture.

Cook, using spatula to lift cooked edges and allow uncooked eggs to ooze underneath, 3-5 minutes.

In separate 8-inch skillet (that can be safely put into the oven), sauté 1 teaspoon of oil. Place hot-oiled skillet upside-down on top of egg mixture skillet. Flip. Cook eggs in new skillet for 2 more minutes.

Pour chopped Roma tomatoes in center of the frittata; spread to edges.

Arrange San Simon on top.

Broil frittata in oven for 3-5 minutes. (Be careful not to burn the cheese.)

Remove from oven (remembering to use a POTHOLDER for hot handle).

Slide frittata onto serving plate.

* * *

Sweet Potato–Nutmeg Quiche

(SERVES 4-6)

    1 cup sweet potatoes (canned, or 2 sweet potatoes
        cooked to tender*)
    2 tablespoons brown sugar
    1 teaspoon nutmeg, plus a dash
    6 ounces (¾ cup) whipping cream
    2 eggs
    1 pie shell (home baked or frozen)
    4 ounces shredded Swiss cheese

Put cooled sweet potatoes in bowl.* Sprinkle with brown sugar and 1 teaspoon of nutmeg.

Mix in cream and eggs. Pour mixture into pie shell.
Sprinkle with Swiss cheese. Dash with more nutmeg.

Bake 35 minutes at 375 until quiche is firm and lightly
brown on top.

*To cook fresh sweet potatoes: Peel two sweet potatoes. Cut
sweet potatoes into quarters. Fill a 6-quart pot three-quarters
full of water. Bring to boiling. Set the sweet potatoes into the
pot. Cook for 15-20 minutes, until a fork slips into the potatoes easily and comes out. Remove the potatoes and let cool.
Mash for quiche.*

* * *

Torpedo Sandwich

Urso's favorite

(MAKES 2)

Torpedo-shaped rolls, 6" each
4 tablespoons mayonnaise (plain; not salad dressing
    style)
2 teaspoons Dijon mustard
2 teaspoons maple syrup
1 teaspoon ground pepper
1 teaspoon salt
2 green onions, white tips only (or scallions)
8 1-ounce slices maple-infused ham
8 1-ounce slices Jarlsburg cheese

Slice the torpedo-shaped rolls lengthwise.

In a bowl, combine the mayonnaise, mustard, syrup,
pepper, salt, and green onion tips.

Slather each side of the torpedo-shaped rolls with the
mayonnaise mixture. Top the bottom half with 4 slices of

ham and 4 slices of cheese. (At this point, you might desire to heat the bottom half. Place under broiler for 2-3 minutes until cheese is bubbling.)

Place the top half on the sandwich and cut the roll on the diagonal.

Serve with crispy potato chips

Turn the page for a preview of
Avery Aames's next
Cheese Shop Mystery . . .

To Brie or Not To Brie

Coming soon
from Berkley Prime Crime!

A blissful moan escaped my lips. Had I died and gone to heaven? I took another bite of the ciabatta, spinach, and goat cheese crostini—one of many appetizers sitting on the granite counter in The Cheese Shop kitchen—and sighed again. Adding minced sun-dried tomatoes to the recipe had done the trick.

I downed the remainder of the scrumptious morsel and eyed the array that I had started preparing at six A.M. The jalapeños packed with mascarpone and seasoned with Cajun spices had nearly seared the roof of my mouth, but the ricotta-stuffed mushrooms had a good balance. All in all, the experiment was a success. I had at least ten winning choices for the taste testing.

As I collected cartons of cream to use in the desserts I planned to make, I paused. Did I smell smoke?

I tore out of the walk-in refrigerator. Flames not only licked upward from the sauté pan on the stove, they spiraled from the twenty-five-pound bag of flour beside it.

"Fire!" I yelled to no one. I was alone in the shop. Lured

by the ciabatta crostini, I had forgotten that I was frying shallots for one more dish. "Shoot, shoot, shoot." I hadn't patted the shallots dry enough. Water must have boiled a spit of oil out of the pan, which had then caught fire and nailed the flour bag.

"You dope, Charlotte." I knew what danger lurked in a kitchen. That would teach me to multitask. Why did I always think I could do everything at once? Wonder Woman, I was not, though at the age of seven I had liked her costume so much that I had begged and pleaded to wear it for Halloween. What girl hadn't?

I dumped the cartons of cream on the counter, swooped to the stove, grabbed a lid, and threw it onto the sauté pan to douse the flame. Then I switched off the gas beneath the burner, snatched one of the oven mitts, and batted the bag of flour. I quenched the fire, but smoke coiled toward the ceiling, and the fire alarm began to bleat.

"Dang." I chucked the oven mitt, hoisted one of the wicker stools nestled under the counter, placed it beneath the alarm, and climbed on.

"*Sacre bleu,*" a woman yelled from the front of the shop. Rebecca galloped into the kitchen. "Charlotte, I smell smoke." She skidded on her heels. "What are you doing?"

"What does it look like?" I teetered on tiptoe, the hem of my pumpkin-colored sweater rising up my midriff, the heels of my loafers loose. "I'm trying to hit the red button." I jabbed at the darned thing with my index finger but missed my target. The smoke alarm began to howl like a banshee.

"You can't turn it off that way." My young assistant covered her ears. "You have to remove the battery."

Swell. Out of spite, I poked at the red button one more time before unclipping the alarm case, which came loose but remained fixed to the ceiling by its wires. I plucked at the battery, breaking a nail in the process—*double swell*— and removed the battery from its slot.

Just as the siren stopped blaring, I felt something give

way beneath my feet. "Oh, no." The seat of the wicker stool burst. I let rip with a yelp, lost my grip on the alarm, and careened heels-first through the seat's hoop. The wicker and rubber matting on the floor cushioned my landing, but the undersides of my bare arms scraped the rim. I would have black-and-blue bruises, but at least I hadn't broken my skin, or worse, my neck.

Rebecca rushed to help, her ponytail flapping behind her, her pencil skirt preventing her lanky legs from making long strides. "Are you all right? Are you hurt?"

"Only my ego."

"What were you thinking? We have a ladder."

"Do you see it nearby?" I said. "No, you do not. I didn't have time. I had an emergency."

"Impulsive," she muttered.

"Proactive," I countered.

"Okay, okay." Rebecca offered a hand to help me out of my confinement.

Spurning her goodwill, I snuggled my feet into my loafers and, balancing both palms on the broken chair's hoop, slipped one leg out, followed by the other. I brushed bits of wicker from my clothes and tugged the hem of my sweater over my chinos. After a stunned second, I burst into giggles.

Rebecca covered her mouth with the back of her hand and sniggered. When she regained control of herself, she said, "What kind of quiche are you making—let me rephrase that—*were* you making?"

"I wasn't." Each day at Fromagerie Bessette—what the locals liked to call The Cheese Shop—we made a different quiche to sell to our customers, but I had finished the dozen long before I had started in on the wedding menu. Every autumn, as the days grew shorter, my inner clock went cuckoo. For weeks, I had been waking before dawn. "I was testing out wedding appetizers."

"*Bien sûr.* But of course."

I smiled. Ever since she had started working at the shop, Rebecca had been practicing her French. She loved the way

my grandparents, who had owned the place before ceding it to my cousin and me, settled into their native tongue. To date, I think she had learned close to a hundred phrases.

"How is the menu coming?" she asked.

"Pretty well, except for one." The shallots—now ruined—were intended to go into a radicchio marmalade that would garnish a filo dough turnover filled with breast of turkey and smoked Gouda.

I headed to the kitchen sink to freshen up.

"Why are there ice cream fixings on the counter?" Rebecca trailed me.

"I'm planning on trying out a few new desserts." I wasn't a caterer—I was a cheese shop owner—but when my best friend had asked me to come up with an eclectic menu for her wedding, I had promised I would do my best.

"Maybe you should have waited until you had more hands to help."

I frowned. The last thing I wanted after a kitchen fiasco was sage advice from a twentysomething who was ten years younger than me. Wonder Woman wouldn't take it, would she?

"I wasn't expecting you," I said as I rinsed my hands and patted them dry on a fluffy white and gold–striped towel. "It's your day off, isn't it? I thought you were spending it with your fiancé and his parents. You were going on a tour of Amish country."

"Speaking of desserts," she said, ineptly changing subjects, "remind me to show you an all-cheese wedding cake that I saw on the Internet."

I glanced over my shoulder. Was there trouble brewing in Romance Land? Was that why she had come to work? "Are you okay?"

"The cake was so cool-looking," she went on, fluttering her fingers to describe the shape. "Wheels upon wheels of assorted cheeses. Cheddar, Smoked Gouda, Cashel Blue, and Ashgrove Double Gloucester, all topped with a wedding couple carved out of cheese."

I raised an eyebrow and pursed my lips, my standard look when demanding an answer to a question.

"I'm fine," she assured me. "Really."

She didn't seem to have been crying. Maybe I was making more of her sudden arrival at the shop than I ought. I turned back to the sun-shaped mirror over the sink and assessed the damage the shock and awe of a kitchen fire had done to my appearance. Thanks to nerves, my short feathery hair had gone as flat as a pancake. I tweaked it but to no avail. Giving up, I dabbed perspiration off my face with the tip of the towel and traipsed back to the main shop.

I fetched a container of Brie from the glass cheese case, set it on the wooden counter, and cut the cheese in half with a carving knife.

Rebecca scooted to my side and tapped the cheese counter with the tips of her hot pink fingernails. "Okay, truth? I don't want to go on the tour. Ever."

"Why?"

"Because I'm afraid I'll run into Papa. He was so shut down the last time we saw each other."

Her Amish father had been as cordial as a bale of straw. He had come to town to bring Rebecca her grandmother's shawl. They had exchanged few words. Anger and disappointment could run deep for the elders of a clan when someone like Rebecca left the fold.

"Was I nuts not to go?" she asked.

"Sometimes you have to protect your heart."

"That's what I told my future in-laws. They seemed to understand. Do you think they understood?"

"I'm sure they did."

"Let's not talk about me anymore"—Rebecca clapped her hands—"I'm here. What can I do to help?"

I loved her no-pity-parties attitude. The day I took ownership of Fromagerie Bessette from my grandparents, I had hired Rebecca. She had helped me through all the renovations. Together we had decided where the wooden display barrels would stand and what jams and other accoutre-

ments would sit on the many shelves around the spacious room, and she had been instrumental in helping me decide on our color scheme of Tuscany gold and burgundy. I don't know what I would have done without her.

I pointed. "Open some windows and let in the fresh air."

"I'm on it." She scurried to the rear of the shop and cranked open the window beside the exit door, then flew to the front door and propped it open with the cheese-shaped doorstop. "Next?"

"Fetch some blueberries from the refrigerator."

Her gaze went from the cartons of cream in the kitchen to the Brie sitting on the cheese counter. "Are you planning to make Brie blueberry ice cream?"

I nodded. "I've been collaborating with the owner of Igloo's Ice Cream Parlor. He's a wizard with flavors."

"And he's willing to share a recipe?" Rebecca whistled.

"Actually, it's my recipe," I said as I rewrapped the remaining Brie. "He—"

"Mystery and magic abound ever since he took ownership, don't you think?" Rebecca's eyes widened; her face flushed.

"Magic?"

"And he's very secretive. He's in and out of town all the time. What's up with that?"

"I don't have a clue." And, to be honest, I hadn't paid attention.

"He's so dishy handsome. He reminds me of Houdini, with that thick black hair and those ebony eyes."

I pushed the Brie to one side. "Rebecca Zook, if I didn't know you better, I'd say you had a crush."

"Oh, no." She crossed her heart. "I'm committed to my man. He is the best, sweetest—"

"Who's the sweetest?" Umberto Urso, our chief of police, appeared in the opened doorway.

"Not you," I teased.

"I am, too. My mother tells me so."

"She's sparing your feelings."

Urso removed his broad-brimmed hat before sauntering

into the shop; otherwise, he was so tall he would have scraped the top on the upper edge of the door. As he moved toward the counter, he smoothed the front of his snug-fitting brown uniform. Had he lost a pound or two? He seemed robust and happy. He perched on one of the ladder-back chairs by the tasting counter and sniffed. "What did you burn?"

"Nothing."

"Don't kid a kidder. I'm guessing onions."

"Scallions."

"Ah, one of my favorite smells." He swatted the Genoa and Cervelat salami hanging on the silver S-hook. The group swayed to and fro. "Hey, I heard you set a wedding date."

"You heard wrong." The love of my life and I had been discussing dates. We hadn't settled on one yet. He had suggested November; I had proposed June, mainly because I didn't want to steal my best friend's thunder and get married too soon after she tied the knot. "Are you here for your usual?" In addition to cheeses and the occasional quiche, we offered sandwiches, made fresh every morning. Urso preferred a Jarlsburg with maple-infused ham on a torpedo-shaped roll. Over the last six months, I couldn't remember a day when he had missed ordering one.

He stopped the salami from swinging. "Actually, I'm going to take two of your heroes made with prosciutto, Morbier, and pesto."

Knock me over with a feather.

"Two." Rebecca winked. "Planning a picnic, Chief?"

"The weather is perfect for it," I said. Autumn in Ohio was one of the most beautiful seasons. I loved the vistas of amber hills and the trees turning burnt orange and gold.

"So who's the girl?" Rebecca asked.

"Girl?" I echoed.

"Picnic means date," Rebecca explained.

I ogled Urso. He avoided making eye contact, but his mouth quirked up ever so slightly.

"C'mon, who is she?" Rebecca pressed. She had no com-

punction when it came to Urso. She ribbed him mercilessly, as if he were her older brother. And he took it. I could banter with him only so long before he turned disagreeable.

He ran the rim of his hat brim through his fingers. "Mine to know," he said, his voice cagey.

"Will she be your plus-one at the wedding?" I said. A select group of the town's residents were invited.

"We'll have to see." He chuckled.

Not eager to pry further for fear he would think I was interested—which I most definitely was not—I grabbed a pair of the requested sandwiches from the glass case, stowed them and a pair of napkins in one of our glossy gold bags, and beckoned Urso to the cash register.

As he paid for his purchase, a group of tourists wearing purple tee shirts with STOMPING THE GRAPES inscribed in cursive writing on the front, crowded into the shop.

Behind them marched Prudence Hart, Providence's self-appointed diva. "Charlotte!" She booted the cheese-shaped wedge from beneath the door and slammed the door shut. The picture display windows rattled with a vengeance. Wagging a bony finger, Prudence made a beeline for me. The mustard-colored sheath she wore matched her dour expression. I swear, I couldn't remember Prudence ever smiling. "You won't believe what I . . . I . . . ." She sputtered.

Oh, dear. I hoped she wasn't going to do what she had done during a previous visit to the shop—pass out. I didn't have any brown paper lunch bags on hand.

"What I"—Prudence drew in a deep breath, tapped on her toothpick-thin leg as if to regulate the intake, and exhaled—"what I heard."

"What?" Rebecca said.

I prodded her not to encourage Prudence. The woman was an uptight authoritarian who rarely came into Fromagerie Bessette unless to spread rumors or make a fuss.

"The Harvest Moon Ranch has been sold," Prudence blurted.

"Oh, no," I said. That was the site for my pal's wedding.

It was a charming red ranch north of the city, with a gazebo and barn and acres of lush grounds. Would the sale cause a postponement?

"Oh, yes," Prudence went on. "I was going to buy it."

I didn't believe her for a second. She was forever blustering about purchasing this and that. She considered herself a real estate mogul in the making. So far she hadn't purchased a thing other than her dress shop, which was situated catty-corner from Fromagerie Bessette.

"Who bought it?" Rebecca said.

"That divorcée," Prudence hissed, the word as distasteful as witchbane.

I didn't have a clue who she meant.

"She snatched it out from under me. Why, I should—" Prudence gestured as if wringing someone's neck but stopped when she spotted Urso, his head tilted, his steely gaze blazing at her. She blanched. "Oh, Chief, I didn't see you there."

How had she missed him? He was almost as large as a grizzly bear.

"I didn't mean . . ." Prudence hesitated. "What I should have said . . . I'll have my attorney speak to her attorney and—"

The door to The Cheese Shop swept open. The grape leaf–shaped chimes jingled.

With murder in her eyes, Prudence bolted toward the woman who entered. "You-u-u-u!"

Someone's out to make a killing . . .

FROM NATIONAL BESTSELLING AUTHOR

PAIGE SHELTON

Crops and Robbers

• **A Farmers' Market Mystery** •

Thanks to her delicious farm-made jams and preserves, Becca Robins's business has been booming.
But when an unhappy customer turns up dead in
Becca's kitchen, she's afraid it will really sour her
reputation . . .

penguin.com

PaigeShelton.com

facebook.com/TheCrimeSceneBooks

M945T0811

"Rich characters, decadent cheeses, and a scrumptious mystery. A bold new series to be savored like a seductive Brie."

—Krista Davis, author of the Domestic Diva Mysteries

"Avery Aames serves up a yummy mystery featuring cheese purveyor Charlotte Bessette, an adorable new character whose love of family rivals her love of good food. Fans of amateur sleuths, prepare to be charmed."

—Joanna Campbell Slan, author of the Agatha Award–nominated *Paper, Scissors, Death*

"Absolutely delicious! This is the triple cream of the crop: a charming heroine, a deceptively cozy little town, and a clever cast of characters. This is more than a fresh and original mystery—Aames's compassion for family and friends shines through, bringing intelligence and depth to this warm and richly rewarding adventure."

—Hank Phillippi Ryan, Agatha Award–winning author of *Drive Time*

"The charm of the story is greatly enhanced by a very rich cast of characters." —*Booklist*

"A fantastic read, this cozy was truly a special treat." —*Romantic Times*

"Not since Agatha Christie has a female author created an amateur sleuth with a penchant for details." —*Suspense Magazine*

PRAISE FOR
THE CHEESE SHOP MYSTERIES

Clobbered by Camembert

"Avery Aames delivers another deliciously fast-paced, twisty mystery filled with lovable, quirky characters and Charlotte's delightful attempts at amateur sleuthing. Come sample what Fromagerie Bessette has to offer. I guarantee you'll be back for more."

—Julie Hyzy, national bestselling author of the White House Chef Mysteries and the Manor House Mysteries

Lost and Fondue

"Avery Aames has cooked up a delectable culinary mystery with a juicy plot and a tasty twist. *Lost and Fondue* is fun, flirty, and full of local flavor. Take an engaging, sassy protagonist willing to do anything for friends and family, add a delicious yet mysterious hero, mix in a yummy setting, top it all with a scrumptious plot with enough twists and turns to keep you guessing to the very end—and voilà! A tasty morsel of a mystery that will leave you hungry for more."

—Kate Carlisle, national bestselling author of the Bibliophile Mysteries

The Long Quiche Goodbye

Agatha Award Nominee for Best First Novel

"[A] delightful debut novel."
—Lorna Barrett, *New York Times* bestselling author

"A delicious read. Charlotte Bessette is a winning new sleuth, and her gorgeously drawn world is one you'll want to revisit again and again. More please."

—Cleo Coyle, national bestselling author of the Coffeehouse Mysteries

continued . . .